I0822839

A Harry Circus Mystery

Before the Leaves Change Colors

By E.D. Ward

Before the Leaves Change Colors

Published by Piscataqua Press
An imprint of RiverRun Bookstore, Inc.
142 Fleet Street | Portsmouth, NH | 03801
www.riverrunbookstore.com
www.piscataquapress.com
ISBN: 978-1-944393-80-9
Printed in the United States of America

NOTICE TO THE READER

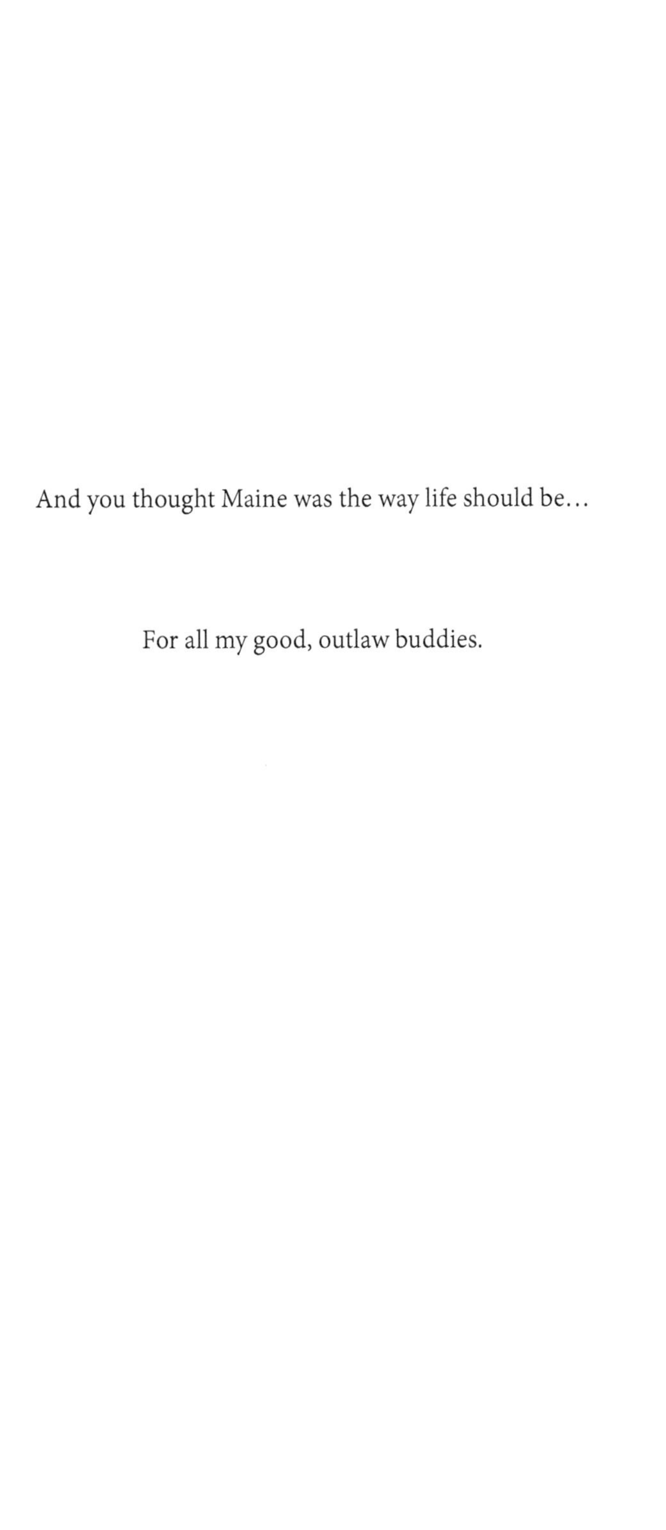

And you thought Maine was the way life should be…

For all my good, outlaw buddies.

Prologue

"When I tell ya ta motha'-fuckin' cut 'em,
I mean ta motha'-fuckin' cut 'em!"

(Zeke Brailey)

1

THE MIDSUMMER RAIN PELTED THE COAST for three solid days. Petey Harriman drove his white 1964 Dodge 880 with its 361 big-block V8 engine, with push-button, torqueflite automatic transmission along Route 1, just north of Dells, Maine. The car was a huge, four-door sedan that everyone called ugly except Petey. He'd bought the car from a good buddy at Bigalow's junkyard over in Sandown and it ran like an old clock. He removed the headliner the same day he bought it. The old felt was hanging all over the interior, and he took a knife and sliced along the edges over the doors, windshield and the rear window, exposing the entire metal roof.

The dampness from the rain outside, compared to the minimal heat from the defroster inside, caused the condensation on the roof's metal interior to drip all over the seats and Petey. It was impossible to get away from it. He kept several red garage wiper rags under the driver's-side seat, and in the process of dabbing the roof directly over his head, he never noticed the car screaming up from behind.

Petey Harriman was a scrawny little shit of about a hundred and twenty pounds, soaked and wet. He appeared too small to be driving such a huge car, but it's where his ego lived. He sat low, with only the top of his head visible to passersby and many friends joked that they saw a run-away car going down some hill whenever he drove by them. He'd recently turned eighteen and just graduated from the Auto-Tech Department at Biddeford High School. Working on cars and being paid for it was something he looked forward to fervently.

"Goddamn it! I can't believe the shit coming in here. One o' these days, I'm gonna have some insulation and a real headliner put in this car," he said, and with the turn of an eye, he caught the vision of the car behind him in his rear-view mirror, about a foot away from his rear bumper; the driver, blinking his high-beams on and off, was obviously either wanting Petey to pull over or speed up.

"What tha' frig?" he said. Petey actually thought it might be the local cop, but for the life of him, he couldn't imagine the cop not having all of the damned lights on, getting folks all stirred up about some fender-bender up the road somewhere. Without hesitation, Petey yanked the wheel to the right, giving the car behind all the room he needed.

From the looks of the headlights, the car was a late-model vehicle, and the moment Petey rolled onto the shoulder, the car passed him, causing the old, heavy Dodge to sway from the force of the wind between the two cars, and it was then that he noticed the Massachusetts license plate on the rear, while the rooster-tail from the tires blinded him.

"You… fuckin'… dim-witted Mass-hole!" he shouted.

Zeke Brailey and Dwight Betters sat quietly sipping their coffee at their usual booth by the window, facing Route 1 on the southbound side of Portland Street in their favorite hang-out, the Little Roady Restaurant. It was a stinky little diner-dive, run by a mother-daughter duo. It had a peculiar smell that hit you the moment you walked in through the front door. You couldn't exactly put your finger on it, but it seemed like rancid meat and dishwasher, if you can imagine that, yet the boys were there every day after school or work, whichever it might be, on any given day. They'd been there about forty-five minutes when Missy, the daughter of the owner-duo, alone at the counter, eyed the two, thinking they should have finished their coffee by now.

"Ya know… this ain't no hang-out for slouches. Ya gonna

order somethin' or what?" she asked in a snooty, yet humorous voice. She was an attractive young woman with shoulder-length blonde hair; she stood about five-foot six inches tall with a well-defined, firm body that she obviously took much pride in by the way she carried herself. She'd run away several years earlier with some drop-out nose-buster from the Portland waterfront. They shacked-up in Bangor for awhile and when they found out she was pregnant, he took off, and she never saw him again. She miscarried shortly after and finally came home to Dells when her mom opened the diner, using what money was left from the death of her father. Her mom was hoping the joint business would keep her little girl at home.

Missy took the steaming coffeepot from the brew-machine and walked toward the two, who never looked up when she approached. Without saying a word, she re-filled their cups and flipped a couple of sugar packs and some little plastic creamer containers on the table in front of them, forcing them to look in her direction.

"Wow, nice creamers ya got there, Missy," Zeke said, examining her from her eyes to her knees. His stare penetrated her entire being and it excited her that a much younger man was checking her out.

"I'm thinkin' ya oughta' pop yaw' eyes back in yaw' head, Zekie-boy."

"Why don't ya pop 'em back in fa' me, little Missy?" he responded without a moment's hesitation.

Dwight, at seventeen and the youngest of the three began laughing, causing Missy to look in his direction. He was fascinated by Zeke's nasty-boy demeanor. Much like any impressionable teen trying to carve out his own identifiable personality niche in the world, he was afraid of Zeke, as most boys his age were, but he was thrilled that Zeke had chosen him to tag along on any adventure, and with Zeke, there was always something new just about to happen.

Dwight, like Petey Harriman, was a skin-and-bones boy who never seemed to fill out physically. Zeke, at twenty-two, on the other hand, had arms the size of Dwight's legs and he stood six feet tall. Dwight stood five foot seven in height. Zeke was no doubt intimidating to younger boys and some of the men he chose to mingle with, fitting the category of typical bully. Missy's eyes darted from the sound of Dwight's laughter back to Zeke, who was now staring at the two open buttons at the top of her white blouse, which revealed the softness of her upper cleavage. Caught, his eyes turned up quickly to meet hers.

"Take a picture. It'll last longer," she said sarcastically, displaying a slight smile that could be considered an invitation, and they both enjoyed the feeling the little back-and-forth gave them deep inside.

"I don't need a camera, Missy. I've got a good memory and I won't be forgettin' that shot real soon," he said, bringing out another burst of laughter from the younger boy. She turned toward the counter and worried that her facial expression gave her away as to the true feeling that came over her from his stare. Without realizing it, his thought was completely opposite. He hoped his facial expression gave his fantasy up for her to ponder.

—

Nigel Linscott, like Zeke Brailey, was one of the original "nasty-boys." They had gone to school together throughout grammar and high school in Sandown and dropped out at almost the same time (within a week of each other). They became as close as any two individuals the same age could be. Since dropping out of school four years before, neither young man had been responsible enough to land a full-time job. Outside of a few menial work ventures, both remained happily unemployed.

Nigel's nickname was Pozy. He had gotten the name from an elderly woman friend of his mother's for whom he used to mow lawns in summer and shovel the walks and driveway in winter. She simply began calling him Pozy one day, and the name stuck. With a nickname like Pozy, until he became more broad at the shoulders and heavier, he withstood an onslaught of ridicule to an almost taunting level from his peers, but that only lasted a short while. After a few bloodied noses and one dislocated shoulder, the name became accepted and respected by all, including Nigel, who came to like the name and the attention it got him from people, especially the young women who loved to say the name.

From the time he was old enough to make his own decisions, around the age of twelve, all he ever wore were black jeans, black T-shirts and black motorcycle boots. When the cold weather set in, he topped it all off with a black leather biker jacket, though he'd never owned a motorcycle. In the coin pocket of the jeans, he always carried a jackknife, part of the handle protruding just above the pocket. With matching heated tempers, he and Zeke could have been twins. A short fuse was an understatement where these two young men were concerned and trouble appeared wherever they went. When it didn't, they had a way of making it appear.

Pozy ambled along southbound on Portland Street toward his daily rendezvous with the boys at the Little Roady. The earlier heavy rain had subsided, yet the road remained wet and the overspray from passing vehicles kept the air damp and moist for pedestrians. He could see the restaurant sign about a quarter-mile in the distance when he heard the rattle of down-shifting from a vehicle he'd come to recognize as Petey Harriman's car. He turned at the sound and gestured with an outstretched thumb, knowing that Petey would never go by without picking him up. As close as they both were to their mutual destination, Pozy appreciated a moment to sit in the front seat and arrive in style.

"Hey, ya little douche-bag, where ya been all day?" Pozy asked, while displaying the broadest shit-eatin' grin for Petey's benefit.

"I was out tryin' to find some parts for this headliner. Most o' these cars went to the crusher by now," Petey said in his high-pitched voice.

The first thing that crossed Pozy's thoughts was to jokingly cut him and his old car up, but for some reason he just couldn't muster the energy to give-a-shit today. He was soaked to the bone after being caught in the heavy downpour earlier and all he wanted was a hot cup of coffee. Hopefully, the little blonde at the

Roady had the heat on and he'd get himself dried. By the time it took the transmission to up-shift through the gears, Petey pulled to a sliding stop in front of the large window of the restaurant.

At the sight of the vehicle, Zeke and Dwight simply turned their heads toward the movement from outside, yet remained expressionless. Zeke's thoughts remained in the depths of Missy's cleavage and his fantasy ran away with him. Dwight, on the other hand, was glad to see Petey; they were closer in age and he was always uncomfortable whenever he found himself alone with one or both of the older boys, though he did his best to hide his true feelings.

"Ya look like somethin' that washed up on the banks o' the Piscataqua River, Pozy-boy," Zeke said with a chuckle as the two walked in from the street.

"Fuck you with a big stick up yaw' pants. If you was out in what I was out in, you'd look like shit, too," Pozy responded. He slid in the booth seat alongside of Zeke, while Petey slid in next to Dwight. This time when Missy approached with two coffee cups, more sugar and creamers, Zeke never broke his attention from Pozy and what he was saying, appearing totally absorbed with what he was hearing. Missy, who felt completely dismissed, frowned and repeated her earlier performance with the packs of sugar and creamers and dutifully filled all four cups with fresh, hot coffee, then returned, without saying a word to anyone seated at the booth, to the counter and the area where the coffee brew machine was, and went about her business. The two younger boys appeared comatose, trying to catch any part of what their older counterparts discussed, but kept their tone low so very little escaped their immediate side of the booth.

The four boys were from varying family backgrounds. The two older boys, nearly young men, were farm stock; Zeke was from up around Casket Mountain, and Pozy hailed from near Lost Corner, north of Sandown. Theirs was a typical scenario: they'd grown up on the farm and left as soon as possible. Neither Zeke nor Pozy had a plan or a clue. The phrase "numb as a pounded spike" applied here, and both ventured back home occasionally when nowhere else was left for a pillow, a blanket or a bowl of soup…when they were homeless. But each one had an evil streak in them that only a vivid imagination could perceive. Work, to each one, was simply a waste of precious time, and when they needed money and transportation, they relied on Petey and Dwight. They had jobs and still lived in family homes, yet were more than willing to be part of the troublesome foursome.

Dwight's father was a successful dentist with a small practice in Biddeford. His mom stayed home and took care of the socialization for their union. They remained distant from their only child, so like most young people, he found security through the comradeship of his closest friends.

Petey Harriman, on the other hand, was completely unlike any of the other three. His parents had been killed in a car crash up in the Moosehead Lake Region on a deserted section of road between Greenville and Kokadjo. His mother, pregnant with him during her final trimester, lived long enough to give birth to her preemie, who remained far underweight and had lived with his grandparents to this day. Befriended by the likes of Zeke Brailey and Nigel (Pozy) Linscott, he was protected against harassment from school-mates the association afforded him.

The two younger boys sat conversing in low tones, with an observant ear trying to pick up a morsel of anything the other two spoke about. Petey overflowed with the need to share his earlier encounter with the car from Massachusetts, knowing how out-of-staters inflamed both Zeke and Pozy's spirit of hate. He was, however, unwilling to bring it up with Dwight, fearing that somehow he would squeeze it in before Petey had the opportunity to do so. Though Petey's feelings were well-reserved most of the time, his age dictated the rise and falls of his hormonal eruptions. During a lull in their conversation, from the corner of one eye he caught the movement from the area of the coffee brew machine and Missy. He envisioned himself at times like this in the back storage closet with her; she allowing his libidinous energy free range over the beautiful pasture, of her exquisitely endowed body. A thousand fantasies fluttered through his imagination and his mind removed him from the moment and ushered him to the brink of sexual arousal, while his eyes followed her every move throughout the restaurant.

Outside, the late afternoon traffic slowed as the occasional camper-trailer—which the boys called mobile toilets—passed the restaurant going north and south on Route 1. The Maine Pike on and off ramps were less than three miles from the restaurant and it was obvious now that the onslaught of tourists was in full swing. Schools everywhere were closed for summer vacation and the floodgates at the York tolls were open. Dwight, at that very moment, forced all three back into the reality of the present.

"Did you guys see that little fuck-of-a-dim-witted Rhode Island Rooster cut old Blaine off goin' into the gas station ova' thea'? Stupid, friggin' rooster," he said.

The unmistakable sound of leather on leather from Pozy's jacket groaned as he turned in his seat for a better look at what Dwight pointed out. The silence created the similarity of deafness in the entire building, forcing Missy to turn in the foursome's direction.

"What in fuck are you lookin' at?" Zeke asked. His temper flared out of control in almost every situation lately that didn't fit in with his own attitude or expectations of others.

"Sorry…I should a' talked faster. That little twit from Rhode Island is gone up the road now," Dwight said, as a nervous knot formed in the pit of his stomach

"What was it, a mobile toilet?" Zeke asked.

"No, some tiny rich car. I thought he'd run old Blaine off the friggin' road."

Zeke simply shook his head in a negative response, but said nothing for several moments, much to the surprise of the other boys, and then he began, "Ya know what pisses me off the most? They come up hea', do what the fuck they want everywhere they go, and the fuckin' law turns their maggot-heads the otha' way, 'cause they come up hea' to spend money."

When he said this, the strangest look came over his face, one that the others had never seen; then he continued staring out onto a now-vacant Route 1. Again, the silence that blanketed the entire restaurant seemed overpowering, and not one of the four people there ventured to speak a single word.

Pozy broke the silence with a soft, yet clear whistle in Missy's direction. Her stare, like the others, was focused on Zeke, and she jerked her head toward the sound.

"Missy...honey... I can't shake the chills from that rain I was in before. Ya got any soup on the flame back there?" Without a word she moved toward the kitchen section of the restaurant and disappeared through the swinging doors, just behind the counter in the center of the room.

"Yep...it pisses me off, too. Those freaks come up here and think they can do whatever they friggin' want and no one gives a shit as long as their flippin' the cash on someone's counter. Let me tell ya how close one o' them came to runnin' me off the friggin' road during that rainstorm this afternoon on my way back..."

"What tha' frig' are you talkin' about?" Zeke asked.

"I was comin' from Sandown..." Petey began and went into detail, adding a few exaggerated facial expressions and phrases to heighten Zeke's already wrathy mood. By the time he finished, it was obvious he'd implanted the seed deep within Zeke's psyche, and when he saw Zeke's entire body beginning to quiver, Petey had a sudden thought that he'd taken it all a bit too far.

2

After a week-long rain, heavy at times, the summer heat encapsulated the entire coast in a deep fog—thick enough to moisten nostril hairs with tiny droplets of dew for those who ventured out-of-doors for summer chores or frolicking on the beaches, waiting for the sun to burn it off. Despite the obscured vision, the bumper-to-bumper traffic was enduring. On days like this, Zeke and Pozy remained at a garage, which was owned by the old woman who had nicknamed Pozy. It was set off by itself about a hundred yards from the blacktop down a winding, gravel road in a deep growth of pines, well hidden from passersby, behind the old woman's house. She was too old and fragile now to venture down and she'd told Pozy, long ago, that as far as she was concerned the "old shed," as she called it, belonged to him for all of the things he'd done for her over the years.

For Zeke and Pozy, the situation couldn't be better for two semi-homeless young men. With an old couch, a fridge, and an outhouse to the side, it was home. The old woman paid for the electricity. The center was always kept open for Petey's car and the ongoing repair needs of an older vehicle. The boys had found a cast-iron box stove and ran a stove pipe out the side wall. Comfy-cozy they were.

"Ya know, you and me, Pozy, we're in the same canoe, we've just lost the fuckin' paddles is all," Zeke said, and followed with an outburst of ear-splitting laughter as he lay on the filthy couch, using Pozy's rolled-up leather jacket for a pillow. Pozy remained quiet; leaning against the door frame of the garage's opened double doors, looking as though his thoughts lifted him to outer space. He looked out on to the thick morning fog and wondered if his life was destined to be forged by the bellows of boredom forever. Although the early morning fog cooled the air, Pozy felt the heat on his face from the partially hidden and dulled sun.

"It's gonna be another hot one. Them friggin' babes on the beach aar' gonna be as slick and shiny as friggin' lollipops." Pozy forced out an exaggerated laugh. Zeke picked up on it immediately.

"What's yaw' problem? Ya sound like some nose-blowin' hyena from Connectaclit," he said.

The rhyming names had been made up long ago by the foursome during an evening of pot and a little beer at the garage, when they agreed that they did hate out-of-staters. The names, made up by each one taking their turn, went something like this… Mass-holes for Massachusetts. Connectaclits for Connecticut. Roosters for Rhode Island. New Jerkeys for guess who? And Pissmyvainias for Pennsylvania. The names remained in their cut-ups of summer vacationers.

Immediately, both young men looked at each other and broke out into uncontrollable laughter that echoed through the thick fog and the trees that surrounded them. After several moments, their laughter faded to chuckles as the familiar sound of Petey's car was heard on its approach to the garage.

"Yeah, baby. Looks like we're gonna ride the coast this afternoon. Take a good look at them lollipops," Zeke said.

"Umm…" was all Pozy offered.

Petey stopped the car about five feet from the opened garage doors, turned the engine off and got out.

"You two had breakfast yet? I brought ya some doughnuts and coffee. You both look a little weak ta me," Petey said.

Neither one said a word; they simply focused a stare toward their breakfast delivery-boy and waited to be served. Petey walked past them and placed the two white bags on the work bench, on the side of the garage opposite the couch. Zeke and

Pozy converged on the food like ravens on a hunk of road kill.

At times, when money was tight, Petey would take in small repair jobs on the side, from friends and word of mouth, but in most cases, the jobs were done for free. Petey just didn't have the ability to ask for or even set a reasonable rate for his labor, just as his breakfast-bearing thoughtfulness would go thankless from the ingratitude of its recipients.

While the two gorged themselves on the doughnuts and large coffees, Petey busied himself by opening drawers in the tool box he kept by the work bench and shuffling through them for what, only he could know. Although the sound of tools being clanked dominated the surroundings, Petey could still hear Zeke's lips popping as he mangled the food. He seldom sat at a table to eat, so table manners were unknown to him. Zeke smashed the cups into the empty bags and tossed them into the woodstove. Suddenly, Pozy erupted with a thunderous burp, which ushered all three into a fit of uncontrollable laughter.

"Did ya get any on yaw' shirt, ya friggin' pig?" Zeke asked, rallying another outburst of near-convulsive laughter. It was strange what these boys found humor in.

There was one small window on the side of the garage with southern exposure. At windowsill level, Zeke kept his pet Black Racer snake. It was illegal in Maine to keep a snake of this type captive. When not coiled, the three-year old had grown to about twenty-five inches long when the boys had last ventured in and stretched him out on the garage floor to measure. He had stolen the cage and the have-a-heart trap which he used to catch mice to feed the snake. The eight-finger, two-thumb discounts became a well-established form of survival for the boys and they were proud of their ability to pull it off every time. "Yankee ingenuity" took on a whole new meaning where this group of young people was concerned.

The garage became quiet following their final outburst of laughter. Petey had obviously found what he'd been looking for and was out under the raised hood, tinkering with something. Pozy returned to his stance against the door frame, facing the driveway and the still, faint summer sun on that side of the building. Zeke appeared to take much pleasure from teasing the snake with the last live mouse which he held by the tail, dangling it in front of the snake through the cage. All seemed normal for a kick-back day at the garage, until the rumbling sound of a rapidly approaching vehicle on the gravel toward them forced the attention of all three to focus on it. From his perch against the door frame, Pozy was the first to notice, and recognized the vehicle.

"What tha' fuck does Queer-Eye want?" he asked. The other two snapped to attention, and Zeke quickly covered the snake's cage with its blanket, before the gravelly voice of Rodney, the town cop, who was known as Queer-Eye, seemed to suffocate them from what little remained of the foggy air.

"Well, if it isn't the three no-goods, up ta no good. What are you three no-goods up to today?" And before anyone could answer, he went on abruptly, staring at Petey.

"Did you steal those doughnuts, you little frig? Just because we have all them summer folks down here doesn't mean you can waltz off without paying because the counter got all clogged up near the register," he said.

As the three boys began looking around and at each other, from where he stood by the hood of his cruiser, Rodney began scanning the inside of Petey's car and the garage for any obvious sign of a donut bag or coffee cups.

Rodney Torrey, a ten-year veteran of the Dells Police Department, had maintained a youthful physique through years of diligence with proper diet and exercise, and prided himself for doing so. His uniform was always pressed to sharpness in the creases and his badge shined to a glare. He was considered by most residents to be a good cop, and he didn't waste time showing up when and where he was needed—and that was pretty much what turned the young folks off. They couldn't get away with anything with him. But, there was one particular thing about Rodney that stood out above all of his wonderful characteristics. Embracing his best police bravado as he stared at Petey, his right eye wandered, unsynchronized to his right, while his left eye penetrated a stare toward the boy, earning him the nickname—with young people anyway—"Queer-Eye."

As he stared at Petey, Zeke focus a sly gaze toward the wood stove. He knew how thorough the cop was when he suspected that something wasn't right or if his little nose for shit sniffed out a turd. It wouldn't be beyond him to walk right over to the stove and open the door to have a look inside if he had a mind to. Suddenly, he thought about the snake.

Rodney's stare appeared to freeze them all in time as a slight breeze began to filter through the thick pines that surrounded them. For the moment, the heat from the partially exposed and hazy sun was felt by all. Even though they were about a mile from the ocean, the salt air and its overpowering scent of iodine filled their senses.

"So, what have you to say for yourself?" Rodney's stare penetrated deep to Petey's soul.

"I…I…don't know what you mean." Petey broke from the fixed stare. Rodney spoke louder.

"Did you steal those doughnuts and coffees?"

With the intensity of his question, Zeke came out from the semi-darkness of the garage. He believed that together, they could take Rodney physically, and he pranced over to stand next to Pozy. They were both of the same mind-set: they simply wanted him to go away, but pissing him off would only prolong his stay and increase his heightened curiosity.

"I didn't steal anything. As a matter of fact, I never was near any donut-shop this morning. I came here from my grandparents' place, and Gram gave me a couple of muffins for the boys here and that's about the extent of my morning, officer," Petey said with confidence.

Rodney shuffled his feet over the gravel, the leather soles of his shoes scratching against the tiny pebbles with an irritating grumble. He moved closer to Petey, who'd remained next to the left fender and the open hood of his car, which, for the first time in a very long time, he'd driven in toward the garage, instead of turning around and backing in. As Rodney approached the car, he began looking first in the back window, then, without a word, he poked his head into the open driver's-side window. His actions seemed designed to provoke the boys into saying something, but all three remained still and quiet.

"I know you took the..." was the first thing he said, then he stopped, returning to his straight-as-an-arrow posture. "I'm going to keep an eye on you boys. It's going to be a long summer for the three of you." With that said, it took all the strength that the three could muster to maintain straight faces and closed lips when Rodney said he'd keep an eye on them. The big question was which eye would it be?

"Look..." Zeke began speaking and Rodney cut him off immediately.

"I'm not talking to you, Zeke. It would be nice if ya kept it shut 'til I'm finished talking to Peter. Like I said before, I'm gonna keep an eye on you, especially, and this white...white, whatever it is," he said as he pointed toward Petey's car.

The officer then walked slowly back to the patrol car, swung himself in the open door, and slammed it. The boys thought he would peel out, kicking all kinds of gravel and dust into the air simply for effect, but he turned the vehicle slowly, never upsetting a single pebble with his tires, and drove slowly, with very little dust stirred into the air.

"Well, ain't that nice. The only thing he wastes is hot air," Zeke bellowed out with laughter. All three, having held their breath for quite a spell, released their pent-up frustration with an outburst of laughter and joined in with a few pointed cut-ups toward the policeman.

"So, where did ya get them friggin' doughnuts, Petey-boy?" Zeke asked.

"I stole 'em," Petey responded, evoking another eruption of laughter from the three. Zeke grabbed for Petey and put him in a headlock and gave him a noogy on the top of his head until he fell to the ground, holding his sides from the foolish behavior.

"Ya know...I'm glad that little twit Dwight wasn't here when Queer Eye said he'd be keepin' an eye on us. I know he would have lost it then," Zeke said.

"Oh, ya…that's all we needed was for him to bust out laughin' while Rodney was handin' us the crap. So...where is that tiny penis?" Pozy chimed in.

"He told me he'd meet us here. He should o' been here by now," Petey said, never looking up from under the hood as he replaced the air cleaner on the top of the carburetor.

"Well, if he ain't here by the time you get done fuckin' with that thing ya call a car…" Zeke choked out laughs between syllables. "Just kiddin', I love that car," he said.

Petey knew very well what most people thought of his car, but it just didn't matter to him any longer. *This big Dodge was quality-built and will most likely outlast the plastic and thin metal cars built now-a-days,* he thought to himself as he slammed the hood, the thud resounding off of the trees. Through the windshield, he saw Dwight ambling his way toward the garage.

"Here comes Silly-Sally now," Pozy said, still leaning against the door frame. It seemed to take forever for Dwight to cross the short expanse between the start of the clearing and the garage, paying no attention to the three who stared or anything else in his immediate surroundings. Finally, at about twenty-five feet from the rear of Petey's car, Dwight began speaking.

"What the hell did old Queer-Eye want? He passed me on the way in here. One eye cut right through me… the other one was lookin' up in a friggin' tree or something."

All four began laughing now, but it was Dwight who seemed to find the most humor in what he'd said. Dwight resembled a street person in the way he dressed. The knees of his jeans were torn out, leaving fragments of material, a much lighter color of the already heavily faded pants hanging loosely and flopping from side to side as he walked. He carried a small white paper bag that might suggest he'd been to a pastry or chocolate shop, yet it was partially hidden by the baggy, long length of the sleeves on his hooded sweatshirt, which was also was torn near one shoulder. The sole of his right sneaker had come unglued and flopped with an irritating plopping sound as he shuffled along, tripping occasionally from the worn-out sole.

"Whataya got in the bag, teeny-peeny?" Pozy asked, but Dwight simply displayed a grin as broad as his lips would allow and said nothing, continuing his amble toward the garage.

After Rodney left, Zeke had returned to the snake cage, removing the blanket again.

"Where's Zeke? I've got something for the snake."

Shortly after catching the Black Racer, Zeke had named him Rowdy. The snake, which everyone continued to call "snake" then and to this day, resented confinement, and Zeke, his only handler, had been bitten many times during feedings.

From inside the garage, Zeke hollered out, "Whatcha' got, big-boy?" Dwight quickened his pace and went directly to the cage, holding the bag out in front of him, the bag moving on its own in his hand.

"I've got three blind mice for ya, snaky," he said and laughed.

He passed the bag over to Zeke, who took it with a broad smile and nodded his head affirmatively.

Dwight enjoyed bringing the snake its regular diet of mice, as he knew it gained him clout with Zeke, yet he could never remain and watch Zeke tease, and then feed Rowdy. The snake would never eat all three mice at one feeding and Zeke, only moments earlier, had fed the snake the mouse he'd been teasing it with. He kept a small menu box (as they called it) for just this reason. Zeke enjoyed watching the tiny lumps as the snake worked them through its system and would, occasionally, if he moved quickly before the snake turned on him, poke at the lump, and took much humor at the way it felt inside the snake.

Dwight stood next to Pozy, slouched by the door, and asked, "What did Queer-Eye want?"

"He wanted to know where Petey-boy there stole the fuckin' doughnuts."

"What…?" Dwight asked, and began looking around for them.

"Neva' mind, ya little fuck-head. Come ea', let me give ya a big kiss. I missed ya so much, ya little shit." Pozy reached for Dwight and gave him a huge, wet kiss on the cheek, causing Dwight to flinch away, wiping his cheek in disgust and whining like a little kid.

With doughnuts and coffee disposed of, the two older boys grew bored. After all, they lived here. The other two came and left at will. Sure, they stayed some nights and hung around for days on end, but they both had homes and family to go to when they'd had enough of the garage.

Rowdy had the mouse halfway down; the other three were snug in the menu box when Zeke hollered out from the cage area, forcing all three to look in his direction.

"Hey! Are we gonna stay here all friggin' day? There's some lollipops out thea' waitin' for our eyeballs to feast on. Besides, I'd like to see just what Queer-Eye plans to do when he sees us out and about after his baby tantrum."

Dwight, Pozy and Zeke were anxious to get going. However, Petey, for the first time since the officer had left, realized a sudden pang of uncertainty for extending himself beyond his comfort zone earlier, when he'd stolen the doughnuts to impress the older guys. He regretted it now. The last thing he wanted was for the others to see a scowl on his face—they might question it. He could not shake the shameful feeling that weighed him down for having been so foolish.

"Petey…darling…are you finished tinkering on thy huge chariot? The rest of us Romans would like to get the fuck outta hea' if ya don't mind," Pozy said in a sing-song voice.

Dwight fidgeted and began duct-taping the floppy sole of his sneaker, unaware of anything going on around him. Now it was Zeke's turn to badger the younger Petey.

"Let's go, Lamb-chop, before the sun goes down."

Within a minute or two, the four were piled into the huge Mopar in a seating arrangement long ago decided by Zeke. No one had a license except Petey, so that seat always remained the same. Zeke always rode shotgun and Pozy's place was always behind him. That side of the car would, for all practical purposes, be the nearer to any sidewalk, keeping them close to any action, whatever it might be. The only window seat remaining belonged to Dwight, directly behind Petey; yet when there was something on the sidewalk side to crow about, he bounced over the huge back seat like an adolescent going to the fair.

The big engine's exhaust and the mild, throaty rumble it made when at an idle, caused it to vibrate over the gravel. Petey went slowly between the garage and the blacktop. It was midday now, the sky cleared and the heat of the sun and the humidity wafting in through the open windows as the clothes of the four passengers clung uncomfortably to their bodies.

3

SUMMER IN MAINE BOILED with the allurement of an unknown treasure. It had drawn millions over the centuries to venture ever deeper into the wilds of the state, even if it was as far up and as isolated as the out-reaches of York County as some from away might say. All along old Route 1, from Kittery and as far as one might venture north, the antique shops, restaurants, motels, gift-shops and thousands of roadside attractions were crammed with visitors with much to do, except for four young men riding up and down the coast with nothing better to do but make a few cat-calls toward scantily-clad young women with firm bodies. The lobsters were red like so many sunburnt vacationers. Tempers flared in heavy traffic, along with an unnatural need to control a situation.

"The way life should be." It's called Vacation-Land for those who don't live here. In most cases, vacation for residents comes when the tourists go home and they get their pink slip handed to them from a dysfunctional, unappreciative employer; then they can settle down for a long winter's nap. No traffic jams, but even Mainers would just as soon kill each other in a traffic squabble than let the other guy get to the red light first, but throw a set of out-of-state plates into the equation, and things get real fired up.

No sooner was the car on the black-top than Zeke popped a CD into the dash player Petey had installed. "Look at Little Sister" blared out of the speakers. At the top of his lungs, from the rear seat, Dwight screamed the name, "Stevie Ray!"

"Listening to this is like visiting the grave, and it's rockin' down there!" he said.

None of the other three responded, entranced by the pounding woofer speakers in the trunk and the door-mounted tweeters. The heads of Petey and Dwight barely reached the dashboard, yet on the opposite side, Zeke and Pozy's heads seemed jammed into the roof.

They traveled on one of the many unnumbered back roads in the area; they preferred these for the lack of traffic they might be subjected to, and the one that the garage was located on made for a quick roll to the coast and Route 1, north and south. With the sun nearly burned through the remaining thin fog, the foursome now saw the entanglement of heavy traffic about an eighth of a mile ahead of them.

"Holy…shit!" Zeke said, and silently shook his head.

"Why do we even bother with this shit? We could be out near Poor-Peoples Pond and takin' somebody's boat out for a spin while they're gone workin'," Pozy said, while tapping Zeke on the shoulder. In an almost growling voice of dissent, Zeke responded.

"Because we can do any fuckin' thing we want. We live here, remember. These fucks come from everywhere but here and I'm not runnin' away and givin' them run-o'-the-mill, ya hear what I'm sayin', Pozy-boy?"

"I hear ya, sorry… I just want ta see some lollipops without havin' ta put up with all this other shit from away just because these fucks are dough-loaded…"

Generally, when the boys arrived at an intersection of Route 1 and whatever back road they chose to venture down to get there, whichever direction the traffic flow was heaviest, they went in the other direction. Today was no different. They went south.

The late morning sun and the humidity it produced seemed to heighten the mood of tourists to venture out. The heat appeared to only bother the locals. Any way you looked at it, them from away…created a stir.

The boys were nearing Punquit Beach and suddenly, the center of town was a bottle-neck of traffic that even bicycles had a problem getting through. They were people from away, mostly, and displayed less patience than locals trapped in the vehicle mire, but most folks from here and the surrounding towns knew from past experience to avoid the coastal routes during prime tourist season. Going around took a longer time and a bit more gas, but standing still in summer swelter was far more aggravating.

Pozy swore at just above a whisper, to which Zeke immediately responded loudly. Generally, an outburst of this sort was sure to draw attention and in most cases, that's exactly what they wanted—and like a time-bomb, right on schedule, Zeke went off with the windows wide open.

"Ya know, all these frigs' from somewhere else come up hea', choke the life outta everything they touch, and look at us like we're the morons." Zeke was staring at a woman and a man in a late-model Volvo wagon in the lane beside them, the windows of which were up tight, obviously with the air conditioner up high and probably not picking up on Zeke's bellowing voice. But Zeke's flailing arms and hand gestures attracted the attention of the car's driver, causing him to push the down button on the electric window, thinking that Zeke might need help with directions. That was the driver's first mistake.

"Hi! Kind of warm, isn't it?" The driver turned toward Zeke and smiled.

"What the fuck do you want?" Zeke demanded in a very angry voice. The driver's eyes bulged from their sockets, and he quickly lifted the window and looked toward the front. After that outburst and without saying a word, Petey began shifting his head discretely from side to side, hoping he wouldn't see Queer-Eye anywhere nearby. This close to Punquit Beach, they were within sight of the town line, giving Rodney free reign over the turf.

The traffic began to move, but ever so slowly; the Volvo remained close, the driver appearing wary of the potential madman in the vehicle next to him. He exchanged concerned looks with the woman next to him. Zeke was hell-bent on starting something with someone, especially after Rodney's earlier visit. He pounded on the side of the car to the beat of the loud music, much to Petey's displeasure.

"I'll bet this thing next to me is a Mass-hole," Zeke said loudly. "Can ya smell that? That's Mass-hole. I'd like ta get outta this car, walk ova' thea' and pull one o' his fuckin' ears ova' the top o' his tiny head and ask 'em if he can hea' me now." And he began laughing and slapping the car door, almost in rhythm with his laughter.

It was this type of behavior that drew the other three boys to Zeke's personality, yet as had time passed, even Pozy had wondered if there might be something wrong, mentally, where Zeke was concerned, though none of the three could find the grapes to say anything about it to him or between themselves about him. Suddenly, without warning, Zeke began a high-pitched whistle toward a scantily clad young woman walking along the heavily congested sidewalk on the opposite side of the road. Dwight, always seeking Pozy and Zeke's approval, chimed in when he noticed that she was ignoring them. Heads began to turn in the direction of the big white Dodge and at least three of the passengers welcomed the attention.

"Look at the freak in that blue Cadillac. His head is as big as a friggin' watermelon," Pozy said, as Dwight flipped the guy off. Petey began to feel boxed in with thoughts of what could happen if they were reported. After all, the car was his and registered to him and eventually it could all fall on his shoulders, and they were still in Queer-Eye's country. His concerned facial expression was noticed by Zeke, and he opened up on him immediately, as if he knew exactly what he was thinking.

"Don't be such a baby-ass. Nothing's gonna happen, and nobody's gonna take your plate number in this traffic." He said it with such sarcasm, Petey felt insignificant, yet it could not prevent his mind's eye from carrying him back to earlier when he did steal the doughnuts and coffees to impress them, and now it all seemed out of control.

At that moment, as Petey became entranced by his mental venture back in time, he didn't notice that Zeke had removed his eight-inch hunting knife from its leather sheath, which always hung from his belt, and was tapping the side of the blade against the palm of his left hand as he stared in the direction of the man and woman in the Volvo. Suddenly, without Petey noticing, the traffic began moving forward. Petey's eyes were riveted to the sheen of the blade from the sunlight in the car. A horn tooted briskly from behind, rousting Petey's consciousness to the present and the overlooked distance in car-length between them and the vehicles ahead. The momentary distraction from the horn allowed the Volvo to move, unnoticed, closer to the curb, the driver slowly distancing it from the Dodge and Zeke's threatening demeanor.

At the first opportunity, the driver peeled out and Zeke caught a glimpse of the rear end as the car sped down a side road, away from Route 1. It didn't seem clear to either Zeke or Petey whether the driver of the Volvo had seen the knife, but Petey could only imagine that the rate of speed at which the car had vanished meant that he had. All this seemed to go undetected by the two in the back seat, and probably for the better as far as Petey was concerned. After several minutes, the traffic moved along at a regular pace and from the back seat, Pozy and Dwight were unaware of the knife tapping.

Obviously calmed by the cool sea breeze filtering in from the movement of the car, Zeke slowly slid the knife into the sheath, snapping the fastener holding it in place. Had Petey exhaled at that moment, the irregular breath of anxiety would certainly fill the interior of the big car, probably giving way for sarcasm from Zeke, Pozy or both. He might not be able to put into words, given the chance, his concerns for the way Zeke projected hate when in close proximity to out-of-staters. Sure, Petey had a hate for them, too; for the way they were and their ability to just fuck up the home-ground, but not to the extent that it bugged Zeke and Pozy. He wondered at times if maybe the tide was right to move on. Zeke and Pozy would never change; you could take that to the bank. But Petey was changing. He had a diploma as an auto-mechanic. He could get a job mostly anywhere and if he got into the right place, like an auto dealership, in most cases they would pay for him to move up the ladder with tech-schools and more certificates. *What is holding me back?* he wondered.

Petey was dragged back into reality by a slap to the back of his head from a giggling Dwight, and the sound caused the other two to burst out, joining Dwight in loud laughter.

"What's tha' matter, pumpkin-head, can't ya see the fuckin' cars up front are gone?" Dwight asked. While his thoughts carried him off to faraway worlds, Petey again lost track of the slow-moving traffic ahead of him and there was now a huge distance between his car and those who moved on. Surprisingly, however, the one most likely to offer comment remained silent in the seat beside the driver. Zeke appeared to be held captive in his own far-off world since he'd placed the knife back into the sheath. He'd been falling off into these moods lately where he'd remain quiet, without a murmur of sound or movement for hours at a spell. Pozy could care less, as the silence made living together in the small confines of the garage somewhat more bearable, but it was causing some concern at this stage. For as long as they'd hung out together, Zeke and Pozy knew everything there was to know about each other. There were things they both liked and disliked and generally, a burger and coffee would work for either breakfast or dinner to smooth things over after a minor disagreement. These days it was obvious to Pozy that his closest friend was going through some sort of change and he just didn't know how to bring the subject up, or he just didn't want to.

"There ain't nothin' goin' on 'round hea' except outta-state traffic assholes," Petey said in hopes of persuading the others to do something else and get away from what appeared to be a nightmare brewing in the secret recesses of Zeke's mind. Besides, the tapping blade remained vivid in Petey's consciousness and he wanted that thought to fade away.

For the first time since he'd hollered at the driver of the Volvo, Zeke spoke out, though his words were inaudible to the two in the back seat. "Let's head over to the Roady. Maybe we can get a free coffee from Blondie, if her old lady ain't there," he said, maintaining a vacant stare out the passenger side window, while his right hand grasped at the handle of the knife. Petey, from the corner of his eye, saw the grasp, yet turned quickly so as not to be noticed, then turned the vehicle sharply to the right, passing several stopped cars, and took the gravel shoulder toward the first turn that would take them away from this middle-of-the-road parking lot of summer traffic, and much to the pleasure of the two in the back, who'd remained silent until now, even though they'd never heard what Zeke said.

The thought of seeing Missy now gave Petey a good feeling inside. He was so attracted to her, yet he kept his feelings to himself, knowing very well how Zeke overflowed with desire when she was around. The big Dodge rumbled as it sliced through the humidity, which became more intense as they wound their way inland a few miles, avoiding the snarled traffic on the coastal route.

The music continued to blare, echoing over the airy countryside through the open windows, forcing an occasional cow or horse to raise its head with abrupt concern as they roared past. There was no telling where Zeke's mind was—he hadn't spoken a word since they'd ventured away from Route 1, and his vacant stare remained focused out the passenger window. The two in back horse-played with punching and verbal cut-ups, keeping the noise level high. Petey remained quiet, not wanting to disturb Zeke, yet hoping that he'd snap out of it soon. Zeke's silence was making him uncomfortable now and he'd just sooner be somewhere else. The ruckus from the back seat suddenly spilled over into the front, kicking Zeke in the shoulder, causing an immediate outburst from him.

"What tha' fuck aar' you morons doin' back thea'? You kick me one more time and I'll smack tha' hell outta both o' ya. See how ya like them apples!" Zeke, fully revived from his trance, became belligerent, demanding that they get going and end this "little queer jaunt through the cow-shit," as he put it.

"A bunch o' cow's asses don't turn me on, so let's go. Get me to the fuckin' Roady. Missy oughta' look pretty good about now," he said.

Petey took the first turn that would head them once again toward the coast and the Little Roady.

Petey was now in a hurry to end their little romp through the fields, although he always enjoyed the sound and feel of his Mopar under the heavy gas-foot he could afford out here with almost no traffic. The engine just got all clogged up in town, but after the run-in with Queer-Eye this morning, Petey maintained a frugal pressure on the go-pedal as they neared the town line once again, this being Rodney Country. The last thing he needed was a set of blue strobes behind them.

As they made their final approach to the route junction, the roadway here was as congested as the parking lot they'd detoured from several miles back, but here, they were only yards from their destination.

On a good day, depending on the direction of the wind, the scent of fresh-brewed coffee and frying eggs wafted through the air, encouraging hunger pangs from all in the immediate proximity. Today was no different except for the lack of parking places out front, as the big Mopar cruised in on the south-bound side of Portland Street.

"I'll tell ya boys, this place is startin' ta give me a real pain in tha' ass," Zeke grumbled. "When ya can't even pull up to a spot out front of yaw' favorite dive, it's time somethin' was done ta get rid o' this traffic shit."

Petey suddenly realized that negativity appeared to be a way of life for Zeke, as not much else passed his lips unless he spoke of Missy or wringing some out-of-stater's neck. He'd talked of doing the latter much more lately.

Though they didn't speak of it, both Petey and Pozy were very surprised that Zeke had remained quiet this morning when Queer-Eye had chastised Petey and tried, with a few suggestive phrases, to irritate them into a verbal confrontation. It remained deep within Zeke's subconscious mind, and it was apparent by his silence and quickened temper toward his friends.

Petey pulled a quick U-turn from the restaurant side of the road to the other, sliding gently against the curb after power-braking. The four jumped from their individual doors simultaneously and slammed them in unison, making for a loud thud. They all met on the roadside, and never looking in either direction before stepping out, caused the oncoming traffic in both north and south-bound lanes to begin panic-braking and horn-tooting to the obvious pleasure of Zeke and Pozy. Petey held back at the first sound of a horn, yet Dwight, ever the jester, jumped and twirled in the center of one lane, forcing an outburst of chaotic laughter from the two older boys. With Zeke's obvious intimidating size, none of the angry motorists ventured a response, nor chose to exit their vehicle in protest. Zeke would have loved it had one tried.

With the commotion outside, faces of stunned diners in the windowed front of the Little Roady turned toward them; it was the type of distraction Missy and her mother would prefer not to take place out front of their restaurant and instigated by anyone about to be considered a patron.

Zeke, Pozy and Dwight stepped onto the sidewalk, never realizing that Petey had held back and was now being prompted by a less-anxious motorist to go ahead and cross. Zeke turned and began taunting him, while the other two bellowed with laughter.

"C-mon...pansy-pants. Ya need me ta come get ya ta cross the big street?"

The razzing gouged deep into Petey's soul, forcing him to recall the taunting he'd been demoralized by long ago at school. As he hurried to catch up, the three boys turned their backs to him and entered the restaurant without saying another word to each other or to Petey. Zeke, as usual, entered first and scanned for the first available booth, and upon seeing the last one next to a window, their favorite, he went immediately to it.

"Hi... Missy," he said as he passed the wedged-open swinging door to the kitchen. Whether she saw or heard the disturbance from outside, she greeted them with her ready smile. Her mother, on the other hand, had seen their little theatrical approach and dismissed them for as long as it was possible for her to do so. But, with Missy at the grill, she wanted them to order, and hoped that their visit would be a short one.

"Well...well, if it isn't the world's unfortunate foursome." she said.

Marcy, Missy's mother, appeared to tower over the table, her eyes focused on Zeke, tapping her order pad with the pencil. Whenever she was away from the restaurant, Zeke referred to her as "Marcy mommy," and Missy as "Missy baby." He never said it in front of her, though of all the things about him she disliked, that one had made her laugh when she first heard it from Missy.

Marcy was in her late fifties, and though at first glance her past offered little that might suggest an attempt to age gracefully, she was a good-natured woman. She was five foot four and somewhat stocky, never revealing her weight to anyone, including Missy. She loved her daughter's cooking, especially the bacon double cheeseburgers with fries. She welcomed that meal for breakfast, lunch or dinner, and fries anytime of the day with a milkshake or large Coke. She often said, "I don't care what I look like. If I'm hungry, I'm eatin'," and that was apparent from the stretched button eyes on her white waitress blouse.

"Whataya need, boys? I ain't got all day."

"Well…well, marvelous Marcy. How we doin' today, dea'?" Zeke asked before ordering a coffee. The other three chimed in immediately with the same.

With an obvious exhalation of anxious breath, she stroked the page briskly, penciling in the order, then turned toward the counter without another word. In her deepest and most personal thoughts, which she shared with no one, she felt an attraction to Zeke. She'd been without male companionship for quite some time and though her feminine capabilities were somewhat evaporated, her longings at times caused depression. She comforted herself with food and drink, though alcohol had long since been removed from the menu to satisfy that need.

The endearing smell of breakfast being cooked and fresh-perked coffee filled the room, and suddenly, pangs of hunger began to tug at Dwight's stomach. He wished he'd been able to order more for himself, yet his purse-strings had long ago frayed with the association of the two older boys. As usual, all four boys ignored each other, as was their habit, Zeke and Pozy looking out through the window, silently; Petey and Dwight, absorbed by their surroundings, said very little to each other, and if they did, it was in low tones, so as not to disturb the other two.

Marcy delivered the steaming cups of coffee, placing each one hard on the table in front of the recipients, never spilling a drop, and like a professional poker dealer, dealt out the packets of cream and sugar. As he stirred the sweetness into his brew, Zeke eyed the fair Missy at the grill through the wedged door and fantasized about them, removing all thoughts of his previous frustrations with Queer-Eye and the scene in traffic with the driver in the Volvo. She seemed to feel his stare, for seconds after his eyes fell upon her, she looked up toward him and immediately smiled, sending a tingle through Zeke's midsection and down to his knees.

4

"OH…I DON'T THINK they're dangerous, Rodney. Remember the old saying, 'boys will be boys.' You know darn well Petey Harriman's family background. I've known his grandparents our entire lives." Police Chief Willard Weaks seemed to drift off for a moment before he continued. "It was tragic when his parents were killed in that crash up in the Moosehead Lake area all those years ago." He fell silent again momentarily, and appeared to contemplate what he might say next, while Rodney Torrey sat across from him on a hard metal chair as the chief sat heavily in his cushioned office chair with his feet crossed and resting on his desk.

Willard Weaks had been appointed Police Chief twenty-five years earlier. The position was for life or until retirement, whichever arrived first, and the chief had vague plans for the latter. Over the years he'd expanded at the belt-line from long luncheon meetings and late-night functions with town officials and community organizers, and he enjoyed the social aspect of his position. The receding hairline and the whiteness of his thinned locks was somewhat premature for a man of sixty, but ultimately reflected the seriousness of the issues a chief was regularly confronted with. His office was filled with memorabilia on tabletops and walls from the past two-and-a-half decades of the awards and honorable mentions he'd received from the community and local civic groups for his involvement and support of their endeavors. He was held in high regard by the police chiefs of surrounding towns and without a doubt, the Maine State Police, for his assistance when called upon.

"Chief…I just have a feeling when it comes to the four of them…" Rodney began, and was immediately interrupted by the chief.

"Rodney, those boys are simply bored from nothing to do during the hot days of summer. I don't believe, for one minute, and I don't mean to undermine your approach with young people, that little Petey Harriman actually got up the balls to steal doughnuts and coffee from that shop."

There was much Rodney could have and wanted to add to the chief's comments, yet now, he thought, would not be the time or the place to vent his disapproval. The chief began to rattle on about things that had nothing to do with Rodney's concerns for the boys' behavior, and he was convinced now that he should excuse himself as soon as the opportunity availed itself. That moment arrived sooner than he expected when the chief's phone rang, and when he reached for it and said hello, Rodney motioned with a lifted finger as he got up from his chair and went directly toward the door.

"Excuse me," the chief said to the caller, cupping his hand over the mouthpiece of the receiver as Rodney reached the door. "Get back to me later with that, will ya, officer?" he said, and Rodney simply nodded his head affirmatively and walked out.

The hallway leading from the chief's office was cool and removed from the sweltering outdoor heat, as it was in the center of the building's innermost area. It was crisscrossed by a maze of intersections along the way, and for anyone not familiar with the building, it would be impossible to walk directly to the chief's office without getting turned around, had there been the intention of wrongdoing toward the chief. Although Willard Weaks had a long list of friends and admirers, he'd made enemies during his rise to chiefdom, and it was his decision to take that inner office the very day he became Chief of Police.

The sound of Rodney's heals tapped out a rhythm as his thoughts traveled at almost the same pace as his feet. The memory of the chief's words, still fresh in his mind—*"boys will be boys"*—haunted him. He'd been on the force long enough to know that small-town politics ruled over the right and wrong of things, depending on who was involved. The fact that the chief had known Petey's grandparents since childhood inspired his need to protect the boy, but first and foremost, he knew the chief wanted to protect the grandparents. Rodney was no one's fool. He knew the power that backed the chief's decision-making ability and the power the chief had to back it all up. He began to question his visit to the chief's office now as he neared the end of his walk through the complex, before returning to the sweltering heat of the early afternoon. As any good cop knows, to go with your gut whenever something doesn't smell quite right was nearly paramount, and the stench coming from those four boys was a little more powerful than just "boys being boys." Rodney accepted the chief's dismissal, yet he knew his surveillance of the four would continue, with or without the chief's support.

5

THE MID-MORNING BREAKFAST CROWD at the Little Roady evaporated along with the early sea-smoke from the heat of the ascending sun. Missy cleaned up around the counter and the kitchen, occasionally casting a flirting stare in Zeke's direction. His eyes never left her and it was clear that both longed for the same scratching of their sexual itch. It was the day after the four jesters' romp through traffic, and it was a whole lot quieter at the Little Roady.

It was never really cool inside of the restaurant, and the only means for taking the edge off was an antiquated ceiling fan that hummed out a noticeable and monotonous drone when the patrons were few. The added heat from their libidinous desires created an inferno of lust.

"How long aar' ya goin' to rub that counter, Missy?" Zeke asked, and from the look he gave her, the rubbing was done as far as she was concerned.

They'd been lovers for quite some time, keeping it surprisingly secret. There wasn't much that Marcy didn't know about what went on in the Little Roady, or in town for that matter, but like everyone else, she knew nothing about the affair. Without a word, and seeing that the restaurant was empty and probably would stay this way for some time, Missy entered the kitchen, kicking the wedged swinging door free. Not one second passed before Zeke was behind her and through the door, heading for the supply closet at the farthest end of the kitchen, away from any exit or entrance to the kitchen. By the time Zeke crossed the restaurant floor and popped the swinger open, Missy was already out of sight. Her eagerness thrilled him to his knees. He remained speechless, going directly to the closet, and upon entering, he gasped as he saw Missy, braless under her opened blouse. His hands were on her quickly. Their bodies, exasperated from need, crashed into each other in a passionate quivering of fulfillment. Their lips pressed tightly together, neither willing to be first to part, making it difficult to breathe. Suddenly, as quickly as it would be to snap fingers, Zeke's jeans fell to the floor around his ankles, revealing the strength of his manhood, and the sight of him always set fire to her libido.

"Oomph," was the only sound that passed her lips.

Although they'd only used the storage closet a couple of times, they obviously never got completely naked in the event that someone did walk in through either the front or kitchen doors. The alarm would sound, whether it was the tinkle-bell on the front door or the swollen-with-humidity wooden back door that needed to be kicked several times at the bottom in order for it to open. No one, however, was expected to enter that one today. All deliveries had come yesterday and today, and Marcy planned to spend the entire day in Portland shopping to restock the restaurant at BB's Wholesale. She was also shopping at the Mall and always had a late-afternoon lunch with the one or two closest friends she went along with to the city.

After fifteen minutes of sexual enjoyment and a final release, they fell against the sacks of flour, panting from the joy of finally being together. Not a word was spoken by either, yet they stared and smiled intently at each other, as his hands roamed freely over her smooth, firm breasts. After several moments of bliss, as if an alarm had gone off silently in Zeke's subconscious mind, he turned his head rapidly toward the closet door.

"Did you hear that?" he asked.

"No…what did you hear?"

"Petey-pants is coming. I'd recognize the sound o' that engine a mile away."

They immediately began to put themselves together, sharing an occasional kiss and hug between snaps of clothes fasteners and the moment they re-entered the kitchen proper, the front door tinkled right along with Petey's easily recognizable voice.

"Hey...where is everyone?"

As usual, when distracted from a closet rendezvous, Zeke came through the swinging door carrying some non-descript box of anything, giving the impression that he was simply helping Missy with something too heavy for her to carry. He was met with Petey's smiling face.

"Hey people...what-ya'll-doin' back there?" Petey asked, a pang of jealousy ripping at his soul. In his heart he knew they were involved sexually, yet his feelings for Missy were genuine, and he was thinking that he could give her what no one else could, but he was no fool. His chances with someone like Missy were slim to none and now he wondered if she ever really noticed him.

"Hey...if it ain't Petey-weety. What in the hell aar' you doin' hea' this time o' day?" Zeke asked, and went about shoving the box he'd toted over the counter, having no obvious place to put it.

"Well, a guy has a need for coffee once in a while and the best place I know... is here," he said. Missy smiled in his direction, causing a flutter in his midsection, and he sat himself at the booth next to the window, looking at his car parked just outside. His thoughts drifted back to when he first saw them come out from the kitchen, but it faded quickly the moment Missy arrived at his side, brushing against him gently, placing the steaming cup of coffee in front of him. She placed the sugar and creamers softly down beside the cup.

"How ya doin', handsome?" she asked.

He looked up at her, speechless, and the fluttering began again, then he found his nuts and spoke up.

"I'm fine, now that I've seen you, darlin'," he said, and smiled up at her. As he did, he couldn't look away from her well-exposed cleavage, visible through the top three buttons of her blouse left undone. Suddenly, she became self-conscious of his stare and moved away, looking down as she did.

Damn, I forgot to button this… she thought.

Just then, Zeke arrived at the table, passing Missy, wondering what the hissy-look was all about, but never asking. He couldn't refrain from saying something sarcastic.

"What'd ya say to her, ya little fuck? She looks pissed off."

Petey turned his stare toward Zeke, and stuttered a few syllables before regaining his composure.

"I… d-d-didn't say anything e-e-except thank you for bringing my c-c-coffee," he stumbled, leaving out not being able to remove his eyes from her exposed cleavage. That, he thought, would not go over well with Zeke, especially if his intuition was on about them and what he thought they'd been up to out back before he arrived. Zeke burst out laughing.

"Ya fuckin' idiot. I was only messin' with ya." But it was the way he said things that kept Petey on his toes, or on the edge of his seat, whenever he was around Zeke. Zeke sat across from Petey with a lumbering thump, and looked out at the big Mopar. They sat without speaking for quite some time, Petey sipping his coffee, staring intently into the cup. Zeke appeared hypnotized by the sun's glare on the bumper of the big car out front. If he was made uncomfortable from the silence, Petey made no outward sign, and suddenly, Zeke began speaking in a low voice.

"So…ya see old Queer-Eye around since he dropped by the garage?"

"Nope… I haven't seen him anywhere; for that matter, I thought by now he'd be on us like flies on your daddy's farm, but no…"

"I'm gettin' a little bored with the shit around hea'. I'm thinkin' we oughta stir somethin' up just fa' the hell of it. I've got a feelin' he ain't as tough as he makes himself out ta be. I think I could take 'em," Zeke boasted.

Petey stifled a breath at hearing what sounded like a possible threat toward Rodney Torrey. He didn't like the police officer either, but he was a cop, and the last thing Petey needed was to get involved in something like that.

"Are you talking about getting into—"

"Nah…nah. I'm just sayin' if I had to, I could wipe his ass with his tie. I ain't scared o' that badge. He gets between me and what I wanna do, and we'll see just how tough he is. He took judo…I took bales o' hay," Zeke smirked.

Without asking, Missy brought the boys each an order of English muffins with loads of butter and fresh coffee.

"On the house," she said, and looked toward Zeke, yet said nothing now that he was in Petey's company. As she walked toward the kitchen, Petey wanted to follow Zeke's stare, obviously directed at her beautiful behind, but thought better of it and began munching on the English muffin, waiting for a muttered description from Zeke, but none came.

"Ya know, Petey-boy, I'm a bit nervous when it comes ta walkin' 'round hea' in the mornin'. Them out-o'-state drivers aar' getting' a little close ta the kneecaps, if ya know what I mean. Somebody oughta teach them little fucks a lesson in manners; like from us locals. If a few o' them get slapped around, maybe they'll spread the word and stop acting like a bunch o' Mass-holes."

"I doubt a little slappin' would do much good." Petey regretted saying the words the moment they left his mouth.

"Well…maybe somethin' that hurts more than just slappin'," Zeke said.

Only seconds after saying that, the remaining duo-combination of the troublesome foursome stumbled in through the front door, much to the surprise of Zeke and Petey. With no one else in the restaurant, the atmosphere that the four created was of such a festive mood, it could have been mistaken for some sort of a party. Zeke was in rare form, and the others would bend over backwards to cool the heat of his aggressive behavior.

Whenever the boys congregated at their favorite booth, Missy would leave them to themselves, knowing it wouldn't be very long before the wanderlust took them on their way, if only a few miles to the north or south—and from the sound of their pent-up energy, she wouldn't have to wait long. The moment they settled down, Missy brought the late arrivals their steaming cups of fresh brew, and they thanked her for it. As usual, Petey, the only one to carry money, slid a five and a one toward the edge of the table after Missy turned away, knowing very well that no one else would. Immediately, Zeke began speaking, and the three heads turned in his direction as he stood over them at the table.

"Ya know…I had this dream last night…" he started, turning his head toward the kitchen and lowering his voice now, so as not to be overheard. "I was drivin' this fuckin' steam-roller…big motha'...and I was flattenin' all the fuckin' out-a'-state cars out on Route 1A." He looked down at Petey, then Dwight, their faces solemn, and by the time he looked toward Pozy, who refused to look up at him, Zeke burst out in guttural laughter, forcing a slight ringing in Petey's ears before he stopped. "You fuckin' nitwits. I was just screwin' with ya."

It was obvious that Pozy knew exactly where Zeke was taking the boys with his dream of a steam-roller story—a good reason for him not to pay any attention to him while he spoke of it. Being so caught up in the story, the two younger boys seemed puzzled at being called nitwits, but not until seeing Pozy's face crooked in a smirk did they realize they'd been made fools of once again.

The traffic out on Route 1 began to increase; both north and southbound lanes pulsed with summer's tourism. Inside the restaurant, the boys were cool under the noisy ceiling fan, yet an angry heat was building within Zeke that not even his closest friends or lover could know the true dimension of.

6

IT HAD BEEN FIVE DAYS since Missy and Zeke's storage-closet fling on the flour sacks. No contact was attempted by either. Missy was used to Zeke's long disappearances, yet recently she'd begun to feel a more intense need to be with him, and the closet romps left her needy for a lasting relationship. But there was something about Zeke that left her in wonderment as to how far he'd be able to take a true commitment with someone, and she knew from experience what bad boys were all about. It was closing time at the Little Roady. The sound of her key tripping the tumblers in the door-lock made her last thoughts of him fade, and he became the least of her concerns as, without realizing it, she was the least of his.

The early evening sun was brushing the edge of the distant horizon. Darkness was slowly encapsulating the heated earth and the silhouettes of two figures on the shoulder of a non-descript, narrow coastal road nearly blended perfectly with their surroundings. Each was clad in black clothing; and had it not been for the remaining light of the setting sun, they would be invisible to any approaching vehicles from either direction. They walked with the traffic flow, not against it, offering no warning to any drivers to beware of the two shadows in the road ahead of them. The black-clad figures were none other than Zeke Brailey and his closest companion since boy-hood, Pozy Linscott. They had, as usual, no intended direction, yet each knew from previous adventures that they were nearing an area known as Biddeford Pool, several miles south from the city of Biddeford. The road was winding and unnumbered, following the coast from Dells and far enough removed from the high traffic of the main routes that they could enjoy a long stroll with no particular place to go while they filled their lungs with the pungent-smelling smoke of a huge, well-rolled joint of pot.

They spoke little during walks such as this, but what was said seemed to bring them down to earth whenever they were troubled with what they perceived as the day-to-day bullshit that life deals out. No one would deny that these two were the two peas in the prosaic pod, but at times such as these and from the onset of their relationship, Zeke had been the fuel and the flame for their counter-culture existence. Pozy was simply along for the ride, and generally was happy to play the part he was given. Tonight however, it was as if Zeke had an unspoken plan, as his stride was long and Pozy felt out of breath at times, trying to keep up. Whatever the plan was, Pozy couldn't wait to find it out.

The evening was cooling down nicely near the water and the smell of salt air filled them with a sense of welcome. The distant sight of the sea was calming, along with the effects of the pot. The dim lights from surrounding cottages added to the feeling of solitude. The only close sound was from the soles of their sneakers against the blacktop and the occasional muffled crash of the distant surf. They hadn't been passed by a single vehicle for close to thirty minutes, which for this time of the day was unusual, but well-received by both. Neither had spoken for quite some time when Zeke stopped suddenly to re-light their smoke.

"Gimme that fuckin' lighter, will ya?"

Pozy carried it in his hand and when Zeke asked, he simply reached out and flicked it. They stood in the center of the lane, completely invisible on the darkened roadway, except for the warm glow encircling their heads from the lighter's flame. As fate would have it, their presence was also hidden by the fact that they were standing at the sharpest point of a curve in the road, but neither of them gave it a single thought.

Zeke drew deep, as the bright tip grew brighter from the gas-hissing flame and the wonderment showing in Pozy's eyes gave no doubt as to whose turn it would be next. A slight breeze kicked up, rustling the branches on the wild rose bushes, blanketing all other sound about them. At the very moment Pozy released his thumb from the fuel button on the lighter, encapsulating them both in near-total darkness; a speeding car wound its way into the curve from a southerly direction, taking the entire lane in which the boys stood, unaware.

They appeared as horror-struck deer in the headlight beam. It was as if a bolt of lightning had pierced them from eternity, freezing them to the spot momentarily; had it not been for Zeke's thunderbolt-like reaction speed as he pulled himself and Pozy onto the gravel shoulder, tumbling onto their backs out of harm's way, they both would have been killed.

The roar of the car's highly revved engine reverberated against their eardrums as the car missed them by mere inches. It never slowed or even swerved, as if the driver never saw either of the two darkened figures in front of him or her in the roadway. The sound of whining tires drilled its way into Zeke and Pozy's heads as the vehicle, which resembled a mid-sized Honda or Nissan with a dark-colored paint job, faded quickly into the darkness. Through all of this, Zeke was observant enough to catch the last three digits from the rear plate: 019, and of all the plates in America, this one just had to be from Massachusetts—one of the New England States the troublesome foursome loved to rhyme their made-up names with.

Getting to his feet quickly, Zeke ran in the direction of the long-gone vehicle, shouting obscenities at the top of his lungs, flaying his arms with clenched fists.

"Ya fucked-up Mass-hole! Ya better keep on goin' back home. I'll find ya. Ya can't hide; you fucked-up Mass-hole!"

Pozy was seated on the gravel shoulder where he'd landed after being pulled to safety, nearly invisible to Zeke now as he turned in his direction. Pozy's legs were pulled up toward his chest with his arms around them. He was motionless.

"What the hell…you alright?" Zeke asked.

"Yah… Ok… You?" Pozy asked, and then began again. "I'd like ta get a hold o' that little fuck's throat, whoever he is."

Zeke remained in the roadway, only now he focused his attention on any sound that might not be of the natural type, like the wind and the bushes, but he was nearer to the shoulder and Pozy.

"Talk about ruining a buzz," Pozy grumbled. "Did ya get a look at who that might o' been?"

"No." Zeke replied flatly.

At that point he joined Pozy on the shoulder, and sat beside him, though considerably closer to the bushes and away from the blacktop.

"My stomach is upside down right now," Pozy said.

"Yeah…I feel a little funny myself. Ya know how close we came to gettin' whacked just then?" Zeke asked. Pozy did not answer. He continued looking toward the shoulder, while inhaling and exhaling shallow breaths.

"I wish Putsy Petey was here right now with the big Mopar. We'd run that fuckin' Mass-hole into the ground. I won't forget that piece o' shit-colored car and those last three numbers." Zeke accentuated the numbers as he said them aloud. "0 1 9." Suddenly, he began patting himself around the shirt pockets and then his jeans.

"Son-a-va-bitch! I think I lost that fuckin' joint when that car flew by," Zeke said.

He'd been the last to have it. He got to his feet, asked Pozy for the lighter and began scanning the shoulder and the area they'd been standing in when the car almost hit them. He went about ten feet from Pozy when he came to full attention, burning his thumb on the overheated lighter and at that same moment came the sound of a vehicle approaching from the direction the car had gone only minutes earlier. Both young men raced away from the sound, well onto the shoulder, pressing hard against the rose bushes, never feeling the pricking from their thorns. They were both wide-eyed and alert when the vehicle came abreast of them, and both wondered whether it was the very same vehicle on its way back from wherever it originally went. But their hopes were dashed with sobering disappointment. It was a small pickup truck with an older man at the wheel. The moment the truck was out of the immediate area, Zeke again flicked the lighter to life and began looking for the lost smoke. Pozy was now bored with the entire event and was ready to continue walking, or hitchhike and get the hell out of this place. *I'd like to get to Biddeford before it gets too late, and see if Zeke decides to tell me what he's planned for the night; besides just getting into trouble. It might be a decent place to hitch a ride back to the garage and the couch,* he thought.

"Let's get the hell outta hea'. This road's startin' ta freak me out. Anyway, by the time we get ta town they'll be rollin' up the fuckin' sidewalks."

"I wanta find that smoke before we leave," Zeke said and continued searching along the shoulder where they'd been closely missed. At that point, simply to appease his friend, knowing well that the chances of finding it now were slim to none, Pozy began to search.

In the distance, someone apparently dropped the metal lid off a trash can, and the sound echoing through the quiet night caused the boys to dash toward the shoulder once again, feeling stupid upon their arrival there. It now became clear that their evening of indulgent relaxation was over. Since they were this close to Biddeford, the solitude would only diminish with each step forward.

They maintained a steady walking speed for several miles and the traffic became heavy in both directions the closer they came to the city, yet it did little to stifle Zeke's outbursts of foul language, at times at the top of his lungs toward anyone driving past who unknowingly was foolish enough to happen to look in his line of vision. Pozy on the other hand said very little and he trembled at times, as the vision of the speeding car and how close they'd come to oblivion replayed over and over in his mind. There was no one on the entire earth who knew where he and Zeke were, and furthermore, he couldn't think of anyone who might even care had they been killed back there near Biddeford Pool.

"You farkin'... fiddlehead... freak. Come back here and I'll pull yaw' freakin' tiny ears over yaw' friggin' head!" Zeke was standing flatfooted at the edge of the gravel shoulder, waving his clenched, right fist toward the driver of a passing vehicle and from what Pozy saw, the driver never noticed that Zeke was even alive.

"What did he do?" Pozy asked.

"He was fuckin' born," Zeke answered.

The clanging sound of someone working with metal echoed from an alleyway, causing them to look in that direction. Pozy thought it might be enough to make Zeke holler out some obscenities, yet seeing nothing, or anyone there, he remained still, much to Pozy's satisfaction. There would be no calming him down now. His rage would magnify with almost every step and Pozy knew better than to offer solace, but as they neared the top of a rise that would offer a view of the downtown, Zeke appeared to calm himself to the point of quietude. They continued their winding path toward the city on a downward trek—this part of town was mapped with crappy little side streets where people sat on front steps and curbs, taking comfort from the stifling heat inside the tiny houses, staring at the two strangers as they passed. Yet no one, not even the boys, offered comments.

The heat of the summer's evening amongst the brick buildings was smothering, while a fever rose up from the blacktop and singed the soles of their sneakers. They walked awhile longer. Suddenly, after a long, quiet spell and without warning, Zeke noticed a discarded brick in the gutter, and picked it up and flung it with all of his strength through the one remaining stained-glass window above the plywood-protected double doors of an abandoned church. The crash resounded through the empty street with a thunderous volume. The shards of splintered glass falling against the sidewalk were ice-like on their eardrums.

As if cued and without speaking a word, both boys began running in a sudden burst of pent-up energy down the narrow street into the prevailing darkness, away from any suspecting, curious eyes. They ran until it felt like their hearts would pound out from their chests and fall to the ground to be cooked on the fervid asphalt beneath their feet. Pozy continuously looked over his shoulder for anyone who might follow or approach quickly. He saw no one as they came upon a railroad crossing, and hearing the sound of a distant siren, Pozy spoke up for the first time since Zeke had thrown the brick.

"Let's take these tracks for a while. They should take us a bit farther and quicker from that window trick o' yours back there, and my feet are killing me. We might find a place we can sit for a while," he said.

"Who gives a shit," was Zeke's response. Pozy shook his head in the negative and they walked onto the tracks, comfortable now that they were not followed.

Biddeford was not a completely strange town to them. They'd been here many times, but never in this particular section. They knew that they could follow the R.R. tracks if they needed to go back to or off any roadway, except for crossings. The track in this section became somewhat hidden from view by the overgrowth of alder, scrub brush and sumac and ushered them into an exclusive jungle all their own and a solitude they craved, and finally, the sound of crashing glass was the farthest thing from their minds. The only clear vision was in the wide clearing where the tracks were laid and at that point, even the light from the tiny houses along the rail line were hidden from their view.

They had gone about a half mile when the tracks began to take a more southerly direction and when they did, Zeke noticed an almost intimidating presence of the silhouette of an archaic, abandoned factory very close to the tracks, indicating the remains of a possible loading dock, clinging to what remained of its life with a splinter or two of rotting timbers. Thinking it might be a good place to take a break, they headed in that direction.

"We must be about ten…maybe… twelve miles from the garage…don't ya think?" Zeke asked.

"Yah, maybe," Pozy responded.

"Let's find a place ta park our asses fa' a while. I'm friggin' tired," Zeke said.

"Fine," was all that Pozy offered, but he would not share with his friend just how tired he was of everything in his life at this point. *What good would it do anyway?* he thought.

They came upon a well-beaten path leading from the tracks toward the old factory. It was obvious to the boys that homeless and possibly young people looking for a secluded place to hang out kept it clear of the surrounding growth.

"Be careful. I'll bet the friggin' poison ivy's thick through hea'," Zeke said as he walked with his arms straight down and pinned to the sides of his upper body and legs. He was extremely allergic. Pozy, having worked in a saw mill a few years before, could smell the rotting, mold-infested wood emitting from the old structure and he wished they were back in the garage, no matter how hot it might be inside, even with the doors open. The evening was so dark that it made walking through this jungle most difficult.

Pozy could hardly make out the back of Zeke's head only a few feet ahead of him as he bobbed and weaved over the narrow path, when suddenly they broke out into a broad clearing in front of the skeletal wooden hulk. What came into view first were the remains of a loading dock. Loose boards hung crudely between rotting support posts, offering no viable place to sit; yet off to one side it was obvious that a small campsite was set up because huge tree stumps were cut and placed as seats encircling a well-used stone fireplace, filled with the charred remains of unburned wood, long since cooled from the flames. Zeke planted himself heavily on one of the stumps, Pozy on one across from him, so they faced each other, their eyes finally accustomed to the faint light.

"I could use a big, fat fuckin' sandwich and an ice-cold Coke about now," Zeke said.

"Yeah…I wish ta hell we neva' came out hea' tonight," Pozy said and threw a stone at the old building. The sound echoed through the hot evening air.

After that talk of food, both their thoughts drifted off to the Little Roady—its sights, sounds, and particularly now, its aromas. It was true; they hadn't eaten for quite some time, and hunger pangs dogged them, yet they were too tired now and tried to dismiss them, unsuccessfully. Neither had a watch, nor did they ever, and they never noticed any clocks on their quick jaunt through town. One thing was refreshing, though, as they sat on their stumps: an unexpected sea breeze kicked up, cooling the smothering heat of earlier. They sat quietly, feeling the sweat drying from their bodies, reviving them quickly. After several minutes, Zeke stood, walked around the fireplace stones, kicking dirt as he went—not at anything in particular, just in any direction it flew.

"What a friggin' hole this is," he said, and walked off through the clearing between the tracks and the old factory. The clearing went for quite a ways past the structure, widening and then narrowing again, indicating a possible storage area for the manufactured goods that were produced here awaiting shipment, obviously by rail. Suddenly, as Pozy looked in his direction—he was vaguely visible in the darkness—Zeke disappeared around the corner of the building. Being alone for a minute was soothing to Pozy's mind and several minutes passed, the solitude broken occasionally with the sound of everyday life coming from the tiny houses hidden by the overgrowth along the tracks. Pozy estimated the time to be around 10:00 p.m., as they'd been in total darkness since their near-hit by the car, and he guessed that had happened around 9:00 p.m.

Suddenly, the sound of Zeke's rapidly approaching footsteps returning from the same corner he'd disappeared around, came in heavy, flopping thumps.

"You ain't gonna believe this, fuck-face. That fuckin' car that almost killed us is parked behind us right now," he sputtered, the words seething from his mouth.

"Are you sure?"

"Sure as a fuckin' heart attack."

"Is anybody in it?" Pozy finally asked.

"Two little Mass-holes as far as I could see. It smells like they could be smokin' a joint, the little fucks."

At that point, and without saying another word, Zeke pulled his hunting knife from its sheath and slapped the blade against the palm of his left hand, the sound echoing through the still night air.

"Put that thing away," Pozy said, and remained standing with a vacant stare in Zeke's direction. Zeke remained silent and continued slapping the blade against his hand.

Zeke was obviously overcome with excitement and he began a slow pacing around the fireplace. He breathed heavily, occasionally looking toward Pozy, apparently contemplating a plan of sorts, yet never speaking a word, his nostrils, flared with anger.

"We need to go and talk to them," Zeke said.

"How do ya know they're even the right ones?" Pozy asked.

"Mass-hole plate… 019," Zeke responded, in reference to the last three numbers of the plate he'd seen at the scene of their near hit.

"You go 'round that way, I'll go back the way I went before. BE QUIET!" he stressed in a hissing voice. "Don't let them little fucks hear ya. You go 'round to the passenger side, I'll face up with the driver," Zeke said.

As willing as Pozy was to even the score, the sight of the knife gave him much to dread. His friend was pissed, and he really didn't know what he planned to do. Pozy's head began to throb at the temples. He could feel the headache coming on with each step toward the back side of the old building. He wanted to believe that Zeke would threaten them, maybe slap them around a little bit, but the sight and sound of that knife whacking against the palm of his hand rang clear in his thoughts as he went. With each snap of a twig underfoot, the simple rustling of leaves, or the whistle of pine needles in the wind, Pozy wished that they were back in the garage; anywhere but here.

He paused briefly upon reaching the far corner of the building and from this point he could faintly see the tail-lights of the car through the darkness; yet no movement came from the vehicle, or from the far end of the factory where Zeke should be right about now. Stepping lightly, he moved slowly around the corner, and it was then that he saw Zeke about fifty feet from the front of the car, walking slowly, nearly invisible in the pitch-blackness. Pozy's breathing was shallow. The pounding in his temples persisted, and now the sudden need to vomit arose from his stomach, pumping hot bile as far up as his esophagus. He stopped, swallowed, took a deep breath and moved forward again. As he moved closer to the car, he couldn't help but wonder what exactly would happen when they surprised the two. Would they start the car and peel out quickly? Was the car still running? Did they have weapons? Would they use them without a second thought? *Why didn't I think of this shit at the fireplace?* he thought.

It was too late. Their distance from the car was measurably equal at this point. They would be upon the two within a few steps, when suddenly, Pozy's mind went blank and they were there. The two young men in the car were taken unexpectedly and overwhelmingly by surprise with the sudden presence of Zeke's huge figure reaching into the driver's side window, and as the driver turned toward his companion to see what was happening, the passenger was grabbed around the neck and shoulders by Pozy, leaving both occupants speechless and bug-eyed. The scent of body odor rose up from the heated interior of the mid-sized car, along with the piquant aroma of pot. The passenger began to speak. Pozy tightened his grasp and the young man became still.

"Well…little Mass-holes been found," Zeke said, while holding the razor-edged blade of his knife against the throat of the driver. They were total opposites—Zeke and Pozy with disheveled, uncut hair and scraggly beards, compared to the clean-shaven and nearly bald-cut young men in the car, with light-colored shorts and T-shirts. With his head-lock firmly in place, the passenger remained quiet and unmoving, yet the driver, despite the placement of the blade, remained defiant to the point of sarcasm.

"You… dumb…fucked-up Mainiac-retard. Take that fuckin' baby-knife off me!"

Zeke never spoke a word in response, taking Pozy completely by surprise. He did however, reach in and over, grabbing the young man by the right ear and slowly sliding the blade over the dude's Adam's apple, producing a slight trickle of blood down the man's neck and onto his clean T-shirt. At that point he became quiet, while his eyes bulged in their sockets. The slice wasn't deep, probably about the depth of a decent paper-cut, but it was enough to get his attention to what Zeke intended to convey. Zeke maintained about a two-inch distance from the driver's face, yet he remained quiet, probably waiting for another round of sarcasm and when none came, he spoke slowly.

"Do… you… know… who… I am, little Mass-hole?"

The driver shook his head in the negative, so slowly and carefully, it was almost missed by Pozy on the passenger side. There was a moment of wretched silence as thick as the heat of the night and then Zeke said, "You almost killed me and my friend, over thea'." And he motioned toward the other side of the car with a jerk of his head. "We weren't doin' nothin' to get run ova' fa' back thea' at the 'Pool'. I want ya ta get outa the caar'…real slow-like," Zeke said.

Zeke reached in and pulled the handle and the door came open. He switched the knife to his right hand and held it to the driver's neck as he'd done with his left in order to allow the door to open and not give the driver an inch of leverage in which to move away. His neck spewed a small amount of blood now, clotting somewhat on the side farthest from where Zeke stood, but it remained open and tender. He slid himself out slowly into Zeke's powerful grasp and his blade and by then, Pozy had the passenger out and around to the driver's side.

"Bring 'em hea'," Zeke grumbled, and never removing the knife from the neck of the driver, he reached out and grabbed the passenger with his free arm into a bear hug and held them both. Zeke and Pozy outweighed them by at least fifty pounds.

"What the fuck do you want with us, anyway? I don't even know what the hell you're talkin' about…at the pool thea'," the driver asked, stressing the word "thea'" as if mimicking the way Zeke spoke, like a Mainer, and Zeke reached out and stuck him in the shoulder with the tip of the blade. It entered the deltoid muscle, driving the poor kid to his knees in painful agony. At this point, his light-colored T-shirt began to dampen and change color rapidly, but if Zeke intended for him to cry, or whimper, he did neither, implanting a broader sliver of anger into Zeke's consciousness.

"Check out the car. See what's inside," Zeke barked, and Pozy complied. Zeke had both boys on the ground, one kneeling, the other seated, and he stood over them with a hand on each head, like a giant tower. His right hand held the knife. All three looked toward Pozy. The first things to fly from the car were four beers held by plastic rings.

"These aar' still cold," Pozy laughed, as he opened one and took a huge swallow, pulled another out and threw it to Zeke. He grabbed it in mid-air and before opening it, kicked the passenger, who was kneeling, to the ground, opened the brew, and within three seconds, the can was empty. "Aaahh… that… was… good. Glad ya brought the beea'… little Mass-holes," he said, stressing the pronunciation of the word "beea'," while looking down at his stabbed victim.

As Pozy rummaged through the car, Zeke realized suddenly that his earlier observation of it back at the Pool area of it being a mid-sized Honda or Nissan with a dark paint job was right on, except for the make. This was a Toyota with shitty brown paint.

"Well…well, looky-hea'," Pozy said.

When Zeke looked up toward the car, Pozy was holding both his hands up. His right contained a baggy filled with what looked to be pot, his left, held up, like a prize trophy, a small-caliber handgun. At that point, and for no apparent reason, Zeke turned and slashed the passenger, who now rested on one knee after being kicked by Zeke moments earlier across the right upper arm, releasing a torrent of blood that rapidly reached his elbow. This one, however, screamed a howling, high-pitched whine, causing Zeke to reach out and smack him hard in the face, and back down to the ground with a thud he went.

"Shut-up, ya cry-baby Mass-hole, before somebody heas' ya," Zeke hissed.

"You boys come up hea' to do a little huntin' or a little…?" Zeke stopped mid-sentence. "Let me see that gun. It might be worth keepin' for ourselves."

While he was in the car, Pozy had missed most of Zeke's knife-wielding tricks, and now he was astonished to see so much blood on the both of them.

"What the hell ya been doin' to those… poor bastards?"

"They ain't poor bastards. Theya Mass-holes, and don't forget it," Zeke said.

While examining the gun more closely, Zeke remembered his father having one similar to this, and he called it a snub-nose .38. It was black steel, matching his attire of all black perfectly. He stuffed it into his belt and then looked down at the driver, who was pressing firmly against his shoulder wound, as the cut on his neck seemed to be somewhat dried up.

"Which one o' ya owns this fuckin' gun?"

Neither one spoke up until he pulled the revolver from his pants and cocked the hammer. Before and after Pozy handed him the gun, neither one checked to see if it was even loaded, but at this point, if he pulled the trigger, it wouldn't much matter if it wasn't. In the condition the two from Massachusetts were in, they could do nothing to harm Zeke or Pozy.

"It's mine…it's mine," the driver spoke up, still a bit cocky. "Look…sir… we really don't know what you mean by 'at the pool'. If we did something to you, we're sorry. We came up here to get this dope from a friend of his," he continued, looking toward his buddy. "We were going back home. We never saw ya before now and I don't even know what you're talking about." With that said, Pozy knew that they would never report this to any cops.

"Oh… Mister Policeman, two bad-boys beat us up and stole our gun and the pot we just bought." He laughed to himself at the thought.

Pozy moved closer to Zeke and without saying a word, motioned with his eyes that they move closer to the car. Zeke, the big man with a gun now, picked up on the gesture and moved toward him, keeping the gun pointed at the two on the ground.

"Ya move, yaw dead," Zeke said. As they leaned against the car, Pozy began in low tones.

"There ain't nothin' left in that car that's worth takin'. Looks like some good dope, nice gun if ya want it, and I think they neva' saw us back there. I figure we oughta' get goin'. Head down the road, then pick up the tracks a bit farther down and get lost. Ya know they're neva' gonna' call the cops." And his earlier thought about why flashed into his mind.

"Ya mean…that's it, we let 'em go?"

"What else we gonna' do, kill 'em?" Pozy asked.

The moment the words were out of his mouth, there appeared to be a flame kindling in Zeke's eyes that led Pozy to believe that he was one step away from something very wrong. They stood motionless and quiet for several minutes, finishing what remained of the last two beers, listening to the passenger's moans of pain. Pozy walked to the driver's door, which remained open, and the faint dome-light illuminated the side of his face. He reached in, took the keys from the ignition, throwing them out into the clearing which led to the road on this side of the building. In his mind, he wanted no more of this, and thought by the time they found the keys, he and Zeke would be well on their way to being a bad memory as far as these two were concerned. Maybe the next time they came to Maine they'd be a little more respectful, even polite.

"C'mon pal, let's get the hell outta hea,'" Pozy said.

7

IT WAS MUCH COOLER A FEW DAYS LATER. A northwest breeze ushered in a cooling, dry air that soothed a Mainer to the soul. In a restless sleep, Pozy twisted and turned on the couch, covered with an old moving quilt he'd stolen long ago. His mind recalled the sequence of events that night in Biddeford. In vivid color, he was back in the old mill yard, only this time, he was the victim several yards from the parked Toyota. In the middle of the clearing, he was now being buried alive in a casket by a faceless group of images, and no one from the tiny houses along the tracks heard his screams of horror.

Even in the dream, his fear of being buried alive created such anxiety; the sweat saturated his entire body as if someone had poured warm water over him. He moaned, strained his vision toward the light from the opened double doors of the garage and as he did, the brightness and the sound of Zeke's distant voice thrust him into an awakened state.

"Yow...What-tha'-fuck... ya dreamin'?" Zeke hollered out.

It had been three days since their encounter with the two from Massachusetts. They hadn't ventured from the garage since their return early that following morning just before dawn. They did not see or speak to anyone, including Petey or Dwight. Had it not been for the small amount of cash they finally took from the duo to purchase some burgers, chips, a loaf of bread and cheese and two gallons of water, they would be very hungry right now; but then they were always hungry.

Pozy rolled onto his side to face his friend. Zeke, sitting on a wooden crate, was fondling the .38 snub-nose as if he might give it a lick with his tongue. For the longest time now, no greater happiness empowered his expressions or his persona as this little revolver did. Zeke was in a world of his own when he held it. It had been loaded when Pozy found it in the car, and they realized it about an hour after leaving the two bleeding and miserable beside the Toyota. The fact that Zeke walked around with a loaded gun was frightening to his closest friend, but the calmness it instilled in him gave Pozy much comfort, as if a loaded gun could ease an already warped mind. Now, while rubbing the gun, Zeke chimed the lyrics from a John Lennon song, "Happiness…is a warm gun," and he giggled like a kid after singing it.

—

Pozy stretched the sleep from his bones and looked away toward the clearing out front of the garage. How Zeke and Pozy lived was their choice, but at times like this, in the garage with nothing to do and no one besides each other to do it with, Pozy often daydreamed about being back on the farm with his parents. Sure, he'd left all that behind him because he hated the simple life of farmers (as he would gladly explain)—playing in the dirt and pullin' on cow's tits, but that was then. As he matured, some of the good things that went on at the farm filtered in on occasion and brought him back to the reality of what had become of his life off the farm. He hated it when people felt sorry for themselves and broadcasted it to the world, and he'd be the last to tell anyone he felt sorry for himself, but at this moment, with Zeke feeling up the .38…

Hunger pangs went unanswered, while the rustling of the snake in the cage gave Pozy a sense of loneliness. An eerie silence came over the entire area surrounding the garage, inside and out. The coolness remained, yet the breeze died down and after a long period, Zeke spoke.

"Ya think yaw' old man would mind if we fired this thing off in the woods out back o' his place?"

At the first thought of it, Pozy wanted to ignore him, but he knew very well that to do so would only pump him up to a point of continuous questions until he got an answer. Right now, Pozy relished the calm of the morning and answered, hoping it might be enough.

"I don't know, we could ask, see what he says."

"Ya…we could ask," Zeke answered abruptly, and the sarcasm in his voice reached out and did what his huge hand might do if he were closer.

The garage was built at the far end of the clearing and it was possible to see anyone on an approach to the building long before they arrived. It was, however, almost impossible to see anyone or their movements in the garage, especially on a bright and sunny day like today, because the garage was so dark inside. Only moments after Zeke's sarcastic remark, the boys heard the approach of a car on the gravel almost as soon as it left the blacktop. At the sound of it, Zeke slid the revolver into the breast pocket of his black leather jacket and went directly to the snake cage and covered it with the blanket. Pozy remained on the couch; at this location he had an unobstructed view of the entire property.

"Who is it?" Zeke asked.

"Yaw' not gonna' believe this shit. It's Queer-Eye, and he looks pissed," Pozy said with a chuckle.

"Which eye ya lookin' at, ya little freak? Ya don't suppose he found out somethin' about Biddeford and them two little…?"

That was the first time Pozy had ever heard Zeke sound worried about something he'd done, and it seemed out of character for him, yet Pozy dismissed it.

"How could he? He's a cop hea'… not thea'. Besides, they got nothin'." Pozy said it with such conviction in his voice that Zeke, without saying another word, nodded his head in agreement. Although Biddeford was a much larger town than Dells, an assault of that nature created radio chatter between police departments from the area. Along the coast, most police officers knew each other as friends, and it helped to get the word out in most cases.

With an obvious attempt at intimidating, Rodney Torrey pulled the vehicle halfway into the garage and left the engine running, and got out, just outside of the building, slamming the door and walking in.

"Well...well. What have we here?" Rodney asked.

Both boys remained silent, staring at the policeman from the same spot they were in before he arrived. Pozy was relaxed on the couch; Zeke's posture was erect upon his return to the crate. All three eyed each other from top to bottom; their facial expressions were the epitome of poker players unwilling to reveal their hands.

"What have you boys been up to? I haven't seen either of you or the other two little... around town for a spell now," Rodney asked, casually glancing around the garage as if looking for something.

"Nice and cool in hea'. No need ta go out much," Zeke responded, while looking deep into Rodney's good eye, the one that stared directly back at Zeke. And then Rodney looked down at Pozy with a penetrating gaze.

"You're awful quiet today. What's on yaw' mind?" he asked.

Pozy never spoke; he simply shrugged his shoulders, looking directly at Rodney. And then, like a bolt of lightning, Rodney came right out and asked, but not in a threatening way.

"You boys get over ta Biddeford much? A good friend o' mine is a policeman up there and..." He was immediately interrupted by Zeke.

"This a free country, or what?"

"Yeah...it's a free country. I just wanted to ask you something, that's all," Rodney said.

Both boys were visibly stone-faced at this point, and an obvious paleness in their cheeks set in, difficult for any policeman to overlook.

"You two look a little sick all of a sudden. Are ya feelin' alright?" he asked.

Both of the boy's minds raced, yet neither one would look toward the other so as not to reveal their surprise at Queer-Eye's question. If they appeared sick, as Rodney suggested, he was right. The bile began to rise up from Pozy's stomach, forcing him to swallow large gulps, attempting to cool the hot liquid. Zeke, on the other hand, became visibly irritated with Rodney and he spoke up quickly.

"Ya got somethin on yaw' mind thea'...mista'... shiny badge?"

Rodney took several steps toward Zeke. The leather heals of his shoes hit firmly against the concrete of the garage floor, forcing Pozy, who remained on the couch, to look down at his feet. Rodney's good eye was focused deep into Zeke's, and he stopped suddenly several feet from where Zeke sat on the crate, never moving from his erect position. The two maintained their stare toward each other. In his mind, Rodney believed he knew these two, almost as he knew himself, but Rodney prided himself on his ability to see things that might be somewhat out of the ordinary—things that an everyday Joe would miss in a heartbeat. As his stare remained focused on Zeke, his peripheral vision inspected the room for anything that might be out of the ordinary and suddenly, it clicked. The young man was noted for carrying a large hunting knife, and for whatever reason it wasn't hanging from his belt. *Not exactly a good cause to question someone, but good enough right now,* he thought.

Rodney had no pretext to believe that these two were involved in anything that had gone on in Biddeford that night; he had simply thought about a conversation he'd had with a close friend and fellow police officer from Biddeford who responded to a call phoned in from one of the tiny houses along the tracks. The resident had heard moaning and at times, some loud talking coming from the direction of the abandoned factory; then saw the silhouettes of two figures going south on the RR tracks. Upon inspection, however, Rodney's friend found what appeared to be dried bloodstains in the gravel, and some tire tracks and footprints all over the area, but that was it. Relaying the incident to his peer over coffee was simply a coincidental conversation, but upon hearing it, saying nothing to his counterpart, the troublesome foursome leaped into Rodney's consciousness immediately. He had nothing on these two here—it was simply his strategy in keeping the coffee-and-donut caper alive without the chief's cooperation. After all, Petey Harriman wasn't here.

For what seemed the longest moment, both starred silently at each other, and it appeared that both Zeke and Rodney were searching for what to say next; from the look on their faces, a stalemate was reached, blocking any attempt by either to move the subject matter forward to resolution. After several strained minutes, Zeke spoke up.

"Aar' we goin' somewhere with this little chat? I'm showa' that you got betta' things ta do than hang out with us college kids, with nothin' betta' ta do."

Rodney seemed stumped at his arrogance and suddenly he felt kind of stupid for being here and using this approach to try and entrap them for no good reason other than knowing they were troublemakers. In his gut, even if Zeke hadn't been so condescending, he felt now more than ever that somehow, they were involved with the incident in Biddeford that night, and the missing knife would be his saving grace in leaving this less-than-accomplished endeavor with at least an ounce of his pride unscathed.

Rodney broke the stare, and shuffled his feet slightly, the scuffing of leather on concrete echoing through the near-empty garage.

He cleared his throat and said, "Zeke… I can't help notice that yaw'… not sportin' yaw' favorite huntin' knife."

Zeke swallowed heavily, yet said nothing. The officer turned and faced him, taking one step toward him, and then stopped. "Did ya lose it somewhere? Because… ever since I've known ya, you've always carried it on yaw' belt." For the first time since Rodney had arrived, Pozy sat upright on the couch looking toward them both, yet he remained quiet.

The building was silent once again, and a dumb look came over Zeke's face. Without saying a word, he pointed toward the workbench on the other side of the garage, jerking his head in that direction. And there it was; resting beside the sheath in plain sight for all to see.

"A knife gets dull…once in a while. Need ta shaapin' 'em now and then," Zeke said.

Pozy hoped his friend had cleaned the knife of any blood residue before leaving it exposed for the world to see. As that thought passed through his mind, Queer-Eye went directly to the bench. Looking down at the knife, though he would do his best not to show it, he'd never felt as foolish in his entire career as he did at this moment. *Had I not been so focused on that little freak…I missed this right out in the open,* he thought. His first intuition was to pick it up, probably intimidating Zeke into… something, he couldn't know what. Suddenly, like a blast from the past, the chief's words came to haunt him.

"Oh… I don't think they're dangerous, Rodney. Boys will be boys."

He turned back to face the boys. In his mind it was as if his thoughts were being broadcast openly, and he became suddenly embarrassed that he was even here. *I will never make this mistake again,* he promised himself at that moment.

Zeke could see the expression on the officer's face. He couldn't know what had brought it to the surface, yet he understood it, and knew he could now be relentless until the officer left.

"So…Ya lookin' fa' a knife like that, aar' ya? That one thea' ain't fa' sale, but I know someone's got one like it if yaw' thinkin…"

"No…no. I'm not…" Rodney could feel the heat come over his face. His mind reached for sarcasm, yet that well was dry now.

"Well…go ahead…pick it up. She feels real good ta the touch," Zeke said with a slight chuckle from his throat. Rodney appeared frozen to the spot, looking back down at the knife, which was clean from the tip of the long, shiny blade to the butt end of the handle. The sheath appeared wet, as if it had been scrubbed, but other than that, it was just a knife.

"Wha-da-ya think, chief… That a good-lookin' knife, or what?"

Pozy and Zeke looked at each other and found it difficult not to laugh. The officer could feel the sarcasm levied in his direction and he searched his mind for a diplomatic way to get himself out of this mess. And like an offering from the gods, his car radio crackled with the sound of the dispatcher's voice, and it was his name being summoned. *Oh…thank Christ,* he thought. He practically ran toward the cruiser.

After a short conversation on the radio, Rodney, staying by the open door of his cruiser, focused a stare toward the boys and made an attempt to get in the car, but stopped short and said, "Sorry I can't stay longer. Maybe next time we can get into the meat and potatoes of a good conversation."

He slid in behind the wheel, slammed the door and began backing the nose of the cruiser out of the garage. At that point, with the vehicle several yards from the building and out of earshot of the policeman, it was Zeke's turn to say goodbye.

"Hey… Mister policeman… Come back when ya can't stay so long. Here's yaw' hat, what's yaw' hurry?"

Then, in a cloud of dust from the huge tires over the gravel, the police car disappeared into the woods beyond the clearing, and the area was quiet once again.

Pozy continued to make jokes about the officer's visit long after his departure, yet Zeke, the one who never worried, ignored the humor, and for a solid hour after Rodney's departure, scrutinized the reason for the stop-by.

"He knows somethin', Pozy. Why would he ask about Biddeford if he didn't? I'm tellin' ya…big-boy, he knows somethin'," Zeke said.

"Really? Maybe he heard something from a cop up there and wanted to bust a little butt, 'cause he ain't got nothin' ta do 'round hea'. If he knew somethin', really knew somethin', ya think we'd be sittin' hea' tryin' ta figure out why he came by?"

Zeke pulled the .38 from his jacket pocket and the moment it was out in plain sight, he returned it quickly, as the sound of an approaching vehicle hit the gravel at a high rate of speed from the blacktop.

Both their heads turned quickly in that direction and as they listened, lightheartedness came over them. It was Petey and Dwight in the big, white Mopar, slinging a bit of gravel as they came.

They'd remained reclusive since Biddeford and this was the first time that either Petey or Dwight had made an appearance, and just as well, Zeke and Pozy thought, but right now, after Queer-Eye's visit, they were a welcomed duo. Petey pulled a U-turn and backed the car toward the open garage door, but stopped short from entering. Both boys jumped from the car simultaneously. Dwight spoke first.

"Hey...ya big douche-bags, what's new?" He was holding the familiar white paper bag out in front of him as he entered the garage. Petey waved to the two older boys, said nothing, went directly to his toolbox and began his usual fishing around, pulled out a set of wrenches, and moved quickly toward his car. An air of good-natured joshing came over the entire area. For all practical purposes, from the volume of their carrying on, it was possible to hear them as far away as the blacktop and perhaps beyond. They rassled around, threw playful punches at each other and just made up stupid little things that forced out chaotic outbursts of laughter.

The prize of the day came not too long after. Petey opened the trunk lid and produced a dorm-sized mini-fridge, and their days of living out of an Igloo Cooler were over. It was like Christmas in the middle of summer. Zeke reached in and with the strength of two men, lifted it without straining, carrying it to the only electrical outlet at the corner of the workbench. It fit like it had always been there, and when he plugged it in, the compressor came to life with a few clicks and a clunk.

It wasn't until much later that Zeke thought the time right to share the story of Queer-Eye's visit, leaving out the intricate part about Biddeford, yet he stressed his anger at being singled out by Rodney for no good reason. A month had passed since Petey's coffee-and-donut caper, although they never measured time in that way—they simply lived for today and no calendar ever hung in the garage except for the remains of a centerfold or two. Because of his personality and of what Zeke relayed to them now, Petey immediately held himself responsible for Queer-Eye's visit, though he never shared his feelings with the others. To do so would be an admission of weakness, generally not tolerated by the older boys, especially Zeke.

It was early afternoon. The cool air remained refreshingly consistent. Generally on days like this the beaches were relatively deserted of sunbathers, and it was the Outlet Stores in Kittery that were congested with summer folks, eager to spend large amounts of cash on all of the supposed good deals being offered, but as cool as it was, Petey found it a bit weird that Zeke wore his leather jacket. He was the one who always complained of the heat.

Dwight, though he would never feed the snake, stood at the uncovered cage alongside of Zeke, holding the white bag out in front of him.

"Hey…little fella. Ready for a bag full o' happiness?" He shook the bag gently over the snake; Zeke took it from him immediately.

"If yaw' gonna feed 'im, feed 'im. Don't tease 'im when he's hungry," Zeke said. He was one to talk, being the biggest teaser of them all.

Through all of the foolishness during the past hour, Pozy had moved very little and remained in the same position he'd been in before Rodney Torrey came, trying to upset the day. His presence shook them psychologically, but very little; however, the agitation in Zeke's voice and demeanor could not be mistaken for anything else, and all three boys would do nothing or say anything to provoke him further. When it finally came time for Zeke to stop teasing the snake and feed him that was Dwight's clue to move from the cage area. He just couldn't handle watching the snake wrap its mouth around the tiny creature and almost massage it down its throat or body; however, one might describe a snake swallowing. It was the lump in the snake that freaked him out. He moved toward the couch.

"What's new?" Dwight asked Pozy, his head now resting on the armrest of the couch.

"Not much, fuck-face. How 'bout you?" Pozy asked, and when he turned to look at Dwight, he was smiling.

"Where you guys been? I came by here the other night and it was so dark down hea', I neva' ventured down from the road," Dwight said.

Pozy looked toward Zeke, who was looking at him, unnoticed by Dwight. Pozy thought quickly. "Ah…Ya… we went up ta the old man's farm. Hung out fa' a couple o' days. We wanted a change o' pace, ya know?"

“Ya…ya. I'd like ta take off fa' a while. Maybe next time you two go up that way, maybe you can take me?” Dwight asked. From the corner of the garage, Zeke grumbled.

“I'd rather take a bag full o' deer-ticks than haul yaw' scrawny ass around farm country,” Zeke said, then he laughed in an attempt to soften the sound of it, but for once, neither Dwight nor anyone else could find humor in the way he spoke to his friend.

After that final comment by Zeke, the entire relationship between the four became strained, not in terms of them going their separate ways—it wasn't that serious—but it did, for about an hour, blanket their mood with a silence they'd never experienced before. Pozy lay on the couch and grunted at whatever Zeke said. Dwight walked out to the front of Petey's car and never looked into the garage. Suddenly, after a deep, loud exhalation of breath, it was Petey who decided to speak up. In his mind, the silence was killing him, emotionally.

“Yow…I sure could go for a hot cup o' coffee. I haven't been down to the Roady for about a week,” he said.

The thought of seeing Missy evoked a sense of urgency in both Petey and Zeke, though Zeke's memory was of a hands-on physical experience, while Petey's thoughts were still in the realm of fantasy. Zeke couldn't help but wonder how Missy would react now that they hadn't seen each other for this long since the closet romp. This had probably been the longest time without any contact between them since then.

“Ya…let's go, Zeke said.

8

"It's like puttin' puh'fume on a pig, chief. Yaw' neva' gonna get rid o' the stink," Rodney said between gulps of his Little Roady coffee. The chief, seated beside him, smiled slightly while sipping on his brew, occasionally looking up at Marcy, who had no idea what the officer spoke about. The policemen sat at the counter between the racks of homemade pies and brownies. Their backs were to the entrance and the road. This was their coffee break. The last thing they wanted was to see what went on outside.

It was mid-afternoon. The lunch crowd, long since gone, allowed for a more relaxing environment in the restaurant and with the occasional regular stopping in for their steaming cup of coffee, it encouraged local conversation to flow. Marcy loved it when it was only locals at the counter. She moved little from her spot by the donut shelf and she enjoyed filling her cup as much as those in front of her, and more times than not, the refills were on the house. She couldn't remember when she'd ever charged the chief for coffee, or a meal for that matter, and she liked him and his ways, but there was something about the pressed shirt and high-gloss Rodney that she just didn't like. He'd get his usual, one free cup, but for eating, he paid. No one ever knew that she and the chief had been lovers long ago. She even believed, though she would never say a word of it, that he was probably

Missy's father. Outside of feminine intuition, she had nothing substantial to verify her belief, only that they had been involved around the time before she had Missy, and during the time the chief courted his current wife, to whom he'd been married for many years. "Leave well enough to itself" was her motto for as long as she could remember, but whenever she was this close to Willard Weaks, his facial expressions and his smile always made her insides turn to mush.

On lazy afternoons like this, coffee-break conversations ranged between the amount of tourists on the road to nit-picking about the minutes of the last Town Manager's meeting, and all points in between. Town business, whatever the dimension, provoked a level of animosity at times between the closest of friends, most generally in a constructive way, but there were events of unruliness where the chief became the divider of the warring factions. The chief's position demanded an extreme level-headedness and a solid view of political correctness that many could not possess. Willard Weaks had all of those qualities and more.

Through the years as chief, he had been tempted, countless times, to place the almighty buck as a barrier between the law for the masses and the law for those of fortune. Although no wrongdoing on the chief's part was ever uncovered, suspicions raged for years that services and goods offered by local merchants were traded to overlook improprieties.

The traffic on Portland Street buzzed both north and southbound with summer's activity. Though the temperature was much cooler, the ceiling fan of the Little Road hummed out a rhythm unnoticed by the patrons at the counter. The chief brought his cup to his mouth for a final gulp and nearly spilled the remaining coffee on his finely pressed shirt at the sudden sound of screeching tires and several loud thumps from directly out in front of the restaurant. Both officers turned in that direction simultaneously, as though they expected to see a massive accident. To their dismay, however, the troublesome foursome appeared.

In the kitchen, Missy had also heard the sound of tires against pavement and was looking through the partially open swinging doors, feeling two emotions at once. The first was her heart-throbbing need to see and be with Zeke, who led the group toward the front entrance of the Little Roady. The second emotion was wondering what reaction the police officers would display toward them, and how Zeke might respond because of his explosive temper.

Zeke burst through the front door in a whirlwind of flying hair and dirty jeans. He saw the policemen long before reaching the door, and his entry was a well-choreographed performance on their behalf. He purposely avoided eye contact with anyone at the counter, looking past them in search of his Missy. She made it easy for him because, before his feet ever touched the threshold, she was past the swinging door and waiting behind the counter with yearning written plainly on her face.

Remembering that their involvement was still hopefully unknown to all present, they avoided any physical contact except for holding each other's eyes, and the four boys, under the watchful scrutiny of the patrons on swivel benches, went to their usual booth by the window, followed closely by an order-pad-toting Missy.

Everyone at the counter returned to their original posture, heads down toward their prospective orders; the policemen, however, held their stare with the sternness of law enforcement.

Missy ambled up to the booth and leaned against Zeke with her hip, ever so slightly, the gesture almost being missed by anyone looking, except for Marcy, who saw through the promiscuous behavior, yet remained speechless. It was the scent of Missy's womanhood Zeke had missed most, and being this close to her after the time apart made it difficult to hide their feelings and mutual need to be together.

"Well...well, if this isn't a sad, but...jolly-lookin' lot. I haven't seen you boys in quite a spell," she said and when she did, she looked down and met Zeke's eyes. For no apparent reason, Zeke brushed his hand against the jacket and felt the gun, and his confidence rose even higher than its usual level. He regained his composure, looking now in the direction of the lawmen, who continued staring toward their corner of the room. He blinked, and when his eyes reopened, his stare was focused on Missy.

"Missy…darling…it's so good to see you. I've had so many sleepless night since being away," Zeke said in a tone that left no doubt in anyone's mind that he was being facetious, and he strained to remove his natural Maine accent from his speech, yet no one at the table dared to challenge him on his behavior.

Missy playfully slapped his shoulder with a smile and said, "Did anyone eva' tell ya that you were full o' shit? I'm thinkin' you could care less if ya eva' saw this place again, but I'll fa'give ya this time. What'll ya boys have, the usual?"

No one spoke a word—they simply nodded their heads yes.

Missy headed for the coffee pot, and when she did, Rodney Torrey left his counter stool and walked slowly with the clacking of his leather heels trailing toward the booth at the far corner of the room. A loose floorboard in the old building creaked under his weight, as a single beam of the mid-afternoon sunlight slanted through the plate-glass window and reflected off the shiny badge on his chest, causing a slight glare in Zeke's eyes, seated facing him. Again, Zeke brushed the area of the jacket that held the .38 and this time Pozy saw the gesture, and felt an instant pang of uncertainty in the pit of his stomach. *I wish I'd neva' found that fuckin' gun in that fuckin' car. I don't see any good comin' o' this shit,* he said to himself, and at that moment, Rodney's shadow fell over the table, yet this time he didn't look at either Zeke or Pozy. His full attention was now focused on Petey.

"Wow! Cowboy! You drive like that all of the time?" he asked, and then stood in silence awaiting a response. Petey, timid as he was at times, feared Rodney, and simply returned a worried stare, his jaw agape as he shook his head slowly in the negative, never removing his gaze from the officer's.

"You do know that there is a Noise Ordinance in Town? I could, if I wanted, give you a ticket." And then he remembered the chief's comment several weeks earlier.

"I've known his grandparents our entire lives."

"Do you suppose your grandparents would enjoy a call about this?"

The officer stood silent now, watching as the boy began to squirm restlessly in his seat by the window. In a nervous voice, Petey spoke up.

"There's no need to involve them in something like this. They worry about me too much already. I'm sorry for the tire squeal. It won't happen again," Petey said.

At that point, Zeke had had enough, and as Missy approached the booth, though it wasn't his intention that she be this close when he exploded, he opened his big mouth.

"Hey…Petey-weety. Ya eva' been to Biddeford with that big… Mopar o' yaw's?"

Rodney's stare went from Petey to Zeke as Zeke continued. "I think ya should arrest the little twit, thea', mista' policeman."

Several moments of silence passed, and seemed to affect the entire room with an incurable disease. Though most everyone wanted to, no one dared to look toward the area where the heavy silence covered the table like a thick fog. Not even the chief turned on his swivel stool.

The sting of embarrassment continued to burn in the pit of Rodney's stomach, and he wouldn't tolerate another fall from grace. Almost casually, Rodney blinked his eyes once and when they opened, his stare was focused on Petey. The dismissal of his gaze angered Zeke so much that he began thumping his boot on the leg of the table, forcing the freshly delivered coffee cups to vibrate and rippling the hot liquid within them, yet Rodney never broke his concentration on the younger boy, and Zeke remained quiet.

A light sweat began to bead on Petey's forehead, visible to everyone, then he spoke up with an undeniable quiver in his voice. "Li- like I said, R-Rodney, it won't happen again. We were just—goofin'."

"You…Save yaw goofin' for somewhere other than behind the wheel of a caar'. What ya did was irresponsible. Ya could have hurt someone or yawself with a stunt like that."

It wasn't as if the officer had witnessed the stunt that caused the screeching tires, for when he and the chief finally turned to look out, Petey's car was parallel parked perfectly against the curb.

"You keep in mind what I said about your grandparents," he said, while maintaining a straight face. He spoke in a low tone, remembering the chief's connection with them.

Silently, from the kitchen, Missy maintained a distracted vigil on the booth in the corner. She moved things around in a semi-noisy manner, giving the appearance—to her mother anyway—that the needed chores were being done, but with an occasional clang of a pot or pan and a few rapid footsteps back and forth, very little was actually done behind the wedged-open swinging doors.

"Something must have happened since the last time I saw him. I can't believe that a tiny incident like tire-squeal would get those boys in trouble to get such a sermon from Rodney," she thought. Then her mind carried her back to the last time she'd seen Zeke. She closed her eyes momentarily and the vision of them making love together in the kitchen storage closet came to life once again as she realized how much she wanted him.

Just then, a sudden darkness came over the outside of the restaurant. A summer squall developed quickly and at the sight of it, without a word spoken, Petey, very unlike himself, jumped over the backrest of the bench seat, causing the officer to flinch defensively at the boy's quick action, yet Petey never noticed. It was the open windows of the big Mopar that drew his attention alfresco. Much to the surprise of those witnessing it, everyone remained speechless, including Zeke, except for an outburst of ear-splitting laughter.

Rodney refused to look toward the remaining threesome at the booth and shook his head in disbelief, walking slowly back to his swivel bench and the chief, who hadn't moved an inch since his officer left to reprimand the boys. He remained silent as Rodney sat himself softly next to him.

"Ya know…Chief…had a policeman stood by at my table when I was their age, no matter what, I would never…" And he was immediately stopped by the chief's slightly lifted hand. While Rodney had stood at the boy's table, Marcy had filled the chief's cup again, and though he preferred less caffeine, he lifted it now to his lips and took a small sip, then began speaking in a low tone.

"Rodney, I'll speak with the boy before we leave. I agree that he needs to be more…vigilant with his driving skills." Then he drifted off from the moment as he did regularly now, and a sudden clang from the kitchen brought him back with a low chuckle.

"Ya know…I wish I'd seen how he did that stunt." And he lifted his shoulders in a type of cringe, nodding his head with a smile.

Rodney exhaled with a pulse in his breath, as his mind churned with frustration, but he remained silent, looking toward Marcy for support, and noticing that she'd already turned and approached the swinging door.

Over in the corner booth, the decibel level rose once again with Petey's return, and the moment he slid in beside Dwight on their side of the bench, a torrential downpour made it difficult to see across Portland Street. The already cool air of the day became chilly in an instant and Marcy, from the kitchen entrance, switched the ceiling fan off. Now, Missy was beside herself for need to be with or simply talk with Zeke—the week since they'd been together had been a long one for her. She looked out occasionally into the restaurant area, and as luck would have it, Zeke was looking in her direction each time, though always under the watchful scrutiny of Marcy, unseen by either one.

As quickly as the rain began, it stopped. The storm moved north along the coast, and from the south came a slight shimmering of sunlight through thinning dark clouds and as it did, an uncomfortable humidity crept in. Summer returned.

Zeke began to show signs now of being agitated by the police presence. He slid the back of his hand over the breast area of his jacket and an instant feeling of calm appeared to come over him as the feel of the revolver lifted his spirit as nothing else could, besides Missy. His eyes shifted between the swinging door to the kitchen and the two officers, who appeared to be readying themselves to leave. Their actions enlivened Zeke's expectations.

As the chief stood, the metallic sound of the swivel bench

turning echoed slightly through the restaurant, which was Marcy's cue to reenter the behind the counter area—and when she did, she immediately asked the chief if there was anything else he wanted.

"No…no, I'm filled to the gills with caffeine, but I'd take a couple o' those sugar doughnuts with me if ya don't mind." As the chief reached into the depths of his pocket, Rodney touched him lightly on the arm and motioned that he had this one, and he placed a five and two ones on the counter, getting up from his stool and moving immediately toward the door, this time never looking in the direction of the foursome in their booth, remembering that the chief mentioned he would speak to Petey before leaving. Marcy returned quickly with the small bag. Her smile seemed exaggerated, and the chief perceived it as a case of nerves after overhearing him say he would speak to the boys.

"Marcy, there's something about yaw' coffee that a man just can't do without." He smiled and as usual, her heart fluttered.

"Thank you, Willard. You come back anytime and the pot'll be hot for ya," she said and reached over the counter and handed him the bag. He turned then, facing the booth across the room. He took a slight breath and walked slowly. The booth was about fifteen or sixteen steps away and his thoughts drifted out to space somewhere, never contemplating what he might say upon his arrival. Rodney stood by the door listening to the creaks in the floorboards as the chief went. He wanted to join the chief at the booth, if only to reinforce his earlier visit, but thought better of it now that Willard Weaks stood like the pillar of law enforcement before the table of young folks, as he often called those of their age from town, with a smile on his face.

"Good afternoon, men. It looks like a meeting o' the minds ova' hea'. What have you young folks got planned for the rest o' this fine day? It feels like the heat is comin' back, yah?" All four remained silent and only nodded their heads in the affirmative; and then the chief looked directly at Petey. "Well…young man. You practicin' stunt drivin'?" Petey's eyes seemed to pop from their sockets, yet he remained still and silent. The chief had a way to bring wonderment into many a conversation, this being one of them. Not knowing if the chief was angered by Petey's little stunt, he though it wise not to offer comment just yet, and he didn't have to wait long to find out the chief's intentions. Rodney, from his place by the door, feeling that a hanging was imminent, focused his stare in that direction.

"You do realize…that you could have popped both those tires when you hit that curb." Petey nodded his head, slowly. The sound of crumpling paper was heard by all as the chief re-gripped the bag. "You know how yaw' grandfather puts a price tag on everything, and your grandparents are pretty lucky to have a grandson like you. 'Course…I'm not sure they'd get much of a kick knowin' you were driven like that in town, hea."' And then he chuckled.

"'Course… I caan't help but wonda' where you learned a stunt like that? You… practice somewhere?" After the chief asked that, you could have heard a pin drop. "Ya know—If I was able to ta pull a few out-o'-staters ova' with a stunt like that, I'm sure it would make quite an impression on 'em. Think you could teach me how ta do that out back o' the station sometime?" he asked.

Petey gulped, but the words simply would not form for him to speak and again he just nodded, yes.

Rodney Torrey could not believe his ears. He expected at least a decent reprimand for the boy's behavior with a motor vehicle. He realized now that the chief was dealing with the grandson of close friends and his thought returned him to that hot afternoon in Willard Weaks' office and how he'd responded to the coffee-and-donut caper, and he thought, *that…little Petey Harriman actually got up the balls ta steal doughnuts and coffee…*

Rodney turned his attention toward the two older boys who were now laughing in near hysteria at the chief's request, and then he turned and looked out onto Portland Street and walked out without saying a word. The two officers were leaving together in the chief's car, and as he walked toward it, Rodney wanted to spit on the sidewalk, his emotions ran that high.

Every time I deal with this group of little turds, I always seem to end up on the shit-end of the stick, he thought. He got in the car and slammed the door.

9

SUMMER'S HEAT BURNED like exposure to poison Ivy. Seacoast Emergency Rooms from Portsmouth, New Hampshire, to Bangor, Maine were filled with the daily needs of tourists and locals alike who overdid the activities of the dog-days. There were sunburns, sprained ankles, upset stomachs from overeating and even drug abuse, to name a few, to the serious trauma victims from inexperienced race-car drivers losing to the competition in a race to be first at the next red light. The locals, no matter how hard they prepared themselves for the onslaught of tourism, were always overwhelmed when vacation season came.

The scene at the Little Roady a few days before had left an imprint on the minds of all who were there. Both policemen contemplated the events from dissimilar agendas. Rodney Torrey continued to feel the sting of embarrassment from the chief's request to learn that stupid, little spin-around stunt from Petey Harriman. And the sound of laughter from the two rogues, as he thought of Zeke and Pozy, ran vividly through his memory. The chief, however, never gave any of it a second thought. Dwight remained numb to most everything, while Petey went home to his grandparents, hoping to deflect the occurrence from them if the need arose. The remaining duo retired to their garage and the sweltering heat that made it difficult to breathe at times

It could appear to anyone trained in psychological evaluation that Pozy, curled up on the couch in a fetal position, might be on a downward spiral toward clinical depression. His long periods of silence were intimidating, and when he did communicate, it was with a series of grunts or moans. He ate very little, and his face had become gaunt and bony-looking. Zeke, on the other hand, seemed to manifest only one problem: with the extreme heat, there was no way he'd be able to wear the leather jacket to conceal the revolver.

"Shit…shit…fuckin' shit!" he said, while dangling a tiny white mouse between the thumb and index finger of his right hand, clutching the black .38 revolver in his left.

"How in the hell am I going to carry this little beauty without wearing that fuckin' leather? It's too goddamned hot," he said.

Pozy roused himself from his stupor in frustration at hearing Zeke bitch all morning, and said, "Why don't ya shove it up yaw' ass? I can't see no-one lookin' fa' it thea.'"

At that very moment, as Zeke looked toward his friend in disbelief, the snake slithered upward and snatched the mouse from his fingers, nearly taking the thumb with it, much to Zeke's astonishment. "Son…o'…va'…bitch, you bastard!" he said.

Pozy, thinking he was speaking to him, not knowing what happened at the snake cage, mumbled something inaudible and rolled over onto his side and faced the back of the couch to resume his downward slide toward his own hell.

—

Petey sat on the porch of his grandparent's house, which had been his home since the loss of his parents. The Little Roady was the farthest thing from his mind. The hot afternoon had cooled considerably from the shade of the towering maple trees lining the front of the old New England farmhouse on the hill. The home had been in the family for three generations now, and most likely would eventually belong to Petey. His grandparents were stay-at-homers nowadays. The old man had retired from the shipyard a couple of years before, and his grandmother had always been a stay-at-home wife, taking care of things around the farm. It wasn't a real farm, but they raised at least one pig every year. They had chickens as long as they were laying eggs, and she always tended to huge vegetable gardens, some of which she cared for through the winter months in cold-frames along the southern-exposed side of the house and barn. With the manicured lawns out front and the tall grass on the sides and back, it was a beautiful country home.

Petey loved being here. The view from the porch, which ran the length of the house on the front and one side, looked out over the largest part of the acreage, which was about one hundred acres. In the old days, surveying was unheard of, and the farm was bordered on three sides by a five-hundred acre bog and swamp, securing their privacy for future generations. On a clear day, from this vantage point, you could see the horizontal outline of the open ocean and the sight of it now gave Petey his first nervous stomach pang, remembering the events at the Roady and his conversation with Officer Rodney Torrey, and the chief. He wondered if he should bring the subject up, not knowing if the old folks had heard anything of it, since word traveled fast around here, or wait until one of them went to town and heard it from someone else spilling the proverbial beans.

As his mind contemplated the thought, he heard the familiar sound of his grandfather's footsteps approaching the porch, from the long hallway beneath the inside stairs. As his grandfather stepped onto the porch, they greeted each other, his grandfather calling him Peter, as usual, and he sat himself on the identical rocking chair beside Petey. Both chairs had been handmade by the old man many years before. They made small talk of current events, because both were news buffs, while the aroma of beef pot-roast and browned potatoes and onions encircled the entire property, inside and out, from the kitchen at the rear of the house. Their hunger pangs were not easily ignored.

As the old man spoke of insignificant, daily struggles, Petey's thoughts carried him away from the moment; the old man's voice became a distant distraction, and he couldn't free himself of the burden of not telling someone of the events at the Little Roady, if only to simply ease his sense of right and wrong that they would hear it from him and no one else that might trump it up to more than what it actually was.

In the middle of an unfinished sentence, observant as the old man was, he stopped speaking, forcing Petey to return to earth, looking toward him now.

"Yaw' thoughts aar' on somethin' all together different than what we were talkin' about, Peter. Anything you want ta share?" he asked.

After a few moments of staring in silence, Petey spoke up. "Well…gramps… there is one thing, but I didn't want ya to worry about it, 'cause I took care of it in the best way I could and it's all good now."

"Ok." The old man responded simply.

Petey began to explain the reason for the conversation between Rodney Torrey and him, telling his grandfather about those who were present and what he explained as a humorous request by the chief to teach him how to spin his police car the same way. The old man's first response was a type of snort. He sat there with a strange grin on his face, yet he said nothing, as if waiting for Petey to say something else. When nothing came, he cleared his throat and spoke.

"Ya know… money doesn't grow on trees. Those tires a' yours… if I remember right, aar' pretty big. You saved quite a while to pay for them. I can't imagine why you'd wanta' burn the tread off 'em like that." And then he remained quiet, but continued looking deep into Petey's eyes for an explanation of sorts.

Knowing his grandfather as he did, and feeling the respect he had for both his grandparents, he knew he would respond, but it would probably take a few moments to get his thoughts together.

A soft afternoon breeze ushered in the scent of the sea, cooling, if only a little, the afternoon heat. While considering his answer, his thoughts drifted back in time, and he wondered how he always seemed to make such dreadful decisions when trying to impress Zeke or Pozy and even Dwight. The doughnut-and-coffee heist, and now the squealing-tire thing suddenly made no sense to him, and looking at his grandfather—as frugal a man as he was—his actions seemed a bit stupid to him now. Perhaps the time was right for him to move on. Suddenly, the sound of his grandfather clearing his throat once again brought him back to the moment.

"Sorry, gramps. You're right. Money doesn't grow on trees and I did save a long time for those tires. I told Rodney Torrey it wouldn't happen again, and it won't. If the chief or Rodney say anything about it to ya, you can tell them I said just that."

—

The day was winding down for Missy at the Little Roady. She prepared to leave by the rear door as usual, looking back over her shoulder, making sure that all of the lights were out. She turned the doorknob and pushed, but it wouldn't budge. With all the humidity, the door had swollen, and a solid kick to the threshold area usually did the trick. She drew her right foot back and was about to let go when the door opened quickly, by itself, forcing her to jump back with a defensive stare. Suddenly, without warning in the fading light of the day, a figure bounded into view, blocking the entire doorway, forcing Missy to inhale a spastic breath. She pulled back quickly and then, with as quick a reaction, she punched Zeke hard in the chest as he stood, laughing hysterically.

"You freak! You almost gave me a heart attack. And where have you been… by the way?"

With a slight shaking of laughter still in his voice he said, "Me and Poz held up for a couple o' days at the garage. Too hot ta get out and about. Miss me?"

"If I said no, what would ya do then?" she asked.

"I…don't know, maybe go home and play with myself, I guess."

"You… freak pig. Is that all you can think about…sex? What about how long it's been since we've just had time to talk and be together?" she asked, although she would not share with him her true feelings of why she was glad he was here.

"Come hea', I'm sorry," he said in a sing-song voice, in what could and should be considered condescending, yet hoping it would be enough to calm her down, and when he reached out with an outstretched arm, she came to him with welcomed abandon.

They stepped back inside the kitchen and closed the door. As much as she wanted and needed to be with him, the storage closet was not going to make it for her this evening. They held on, it seemed, for dear life—neither attempted to let the other go for a long period of time. Their lips pressed tightly; their breath against each other's faces was a turn-on. His hands felt her from top to bottom, and twice he tried, unsuccessfully, to unfasten the snap on her pants, but she pushed his hand away and he returned it to her breast, while she masterfully yet callously groped his groin.

Even though she lived at home with her mother, Marcy's frequent Portland trips to freedom from the restaurant left Missy with the run of the place. Since this was one of those escape-times, they would have Missy's bed to frolic in as long as Zeke hadn't planned one of his disappearing acts again. After a long spell of lip-locking, she finally pulled herself away long enough to get a word in edgewise before Mr. Mouth cranked up again.

"We've got the house to ourselves if we want it. My bed is softer than those sacks o' flour in that closet." She stopped then, focusing her stare into his eyes, leaving no doubt as to her intentions. His thoughts drifted swiftly to how long it was since he'd slept in a real bed, never mind falling off to sleep after sex without having to get up and leave. He pulled her body tight to his, feeling the firmness of her butt in his hands.

"What aar' we waitin' fa'? Let's get goin'." *It'll be good ta get old Dr. Ramachuck out o' my pants and not be the one grabbin' him,* he thought.

—

It had been about an hour since Zeke left; Pozy enjoyed every moment of the solitude without any interruptions from his friend and garage-mate. His thoughts drifted in and out of reality; daydreams were now a very real part of his day-to-day existence. The old farm. Rodney Torrey bawling them out at the restaurant; and Zeke sliding his hand over the .38 in his jacket. Even the bloody mess they'd left those two guys from Massachusetts in that night in Biddeford. He looked out onto the clearing in front of the garage. The setting sun cast an almost angry, red glow on everything beneath it. The stillness of his surroundings gave him comfort and he thanked his lucky stars that the old woman had given this place to him to lay his weary head, even if it was on this stinky, stained couch on a cement floor.

The gang can't stay together forever, Pozy thought. *Sooner or later all things come to an end. I'm not sure how long I can go on like this. Maybe a job? Get a real place o' my own. Sure, Zeke and me've been through a lot together. Petey and Dwight are my friends, but it just doesn't feel the same anymore.*

10

The dawning of Saturday appeared to scorch the earth with an incandescent red; as if last evening's setting sun had purposely left it behind to finish what it began.

Most tourists had arrived the previous day, seeking the wonderment of a long Maine weekend. Along with their joy they brought with them an overpowering sense of territorial dominance that drove the locals out of their skulls. But money talks and shit walks, and the legal tender speaks for all men, no matter where they're from.

Zeke and Missy had slept locked in a firm embrace. A light film of perspiration developed where their skin touched, although they hadn't noticed yet. A cool, early morning breeze allowed the window sheer to float nimbly through the air. Zeke opened his eyes to the distant sound of an eighteen-wheeler chugging up the Maine Pike. The house was less than a mile from the highway—at times, the groan over the asphalt was disconcerting, but for those who lived that close it became somewhat nonexistent.

He wanted to move. Get out of bed, take a piss and start the coffee. Missy had told him how the coffee-pot worked before going to sleep, but the soft expression of pleasure on her face would not allow him to disturb her from sleep. Having slept in a real bed with smooth, soft sheets and a fluffy pillow, Zeke began to consider the vagabond type of life he'd lived for what seemed like forever now with Pozy. Unknown to him at this moment, his thoughts were identical to his closest friend's last night.

Sure, Pozy and me've been through a lot together. Petey and Dwight are my friends, but it just doesn't feel the same any more, he thought.

"Hey… three cents fa' yaw' thoughts." Missy was awake.

"You'd pay that much?" he asked.

She remained still, except to reach out for him with one arm pulling him tighter to her. As they came together, his thoughts, for no apparent reason—and he would never share them with her—suddenly traveled back to that night in Biddeford when he'd put a real hurt on those two from Massachusetts, and it gave him a sudden tingle of satisfaction to know he had had such control over them. He now longed for autumn when he could conveniently carry the .38 in the lapel pocket of his leather jacket again.

11

Zeke came away with a heady new attitude about himself after spending the night with Missy. He was always confident in most aspects about himself, but lately, he'd questioned all things that he did by himself or with Pozy, causing them both to doubt themselves, though they never shared most of their personal thoughts with one another. Now, it was the old Zeke reincarnated. Today, he didn't give a shit what anyone thought. He intended to sharpen his knife, and keep his gun loaded.

They spent the forenoon together with coffee and muffins on the sunny side-porch of Missy and Marcy's home. Marcy called to confirm her early arrival at the restaurant, going directly there from her little escape trip to Portland yesterday. It was agreed that Missy would come in around 1:00 or 2:00 p.m. to spell her mother, giving the two love-birds more time in their little nest.

For Missy, having him here like this heightened the possibilities of being together as a couple. In her heart she felt that in Zeke, down deep, was a hidden goodness and she thought she had the tools to harvest that rectitude. Unfortunately, Zeke was overcome with the release of his sexual frustration and the closest thing that might resemble love was his thought of maybe having a quickie after breakfast before going their separate ways until whenever.

The morning flew by, they went their separate ways, Zeke refusing a ride, and he headed north in the opposite direction from Missy and Route 1. She had only two thoughts as she drove: Zeke and last night. He had only one: the black .38 caliber revolver he'd left back at the garage.

He changed directions at the first side-road he came upon, one that would parallel Route 1, and the minute he did, now that he was well out of sight of Missy and the love-nest, his thumb went out to every passing vehicle going his way. The sun was at high-noon. With no apparent takers for a rider, he removed his T-shirt and worked on his tan, while the thought of the night in Biddeford raged in his subconscious mind between toned-down outbursts of vulgarity directed at those passersby who didn't stop. At this point, he was less than three or four miles from the garage, and realized that for the first time in many months, he hadn't spent the night at the garage with Pozy. It wasn't as if either one cared where the other was or went, it was simply that they were always together most of the time.

When he returned, he always made up little parables for Pozy about his time spent with Missy. There were no limits to the extent of the exaggeration which both of them looked forward to; Zeke telling and Pozy hearing the tall tales.

There were still no takers for the outstretched arm and thumb. Zeke walked the entire way to the garage, drained of energy from the heat by the time he arrived. The moment he stepped onto the gravel and caught first sight of the building, he knew then that no one was inside or on the property.

"Well… Where the fuck did he go?" he asked himself in a low, but audible tone. It was unlike Pozy to go off for long periods by himself; it wasn't that he didn't, it just seemed strange to Zeke. Besides, Zeke knew that being alone made him feel good.

Zeke opened the two garage doors and immediately felt a coolness that generally settled inside overnight. He went in, going directly to his leather jacket which he kept behind the snake cage whenever he was away and immediately reached for the revolver. The moment his hand was upon it, a feeling of intense satisfaction came over him, and he exhaled a breath of relief knowing it was untouched. He wanted to shoot it so badly, but bullets cost money and right now, with the state of his finances, if it cost a nickel to go around the world, Zeke couldn't get up enough to leave the garage yard. The bullets that were in the gun when he stole it would have to stay there for a while longer. Knowing he was alone, he pretended to take pot-shots toward things at random. He even pointed the gun at the snake, wondering how big of a splatter he'd make at this close range.

"Sorry…sorry little guy. I was just fuckin' kiddin' with ya," he said, as if the Black Racer understood what had just happened. He immediately reached for the box he kept mice in for Rowdy, realizing there was only one left; he knew he'd be spending part of the day "shopping" for the snake's groceries. Instead of his usual teasing of the snake by dangling the mouse in front of it, he simply dumped the tiny critter into the cage to fend for itself. Because the cage was filled with grass, twigs and sawdust, the mouse burrowed deep into the ecological environment of its surroundings quickly, the snake, though it hadn't been fed for at least a day, maintained its focus on Zeke.

"Well, ya little fuck…Whaddaya gonna' do, bite the hand that feeds ya?"

He looked down at the snake as if it might answer and the staring continued for several moments without a single movement from either Zeke or the Black Racer. He felt a slight pull suddenly from the skin around his shoulders; reaching for the area now, he realized he'd been sunburned during his walk without a shirt. He liked being in the sun and another burn would mean darker skin as the summer faded.

Ennui became overwhelming. He grabbed the tiny box, stuffed the revolver in his belt and went out to check the little have-a-heart traps he caught mice in throughout the surrounding woods. He thought to himself as he went, *I'll make plans for a jaunt to the coast later, by myself if no one shows up before I get ready to leave.*

The moment he exited the building, he felt and smelled the incoming freshness of an afternoon sea breeze, cooling everything smothered under the scorching, early-day sun. Although it remained warm, if the temperature continued to drop, the evening would be nice and cool.

—

For the first time in months, Pozy had gone home to the farm. He'd left shortly after Zeke on Friday, hitching rides all the way. The Friday evening travelers were far more generous with someone needing transportation then than they'd been earlier today with Zeke. His second ride dropped him within a mile from the old homestead, giving him very little time to reconsider a stay with his parents. Down deep, however, he knew it would be for the better.

Well... some good old home cookin' z' gotta' be betta' than a shaap' stick in the eye, he thought as he approached the long gravel road that would lead him home. The farm proper was hidden over the top of a rise some two hundred yards from the road by a field, where a dense crop of summer hay swayed gently in a light breeze. The hard work of haying in the hottest time of summer associated with this beautiful landscape gave him a slight twitch of uncertainty, yet he continued on his way toward the house.

It was, however, without a doubt, a most peculiar moment in time, for as Pozy crested the hill and the farm buildings sprawled across the terrain two figures came into view, as if a sixth-sense enveloped his parents into thinking something was about to happen. They stood, motionless, in front of the house, both staring out across the field in Pozy's direction, all three seeing each other at the same instant. A sudden feeling of warmth came over him; he stopped, and began to feel a little sick in his gut, yet a mere second passed before he continued his slow jaunt downhill toward where the two people who hadn't moved as much as an eyebrow waited expressionlessly for their son.

—

After the tire-squealing incident at the Little Roady, it was as if a blanket of skepticism had covered the four boys during the past week or so. Dwight also returned home for an extended visit. Although he was not welcomed with open arms, he was shown to his room by both parents, and as they stood silently watching, Dwight appeared to float over his almost-forgotten possessions. They left him to them, making their way downstairs, unnoticed by him. He remained that day in his room for several hours contemplating his self-imposed truancy from the life he'd come to know as he followed the misguided traits of the outlaws, Zeke and Pozy.

At the far reaches of the county, Petey remained at home with his grandparents. The simple chores around the place kept him focuses and planted, unwilling now to return quickly to the impolitic ways of his two older friends.

Three young men suddenly found themselves on separate paths. Maturity comes when least expected, and nothing lasts forever.

12

THE INFECTIOUS HUM FROM the weekend traffic into Maine quelled somewhat now that the out-of-staters were nestled in their vacation homes. Most folks went about their normal daily affairs, permanent residents and vacationers alike. Zeke had almost completed his rounds of the have-a-hearts, gathering a full supply of mice, and boredom itched at the core of his existence. With no one around, Zeke had no audience to fill his ego; however, his antics of throwing things about gave little rise to what he needed most: attention.

He couldn't handle being alone. Upon his return, he immediately went to a small stash of pot—though none of the four boys were regular smokers of weed, they had, long ago, agreed to maintain a small amount at the garage just in case. The "just in case" could be as little as a rainy day with nothing to do but stare at each other. For Zeke, the "just in case" was now. No one ever remembered to buy rolling papers, so a small corncob pipe was placed with the herb, and because of the woodstove, there were always matches or a lighter left in the baggy. Zeke was set.

A sea breeze continued to cool the afternoon, and with both garage doors open, it was as if the place was air-conditioned. Zeke loved the sun, but he melted in the usually high humid summers on the Maine coast. The cooler air was a great comfort to him. He packed the pipe and propped himself in a chair leaning against the frame of the open doors and gave very little thought to the other boys.

Occasionally, he saw Missy through his mind's eye, and himself being naked with her the night before, but clearly his mental exercise consisted of pretending to cock and fire the revolver. Until he actually shot it, he would not rest easy. He held it now, examining it from barrel to pistol grip, and between puffs on the pipe, he pretended to take pot-shots at tree limbs, rocks out front and occasionally, trailing an aim toward an unseen passing vehicle out on the road behind the thick growth of trees.

Although he never wore a watch, Zeke was an excellent judge of time. It seemed a natural instinct to be within minutes of the actual time whenever someone asked or he simply needed to know and guessed. His boredom passed with the time, as he relaxed under the effects from the happy-pipe.

Suddenly, he found much humor in the sound of the mouse he'd thrown the snake earlier, rustling through the man-made carpet of underbrush in the cage, listening to its final attempt to save its life by eluding the inevitable end. And then the only sound was from the wind through the pine boughs of the surrounding forest.

The afternoon slipped away and the late-day shadows extended across the clearing out front where Zeke sat. He was relaxed, something that wasn't usual for Zeke. He mumbled a few words of unhappiness at the speed at which the day faded without any of the other boys showing up.

"Those little twerps! The last thing I wanted was to have ta walk ta town tonight," he spat.

He kicked himself forward on the chair and got to his feet quickly. He'd been shirtless since returning to the garage; now with the sea breeze and the slowly setting sun, the air was cool and comfortable. As he pulled his shirt on, the earlier effects of sun greatly enhanced his tan, and he was ready for a walk.

A sudden pang of hunger erupted and he went toward the tiny fridge at the corner of the work bench. As the door swung open, the rancid aroma of what appeared to him as baby vomit emitted itself from an open and long-forgotten container of cottage cheese. Although Zeke had a cast-iron stomach, he damned near heaved up what little remained of the morning's breakfast with Missy.

"What-tha'-fuck'! Am I the only one that finds shit like this? Nobody gives a fuck around hea." He reached in to grab the container, and without thinking it through, opened the door of the wood stove and threw the container and its ill fated contents in and slammed the door, bringing the lever down sharply. He returned to the fridge, removed the last of its contents—a tall, plastic bottle of Pepsi, which was nice and cold. He removed the cap and guzzled, wishing it were beer. He looked out at the sun, low in the sky, and wondered where in hell the day had gone, never thinking that he'd spent most of it under the effects of the pipe, which allowed him to nap for several hours. He was wide-awake now, ready for a trip to town. He gave a quick thought of dropping in on Missy; he could even invite her back here for the night. But he remembered she'd been here once and looked around with an expression of distaste. Then, he looked around himself.

"Fuck...I don't even like this hole that much anymore," he said.

Besides, he couldn't picture her on that stinky couch after the night they'd spent in her soft, cuddly bed. *No...this is no place for her,* he thought.

His thoughts quickly went to the revolver. Stepping out through the garage doors he felt a steady off-shore breeze bringing with it heavy, damp sea smoke with the tell-tale sign of rain. A thrill came over him—he knew it wasn't exactly cool enough for the leather jacket, but the gun and the leather would be reunited tonight and the thought of that led him back to the happy-pipe and a generous refill to start the evening. The Pepsi quelled the hunger pang he'd had earlier, but with Zeke's appetite, it wouldn't last for long, especially when the effects from smoking wore off. The need for food would probably be overwhelming then. The distant sound of cars on the road began to instill the need to wander, and he looked around the garage in disgust, threw on the leather, and slid the .38 into the lapel pocket, closed the doors and left. Clutching the small baggy, pipe and lighter in his hand, he headed for town. Although he would never admit it even to himself, he missed the company of his friends, and for no explainable reason, Zeke felt a pang of loneliness.

—

For the most part, Missy simply went through the motions after her mother left the Little Roady. Her thoughts were only of Zeke and their evening together. Every time the front door opened, she hoped it was him. Each time the rear door was forced open for a delivery of any kind, her heart thumped in her chest, thinking it might be him. She would never understand how he could be so incredible in bed while they were together in every way and then just disappear for days or even weeks on end, then reappear like he'd never left. Through all of their conversations about each other and their past, she knew how troubled he was emotionally; hell, she had her own baggage and he knew that. It's probably what attracted each one to the other, but lately he was consumed by something he was unwilling to talk about and the last thing she would do was pry.

On Saturday, the restaurant always closed early. People just didn't want coffee and eggs and bacon for dinner. They all headed for the Clam Shacks, Lobster Pounds and Steak Houses along Route 1, while Sunday morning and breakfast would come soon enough. She cleaned the counter, hopefully for the last time—no customers had ventured in for at least the last hour. The coffee pots were cleaned except one, just in case, and closing time was only a twist of the door-key away.

She wanted to be with him; so much so that she considered going to the garage on her way home, as much as she hated that stinky place. If the other three nerds weren't there, she might even consider staying the night, and if they got together again after last night, there'd be no doubt in her mind that they would be a couple tonight. Not wanting to push, she drove the thought from her mind and continued to close.

Call it intuition, but as Zeke strolled down the shaded country lane, his thoughts were of Missy. He'd never felt this way about a woman or a girl before. He never considered a woman as a close friend or companion, someone he could share his most private thoughts with besides Pozy. A woman's purpose was to satisfy her man—whether they were together for the night or just long enough to take care of business—it was all the same to Zeke. The only time he thought of them again was in time of need—his. It was different with Missy. He couldn't get her out of his mind and it was killing him. He didn't want someone latched onto him; that kind of responsibility was for the saps who got hooked up with a chick at too young of an age and didn't have the grapes to tell her to get lost when it came time to go… period. He shook his head now, trying to dispel the agony of his thinking. He just didn't want to be bothered with that tonight.

Everything was fine until he closed in on Route 1. The traffic became heavy, and several times cars came very close to him, yet he never gave it a thought that he was wearing all black, walking in the same direction as traffic, and he probably didn't care. It was normal for Zeke, if normal is to become agitated when finding oneself in a throng of people. Sure, there's a certain amount of frustration that builds in most people when confined in a crowded situation, but with Zeke, it was not healthy. His laid-back, buzzed-out demeanor began to fade, and with the occasional derogatory slur directed at a passing motorist, Zeke was again his unhappy self. With the gun in his jacket however, he became a force to be reckoned with. His facial expression took on a new dimension that could almost allow anyone who knew him to mistake him for someone else. Evening began to settle in. Lights from houses along the way were being turned on, while screened-in porches held boisterous vacationers, enjoying their stay in Maine.

At this point in time, with his attitude plunging rapidly, the last thing he needed—or what he needed most to continue his downward spiral—was to have Queer-Eye pull alongside in his shiny cruiser. With the illegal .38 revolver concealed in his leather, the term, "So near, yet so far away" took on an all-new level of satisfaction for Zeke. At the very first sound of tires on the gravel shoulder, Zeke made a quick lunge toward someone's lawn, stopping and turning in the direction of the oncoming vehicle. He could just puke at seeing who it was.

"Well…well, out fa' an evenin' stroll, are we?" Rodney asked.

Zeke didn't respond immediately to the officer's question, he simply looked into the car and made eye contact. "Free country… right?"

"Oh…yah! Just askin'."

"That's nice. Slow night fa' tickets?" Zeke asked.

Rodney ignored the question and followed up with one of his own. "Where's the rest o' yaw' little band? No big Mopar ta drag around in?"

"I ain't their old man. I don't keep tabs on them. Besides, ain't that yaw' job, to keep tabs on the local riffraff?" Rodney shook his head and immediately pulled back onto the roadway.

Zeke remained on the lawn, watching as the cruiser's rear lights disappeared over a slope in the road. In his heart, Zeke knew that tonight would be one to remember. Missy would not be there to calm his hormones. There was no one to say no.

He slid his open palm over the concealed gun, and he knew then it would become a part of history this night. Zeke arrived at Route 1 just after dark. The road was busy with north and southbound traffic; the aroma from busy food-joints was almost toxic for a hungry person—at times even those who weren't hungry fell to the temptation.

Zeke had stolen a small folded wad of cash from Missy's this morning before leaving. What he thought was a successful heist was actually a plant by her. She knew he had no cash and if her hunch was right, and it was, she figured he would take it. There were twenty-five dollars in mixed bills. His hand squeezed it now, knowing very well he'd indulge in that aroma sooner, rather than later. There was a Chinese place not far from where he was and they had a bar. The egg rolls and the Crab Rangoon appetizers were the best and the price was right for a bottle of beer to wash it all down.

Zeke had worked for the owners every once in a while, and they were on speaking terms, unlike most former employers of his. He arrived sooner than he thought and walked in through the large Chinese Temple-like doors, and was immediately greeted by the wife of the co-owner duo. Her face carried a look of curiosity, thinking he might be looking for some type of work, and she was surprised when Zeke pointed toward the bar, moving unescorted toward the dim lights of the lounge. He put on a long face when hearing the accents of those folks seated around the bar. He moved toward the far end, where it opened for wait staff to enter and exit with orders, and finding a solitary stool, he sat himself heavily on it. He looked at the draft-beer spouts, their handles displaying the brands, and when asked his pleasure, he responded simply, "Bottle o' Bud." The bartender didn't ask for ID, as he'd served him many times after work, when he worked.

They made small talk, and then he reached for the brew. "Here ya go, big guy."

"Thanks," was all Zeke responded.

He looked up at the huge, flat-screen TV over the shelves of bottles while taking his first pull on the beer. The Red Sox were at bat, the Yankees out in the field at Boston. He could hear the tourists chime with the announcer's strike and ball calls.

Zeke was a baseball fan whenever he sat at a bar; outside of that, he didn't give a shit about the game. He felt a bit out of place with the leather, since everyone in the joint was wearing summer clothes, but when he slid his hand into the lapel pocket, he smiled slightly and was again comfortable in his own skin. He took much humor in the sounds of the patrons, thinking them more Connectaclits than Mass-holes.

The effects of the pot lingered and the alcohol gave the feeling a new perspective, and as expected, the hunger pangs returned. He guzzled what remained of the beer, motioned for the bar-keep and ordered another one; this time added an egg roll and an order of the Crab Rangoon he'd been thinking of earlier. The glistening bottles and glasses under the lounge lighting drew his attention, distracting him temporarily from his surroundings. His mind drifted to the other three boys, wondering where they'd gone. Pozy especially; he was closer to him than the other two. Missy popped into his thoughts momentarily; then suddenly, he and Pozy were back in Biddeford that night several weeks ago. He reached into the jacket again, wrapping his right hand around the pistol grip. The sensation was uplifting to simply hold onto it. His thoughts continued to carry him away somewhere, when suddenly, without warning, the fresh bottle of beer being placed in front of him sped him back to reality and the moment. The bartender stared briefly, thinking the young man was having trouble holding his beer. Most bartenders are aware of when a drinker is ready to fall over the edge. Zeke had that look on his face, but as he returned to reality, the guy dismissed it as daydreaming and went about his business.

The food came quickly; it was devoured, and the beer went with it. Refreshed, Zeke's thoughts went to rabble-rousing. Taunting out-of-staters was a high for him and the others, and there were thousands of them to choose from. He looked across the length of the polished wooden bar and mentally singled out those he thought could be easily agitated. Doing so here, however, could jeopardize his future work arrangement, and he gestured for his tab, while making mental notes of the faces. Who knew, they might just cross paths later.

After paying his bill, knowing the back way out, he left unnoticed by anyone in the lounge, including the bartender. Upon exiting he realized the air was considerably cooler. The leather jacket was a happy experience. The traffic was heavier and the evening crowd was out in force, creating a buzz that permeated the atmosphere of the entire seacoast. He walked southbound, thinking he might hitch a ride toward Punquit Beach and get a look at some lollipops there. That area was full of tourists.

"That should make for a few laughs," he thought.

In spite of being alone, he refused to dwell on the matter. He did, however, wish he had Petey's wheels right now. Walking these days was too slow for the way Zeke wanted things done.

As the crow flies, he was about five miles from the beach. His thumb went out only feet from the restaurant, and within a minute a vehicle with Maine plates stopped. It was two young chicks in what looked to be an old farm truck and as he passed the open bed, there were tell-tale signs of manure in the corners near the wheel.

"I ain't ridin' in the back o' that fucker," he thought as he passed.

The front passenger door swung open as he arrived, the girl sliding toward the middle. Zeke got in. "Well…well. If it ain't a couple o' angels come down from heaven to help me on my way," he said. The young girls, probably in their mid-to-late teens, giggled.

"Where ya goin', sir?" the driver asked.

Zeke recognized the farm stock and lingo immediately. "Punquit Beach," he said.

"Ok." The driver responded and accelerated heavily back into the flow of traffic.

Zeke began to examine the two, straining his vision from the corner of one eye. He laughed to himself, thinking, *I wonder if Queer-Eye got started this way?*

He felt the heat rise within him being this close to the girl next to him. He wondered just how old they were, and right now, a threesome out on the beach would do wonders for his ego. Suddenly, no more than a mile from where he was picked up, the driver recognized someone in a passing vehicle going in the opposite direction, and at once their ages and maturity made itself known, the driver, without warning, pulled a ferocious U-turn amidst the oncoming flow of cars. The horn-blasting and tire-squealing was deafening, and immediately upon completion of her turn, Zeke hollered wildly, "Let me the fuck outta this truck," and as the vehicle began to slow, he kicked the door open and jumped before it came to a full stop. Although he was pissed, he couldn't keep from thinking that she'd pulled the stunt off nicely, but she was no Petey. He'd become accustomed to Petey's driving and right now, nothing else would do. With the girls, it was as if nothing out of the ordinary had happened. Both girls turned to watch their passenger jump and when he was out, they simply returned their focus on the vehicle they'd turned to meet and took off after it.

Zeke was alone again. He refused to stick his thumb out a second time, fearing what type of idiot might stop. He began talking to himself in his thoughts.

Another trick like that and I might blow the little twit away when she's drivin'. How could I be so stupid to think that those kids back there were more than just rug-rats? The little bitch shouldn't even be drivin'. Ta pull a fuckin' stunt like that with me in the truck… I shoulda' shot both them bitches. If that friggin' idiot… Petey showed up I'd a' never got into that piece o' shit truck in the first place. That bitch coulda killed us all.

As that thought melted away and with several miles behind him, he reached into the jacket and actually cocked the hammer of the revolver. With the hammer drawn back, a single screw-up could be fatal, probably for him, as he carried it with the barrel facing down. A shot from that distance and direction could go through his abdomen or catch him in the upper thigh, taking out an artery. With the gun cocked, it was a deadly weapon in his pocket. Zeke had handled the pistol every day since he'd stolen it. He knew that to make the revolver safe again, he had to hold the hammer with his thumb while simultaneously squeezing the trigger and gently returning the hammer to its safe resting place. To do that, he'd have to remove the gun from his jacket, and he wasn't ready to do that now with as many tourists as there were about the area.

He could smell the ocean. Route 1 followed the coast throughout Maine. It was just at specific times and locations when you got a good whiff of the iodine.

There was a dead-end road ahead on the left. From it, there was a narrow, tree-lined trail that ran down to and skirted the water's edge for miles. It was a path for the sure-footed, and Zeke and Pozy had traveled it often, in daylight and dark. Upon entering, houses were set far back and very little light showed, except from the evening sky. Zeke removed the revolver and carried it alongside his right leg, with the hammer still cocked. It was along this trail one night that he and Pozy had stumbled upon a huge raccoon and her three young. The sudden appearance of the animal jolted them into a fright; but since they were country boys, neither was afraid of the creature, though they knew enough to leave it alone. Tonight, Zeke wished a raccoon to appear, for only one reason. Zeke was going to get his gun off tonight, one way or another.

In the distance the surf crashed against the rocks, and a multitude of summer sounds buzzed in the tall grasses. His mind raced from one ridiculous thought to another. Silly things like… *What if I took the gun out back there when Queer-Eye stopped and plugged 'im in the stomach?* He laughed to himself. He stopped walking. He thought he'd heard giggling of sorts coming from the tall grass and goldenrod, vaguely visible in the reduced light. Standing fast in the middle of the path, his ears perked like a predator, he focused on a direction and then he heard it again. It was the smooth sound of a female, *being tickled,* he thought, and then catching the deep sound of a male's voice, he was certain he was right on.

He moved flat-footed and slow toward the laughter. It appeared to resurrect a deep sense of anger in him for reasons only he could know toward whomever these voices belonged; they hadn't invited Zeke for the festivities. Then, it became deafeningly quiet. He was close enough now to hear the woman panting with moans of satisfaction, which seemed to anger him more.

They're hidden well, he thought and as the notion passed, he immediately saw the back of the woman's long, silky hair and her bare shoulders, bouncing up and down as if enjoying a pony ride at an end-of-summer state fair. He watched them silently for several minutes, unseen by the lovers. She was completely naked and his mouth moistened at the beautiful physique before him. He couldn't see the guy except for part of a knee and leg. He was fully dressed, his pants down around his ankles. At the sight of her, Zeke began to feel the urge with a tingle through his scrotum and the moment he felt the turn-on, he shifted his weight slightly and a twig snapped beneath his foot. The young woman jerked in a sudden spasm of fear, hiding her bare breasts with encircling arms in a natural reaction to conceal her nudity from the strange intruder. The young man rose quickly, almost flipping her off his legs onto the ground. She bunched her scattered clothing in her arms and retreated behind her beau and began dressing, only to be halted by Zeke. "You stand right where you are, honey, and don't move any pretty parts yet," he said. Cowering behind her man; she clung to her bundle of clothes.

"What-tha'-fuck you doin', you little pervert? You get your cookies off watchin' other people do it?" the guy asked. He couldn't be more than twenty, Zeke thought, but from the attitude and accent, he had to be an out-o'-stater. Surprisingly enough, neither one noticed Zeke's gun as of yet, for the young man continued his verbal barrage of belittlement, while Zeke remained in the same spot he was when they first noticed him, silently displaying a stupid-looking grin.

"Wha-da-ya, stupid?" the young man asked.

Zeke spoke for only the second time.

"Stupid? No. Crazy…Yes." Then he raised the gun in their direction, forcing a pale silence over the couple.

"You want money?" the young man asked, and he reached for his back pocket, forcing Zeke to level the .38 in his direction.

"Ya move another inch and I'll blow yaw' fuckin' head off," Zeke said.

He froze in that spot, dropping the hand he'd reached for the wallet to his side. The girl whimpered and remained motionless.

Suddenly, Zeke felt sick to his stomach, *Chink food,* he thought. It wasn't that, however. He'd always wanted to hold a gun on someone and now that he did, it was the strangest feeling. He loved the fact that they were scared shitless. He thought he'd keep the chick naked and have a little fun with her, just for the hell of it. All of this felt extremely surreal to him, and while thinking this, he let his guard down for a millisecond and the young dude was on him. Out of nowhere, he smashed Zeke in the face, almost causing him to drop the gun, and he continued to hammer at his face and head.

Zeke was so stunned by the attack; the guy being lesser in stature he felt he would certainly fall from the fierce assault. Surely the young man was trained in the fight game. His speed and accuracy at placing the blows for the most benefit enlivened Zeke's need to return some punishment of his own. At the very moment of a possible victory by the younger aggressor, Zeke pointed the gun, without aiming, and fired, taking the boxer in the knee of his right leg, dropping him like a fifty-pound sack of Maine potatoes. He made no attempt to hide his pain and his still-naked companion went directly to his side after a compelling whine.

"Oh...does that hurt...fuck-face?" Zeke asked with a slight laugh, yet the sound of his voice had changed by at least an octave lower from only minutes earlier, as if he were a completely different person.

Without looking up, the woman blurted out, "You fuckin' idiot, you shot him."

Zeke, in response, swung his arm and took her on the side of the head with an open hand, knocking her unconscious to the ground and on her back. Dismissing his pain, the boxer, angered by the assault on his girlfriend, rose in an attempt to get at Zeke. When he did, Zeke grinned and allowed him several steps forward then he shot him in the stomach. He fell backward this time, lifeless.

Zeke looked toward the girl; she remained on her back, completely unaware of what had just taken place. He moved quickly, going through the man's pockets, removing his wallet and car keys, and taking a watch from his wrist and a ring from his finger.

Suddenly, without a moment of thought, the scene from that night in Biddeford flashed in his mind's eye, and he was filled with an adrenaline rush, heightening his senses. He looked toward the girl who hadn't moved, then looked for a purse, but found none. He gave his former opponent a quick kick to the shoulder and getting no response, he focused his attention on the nudity at his side. He wanted to just touch her, all over, but since she lay unconscious, he saw no thrill coming from it. He scanned the entire area, saw nothing and no one, and left quickly on the path toward the water.

—

Less than an hour later, Zeke sat in the semi-darkness of the closed garage, the only light from a candle burning on top of the wood stove. He rubbed his fingertips lightly over the swelling of his right eye from the blows he'd received from a young man, lying dead from his gunshot wound. His thoughts raced through the scenes of the assault and shooting, feeling like minutes ago. He shook at times in spasms of fear for what he'd done, and he could still feel the burn through his windpipe to his lungs as he sped from the path, taking no direct or plainly visible route away from his pitiless attack on the couple. At one point he closed his eyes and saw the scene in his mind awash in blood splatter, and as quickly as the spasms of fear had come moments before, his eyes suddenly opened wide with glee as a child might display on Christmas morning seeing his presents under the tree. He could never imagine that a single bullet could blast blood from a man in so many directions at once. Even though he'd been several feet from his victim, Zeke found splatters on the tips of his boots and the shooting arm of his jacket. He was holding the gun with both hands, looking at it, and realized he'd fired off two rounds. In his mind, knowing he still wouldn't be able to buy more ammo even with the cash he had, until this all cooled down, he no longer had a six-shooter. There were only four bullets left. He breathed heavily at times, nearly hyperventilating, then sweating profusely.

"Fuck me!" he hollered out suddenly, looking around, thinking he'd heard sounds from outside. No one was there. The light rain was tapping on the roof or perhaps the carpet of pine needles on the ground. Meticulously, he'd placed the wallet, watch and ring he'd lifted from the young man before leaving the scene at equal distances apart from each other on the work bench within an arm's reach, directly in front of him. He glanced occasionally at them. He placed the revolver on the bench to his right and began a closer examination of the items, for the first time since he'd placed them there. It was still quite early Sunday morning—4:00 a.m., he noticed as he picked up the watch. He felt a sudden chill in the air. His clothes were soaked from his jog through the rain, a dampness that went to the bone. Again, without warning as he breathed deeply, eyes closed, exhaling in jerky breaths, the young man's face reappeared with a torrent of blood flowing from the corners of his tightly stretched lips, formed from an obvious expenditure of pain. He tossed the watch back on the bench as if it were infected with a disease.

"Fuck…Me!" he hollered again, this time smacking an open hand on top of the bench, unleashing a sting of pain in his fingertips. He'd felt that same sensation last night after knocking the girl to the ground. *No wonder she didn't get up*, he thought. Reaching for the wallet, he opened it, and his eyes bulged abruptly at the sight of two one-hundred dollar bills and an assortment of ones, fives, and tens. He pulled the bills, placing them in a stack in front of him.

I'll count this later, he thought, and rummaged through the remaining contents. The driver's license confirmed his last night's belief that they, or at least he was from away—the word Connecticut made it perfectly clear, and the name, Melvin Nisbet. "Connectaclit, I knew that shit-face was an out-o-stata," he said aloud, never bothering to look at a name. Suddenly, he had no feelings for what he'd done. As far as he knew, he'd killed a man and severely injured his friend, yet now he showed no remorse.

He stood, opened the stove door, which was an arm's distance away, and threw the wallet in along with several credit cards, a Maine hunting license, which he never gave a second thought to, and a cloth Saint Christopher medal. Zeke had no religious affiliation. Anything that could burn followed. He counted the money: two-hundred and thirty-five dollars—folded the bills and stuffed them into his damp jeans pocket along with the few remaining from last night's supper, never bothering to sort the folds. Without regret, he moved back to the watch. He remembered very little of removing it from the guy's arm except the flexibility of the band, which made taking it easy. He didn't know what to do with it except pawn the thing. That would have to wait until the heat was off. He shoved the watch into his jacket pocket. His eyes now fell upon the ring. It was gaudy looking, of Bali design, with a square, turquoise stone. Then he spotted the dried blood along the setting. He reached for a rag, draped over the edge of the bench, and spitting on it, he began rubbing to remove what blood he could. The more he rubbed, the more blood appeared. Turning the ring over, he found the indentation where the stone was set to be filled with dried blood. His saliva simply liquefied the matter allowing it to seep through the setting.

"Fuck... Me!" he hollered a final time before getting up and throwing the ring out into the now heavy, driving rain, hoping for a cleansing. He walked toward the kindling pile behind the stove, picked up several sticks, and threw them into the stove. He squirted a good dose of lighter fluid in and struck a match. Inside the stove was an instant blaze from the collection of summer refuse, like the donut bag and cups of Petey's crime. He removed the candle from the stove top and placed it on the workbench, then sat down heavily on the stool. Not having slept since his pot-induced naps the previous afternoon, his need for sleep was overpowering, especially with the heat from the clinking stove, causing blurred vision at times, and creating sounds from all around him that weren't there. He looked toward the couch and wanted to gag. Crouching over, he placed his head onto his folded arms on the bench, closed his eyes and hoped for sleep.

13

The little town of Dells was in a panic. The TV news vans with their extended remote antennas lined the road at the start of the little path that led to the water. With their microphones stuck in the faces of locals and vacationers alike, they asked pointed questions that couldn't be answered by the average John Q. Someone had to know something about this young man from Connecticut who was shot and killed. His girlfriend, now at the Southern Maine Medical Center in Biddeford for observation, had been assaulted with a hard blow to the head. A murderer was at large in Vacation Land.

A light rain had begun shortly after the murder last evening. It continued today, Sunday; heavy at times, hampering local and State Police investigators. They cordoned off the entrance and exit to and from the path, studying every rock and twig that seemed out of place, yet with the rain, evidence was not easily found. The main focus of their detective work would be the young woman, as soon as doctors allowed her to be questioned, hopefully later this morning.

Without a doubt, the subject of all conversation at the Little Roady was the kid from away who got killed. Reasons the locals gave were things like, love triangle gone bad, botched drug deal, no one thinking about what really happened. The locals had it all figured out before the chief or his officer ever stopped in for a refresher cup of coffee and their usual donut. Marcy's patience wore thin, yet she'd wait to hear anything from the chief himself, if he could share something. Gossip always made for big news in a small town, but a murder—something that happened maybe once in a decade or so—that was really big.

Missy had received a call early on from her mother; now she sat thinking of how the loss of a loved one affects each and every person in what once was their life. She remained by the phone quietly, silently. Suddenly, she thought of Zeke. He was a never-ending consideration now. She wondered how he might absorb this murder. He hated folks from away. He might simply respond with sarcasm, as empathy was not his virtue. She wondered how she might get in touch with him, wanting to share her thoughts with someone other than her mother. It was weird in so many ways. Not only did Missy wonder what Zeke might think of this atrocity, but all three boys of the original gang, now in the comfort of their parents' and grandparents' homes, also wondered where Zeke was and what he thought of the murder.

The boys were gone for several days, without contact with the outside world, yet the Sunday morning headlines and TV news reports overflowed at every breakfast table. All three, without knowing, had the same thought: rounding each other up and getting as much dirt as could be shoveled on this out-of-state stiff. Whatever thoughts they'd considered of freeing themselves from the shackles of their comradeship, while in the homes of the families who raised them, they were suddenly flushed by the realization of their lives as companions of big Zeke Brailey.

—

For no apparent reason while in the middle of the path, the site of last night's murder; where bloodstains from the victim remained somewhat darkened on the matted grass and goldenrod, Queer-Eye envisioned the outline of Zeke Brailey's hulk as it had appeared last evening just outside of his police cruiser door. *Where was he going and where did he end up?* he wondered. Not that he even considered him a possible suspect, but when shit happened, Zeke usually wasn't very far from the stink. The fact that he hadn't seen any of the troublesome foursome together for this long felt a bit unsettling for the officer, but he would not allow his suspicious police mind to go that far. He shrugged the thought off. There was work to do here now. He had to get it done before moving on to question locals. Besides, there was a young woman in Biddeford he'd see, with the troopers and the chief, first.

—

Sunday afternoon came quickly. Chief Willard Weaks, Officer Rodney Torrey and a Maine State Police investigator from the Major Crime Unit stood in the hallway just outside the young woman's hospital room door. The questioning, when her doctor believed the time right, would be done by the State Police as the MCU is responsible for major investigations, including homicides, suspicious deaths, and child abuse cases throughout the state, except in Portland and Bangor. There was little small talk between the men, while a thousand thoughts ran through the chief's mind. Right now, the last thing he wanted (selfish or not) was an unsolved murder in town, this close to his possible retirement, and an unstained record.

Rodney Torrey was pumped. This was his first in-town murder. His thoughts were jumbled with anticipation. The trooper simply studied from and wrote in a huge, black leather binder, appearing oblivious to what went on around him in the busy corridor. After a half-hour wait, the doctor opened the door and looked out, motioning for the three men to come closer. As he stepped just outside, holding the door partially open, he whispered that the girl was quite frail. She'd suffered a concussion and they'd have to take their time with her, and not stay too long. All three agreed with nods of their heads, following the doctor in.

The walls were pleasantly painted and decorated; the medical equipment was relatively new. Rodney was the last to enter, and even with her head bandaged, he immediately was attracted to the young woman's beauty. Her features were soft and delicate and he instantly loved her skin tone. Her deep blue eyes focused on the three uniformed men at the foot of her bed, while the doctor went directly to the side nearest her shoulder as she rested in an elevated position. The doctor maintained a stern and concerned expression and motioned to the inspector with a nod to proceed.

In a soft, reassuring voice, the trooper began with a greeting.

"Good morning, I'm Investigator Moody, Maine State Police Major Crime Unit." Then, he introduced the others.

"Your chart indicates that your name is Lillian Crandlemyer, is that right?"

"Yes," she responded.

"Would it be ok if I call you Lil, and are you ok to answer a few questions about last night?" he asked.

Without a verbal response, the young woman nodded her head in the affirmative and then looked down to the entwined fingers of her hands and waited for a question. The investigator was seasoned at this sort of thing. He knew she'd been through an impossibly frightening chapter of her young life. *She will have nightmares about what she's witnessed for years to come,* he thought. He proceeded slowly.

"Do you remember what time you and Melvin arrived on the path?" He scanned his notes as to the time of the call to the police.

"No, but it was after dark," she said. "You can't imagine how afraid I was. I thought he would shoot me too." She paused for a moment, as if gathering her thoughts. "No," she said simply. And then she began to cry. Not wailing, but whimpering. You could have heard a pin drop on the floor had someone dropped one, and now the trooper turned toward the two men with him with an open hand that might suggest taking a moment. After several minutes, the trooper looked toward the doctor by her side, and he gestured with an affirmative nod. The trooper began in a low voice.

"Are you ok to continue, Lil?" He asked softly.

"I think so," she answered hoarsely.

"Besides the person who..." he hesitated a long moment,

"assaulted you, did you see any other people on the path who may have seen something?"

This time she simply shook her head in the negative.

After several hesitant responses to more questions, all three men wrote frantically when she did offer a cohesive answer. The fact that she'd reported the murder left no indication as to what she and the victim had been doing on the path the previous night, and she would offer none of it if she had her way. After all, no one had found her naked except for the creep, so there was no need to go there.

The questioning went on for about thirty minutes, and when the doctor observed a slight slowness in several responses, he immediately motioned to the trooper that time was running out. He'd saved the best for last. This could be the last question if she answered it right.

"To the best of your ability, can you give us a description of this guy?"

She'd already envisioned him during parts of the questioning about how it all came to be, leaving out her sexual encounter with her lover. The thought of having to bring him fully visible in her mind again filled her with anxiety and it showed on her face. The room became eerily silent; even the doctor looked away from her so as not to heighten her apprehension.

In a low, hopefully reassuring tone the investigator asked, "Do you think you can do that for me? Take your time. Give it your best shot…" And he hated himself for that terrible choice of words, but it was too late to call them back.

She took a deep breath, exhaling slowly, and as she closed her eyes, the nightmare became vivid, yet it was as if she'd entered a foggy night all over again. The sound of their voices seemed far off on the path, somewhere she didn't want to go back to revisit. A slight headache began to throb at her temples and her stomach turned, yet she would not allow herself to be beaten by this pervert monster who'd killed her boyfriend. She entered a daydream now. His voice came to her thoughts first, but it spoke with a southern twang—that much she knew he did not have:

"Well…Bobby, life's a bitch…ya die…and it's still a bitch."

And then, the deafening shot rang out once again in her subconscious mind. She jumped in response (much to the wonderment of the men) and returned to the present. Her eyes were wide open. She looked around to each person in the room as if studying their faces for some sort of recognition, yet found none.

The hospital room was flooded with natural light from the window to the left of the bed. A glare formed from the shiny, hallway floor through the space at the bottom of the door, while a single light showed from the partially open toilet door in the corner of the room. She was covered to her midsection with a thin blanket, allowing a faint outline of her breasts to form through the hospital Johnny, and she nervously yet gently stroked the IV bandage near her wrist. A pin falling to the floor now would probably sound like thunder. She looked up as the doctor, still at her side, reached out and took her pulse. As he did, she began speaking.

"We…were holding each other… when we heard a snapping sound, then we saw him looking at us. He was just standing there, like a big…tree."

The room went ghostly quiet once again, then she went on.

"Mel… asked him if he was a pervert watching other people… or something like that." She whimpered at that point, sniffed a tear back and went on.

"Mel offered him money and when he reached for his wallet, is when we saw the gun," she said, then went silent again.

Rodney listened attentively, keeping in mind how the trooper eased his way through the questions. He liked to move things along when questioning someone. This was his first murder, however. He really didn't have a clue how it all worked, so he took a deep breath and waited. His curious mind wanted to know, however, why he'd found the tall grass matted down so firmly, only several feet from where they found the body, but as the doctor's question interrupted his train of thought, he gave it up for the rain or simply she or the culprit had stomped about after the shooting. "Are you alright?" the doctor asked. She nodded her head, looked around the room and spoke again.

"I'm not sure what happened next...but Mel flew at him real fast and started smashing him in the face and head. The jerk never moved; he just let Mel beat the hell out of him. All of a sudden, when I thought Mel had won, he...he shot him," she said and went into convulsive crying.

The doctor raised an arm, attempting to put an end to this, but the investigator produced an imitation rising of his own arm in response, taking the doctor completely by surprise.

"I know that I said the last question would hopefully be the last one, but I think I need one more thing and maybe we can take a little break," the trooper said.

"No!" the young woman responded. "I want this asshole caught. He killed Mel. I want him!" And she spoke again immediately. "He shot him in the leg and I went to him." Suddenly she remembered him saying something, and she said it out loud: "Then the jerk asked him if it hurt. What kind of asshole would ask that? Then I went to Mel and he was bleeding, bad. I remember calling the guy an idiot and he hit me, hard, and I went out, I think. I don't remember anything else," she said. She remained staring at the trooper who continued his vigilant gaze.

Then he said, "I want you to think about this. Take your time and think about it for a minute. Can you remember anything about him—and I don't care how insignificant you may think it is—it may be far more helpful than you know."

Without hesitation she said, "It was so dark. He was like a big, black tree standing in front of us. Maybe...six feet tall, I'm not sure. He was like the silhouette of a tree."

The trooper thought for a moment, looking around the room, seeing a dust ball clinging to one of the wheels of the bed. *Hospital clean,* he thought.

"Do you think he was dressed in dark clothing, making you think of a silhouette?" He maintained eye contact with her.

"You know... he may have had a leather jacket on. Yes... he wore a leather jacket, now that I think of it. There was a faint glow, like leather has at night. Yes! I think he wore a leather jacket."

She appeared pleased with herself for the first time since the questioning began.

Not much to go with, and not many people wear leather in the middle of summer, but the fact that it was raining or about to start, means that a leather jacket could act as a rain coat, the trooper thought. Rodney's eyes bulged in their sockets with the description of a leather jacket, yet he remained still. Several minutes went by. The last thing anyone wanted was to rush her. Finally the trooper asked, "Is there anything else you can think of about what he looked like or what he wore?" She shook her head slowly in the negative.

The trooper thanked her, then the doctor, and nodded toward the chief and the officer. They moved into a tight circle, conversing in low tones, the trooper asking if either man had any questions for her or if anything she said led to any insight on their part. The doctor checked the IV drip and pulse and joined the three still in conference. Without sharing his thoughts, Rodney's memory of Saturday evening ushered him away from the circle of men and back to his stop on the shoulder of the road and troublemaker Zeke. He'd worn a leather jacket that night and he'd seen him wear one many times before, but he never thought of it until the young woman mentioned a leather jacket. The last thing he could actually believe or try to pin on Zeke was a murder. He was a punk, no doubt about that, but a murderer…?

He knew much about the four boys, being from the area and all, but the subject of one of them owning or having a gun—this would have changed things had he known or suspected them of that. Suddenly, the doctor broke from the group, going toward the bed, and the lawmen turned toward the door to leave. As they did, they were stopped dead in their tracks as the young woman spoke up from the opposite side of the room.

"He had a strong Maine accent," she said.

14

THE SUN BEGAN TO BREAK THROUGH the rapidly thinning clouds from the west, and with it came refreshing, cooling air. The humidity of the previous week was a memory, yet the events of the previous evening were still fresh in everyone's mind. Sundays were usually dull around the farms and homes of the parents and grandparents the boys had visited during the past several days. Gone now was a mutual thought of breaking up the old gang, although none of the members knew their thoughts were the same. The need for them to be together far outweighed the demands of the friendship and the occasional temper outbursts from Zeke.

Petey made several calls, simply from intuition, and began rounding up the boys, taking the long way; he went in the direction of their meeting place, the garage. It was a good thing Petey came when he did. The boys were restless.

It was like a childhood reunion. Without knowing them, one might think when seeing them that years had passed since their last meeting, yet it was merely days. Petey had again found his lead foot, neglecting to remember the responsible conversation with his grandfather only days earlier. Pozy appeared detached as usual, but he made attempts at conversing and since he was first to be picked up, he took the shotgun position in front in Zeke's absence. Dwight, when they found him walking along the road to

Dells, jumped in the back as would be expected of him. In order for the boys to finalize the gathering, only one member remained absent, Zeke. Soon they would converge on where they expected him to be.

All three babbled on, sometimes all at once, speeding toward Dells along Route 1 south. The late afternoon traffic was heavy in both directions, yet it didn't seem to bother them as it might if Zeke was along. Although no one spoke of the past several days, it appeared to the two in front that some things had changed with their demeanor—neither being able to put it into words or willing to bring up the real subject, their maturity.

The cool air felt good. The old Mopar roared down the blacktop with all the windows down and the radio blaring, but it wasn't as loud as usual, and all three appeared good with that and continued their eclectic conversations vigorously, without inhibition. With everything considered, the boys were happy to be reunited. While driving, Petey had a keen eye for his surroundings. He was also aware of what went on behind, making good use of the rear-view mirror. That's how he spotted the chief's car as soon as it appeared about six car lengths back. With both hands on the wheel, he kept the car within eyesight, and it wasn't until they'd gone a mile or so down that he noticed the roof-lights of Queer-Eye's cruiser about six cars back from the chief's. He lowered the sound on the radio and shared his knowledge with the other two.

"Well, boys…looks as though we're at the front of the parade."

They both looked at him as if he had two heads, not knowing what he was talking about. Then he said, "Don't look back, but the chief and Queer-Eye are trailing us about six and ten cars back."

"They must be out together 'cause o' that murder. Looks like a little Connectaclit bought the farm last night," Pozy said.

"Yah…gramps had the TV news and the papers splattered all ova' the dinning room this mornin'," Petey responded.

It appeared that Dwight was oblivious to what the others said as he fooled around with something he'd brought from home, paying no attention to anything going on around him.

"I can't wait to hear what Zeke's heard, being hea' just down the road from it. Maybe he saw something," Pozy said.

Through the corner of his right eye in the mirror, Petey noticed the chief's car move slightly to the right. The car was not equipped with roof lights. The chief's blue lights were embedded in the front grill, which gave it more of an official look and made it easy to distinguish both cars. When the right light in the grill became visible, the car made a quick right turn onto a side road, eliminating one of the police cars behind them.

"Minus, one. The chief just turned off," Petey said.

The second it did, Queer-Eye's car resembled a shark smelling blood. The roof lights came on. A single bleep from the siren, and the cars in front peeled to the shoulder, exposing the big Mopar like a hemorrhaging hunk of meat in water. He came on them like they were standing still, motioning for Petey to pull over. It was obvious he'd been waiting for the moment, probably knowing the chief's plan to turn there.

"Shit…he's pulling us over," Petey said. To say the least, the other two were confused. It was minutes since he'd told them they were there, now they were being stopped. From experience, neither passenger looked back. Being nervous around the police was not their style. Petey however, just having had the conversation with his grandfather about frugality and car ownership, was not eager to share information of a traffic stop with him, especially by… Rodney Torrey. He wasn't quite ready for that. Besides, he hadn't done anything wrong to be pulled over. He nudged the car onto the shoulder after placing his directional light on, leaving plenty of room in the roadway for the flow of traffic. Rodney pulled his cruiser in behind, edging the nose out slightly and turning the wheels toward the roadway as a protection for himself. He didn't, however, approach the car on the driver's side. He walked around back of the Mopar, looking like John Wayne ready for a gunfight, and headed for the door and Pozy's open window. He actually appeared surprised when it was Pozy's face he came to meet.

No one had thought to turn the radio down, so it still blared as Rodney came alongside the car, and he hollered out to shut it off.

"Well, well, it seems that one of ya is missing. Where's the big guy?" he asked.

All three looked at the officer and raised their shoulders simultaneously, indicating they had no response to the question. Then it was Petey's turn to ask a question.

"What was it that I did for you to stop me, Officer Torrey?"

The officer ignored him, or he didn't hear the question. His focus now appeared to be Pozy's black leather jacket. He kept staring at the jacket, as if it might be the first one he'd ever seen. Pozy began to feel a bit uncomfortable under the officer's gaze. "Somethin' wrong…with my jacket? It ain't fa' sale, but if ya wanna' try it on, we can work somethin' out," he said.

It was as if Rodney had never heard a word. Without a doubt, the officer was completely curious about the jacket, but without something substantial, he wasn't sure of how to start the questions. He looked toward Petey and answered his earlier question.

"Young man, I may have made a mistake. The sunlight at the angle it was in a few minutes ago led me to believe that you had a taillight out, but as I walked around the back to get here…I guess I was wrong," he said, and he appeared to snicker at his own comment. He was looking down at the jacket and Pozy once again. "Ah, you and Zeke, you both have the same kind of jacket, don't you?" Suddenly, he was being sickeningly polite. It was not his way. When Queer-Eye wanted to know something, he blurted it out in a way that left no doubt as to whom he spoke to or what he meant. Right now, he was like a spring peeper in a frog pond. The boys couldn't figure out what in hell he was tweeting about.

"Ah, ya, they're the same." And unlike himself, he offered more. "We bought them from some guy…who was sellin' 'em at the Acton Fair, couple o' years back, why?" he asked.

"Gee, I'll bet a jacket like that must have cost a lot of money. You boys don't work that much. Where'd you get that kind of cash?" he asked.

They stared into each other's eyes for an uncomfortable length of time. It didn't appear to bother Pozy much, but the officer and the other two boys became noticeably uneasy.

"Ah…" Pozy began and the officer interrupted.

"Never mind, it's not important. So, where is Geek?" he asked, knowing that by using the word Geek he was pushing buttons. No one answered. They simply continued to stare at the officer.

"Let me ask you another question, if you don't mind." He wouldn't give up. "Being summer, nice warm days and all, do you wear that leather all year around?" Again there was a lengthy pause between the question and Pozy's response as he looked around the interior of the car, making faces at his friends that the officer couldn't see, and then he answered.

"I don't want to carry it, besides, the boys have the windows open. I don't want to get a stiff neck from the draft." He was simply returning the sarcasm, and the two boys appeared to choke when holding their laughter in. Rodney picked up on his cynicism. *Shot down, crashed and burned.*

Although the officer felt a slight prickle of "piss me off" in the neck, he refused to be outdone by this little punk. *Zeke is the one with the mouth, not this one,* he thought.

"So… ya never answered my question, and you all can save the crap-mouth for someone else. I asked where Zeke was and I'm still waiting for an answer." Again, Pozy offered a satiric response.

"Oh…Geek, you asked. What…is that? You asked where Geek is. What…is…that?" He said it again then looked around the interior, but receiving no response from his audience, he looked back at the officer with a stupid grin.

The red that began to creep up from Rodney's neck flowed quickly throughout his face, giving the impression he stood in a reflection of something bright red. Their stare intensified; neither would blink first. The sound of slowing traffic making its way around the two stopped vehicles began to weigh heavily on Petey's thoughts. Sooner or later someone he or his grandparents knew would happen by, and the news of the traffic stop in Dells would get home before he did.

"We can do this the easy way or the hard way, but I have all day and I don't care how long I back traffic up on this spot," Rodney said. With that, Petey chimed in.

"We haven't seen Zeke for three or four days. We all went

home for the weekend and we haven't seen 'im." The officer's eyes thinned, looking around at the snotty faces staring back at him. He seemed amused now when looking in the back seat. It was as if the kid back there never knew they'd been stopped. At this point, the officer had no real reason to disbelieve Petey. He didn't trust these boys, but he figured this one was probably the most trustworthy of the group. Simply out of curiosity he had looked into the boy's school record.

A long, silent moment passed, blanketing them with uncertainty, the officer unwilling to end the questioning. What he wanted was more on Zeke and his leather jacket, where he'd spent Saturday night and where he was now. That much he knew would not be revealed by this vagabond group from up-river.

He looked toward Pozy now and asked, "Did you go home for the weekend and stay there all this time?"

"Yup," was all Pozy replied.

Rodney knew he had nothing to connect Pozy and his leather jacket to the crime, and decided to let it go for now.

"Tell ya what. You get on down the road and when ya see… Geek…"—he had to push the button one more time—"let him know that I'd like to speak with him. Can you do that, boys?" When he said that, he looked directly into Petey's eyes, knowing that the jerk closest to him would probably not get it at all or would simply make a derogatory remark, infuriating him further.

"Yah…I'll do that," Petey responded.

It seemed to take forever for Queer-Eye to leave. He remained crouched on the side of the big Mopar for the longest time, simply looking in, shifting his gaze between the three inside, occasionally looking out on to the traffic for no apparent reason. The he said, "Remember, tell him I'd like to speak with him as soon as you see him," and he stood up straight, tugged at his shirt to pull the wrinkles out and walked slowly back to his cruiser. A moment passed and he pulled out quickly, turning his roof-lights out while alongside Petey's car.

"Whoa! I thought he'd neva' leave. I gotta' piss like a moose. What-tha'-fuck was that all about? Zeke's and my leather jackets?"

Pozy said. Petey shook his head. He had no idea.

He remained parked on the shoulder for a few more minutes, he and Pozy trying to put the pieces of the conversation into a reasonable, what-in-hell-was-the conclusion, yet they came up with nothing. Without warning, Dwight chimed in from the back seat. "Maybe he thinks Zeke killed that Pissmyvania?" And then he fell silent once again, toying with whatever it was he'd brought from home. The boys in front gazed into each other's eyes, and then burst out into laughter. Petey started the big engine, and looking into the side-view mirror, pulled out in to the flow of traffic, which was much heavier now. As the car reached the posted speed, catching up with the flow, Pozy's thoughts whisked him back in time to the night in Biddeford and Zeke's brutal assault on the dudes from out-of-state. He had a gun and he knew Zeke couldn't wait to fire it off. As the car's throaty exhaust rumbled down the road, entrancing Pozy, it allowed the uncertainty that had plagued his mind last week, which forced him to return home, to once again haunt his entire being.

One dreadful scene after another came vividly into his imagination, all the memories of Zeke's uncanny ability to blow a mental gasket without warning: his anger tantrums, and his hate for and reaction to an out-of-stater; even the simple pleasure he took out of watching the snake feed and the way he teased it for its food. He was happy to see Petey and Dwight, but he now wished he'd never been called this morning. He'd probably still be on the stinkin' farm and glad to be eatin' his mother's hot meals, even listening to his old man's theories on the world, consuming them with deaf ears. *Oh...why did I leave?* he thought.

The traffic thinned in places, allowing Petey to speed it up toward their planned destination, the garage and their old pal, Zeke. The radio blared once again, distracting Pozy from his daydream desires to be free of this mess he called friends. Maturity... *The gang can't stay together forever*, he thought.

It wasn't as if the boys were shaken by the unexpected and truly unwarranted traffic stop, but it was obvious by both Petey's and Pozy's swiveling heads that they would not be surprised by Queer-

Eye again today, if they could help it. Dwight, however, remained in a world of his own. He spoke to the boys in front occasionally, but stayed preoccupied with his back-seat fascination, whatever it was. Just as the traffic began to intensify, Petey took a hard right turn, putting them on the back road to the garage. Although all three of their feelings about being there were different, they all felt a sense of belonging when they were here.

It's good to see these types of trees. They're different than those on the farm, Petey thought.

Yeah, it is good to be back here at the old garage, Pozy thought.

Where in hell are we, anyway? Dwight thought after looking up from his distraction in back.

Within a minute or two, Petey pulled the big Dodge onto the gravel and headed to the garage. The instant their eyes fell upon the building, it became obvious to all that it was deserted. The rainstorm of the weekend had left the gravel somewhat roughened, whereas regular traffic would generally smoothen out the area traveled over. No one had come or gone for a reasonable length of time, or at least since the downpours of the early weekend. They remained silent on their approach, even then thinking that Zeke would pop his head out at any moment. Petey swung the car around wide with his usual one-handed crank of the wheel in order to back in toward the doors, and there was still no appearance by their friend.

"Yo!" The sound of Pozy's call echoed around the property. He thought that Zeke might be napping, yet no response came from inside. Petey went directly to the doors and swung them open, revealing what they expected: an empty garage. It was obvious to all three that Zeke was there, as the smell of burning wood and an unfamiliar odor filled the inside. Dwight, being the only one to share Zeke's attachment to the snake, went directly to the cage and removed the blanket. The Black Racer, startled, struck the side of the cage then recoiled in a defensive stance.

"Whoa, little buddy! Looks like you're pretty hungry. Ain't Zeke feedin' ya?" he asked, looking at the snake as if awaiting a response. He knew instantly when reaching for the menu box that

Zeke had been in the garage, at least for a while. It was full of tiny critters and at least one would be offered now. Unlike Zeke, Dwight would not stay to watch the devouring.

Petey began a clamorous sorting of tools from the roll-away tool box near the door. Pozy walked around aimlessly. The afternoon flew by and Zeke never showed up.

The weekend away had given the garage and its surroundings an almost alien feel, even though it was the most familiar second home all three boys had. Their feeling for moving on with their lives could not be re-masked with this short visit to the empty space. Each one, through a voice from within, heard the calling for a new beginning.

They weren't there more than an hour when the sound of rapidly approaching tires on the gravel forced all three, encircled around the open hood of Petey's car, to look in that direction. To their surprise, it was Missy. All three were here the one time she'd stopped by with Zeke and it was definitely out of character for her to appear without him. She slowed the car at the sight of them, swinging wide in a direction to bring her open window alongside the small group.

"Wow. If this isn't a motley crew, I don't know what might be," she said.

"Hi, beautiful, what brings you out hea', ya lost?" Pozy asked.

Petey wanted to be the one talking to her, but he was just happy to see her anyway.

"Hello, handsome." She was looking at Petey now. His stomach did flip-flops.

"Hi…Missy, I haven't seen ya in quite a spell. Looking as good as usual," he added.

"Right back at ya, handsome. I haven't seen any of you, it seems for weeks. Where've you all been?"

They shrugged their shoulders simultaneously for the second time today.

"Well, I've been looking for Zeke, but he seems to have vanished from the face… if ya know what I mean?" she said.

"Yeah, we came down hea' lookin' for 'im, too. The place has been empty for a while, looks like," Pozy said.

"Ya think he went home?" she asked.

"I doubt that, besides he don't like goin' home. Says there's nothin' there for 'im anymore." It was Dwight that responded this time.

For a few moments, it was as if time stood still. Without Zeke there, they seemed to have nothing to say to each other. The only sound was the wind through the pines and the idling engine of Missy's car. Several moments passed—the silence was uncomfortable and it felt weird to the boys having Missy out here as opposed to behind her counter or waiting on the tables. Then she asked the big question. "I suppose you've heard about that kid from Connecticut who was murdered last night. What a shock—everyone at the Roady has an opinion about why, but I'll wait... see what happens. Any word on the girl they found with him?"

"Nope," Pozy said, while the other boys simply shook their heads in the negative. Petey looked in the car and realized Missy was smiling at him, sending butterflies through his midsection.

"Well, I've got to go. If you see him before I do, tell him I'm looking for him, would you?"

"Ayah'... no problem. You do the same, ok?" Pozy asked.

She put the car in gear, driving past the front of the Dodge, swung wide and drove out toward the blacktop, and she wasn't even out of sight when Petey's mind took him on a fantasy.

I can't believe the way she looked at me. I know the day will come when she realizes that Zeke is only playin' her a tune. No one could take care of her the way I could. We could live out on the farm. Make a good life for ourselves.

"Wake up...fuck-head! She's gone." Pozy was punching him in the upper arm and both boys were laughing at him.

Missy hadn't made it to the blacktop before a powerful feeling of dread came over her. Not knowing where Zeke was or why he hadn't called her, she just wanted to pull over and wait it out. However long it took for him to return, she would wait, but she knew that wasn't how the relationship worked.

In her mind, she could see him appear before her at the bend of every curve in the road. She flinched each time she mistook something to be the figure of a man beside a solitary tree. She wished they'd never parted yesterday morning. Had her mother not gone away, they might still be together. Then she spoke to herself. "Get real, Missy. That's not the way this relationship works. You can't hold him down no matter how much you want him with you."

15

SUMMER MOVED ALONG as it always did, like a rocket. The Fourth of July was next week and the old-timers always said, "It's all downhill from there." It was, or at least it felt that way. After the Fourth, if you blinked once too often, it was Labor Day and after that...Well, you'd better have your firewood under cover.

Several weeks passed and a definite lull fell over the murder investigation, while local and state police continued their work. Officer Rodney Torrey became somewhat obsessed with finding an elusive piece of the puzzle that remained unplaced: the one person on his list to be questioned. Zeke Brailey. He had seen him the very night of the murder and he was wearing his leather jacket.

He returned, time and time again at all hours of the day and early evening. He'd walked the path from the road to the water and back so many times now, wishing he'd logged the amounts, if only for his own benefit. Each time he would stop at the exact spot where the murder happened, sometimes going down on hands and knees looking at blades of grass, thinking he'd missed something. Time and weather, however, took its toll, and it seemed that nothing was left that could be used as evidence. He did maintain an extensive notepad, writing everything he saw or thought; even people who crossed the path while he was on it became the subjects of his questioning and a record was entered in the pad with everything about that person or persons he spoke with at that time. A police officer's worse enemy is frustration. Patience, on the other hand, is the laws' virtue. He would need to keep his cool and a flame burning on this one and he knew that better than anyone.

He read his notes over and over again each time he was on the path. He concluded with the fact that the young man was shot twice and the fact that there were no spent casings indicated the murderer took the time to retrieve them, or it was a revolver where the casings remained in the gun after firing, being removed manually at a later time. Under the obvious stress of just having killed a man, only a pro would risk picking up after themselves.

No...this had to be a revolver. Nothing from this young man's past would lead anyone to think he or his girlfriend were involved in something that would call for a professional hit. No...this was a random act, by some punk thinking of themselves as judge and jury for whatever reason. He looked back to his notes and saw that the girl had said the victim gave the guy a good pounding about the head and face. *That would piss me off. No, I'll wait for the ballistics report to come back from Augusta. That will tell all,* he thought, and left the area.

It had been quite some time since the chief stopped by the Little Roady. It became obvious that Marcy, with her high energy and constant doting, was more than pleased to see him. He sat at the far end of the breakfast counter, out of the way of the in-and-out traffic. Missy remained in the kitchen, giving the two out front more time to just chat between customers. They had been an item once, unknown to Missy. Now that the chief neared retirement, things at home weren't going as smooth as one might plan at this stage of his life. His wife was having some medical problems he wasn't ready to share, but it didn't take a marriage counselor to know there was frost on their sexual pumpkins. Marcy was perceived to be celibate, though she denied it vehemently when teased by close friends who had sex regularly. No one knew she indulged in the occasional one-night stand.

They spoke of many things in low tones; the conversation was private. The chief shared thoughts with her he would never offer anyone; not even his wife. Although Marcy was still attracted to him, she would never start anything to break them up. No one would ever accuse her of being a home-wrecker, but she would never deny him if it came to that. After all, in her heart she believed it was a very real possibility that the chief was Missy's father. There would always be a place in her heart for him, even if she was the only one that knew it.

Missy had been in the kitchen for a long time, and needed to get out into the restaurant area for a cold drink and something to nibble. She also wanted to quiz the chief on anything he knew about the murder, but as she entered the dining area, the first thing that popped into her mind at the sight of the last booth in the corner was Zeke.

Where in hell is he and why hasn't he called me? she thought.

She came to a sudden stop, looking toward the booth. It was as if she'd fallen into a trance of sorts, still unnoticed by the two at the far end of the counter. At that point, Missy's dazed posture and expression were noticed by her mother and she spoke up.

"Whataya lookin' at, Missy?"

"Oh…nothin', just thinking," she said, though she looked somewhat removed from the moment. She shook it off quickly and moved closer to her mother and the chief.

"Hi, chief," Missy said.

"Right back at ya," he responded.

Missy, not knowing the right approach to get the chief started on the murder, drew herself a tall Pepsi from the fountain. She gulped twice then breathed a sigh of being refreshed, her thoughts floating in a dozen directions, one after another, and it became obvious that she was stalling for something. The chief looked at her, and then spoke.

"Missy…if my sixth sense hasn't failed me, I'd say you had something on your mind."

"Well, that murder still has me feeling a bit uneasy," she said.

She surprised herself with the quickness of her response. There was a moment of silence; it appeared that the chief didn't want to discuss the matter. Both women stood looking at him, wondering if he might share what he knew with them. Throughout their palavering, Marcy had avoided the subject, but she was thrilled when Missy brought it up.

"Ladies…without going into areas that might…in some way compromise the investigation…and if I could, I wouldn't mind sharing with the both of you, if I'd share anything with anyone…" It appeared that the chief was stalling for time now. He looked down at his half-filled cup of coffee, then back at the two women, suddenly shaking his head in the negative. "We really have nothing right now," he said. For whatever reason, Missy was pleased with herself for asking, to whatever end it got her.

OK! I still know as much now as when I started, she thought. *He didn't say they knew who did it. So that leaves the one or those who did still out there, maybe right here in Dells."* And her mind took her on another excursion to wherever Zeke might be. She began to feel a sense of anger now. He'd spent the night with her and that was good, but to disappear like this without saying a word, knowing now that he was alone after seeing the boys at the garage…

Maybe he's not alone. That little twerp! He's probably shacking up with some little slut, somewhere… As that thought crossed her mind, Zeke, as big as life, walked in through the front door.

"Hail Jehovah! And all you little saints," he cried, looking at the chief, who paid no attention to him, with his usual stupid-looking grin.

Everyone in the room was speechless.

—

Several weeks had passed since Missy had laid eyes on him. She was out of breath and breathing heavily at the same time. She looked him over from head to toe. As he walked slowly toward her, she made her way to the opposite end of the counter to meet him. He'd gotten a haircut and shave and he wore what appeared to be all-new clothes. He looked awesome. He had a blue-jean jacket that fit him beautifully over a white T-shirt. He had blue jeans on and to top it off, white sneakers. He looked like a different person.

"What…in hell?" she asked. Going to him and suddenly not giving a damn what anyone thought, she put her arms around his neck and pulled him to herself. As she held him, she thought she detected a slight bruising around the cheekbone, but dismissed it.

"Where have you been?" she whispered.

"I'll tell ya later," he whispered back. "Right now, I'd love a cup o' yaw' delicious coffee, darlin'."

Marcy and the chief simply stared into each other's eyes and remained silent, while nonchalantly trying to pick up tid-bits of the conversation between the two at the opposite end of the counter. Occasionally, Zeke would look down in their direction, smile and then look back at Missy. He downed the first cup so quickly the chief wondered how he could do that without a serious burn to his esophagus. When Missy brought him his second cup, they walked toward the window booth.

"Mom, I'm taking a little break, ok?" she said.

Marcy simply gave an upward nod of her head.

He sipped his hot coffee. Missy had brought along a couple of plain doughnuts, since they were his favorites. "Where have you been? I've been worried sick about you."

"Now…that's not the type o' relationship you or me wanted. At least that's what I remember you tellin' me, anyway," he said. She put up a hand with the palm facing him.

"I know…I know what I said, but after that Friday night together…"

They remained silent, looking deep into each other's eyes. She was glad that he was here, that he wanted her now. They remained still for a while longer; the sound of the ceiling fan droned along and so did the afternoon. Finally, she spoke up.

"So, where'd ya get the new duds, big boy? I like the new look with the haircut and all."

"I thought it was time for a change. Besides, I'm sick o' hangin' around with them kids at that…"—he lowered his voice—"fuckin' garage. It's goin' nowhere for me, ya know."

She intended to tell him that she'd been there looking for him, but thought better of it now, after he said what he did. Sooner rather than later, the boys would find him and she'd see how far his statement "goin' nowhere" went, but she was happy he was here with her. That was all that mattered.

It was slow now in the restaurant and Marcy would leave soon. She'd cook something for them and they could sit in the booth together after she closed the place for a quiet, early evening meal. She also knew that being around Zeke, there was never a dull moment, so she simply hoped for the best. She wanted to know where he'd been since they were together last, but pushing the issue would only piss him off, distancing him from her, and possibly causing him to leave again. She listened to him chatter, half-listening while picking up tiny bits of her mother's conversation with the chief. It appeared their get-together was coming to an end, as Marcy clanged around the area, picking things up and tidying. The chief stood up suddenly, reached over the counter and took Marcy's hand in his. He spoke softly to her mother, making it impossible for Missy to hear. It wasn't exactly a romantic type of touch, Missy thought, but it wasn't exactly a handshake either. She watched from the corner of her vision. It was her mother's facial expressions that forced Missy's imagination to run wild with her thoughts.

Wow…Mom and the chief fooling around? No way. He's a married man. Mom would neva'… And then the chief sauntered out, never noticing the two in the booth, making for a very unusual departure for him. Missy glanced around the restaurant as if in a state of shock. *It's as if the chief never recognized Zeke in his new clothes. He never acknowledged him when he came in and he never looked toward us when he left. That's weird,* she thought.

What Missy didn't know was that the chief certainly did recognize Zeke, yet was keeping it to himself; he was most curious as to why the young man would make such a drastic change to his appearance. The second he got into his car, which was parked directly out front, he got on his phone and called Rodney. Rodney had made his intentions to speak with Zeke known to the chief earlier that morning and told him why. It was important now that Rodney know that the young man looked completely different since either of them had seen him last. The chief gave his officer, from memory, a full description of what Zeke wore and where he was at the moment, but to the chief's surprise, Rodney told him it would have to wait. He'd found something upon his return to the murder scene and wanted to meet the chief there, ASAP.

16

When the chief arrived at the entrance to the walking path, the Route-One traffic was heavy in both north and southbound directions. He pulled his car alongside Rodney's cruiser which was near the curb and double-parked beside it, slowing the traffic around him. The towns of Punquit and Dells, bordering each other with a beach between them, overflowed with tourists, sometimes all year long. The constant drone from the traffic could confuse even a local into wondering whether it might be that or the crashing surf, some one-hundred yards from the road. Today was one of those days. The chief however, overflowed with anticipation after his phone call with Rodney and never noticed.

As the chief got out, seeing the two police cars caused some rubber-necking from passing motorists, some frowning at the chief for causing them to slow down, as neither vehicle displayed lights to indicate an emergency. The chief, being a true local since birth, couldn't help expelling a slight chuckle at seeing them.

"They'll get over it as soon as they spend a little cash on something," he said at just above a whisper. He crossed the sidewalk and stepped onto the dirt pathway. He groaned when having to negotiate a slight incline at the start of the walk.

The town outta pave this ankle-busta' someday, he thought. *Oh...yah', they'll probably wait 'til I retire ta do it. Well, that won't be that bad, I guess. I might be able to take a leisurely walk down hea' to calm my nerves. Oh well, business as usual 'til then.*

He and the other officers had walked this path several times during the initial stages of the investigation and as things cooled, and information ended up in notepads and police logs, then he'd backed off and let Rodney run with it. Today, for whatever reason, he found the walking arduous, wishing now that he'd had only one donut. He neared the midway point of the path when he noticed the uniform of his officer just ahead. Rodney appeared preoccupied with something he held in his hand. He never noticed the chief's approach, which was unusual for Rodney Torrey. He prided himself on seeing what most people missed. Rodney perked up now, hearing the footsteps.

Both men displayed similar facial expressions of confusion, but eagerness to share on Rodney's part and to be informed on the chief's.

"What in hell do you have there, Rodney?" the chief asked, as he looked intently into his officer's open palm.

"It looks to me like a screw from a pistol grip," Rodney responded.

"Where in hell did you find that?"

"Funny…all this time it was right under my nose, literally."

The chief looked into his eyes for an explanation.

"Chief—I came down here every chance I had, you know that. All that rain…ya know. The grasses were matted down, but every day that it didn't rain and with the wind and sun down here, that grass stood upright. I poked around 'til this showed up just awhile ago. I tell ya, chief, it's a screw from a pistol grip, probably from the gun that shot that kid, right here," and he pointed to the spot they found him.

"Well, we'll want to share that with the staties. I'm sure their lab will be able to pin it down to a type of gun, ya know?"

Rodney knew the chief was right about turning it over to the MCU lab, which was a must-do; he just didn't want to let it out of his sight. After all this time invested in finding the damned thing, he wished there was more he could do on his own. They looked around the area one last time. It was as if each man realized, but didn't share their thoughts with the other, that their work here on the walking path was over, and that they now had what they hoped was the final piece to Officer Rodney Torrey's puzzle which he'd worked so diligently to recover.

"Whaddaya think, Rod, let's head back to the station and get this thing wrapped up."

"Yah..." was all Rodney offered.

What neither man could know was that at the very moment they met on the path, a fax from the MCU in Augusta printed out in the office of the Dells Police Department. It indicated that the weapon used to kill the young man from Connecticut was a .38-caliber handgun. Although the trickle of information came slowly, the dribble would continue. Along with the ballistics report was a request for more information about the victim. At the time of the autopsy, the medical examiner had found no wallet or any other form of ID. Basically, there was nothing in his pockets nor was there any jewelry on the body, but there were obvious suntan lines where a watch and ring were worn. At the bottom of the fax in bold print were the words, "PLEASE CONTACT THE MAJOR CRIME UNIT AS SOON AS POSSIBLE."

—

Across town, Marcy left through the rear kitchen door, slamming it, not intentionally to distract the two out front, but it was swollen from the rain and humidity and needed to be slammed shut. Upon hearing the door, Missy immediately realized her mother was at least a little pissed off, as she had never said goodbye.

She'll get over it, she thought.

"Wow...she slams good," Zeke said out loud.

Missy ignored the comment, stood and went to the front door, flipping the open/closed sign to "Officially Closed," and pulled the shade down. "Hey...ya want somethin' to eat?" she asked.

He looked up, and his need for food was plain on his face.

"How 'bout a fat bacon cheeseburger with fries?" he asked.

He watched her walk toward the kitchen, but instead of thinking about sex, perhaps in the back closet, for no apparent reason the blood-splattering of his dirty work appeared in his subconscious mind once again—a vision that continued to haunt him. He fought to minimize the apparition, and looking out onto the flow of traffic, he spoke to himself in his thoughts.

Fuck…Me! Get out o' my mind, bag-face. You're dead. The blood's dry. I cleaned it up myself. Leave me the fuck alone! Then he looked around as if he'd been heard by Missy or someone passing by. Suddenly, he was distracted by the smell of grilling meat and it was more than he could stand, going to meet Missy as she prepared a meal for them. What Missy couldn't know was that Zeke had no plans for a long evening together.

—

The weeks passed quickly. Petey worked regularly now and so did Dwight. Without their long-lost companion Zeke, meeting at the garage became a rare event. Pozy stayed alone most of the time. He made changes in the garage to suit him. The old, stinky couch went to the dump along with a few other things no longer needed. He used his father's pickup as they had remained on speaking terms since Pozy's long weekend at the farm. He returned regularly for things his mother gave him to refurnish his place, as they all called it now.

The old woman who lived by the road and gave him run of the place was in a nursing home in Kittery. She had money, but no family so, without a will made known, Pozy's life at the garage was one day at a time. He stood by the snake cage. He fed it regularly, but not knowing where Zeke was or if he ever intended to make an appearance, he contemplated Rowdy's release, giving it a well deserved freedom from captivity. As he watched a mouse being ingested by the snake, he heard the sudden sound of a faint whistle from the far end of the driveway. There was only one person who whistled like that. When he turned his head in that direction, none other than big, old Zeke Brailey made his way down the driveway toward the garage.

At first glance it wasn't an instant recognition on Pozy's part. The new rags and haircut threw him a slight curve, but there was no denying the stupid facial expression that only Zeke could produce. From inside the garage, Pozy saw his mouth moving, but because of a slight breeze blowing into the garage, he never heard a word of what his friend said on his approach.

"Where ya been…beaver-face?" Pozy asked.

Zeke simply responded with a shrug of his shoulders and another stupid look.

He walked in like he'd never left, going straight toward Pozy. They met with a strong, bro-type handshake and hug. After a few well-chosen cut-ups toward each other and Zeke's inspection of the snake and the bulge halfway down its body, it became apparent that Zeke was glad to be back. He commented on the new look that Pozy had given the garage, but it was neither complimentary nor derogatory. Zeke's new look made him look like a completely different person, but Pozy kept that to himself. Pozy wondered where he got the money for the new clothes and he kept that to himself also. They made small talk about everyday things in general, as if nothing had changed since they'd gone their separate ways several weeks ago. It had been a couple of hours since Zeke had left the Little Roady and one might wonder if Missy actually fed him, because Zeke had arrived with a Pu Pu Platter in a bag and two sixteen-ounce Budweisers, and he handed one to Pozy. The beers weren't as cold now, but it felt good going down, as neither had partaken for a while. They remained by the snake cage, gulping the brew, and neither one spoke.

It was strange how all three young men intended to leave the gang of four, each for their own reasons; yet all four had found their way back to the garage and the relationship in their own way and time. Zeke portrayed himself as a loner and the big, bad guy, but in reality he needed his companions as much as they needed him.

Nothing feels as catastrophic as the moment of or the revealing of something as horrific as a murder, but as time passes, the sting heals to a measurable level of control for everyone involved. For

Zeke, time allowed him to temporarily purge the visions of the blood-splattered images that cursed his existence day after day following the murder.

17

Much to Missy's surprise, Zeke offered to take her to the Fourth of July Parade, arriving at her place after a day at the garage with Pozy. Showing up the day before the parade, knowing the restaurant was closed for the Fourth, would give them at least two full days together. The first day, as they'd been apart for this long, they concentrated for obvious reasons on sex. They had much catching up to do. Zeke knew Marcy's and Missy's schedule for the Roady, so showing up while Missy was home alone was no big surprise for either of them. Although she was as usual thrilled to see him, she offered a cold shoulder, just stand-off-ish enough to hold him at bay, yet not enough to cause him to charge off and leave again. At this point in her frustration however, if he'd wanted to leave, she'd promised herself not to put up any fight at all, but they were both right on as far as the timing of his visit.

From the moment he arrived, he couldn't keep his hands off her. She delighted in the touching as much as he did, but she sometimes wished that he could be more affectionate instead of just grabby. The heat rose rapidly between them. Within a few minutes of his arrival, they were naked in bed and pleasuring each other with masterful fingertips and moist lips, kissing every part of each other's bodies from their heads to their toes.

They spent the entire first day in bed, eating snacks to maintain the essential strength to continue the marathon sex that both welcomed and enjoyed to the maximum of their bodies' abilities. They wore themselves out and loved every second of it. After hours of making love, they lay in an entwined, frazzled heap of tired bodies in the center of her bed. Fulfillment eased the tension that had built between them during his absences; Missy's source of embitterment came from never knowing for sure if he was unfaithful during his bouts with wanderlust. Being here, like this, soothed her fears of infidelity and she wanted him more than ever before. She would do anything for him. He only needed to ask.

Conversations flowed easily when it was only the two of them alone. Unlike being at the restaurant where interruptions were a sure thing and eavesdropping was a way of life, they were able to share their most private feelings about everything. Well, almost everything. For the first time that she could remember, Missy steered the conversation in a direction that might open the door to where he'd been for such a long time without contact with her or his closest friends. The last thing she wanted to do was piss him off, so treading lightly now during the enjoyable verbal intercourse would minimize an explosive result, although she noticed he was more relaxed than normal.

"So...did you enjoy your vacation?" she asked, displaying her best smile.

"Why, yes I did," he said, but made no attempt to add more. Her curiosity encouraged her to dig deeper, but her knowledge of his true personality urged her to tread lightly.

"Did you get to see any of the guys? We met...only once and they wondered where you might be. I had to laugh, you know... we do our own thing, you and me, right?" she said, evoking a stare that might suggest she'd taken a step too far, but his response calmed her concern.

"Yeah...yeah, sure, Missy. You and me are like this," and he lifted his middle and index fingers, twisted to indicate togetherness.

They sipped on a shared, ice-cold Pepsi, he reaching out occasionally to fondle her breasts and to tell her how beautiful her body was. Those gestures and comments made her investigatory task all the more difficult. Then, suddenly, for no apparent reason other than to chit-chat, Missy said that she would love to get away for a couple of days, somewhere no one would find her, to just relax… And the moment she probed for was at hand.

His wide open eyes indicated that he was at least attentive to her desires other than sexual. As she spoke of her need to go off somewhere, she noticed a slight grin appear, and he shook his head in the affirmative, as if prepared to offer a solution.

"What…?" she asked.

"Baby…In case you were wondering where I'd been for the last week or so, I stayed at a place you'd love."

She stared in disbelief, never intending, other than to honestly tell him she needed time away, to uncover the answer to the question that had haunted her for so long. Had she foreseen the task to be of such remedial proportions over her concerns, she would have blurted out her need to know long before this.

After his last comment about staying at a place she'd love, she remained silent, staring directly into his searching eyes and waiting patiently for the story she knew would come.

He told her of a long-forgotten family camp, on some remote lake she'd never heard about where he'd spent all of his time away. He spoke of his need for the quiet space it offered. It had been built by his maternal grandfather when his mother was a child, and was rustic, yet remained comfortable through the many years of non-use. She listened attentively to all that he told her, yet she could not put a finger on everything that he said. He just wasn't the type to go off alone to be quiet—or at least she'd never realized that about him until now.

And the twenty-five dollars I left him that day when I saw him last was not enough to get the clothes and haircut he's sporting. There's something about this story that just doesn't add up, she thought.

—

The Fourth of July parade with the marching bands from area high schools and VFW posts half-stepped past the entrance to the walking path where less than a month ago, a young man from away lay dead from a couple of gunshot wounds. A crowd stood blocking the entrance to that path, and it went unnoticed by the celebrators. Independence Day came and went, and the East Coast sweltered under the heat of a scorching July sun. Missy and Zeke never made it to the parade.

Monday, the fifth of July, was overcast and sticky-hot. The finely pressed shirt stuck to Rodney's back as he exited his cruiser and walked toward to entrance to the Dells Police Department. At the top of his schedule were two asterisks. Alongside of the first—call the young woman in Connecticut—the second was to find Zeke Brailey. For the past couple of weeks, Rodney had been overwhelmed with local calls for the stupid stuff, as he called it, but nonetheless important to a small town police officer in tourist season: fender benders on Route One, sliced toes at the beach, and some kid caught shoplifting at the Saltwater Taffy Shop. It all came with summer on the coast of Maine and he wouldn't change his job for any one or thing. He did, however, want more time on the case, knowing very well that the MCU was in charge of the investigation, but it all seemed to be going dry over the last several weeks. At the request of the MCU for more information, he'd attempted contact with the young woman on a regular basis, but as of yet, she was nowhere to be found. Today, he hoped, would be different.

A faint sun poked its way through a low ceiling of haze, and he longed for the cooling air inside. He was greeted by the dispatcher immediately upon entering and he responded in kind, yet his concentration was on the questions he wanted to ask the young woman about her knowledge of the missing jewelry mentioned on the MCU fax. At that moment, another question popped into his head—that of not having heard from the MCU regarding the screw he'd found on the path, which he believed was from a pistol grip. Sometimes it was all very frustrating to him. He felt his patience running out quicker now; a murder investigation was not your run-of-the-mill stuff. *Why couldn't there be more involvement with the State Police?* he wondered.

The deeper he moved toward the center of the building, the cooler it felt and with each step, he became rejuvenated with a fresh energy.

Today will be productive. I'll make it happen, he thought.

Rodney maintained a desk in the corner of a mid-sized office containing two other desks placed back to back near the only window. They called it the meeting room, where the chief would meet with his officers twice a week in summer when the town hired part-time rookies on bicycles to help with the onslaught of tourists. He sorted his notes and shuffled around in an attempt to be comfortable for his daily filling out of reports and checking his notes from the previous day, most of which he never shared. He was a private person. His parents had instilled that in him his entire life with them.

There are things ya don't wanta' share with them from outside the family. His father had driven that into his head day after day. It was probably the reason he was unable to find a nice girl and settle down, as his mother had planted that seed into his young skull, day after day, but it was that type of discipline that allowed him to maintain his strict approach to law enforcement. He flipped the notepad open and there was her name and telephone number. Her face instantly appeared in his mind's eye. *Lillian Crandlemyer,* he thought.

Suddenly, he was back in the hospital room the day of her questioning about the murder. Her soft, delicate features and skin tone and the image of her intoxicating blue eyes appeared and a pang of butterflies bolted through his midsection, forcing him to look out the window on the other side of the room for a momentary distraction. He spoke her name to himself, thinking, *she doesn't look like a Lillian.*

What the fuck does a Lillian look like? he asked himself at just above a whisper, then he felt stupid for even thinking it. His nerves had the best of him at the moment. The word fuck was not in his vocabulary, but it flowed instantly with the thought of having to speak to her, probably within the next few minutes. He went to the coffee pot, thinking that a clear head would put his thoughts in motion with an approach, when and if she answered the phone, to a cohesive line of questions that wouldn't make him look the fool with the young woman he was infatuated with. Sipping from the hot brew, he was grateful that he and the dispatcher were the only people in the building, as it would be difficult for him to handle the distraction when the rookies blanketed the station with their endless questions.

Placing the notepad in front of him, he reached for the phone, instantly punching out the numbers on the keypad. As if she might see him through the fiber-optics of the phone lines, he straightened his tie and posture at the first sound of the ring-tone. Had someone been watching, they might mistake him for a schoolboy during his first attempt to convince a beautiful young classmate to accompany him to the prom. He appeared extremely uncomfortable.

It rang…rang again, and he nervously tapped his pen, held between his index and middle fingers against the notepad, and after the third ring, he instantly recognized her voice when she answered. "Hello."

"Good morning… Miss Crandlemyer?"

"Yes?"

"Good morning." And he suddenly felt stupid for saying it again. "This is Officer Rodney Torrey of the Dells Police Department. How are you?"

"Oh… I'm fine, thank you for asking. Did you catch that freak?" she asked.

"No, I'm sorry. I do wish that was why I called. I wanted to ask you a couple of questions, if that's ok. It's about some jewelry we think Melvin was wearing…that night." He worried if the last question came out sounding a bit coarse, knowing what she'd been through that night. There was an uncomfortable pause on her end, then a slight sigh that would indicate sadness, and he was convinced it had come out wrong.

"Oh, yeah… I forgot all about his stuff. You must think I'm so cruel. That's stupid. I bought him that ring. Do you have it?" she asked.

"I'm sorry, I don't," he said straight out. "I am wondering if you might tell me what he did have on for jewelry, maybe what he kept in his pockets, anything at all? Nothing is insignificant. Whatever you know might help," he added.

"So… I guess you didn't call me with good news," she said.

"I wish this call was for just that reason. We've been working on everything, day and night. You can be sure of that."

They shared another uncomfortable pause in the conversation. He wanted to say something that would assure her that the "freak," as she called him, would be caught, but that couldn't happen right now. "Is there anything you might be able to tell me about what he wore? Whatever you can, could help, enormously." Again…a dreadful pause, then she began.

"I bought him that silver ring with the turquoise stone…" her voice faded with the word, then, she began again, this time with vigor, going into detail with a graphic description of the ring, where she'd bought it and things that went beyond what Rodney expected from her. She went into detail about the silver watch, also saying, "It was kind of large; he put it on his grandfather's old Twist-O-Flex band. He said it was easy on, easy off with that." Rodney wrote like a schoolboy at final exam time.

That seems to take care of the jewelry the MCU asked about, he thought.

What he knew nothing about was a wallet, but while she carried on with things that didn't concern the case or the officer, he remained quiet, thinking it was a type of release for her to speak with someone who knew something about the situation.

Then, she said, "Oh…his wallet. Did you find that? He had several hundred dollars and he carried a bunch of stuff in it. I told him he should clean out the unwanted things, but he said he needed everything that was in there, ya know."

"Well, what exactly did he have in there, do you know?" Rodney asked.

"Driver's license, like I said, the cash and…ah… hunting license for Maine and…oh yeah, he was a little religious on his mother's side, I think. He carried a Saint Christopher medal. He said it kept him safe, whatever."

Rodney wrote everything down, as fast as his fingers could push the pen. She had his interest and he knew it would be the same when he shared it with the MCU and the chief.

Their pauses came less frequently now, as they found a comfort zone between them. He couldn't deny that he was attracted to the sound of her voice, especially when his memory of her facial expressions was added. Suddenly, the little voice inside his head screamed at him.

Wake up, bubba! Ask her if she gets up to Maine occasionally.

He took a final gulp of Java—it was cold and he grimaced as it went down, listening to her voice and regaining his composure. The second she stopped for a breath, he asked.

"Um… do you ever get down to this part o' Maine, once in a while?"

There was another, slight pause, then, "Yeah, I do. I'm not planning anything real soon, but…you know."

"Oh yah, sure I know. I just thought, if you do…we might take time for lunch or take in the sights along the coast, no pressure," he said. Another somewhat uncomfortable pause rang silent in his ear.

"That would be nice," she said suddenly, and his spirit soared through the window across the room. She carried on about things she loved when in Maine, and then suddenly, her voice broke, sending him into a spiraling sensation of guilt.

Oh, shit. Here I am puttin' the make on 'er and 'er boyfriend ain't even cold yet, he thought. His confidence of seconds earlier was smashed against that same window across the room. He had to say something, quick.

"I…I'm sorry. Maybe this is still too soon for you. I can call you later this month, see how things are then," and the moment the words left his mouth, he called himself every cut-up in his vocabulary, just under his breath.

"Sure, that would be fine. Call me toward the end of the month. I might be ready for a trip to Maine," she said and there was something in the way she said it that allowed him to regain his presence of mind.

"Ok! I'll call you later in the month; see how things are for you then. Although, if I turn something in…you know…the case, I'll call you immediately, ok?"

"Absolutely," and with that, they said their goodbyes and he waited for her to hang up. Even then, he found it difficult to remove the receiver from his ear. He could not remember, except maybe in high school, being smitten with a young girl or a young woman as he was now. He couldn't get her out of his mind, nor did he want to be where he was. Suddenly, the clamor of incoming rookies brought him back to the reality of the moment.

—

The heat in the garage was suffocating. Pozy lay on the concrete floor for the cooling effect it offered, while beads of sweat covered him. He'd been alone for several days, and boredom had begun to feel like an incubator, intensifying his need to grow and go. His mother had packed him a variety of foods the last time he went home. The mini-fridge was full, along with an assortment of fruit and packaged snacks in plastic bags, which now sat on the end of the workbench nearest the fridge. It was just too hot to eat. He cat-napped all afternoon, dreaming of things that seemed too far afield to think they could actually happen, especially to someone like him. *If ya dream about it, it probably won't happen.* That was a saying his mother lived by and often said when he'd told her his dreams as a boy. Alone, he regarded himself with such low self-esteem that lying on the floor seemed productive.

The late-day shadows began to shade parts of the garage-yard and with the turning of the tides, a cooling sea breeze quelled the flames of the earlier heat. At the very moment he felt the cooling air, he heard Petey's Mopar rumble down the dirt driveway. He was surprised and pleased to see all three buddies in the approaching car. Petey popped the horn in short blasts on their advance, enlivening the moment.

Pozy was starved for companionship. He rolled to one side,

getting up slowly, and he saw Zeke holding something up through the windshield, but from where he stood, the natural light from a fading sun made it impossible to see what it was. Petey turned the car hard to the right, the front tires spitting gravel to the side, like a grader with the plow down. The only time he'd seen Petey drive like that was when they all had one too many beers, and then like a light bulb being turned on, he realized what Zeke wanted him to see. They had beer. Petey didn't back the car up to the garage as usual. He left it broadside to the front and all three piled out; two carried a large cooler and Zeke brandished a plastic bag.

Their reunion was similar to the one before, when only the three met at the garage, while Zeke was nowhere to be found. They hugged then punched each other in the upper arms and laughed like schoolboys. It didn't take long for one of them to break out the brew and they drank like old salts on the dock after a long sea voyage. The afternoon shadows began to elongate across the front garage-yard, and no one noticed the cooling effect that the sea breeze offered.

Zeke partied hearty, but throughout the remainder of the afternoon and early evening light, he kept an alert ear and eye on the upper part of the driveway. No one knew the baggage he carried, and after a nondescript question-and-answer period, the boys were satisfied with what Zeke shared about his far-off camp hideaway, and most of what he offered was forgotten after their second beer.

The clock ticked on, and night came before they realized. They gathered at the side of the garage, where stones were piled high in a circle and in turn, each did a part to build a fire. If anything, the smoke would help to keep the mosquitoes and biting flies down to a swatting level of control. With a roaring fire, it was time to bring out a couple of the small bags brought with the cooler. There were several large Italian subs, chips and some small boxes of pies for dessert and more beer. With the false hunger pangs the drinking caused, it was gone in minutes.

"This is the way life should be all the time," Zeke said.

"Yah…It used to be," Petey chimed in.

Zeke looked around for opinions from the other two, but Dwight was already lying down and Pozy appeared to be off on cloud nine, somewhere.

The flames were somewhat hypnotic to begin with, and probably the last thing they all needed was pot. Zeke, displaying a naughty grin, packed the corncob pipe with the weed, passing it around while telling the boys they needed to consecrate the evening, for whatever reason he needed to convey that. Without giving it any thought, they agreed and drew heavily from the old cob.

The beer was gone, finally, the empties thrown into the woods behind the building, and Zeke returned the pot to his jean-jacket pocket. They sat around a low flame now—no one fed the fire, as their faces glowed with less fervor and their mood calmed. No one knew or even cared to ask what time it was, but it was obviously in the late-evening hours, as the distant sound of traffic was nearly non-existent. They were subdued from the effects of the substance and the silence was a good indicator. Only Zeke babbled on of things the other three didn't understand, and half of what he said was gibberish, but they nodded their heads occasionally to appease him. All in all, it was a peaceful reunion.

Without a warning of sound from the blacktop, the pelting gravel against the fender of a rapidly approaching vehicle gave the boys a stark awakening, and all heads turned to see Queer-Eye's glistening cruiser bearing down on the little party at a high rate of speed. As usual, they turned to Zeke for guidance, but he was gone. No one saw or heard him leave, and no sound was heard from whatever direction he'd taken.

"What-tha'..." was all Pozy had time to mutter. The cruiser stopped just short of hitting the corner of the garage, then Queer-Eye got out and started quick-stepping toward them. The only thing that gave him direction in the darkness was the bright, smoldering embers of the fading fire, which glowed several feet from the stones.

"What do we have here, the sorority of camp-fire girls?"

None of the three responded, taking no offense to the sarcasm—but they did wonder why Zeke had left them so quickly.

18

THE SEASONAL BUSINESSES WERE BOOMING and the tourist dollars were projected by the Department of Tourism to produce a gold-banner year. Not many even remembered the murder, which had occurred only weeks earlier. Most travelers who arrived these days never heard about the young man from Connecticut. The walking path on which he lay was at times shoulder-to-shoulder with hikers, and the area of the exact scene looked like any other along the way to the water.

There were those however, who did not forget. The young woman companion of the victim would never forget. Rodney Torrey would remain involved to the case's conclusion and even then, he would probably never forget. The members of the MCU investigation team would go on to other things eventually; although deeply devoted to their work, they would soon forget the body of a young male found on the walkway path that rainy night, near Dells and Punquit Beach. There was one person, however, who would never forget for as long as he lived—Zeke Brailey—and right now, he was the topic of many conversations.

The three boys had stayed on at the garage after Queer-Eye left that night; Petey was in no condition to drive, taunting the officer was not advisable, and Rodney wasn't in the best of moods, not having found the subject of his questioning desires. He knew they'd been drinking beer—their breath gave that away—but with no empty containers around, he'd be damned if he would search the property in darkness, even if he used his flashlight, when his goal was to find and speak with Zeke. This had gone on long enough and he was pissed. He told the boys before leaving that it was in their best interest to tell Zeke the officer wanted to see him, but not knowing where he went when he disappeared these days, not even they could help with that request. After Rodney left, the evening faded into early morning and the boys finally crashed heavily wherever they could; on the seats of the Mopar. Daylight came quickly.

They spoke of Zeke's magician-like disappearance for the best part of the forenoon. Their biggest question was…WHY? No one knew him to run from anything, especially Rodney Torrey. He'd always boasted that he could take him in a fight, yet running the way that he did left much for them to vex over.

—

The morning started as usual for Missy and Marcy. They arrived at the Little Roady before the sun came over the horizon. Missy parked in her regular spot, followed closely by her mother in her car. Marcy, for whatever reason, always blocked the rear entrance, so when she opened her car door, she was only a few steps from entering. At times, parking so close, her door hit the building, so she had to move it several feet, expelling a burst of profanity heard only by her daughter, who had all that she could do to hold the laughter in while shaking with convulsions of hysteria. It was a routine with them. They mulled over the familiarity of their daily chores of opening the restaurant and preparing themselves for the regulars, who at times bored the hell out of them, but being their bread and butter, they welcomed all with open arms, and the hot coffee and fresh, homemade doughnuts the patrons expected and loved.

Missy was exceptionally glum this morning. Zeke had disappeared once again, and this time she'd lost hope. She remained quiet throughout her work, and Marcy never questioned her silence. She liked it quiet before coffee. Had she been angry, things would be tossed and clanged about, that was the norm with Missy, but contemplation overwhelmed her and overpowered her actions. It took about an hour to ready the place to open. Once the coffee was perking, Marcy began deep-frying the famous doughnuts—those were her babies. She loved to make them, and took her share as they drip-dried hot, on racks beside the fry-o-later.

They only spoke while passing, reaching around each other for whatever they needed. Finally, the morning chores were done and they met at their customary places at the breakfast counter—Marcy, standing behind it and facing the front door, Missy, seated at the first bench at the edge of the counter. After a second cup each, Missy's tongue began to loosen and the Roady felt normal again. No more than five minutes passed and the conversation began, then ended with the arrival of the day's first customers. Marcy, from her perch, saw them approach long before they entered. She summed it up as early-morning transients; their appearances confirmed that they weren't locals.

Missy never bothered to turn at the sound of the front door being opened. She simply got up without saying a word and returned to her place in the kitchen and got ready for the obvious bacon and eggs order. Whenever she was in the kitchen alone, Missy often pretended she was a little girl again, and imagined herself in her Queendom. Whether she was flipping eggs or scraping the grill at the end of the day, her thoughts belonged to only her, and could lift her to a plateau where no one could reach and find her. She was there now, though in the background; the sound of her mother making small-talk with their patrons gave her no inkling as to what transpired between them. And there he was again…

Missy couldn't get Zeke out of her mind. He was gone once more. She rummaged around in the fridge, for nothing really, then brought out a dozen eggs as her thought of him carried her away.

How could I have been so naïve to think I could bring him around to my way of thinking? No…no I didn't try to save him, he'd never let me or anyone else do something like that. Oh, no…

that could be a good thing, sensible even. I'd give my week's pay to know where he's gone this time; probably to that made-up camp he told me about…the little liar. Maybe I should leave well enough alone. Be glad that he's gone. 'Too late ta lock the barn door, once the horse is already out.' You always seem ta find the stray cat and bring 'im home and feed 'im, keep 'im warm, then he scratches and bites ya and runs off and yaw' left with the scars."

"Missy… Goddamned girl, you gone deaf or what? This is the third time I tell ya. Two orders bacon and eggs over easy and white toast. Can ya handle it?"

When Missy finally looked up with a start, Marcy was gone and the swinging door was flapping back and forth.

—

Across town, the fax machine began spitting out several pages at the same instant the phone on Officer Rodney Torrey's desk rang. It was Investigator Moody, the trooper who had questioned Lillian Crandlemyer the night of the shooting at the hospital in Biddeford.

"How're ya, officer?"

"Good, yourself, trooper?"

"Fine…thank you for asking. I've just sent a fax along for you. I wonder if you've gotten it yet?"

"Well… there's something printing as we speak. That's probably it."

"OK, I can give you a brief as it prints; you can read it later if that's ok with you."

"Fine," Rodney answered.

"About that pistol grip screw you'd sent up. It sure fits with what else I'm about to tell you."

Rodney perked up in his seat, then with a nervous twitch, he stood up and began swaying in anticipation of what the trooper was about to share.

"I'm all ears," Rodney responded.

Without hesitation the trooper relayed the information. The

screw was identified as being a match to a Smith and Wesson .38 special, the exact type of gun used in the murder. Also, the weapon had been used in a convenience store robbery in Lawrence, Massachusetts, where the clerk was shot and killed several months earlier. That was confirmed through ballistics on the bullets taken from the young man's body.

"It looks as though we have a pretty hot piece here, officer. Good job in finding it—the screw I mean," the trooper added. He continued with small talk about the case and things that enlivened Rodney's interest and his thoughts soared higher, yet the sound of the trooper's voice seemed to fade the longer he spoke. Rodney was not dismissing the trooper, far from that, it was simply his mind working overtime with the possibilities of where it all was going and how he would make a difference in the outcome of the investigation. Finally, the trooper came up for air and Rodney immediately shared with him the conversation with Ms. Crandlemyer, of what seemed to be only a couple of days ago. He shared that information with all who needed to know, but there was nothing like a telephone conversation to get one's feelings in detail out to hopefully be felt by those on the receiving end of the talk. He could project his impression much better over the phone, as the trooper remained silent during Rodney's recounting of that conversation with her.

"So..." The trooper began. "What we have here is a missing gun, minus a screw from the grip, a wallet, a ring with a turquoise stone and an old watch with a Twist-O-Flex band. Do you think this entire thing was based on a robbery?"

"I'm not sure of anything right now," Rodney said, and the trooper went off on a tangent of new ideas which confused the officer somewhat, since they were an altogether different approach to their previous thought process concerning the case. They continued to chat for some time, as the subject varied from the case to everyday stuff that law enforcement people face. Rodney enjoyed speaking with someone from the State Police. After all, they are the state's elite and their approach to maintaining law and order was consummate.

As a boy, growing up in a small town in northern Maine, in most cases, outside of a constable here and there, a trooper was the law, no matter how far away he was. He remembered an old saying about a trooper: "Ya don't see 'em that much, but they're always around." That expression rang true, even today. Rodney, at times, envisioned himself as a trooper. He was young enough, and with his background as a police officer and the fact that he had graduated from the Maine Criminal Justice Academy could only support his attempt if he chose to move in that direction. There were some things to consider, however. His relationship with the chief was beyond reproach, and the fact that Willard Weaks was this close to retirement could, because of Rodney's tenure on the Dells Police Department, open the door to his own chiefdom. The position of chief in a small town like Dells was generally for life or retirement, whichever came first. At Rodney's age, that could mean a long, profitable stay at the top. The rewards for being chief of police were enormous.

Rodney suddenly felt a surge of impatience building within him. He had his limitation for how long he could hold onto a phone receiver. Long talks were not his forte. He began fiddling with things on his desk and couldn't wait for the trooper to break from his palavering. The second the trooper took a breath, Rodney interjected with an observation he'd kept to himself until this moment.

"Trooper… I have a person of interest I've been trying to question since the onset of the investigation. He simply seems to vanish each time I close in to speak to him."

"What's the source of your interest?"

"Well, he's a bit of a local troublemaker. I find it hard to think he'd murder someone, but the night the young man was killed, I came across this individual while driving through town on a regular cruising. His outfit was similar to how the young woman described the assailant's clothes as she remembered them during your questioning at the hospital."

He relayed his thoughts to the trooper about his conversation with a fellow officer from Biddeford a while back and the ruckus that had gone on at the abandoned old factory near the RR tracks; he spoke of his gut feelings about all of it and for the first time since the beginning of the call, it was Rodney who spoke and the trooper listened. Both men realized, yet neither shared with the other that gut instincts at times played a major role in good police work, but it went only so far if there was nothing solid to back it up.

"Do you want me to make the rounds with you some night… see if we can dig up a little rodent from the woodwork?"

"I'd like to continue on my own for a bit, if you don't mind. After all, I haven't got anything solid yet, so…"Rodney said.

"No problem, Rodney. I'll wait on your call."

That was the first time the trooper had called him by his first name. It felt good.

"Thanks. I'll keep you on the same page as I go."

With that said, the trooper told him of another call he needed to make, and they said goodbye.

Rodney sat back in his chair, picking over parts of the conversation and second-guessing himself for not inviting the trooper along to help find and question Zeke Brailey. He even wondered why the trooper didn't get into more questions about who the person was.

Well…It doesn't matter. You know who you want, now go and find 'im, he thought.

—

Those close to Zeke were filled with disenchantment and wonderment as to why he chose to act the way that he did. Zeke, on the other hand, hadn't a care in the world. He rested his head on a stump by the lake, fishing pole propped on a lifted knee, while the sun darkened his features more. He couldn't be bothered less by what others thought of him. Furthermore, not one minute passed that he considered any of them.

"I'm as busy as a renegade faart at a Saturday night bean suppa," he said, while twitching the pole in an attempt to attract what he hoped would be supper for him. He'd been at the hide-out, as he called it now, the camp he'd told Missy about, never saying where it was. He'd arrived here in the early morning as the sun was just clearing the horizon in the east. He'd been without sleep since the day before, yet he felt no ill effects from the heavy drinking and smoking with his so-called friends—the ones he'd counted on so much before, yet abandoned so often. Zeke lay out in only his underwear, enjoying the seclusion. The only thing he'd left the camp with was the fishing pole and the .38 special. It was on the stump.

The money he'd taken from his young victim and frugally spent on food for the camp and beer and pot for his friends that night was near depleted. He'd also spent twenty-dollars on some ammunition, so he was well stocked with bullets now. He simply needed more cash to extend his stay. He called himself frugal because he'd stolen most of the canned goods and pocket-sized items from the small convenience store several miles from the camp. The owners knew who Zeke was, but as familiar to the area as they were, not even they knew where the camp was or that it even existed, or that Zeke was staying there.

He knew that Queer-Eye wanted to speak with him, but about what, he wasn't sure. He had no reason to think that he was a suspect in the Connecticut boy's death. *People of little towns…* he thought. Right now, however, the only thing Zeke thought of was catching fish. The world went around him, as far as he was concerned.

19

THE MOIST, PUTRID AROMA OF RANK, empty lobster shells filled the air as it oozed from punctured trash bags and leaked from the back of dumpster trucks all along Coastal Route 1. The hot sun baked it to the blacktop. If smell had sound, it would be "ca-ching" in the ears of restaurateurs and lobster-pound owners, as the summer catch had been bountiful. Everyone wanted a taste of Maine's official crustacean while in Vacationland.

The heat of the day was suffocating. Petey sat alone in the booth in the corner gazing out the window at nothing in particular. An empty coffee cup sat in front of him and his thoughts were of his three closest friends who had seemed to vanish without a trace. A glimmer of sunlight reflected from the bumper of the big Mopar out front and at that very moment, he was distracted by the sound of Missy sliding in the booth bench across from him.

"Hi…handsome, penny for your thoughts," she said as she placed a fresh pot of hot coffee on a trivet in the center of the table with a plate of fresh doughnuts beside it.

"Oh, you didn't have to do that, Missy. I'd of gotten by with just the coffee."

"Well, I want some, too," she said, then laughed.

He loved the sound of her laugh, but he'd never tell her that. They remained uncomfortably quiet for several minutes—Petey, because of his attraction to her, something he never felt ready to discuss with anyone, especially her, knowing very well the relationship between her and Zeke, who he still feared in many ways. She was of a similar disposition, but not for the same reason. She had been played for a fool and could not bring herself to speak of it, and so she didn't. It was his turn now.

"Penny for your… thoughts," he said, and smiled across at her, and without hesitation she responded softly, "Zeke."

That name and the fact she was thinking of him gave Petey a twinge of discomfort in the midsection, yet here he sat alone with her in what once was a group of outcasts at their meeting place.

"Yeah… funny, I was thinking of him and the other two myself," he said.

They sipped from the hot brew, which appeared to equalize their body temperature to the heat of the day. Petey devoured a couple of the doughnuts in just a couple of bites, but Missy never reached for one. Her desire to eat went out the plate-glass window into the stratosphere, where as far as she was concerned was where Zeke was. Suddenly, as if a switch were turned on in Missy's vocal cords, she began unloading the whole thing on Petey. All he could do was to eat the remaining doughnuts and listen, which was what he did best.

At this time of the day the restaurant was generally quiet. Marcy puttered around with things, paying no attention to the couple at the corner booth. When a customer did come in, it was usually a single for a coffee or a cold drink and Marcy could handle that.

As Missy spoke, Petey noticed a visible level of agitation in the tone she displayed, while going into much detail of her feelings for Zeke and how badly he'd let her down. Petey's feelings were similar, but the last thing he wanted was to interrupt her now. She shared things he'd perceived before, but never to this extent. He began to feel slighted at the ways he'd been treated by Zeke and sometimes Pozy, and a new picture of that relationship was being painted through his mind's eye, in vibrant colors.

Several times now, from the farthest corner of the restaurant or while exiting the kitchen, Marcy stared in their direction, finding it somewhat peculiar that Petey was spending this much time with her daughter—who was quite a bit older than he—and that they were so engrossed in conversation. She had no idea what went on within their group, and knew nothing of Zeke's disappearances, as she and Missy never spoke of her involvement with him. Missy talked while gazing out through the window. Petey reached for that last doughnut and without looking, she slapped his hand away. It was more of a playful tapping than an angry hit, and when their eyes met, neither could break the stare, nor could either find the words to continue the conversation they'd begun. Again, an uncomfortable silence came over them.

Suddenly, Petey asked with no hesitation, "Do you love him?"

Without a moment to think, she responded. "I thought I did. I don't know anything anymore. He just…" And, not another word came out of her. Her face went limp and pale, and it seemed to Petey as though she wanted to be held by someone who could tell her everything would be all right, but he lacked the self-confidence to get up, go to her, and be the one she needed at that moment.

—

"Well…You fuckin' chimp. You been out hea' all this time? What the fuck was that vanishin' act the otha' night?" Pozy asked.

He had surprised the hell out of Zeke. The last thing he expected was someone sneaking up on him here at the camp. Zeke was out in the sun again with his fishing pole and the .38 on the stump when Pozy walked up as quiet as a church mouse. Both were silent when walking in the woods.

"What in hell...you doin' hea'?"

"I figured you weren't comin' back any time soon, and the way you slithered off when Queer-Eye pulled in, any fool would think somethin' was up." Pozy didn't say another word, he simply reached into the paper bag he carried and pulled out a tall Budweiser and passed it to his friend, taking one for himself.

"Didja tell anybody where you were goin'?" Zeke asked.

"No… you… fuckin' idiot. No one knows about this place but

you, me and your parents. Whatddaya think, I'm nuts?"

They guzzled from the cans and it appeared that Zeke hadn't had a drink of alcohol since his stop at the garage. He inhaled the liquid. Without saying a word, Pozy reached for the .38 on the stump under the silent scrutiny of his friend's watchful eye.

"Is this in case the monster from the pond slithers out and tries ta suck ya off?" Pozy asked sarcastically.

"He comes out now, and it's yaw' ass he's gonna suck on," Zeke responded. Pozy answered with a huge burp and they burst out in laughter, echoing across the pond.

—

The phone rang incessantly at the dispatch desk of the Dells Police Department. When summer was in full swing, Tylenol and Advil were on almost everyone's desk, at least during tourist season. Most calls were answered by the rookies—two had bicycles, and the one with time and grade drove the spare cruiser, leaving the chief and Rodney to pursue the actual nitty-gritty of the goings-on of the Department. Rodney continued to live and breathe the so-far unsolved murder, and his thoughts remained on Lillian Crandlemyer.

The weekends were generally time-off for Rodney and the chief. Today, Monday, Rodney came alive with a rejuvenated vitality for the case and a resolve to move forward. Generally, he arrived before anyone, as an empty office gave him time to think things out without interruption, not to say that he hadn't accustomed himself to work well under the pressure of distraction. The lines of his readily available notepad began to fill with to-do's, the number 1 being his top priority, Zeke. During the past several weeks, his thoughts had been overpowering with the similarities of Lillian Crandlemyer's description of the murderer's clothes and the way he remembered seeing Zeke Brailey dressed only a short time before the murder supposedly took place, according to the Medical Examiner's report on the time of death.

The thought of this local rascal killing someone for a watch, a ring and a few hundred dollars didn't make sense, but when speaking with several older people who knew him, their description of Zeke painted a far darker side than just an around-town trouble-maker. Rodney also knew that it would do no good to speak further with the remainder of the troublesome-foursome—they would never give him up—yet that evening he'd broken in on the beer-party, his gut told him that Zeke had been there, but they really didn't know what was going on with their buddy. He scanned the list and added two more names.

Suddenly, out of thin air, his imagination formed the imageless faces of Zeke Brailey's parents. As far back as he could remember, in dealing with Zeke's and the other boys' shenanigans, he had met only Petey's grandparents and Pozy's parents once at a church breakfast. They were from up-river, and were there because family members had invited them. He sat in silence now, shaking his head at having taken this long to brain-fart this one out. He looked down at the list suddenly, and seeing Lillian's name, her likeness appeared through his mind's eye and he longed to hear her voice. He was smitten with a woman he really didn't know and for the most part, had not had contact with since their last telephone conversation several weeks before. For all he knew, she'd never given him a second thought after hanging up that day, yet his feelings remained strong for her.

He put his thoughts together now as to whom he'd speak with first about finding Zeke's parents, if they were from around here or if they were even still alive—probably the chief. Rodney knew nothing of them or of Zeke's past. The chief, however, knew a little something about most folks from this part of Maine. Rodney had the proclivity to keep notes on everything he did or planned to do. He filled several pages of the notepad, and then suddenly realized he'd been working at his desk for two hours when the clamor of incoming rookies got his attention.

"Mornin' chief!" the rookie with the shiny, bald head greeted him.

"I'm not the chief," he answered and continued staring at the young officer with questioning eyes.

"Sorry… I didn't mean anything by it," the rookie answered.

—

The sun was hot and it had been a long time since Pozy had ventured out to the camp. After the little reunion and a couple of beers, Zeke settled in to fishing; supplies were low and fish became a viable dietary supplement. Pozy stripped naked and enjoyed the cooling water of the isolated pond in the late afternoon sun. The camp and pond were nestled deep in the woods at the base of Casket Mountain, where Zeke had been brought up, and mid-way to Lost Corner where Pozy had lived as a boy and where his parents remained to this day. Over the years, the pond had been christened with many names, yet it became lost in the everyday shuffle of a hectically wound world. The boys called it the Pond. The elder locals long ago, for lack of a better name, had dubbed it Poor Peoples Pond, while over the years of non-use, the road had become overgrown and forgotten and impassible by vehicle; the only way in now was over a hand-cut trail by foot that wound its way through the thickets. The master architects of the path were Zeke and Pozy.

Pozy dove and resurfaced time and again; his pale, white butt-cheeks appeared to glow in the mineral-rich mountain water. He was far enough from the bobber not to obstruct Zeke's attempt at fishing, but not far enough to escape his pondering eye. Zeke's thoughts brought him back to that night in Biddeford and how easily the two of them—together— had overpowered those two young men. Then, the memory of the murder came into his mind.

Being alone makes everything tougher, he thought. *I'm used to having my partner in crime, even if he's just along for the ride. I need more money and with Pozy here and…I don't have to tell 'im my plan, it'll be like the old days. The two of us will score tonight. Some out-o'-state fuck will pay for the rest o' my summer vacation at camp and before he knows it, Pozy'll be in on it, too.*

Throughout the remainder of the afternoon, Zeke kept to himself; his focus was on the possibilities of getting to use the gun again. His need to dominate someone was irresistible now and the potential for easy money was only a pointed revolver away. With Pozy here at camp, Zeke was free to think the time away, as he bullied his friend into sweeping out the filthy, unattended camp, and the chore of cooking the fish and canned beans, which was all that remained to eat, became Pozy's. The shadows lengthened across the smooth surface of the pond as their appetites became troublesome. Pozy cleaned the several trout and one bass and opened a large jar of B&M baked beans, while the kindling in the open-pit fireplace crackled through the still air of their surroundings.

Zeke helped himself to another beer, the remainder of which was set in the cooler water, about six to eight feet from the pit. He pranced around with the beer in one hand, the revolver in the other. When Pozy looked up to see the commotion, Zeke resembled a horny rooster chasing the sought-after hen. Pozy simply shook his head in disbelief. He'd never fire the gun here, not wanting to alarm anyone of his presence, but his trigger finger was itchy and he longed to pop a few rounds off. It didn't really matter now what the target might be. All he wanted was to hurt someone.

Although Pozy had noticed the change in his friend's behavior coming for some time, he could never know fully the extent of Zeke's illness. The drinking and pot smoking only added to it through bouts of paranoia and depression. If Pozy had only known, he would have realized it was the perfect time to head on down that path to his own freedom; for he could never imagine what Zeke planned for them this evening.

—

After an hour of putzing around and looking over at Missy and Petey, Marcy began to show signs of irritability, and she made no effort to conceal it. It was late afternoon; she expected someone, and hoped to have Missy and Petey-boy long gone when the person arrived. With a few clangs from the kitchen, Missy received the message without a single word coming from her mother.

"Well...Missy-girl. You're burnin' daylight if you were thinkin' o' doin' somethin' on yaw' free time. Mind-ya, I ain't suggestin' that the two of ya leave or nothin', if ya know what I mean. And what about Mopar-boy there—you've got places ta go and people ta see...don't ya?" One wouldn't need more than a half of a brain to figure they were being asked to leave.

"Well, handsome, it sounds like we've outstayed our welcome," Missy said.

"Oh...no problem, Missy. I've enjoyed every minute of our conversation. By the way, I've got a bunch o' stuff to do and we have burned a lot o' daylight just chattin'. You do know that I'm always around if you need someone to talk to."

"Thanks, handsome. You've been a huge help just listening to me ramble on about nothing...really."

"It wasn't nothing. You needed to unload and it just happened to be me. It's all good. What are friends for?" he asked. She smiled back at him, sending a tingle to the bottom of his feet.

"C'mon, we'll let the old girl have her company."

Within a few moments and with a simple wave of his arm, Petey was gone. All that remained of his visit was the fading sound of the big Mopar's throaty exhaust down Route 1. Missy displayed a smirk toward her mother, yet said nothing and left through the rear door.

"Well, I thought they'd neva' leave." Marcy appeared a bit on edge, as she stood before the mirror, fluffing her hair and sprucing up her white uniform shirt, keeping one eye on the front door. She went to the coffee brewer and fired up a fresh pot, looking around to make sure that nothing was out of place. Suddenly, the vehicle she'd obviously waited for pulled up to the front of the building. Her heart raced at the sight of it. Then, Chief Willard Weaks walked in through the front door. Marcy watched him saunter across the main portion of the restaurant, their eyes in a dead-on stare. Marcy beamed with a sentimental glow and watched him as he arrived at his usual end-of-the-counter stool.

Missy's intuition of several weeks earlier was right on. Her mother was involved with the chief, but she wasn't about to find out today.

"Hi," Marcy said.

"Hi to you," he responded.

He didn't have to ask; she poured the hot coffee into both cups and remained standing on her side of the counter. The faint smile and glow never left her face.

"Is everyone gone for the day?" he asked.

"Oh…gee, while I think of it," Marcy said and walked around the counter, sliding her hand over the top of his shoulders as she passed, and going directly to the closed sign on the front door, flipped it, drawing the shade and locking the door before returning to the counter. The Little Roady was officially closed for the day.

—

Across town, Missy sat on the edge of her bed staring out her bedroom window. After speaking with Petey for as long as she had and touching base on the things that consumed her, and then finding out through Petey's interjections that she was not alone in her concerns for the way she'd been treated by Zeke, she was overwhelmed now with melancholy. She was unable to move from the spot, occasionally looking and feeling around the very bedspread that Zeke and she had made such passionate love on only several weeks earlier.

—

After finishing a supper of baked beans and fish, an aggressive restlessness began to tug on Zeke's stored adrenaline. He pitched a few stones onto the lake's surface, challenging Pozy to beat the amount of skims he'd achieved, but getting no response, he began pitching the flat stones at Pozy, finding much humor in it and angering his friend to the point of almost coming to blows. The two were a comparable match physically in both height and weight, which would make it difficult for either to back down, but as weird as Zeke was acting lately, Pozy was not prepared to test the level to which he'd degenerated mentally.

"Ok…ok, big boy. How 'bout we quit throwin' stones and maybe head to town or somethin'?" Pozy said.

Zeke's plan had worked perfectly. He knew if he agitated Pozy enough he would make the call to head to town—whatever town that might be was of no concern to Zeke. The sun had long since fallen behind the trees at the western end of the pond. Darkness would envelop them soon. The night was Zeke's time. He fired up the small amount of weed left in the pipe and shared it with his closest friend, who accepted it willingly. The attitude that each would develop under the effects of THC was similar—wisecracking, mouthy and just plain smart-ass demeanor, but Zeke's, however, became criminal, and his friend would soon find out the extent of his brutality.

—

Before the chief left, hopefully for the day, he'd given Rodney some valuable information about Zeke and Pozy's parents. He'd told him that he'd gone to school with Zeke's grandfather, who was several years passed on now, and the old man's farm had been left to Zeke's father. As he recalled, the family were back-country farm stock who gave little regard to the laws of the land. Whenever the old man thought they needed meat, and none of the farm critters was ready for killin', deer meat, Canada Geese, partridge and any one of the vast number of wild game to ramble over their hundred-acre spread was killed and prepared for the table. Like most locals from that generation, they had large families, and the local game wardens kept their distance, especially knowing that they seldom ventured off their own land.

Rodney was on his way to meet Zeke's parents—after all, it was Zeke he was most interested in speaking with, but along with the summer traffic, a road-resurfacing crew had hundreds of vehicles backed up on both north and southbound lanes of Route 1, while the many arteries that connected to it in all directions were in gridlock. Rodney was beside himself with frustration, locked in behind a smelly bait truck leaking gut juice and splashing it onto the front bumper of his shiny cruiser. Behind him was a carload of screaming kids and two confounded-looking chicks, obviously beach-bound. From their facial expressions, their headaches matched his.

Damn it all. It seems that every time I have anything to do with… Zeke, I find myself between a boulder and a goddamned stone wall, he thought. *I don't care how long this lasts. I'm going to get there today.*

20

The late August sun seemed less hot than only a couple of weeks before, yet summer remained. A dry cold front had moved in from Canada, leaving the beach-goers stunned to find themselves wrapped in sweaters and long pants at this time of their vacation's evenings. This was however, Maine. Even at the southernmost reaches of the state, it always seemed cooler than most of the states to the south. And… that's where most of the vacationers came from.

It was well after sunset when Rodney wound his way down the narrow gravel driveway that led to the Brailey farm. During the lengthy traffic snarl, he had thought of some questions for whomever he found at the residence. *They'll be complete strangers to me,* he thought, never having met them, but what he could not know was that he'd be met with the extreme opposite of him being a stranger to them. He drove through a final curve in the road, and the faintly lit farmhouse came into view from across an expanse of clearing. It was not evident to the officer whether or not it was cultivated. The road swung around it and came to a wide turn-around driveway, directly in front of the house, with a huge colonial barn off to the left in the distance.

As he stopped the car, the front door opened and the silhouette of an individual appeared, but Rodney could not tell if it was a man or woman. It was as if he were expected, yet he hadn't called or let anyone other than the chief know his plans to come out here. The person at the door now closed it and moved toward the front steps as Rodney parked the car, got out and made his way toward the house. As he approached, he realized it was a man standing before him, and as he went closer, he discovered it was a pretty big man at that. In fact, as the light from the house glowed dimly behind him, Rodney could have sworn it was an older Zeke standing before him. They were built on the same type of frame. His long, dark hair was combed back slick against his head as if it were wet and he wore a pair of bibbed farmer jeans and a pale blue work shirt, as if he'd recently returned from the fields. On his feet, however, he wore a comfortable-looking pair of house slippers.

"We've been expectin' ya, not this late, though."

"What do you mean…you've been expecting me?" Rodney asked, somewhat confused.

"Word gets 'round these paa'ts just like nea' the water where yaw' from," he answered.

Rodney thought it best to remain silent so as not to alienate the gentleman, although from the sound of his voice and comments already shared, he wouldn't have to stretch it very far to accomplish that.

"Ok…then. You obviously know who I am and why I came out hea'," Rodney said.

"I suppose it's about our dirt-bag son who's… got himself in some more trouble. The boy seems ta suck it in like the air he breathes. Ratha' sleep than eat, that one, but I'd guess he'd ratha' eat than do anything. As far as you, you're the cop from down Dells. I heard it said that folks call ya…Queer-Eye, ain't it?"

Rodney'd heard the term and it didn't set well with him; mostly it was the kids that called him that behind his back, but saving it for a later time, he thought, might prove to be more advantageous right now. Besides, the guy appeared to be as serious as a heart attack and there didn't seem to be an ounce of cocky sarcasm in the way he said it, as if it were an accepted term to identify with the cop.

"Ya…I've heard that cognomen before," Rodney exclaimed.

"What's that?" the older man asked quickly, obviously not

knowing what the word meant.

"Oh…nothin'," Rodney said. "I wonder if we might touch on Zeke a bit. I don't want ta keep ya longer than need be."

"Whatever," he responded.

Rodney could see where Zeke's attitude might have come from, but he reminded himself of the reason he was here and to keep tabs on his own attitude if it wasn't absolutely necessary to expose it now. Rodney began, "Because I've never met you before, I'm assuming by what you've said that Zeke is your son. I've been looking to speak with him for some time, but he seems to vanish whenever I get close. I wonder if you might tell me the last time you saw Zeke and where you think he may be."

"Ha…vanish…Ya, he knows how ta vanish alright. Whenever there's work to be done or some shit-shovelin' he knows how ta vanish alright. We ain't seen hide nor hair o' that boy for months now. Usually…when he needs somethin'—money, food, someplace to lay his head—he stops by for a couple o' days. No… he ain't been around."

"What about, oh…you know…a place he might hi—" he began to say hide out, but caught himself and said, "hang out, or maybe someone he might stay with when not here?"

"Nope," is what his father offered.

At that point, a woman came out onto the porch without saying a word, and he assumed it was Zeke's mother. She came to stand next to the gentleman. "Good evening," Rodney said. The woman remained silent with a blank expression and simply nodded her head in the affirmative, then looped her arm through her husband's.

"This here is Queer-Eye from Dells," Zeke's father said. The woman, who remained silent, poked her man in the ribs, obviously to remind him of his disrespect. He simply grunted, but never looked in her direction. "He says he's lookin' fa' Zeke. He says he can't find 'im. That sound familia'?" he asked. Again, she remained silent, but the faint expression of concern she now displayed through the dim light suggested to Rodney that she might be ready to offer her two-cents worth. Rodney's intuition was right on, but nothing could have prepared him for when she did begin to speak. Her voice emitted a type of elegance indicative of an upper-class education—as if she'd been brought up with formal values—and she got right to the point.

"You should know the level of disappointment we have for our son, officer. You can see for yourself, my husband works very hard to maintain this huge property, left to us by his father, who remained diligent and hard-working to his final days. This has been a family of proud, working farmers for several generations. Zeke, on the other hand, decided it was not for him. Although I wish he would have considered a more normal approach to life, there is a point when parents have to accept what their children become as adults. No…we have no idea where Zeke is or how to reach him if need be. Even his closest friends don't stop by anymore. I'm very sorry, but we cannot offer you anything to help you find him."

Her sincerity drove the point home. Rodney was so taken by her presence alone, he never wrote in his notes and his mind was suddenly a blank. The difference between the two standing before him was literally night and day. For the life of him he couldn't begin to figure out how this union, appearing to be very close, could ever come about. It wasn't as if they were deliberately standoffish; it seemed more like a stance of self-protection or preservation. Country folks are that way with strangers until they get to know them. Rodney tried to keep the conversation going in any direction that would lead to anything about Zeke, but it was obvious they knew nothing of their son's whereabouts.

After several uncomfortable minutes, Rodney said, "Well, I won't keep you. I know how early you folks must be up in the morning. By the way, I did notice how well-kept your land is and how much effort it must take to maintain a property this size. Thank you for your time and much good luck with everything," he finished. He turned, leaving the two in their arm-in-arm embrace and walked quickly toward his waiting cruiser. He was about to open the door when the woman spoke, forcing Rodney to immediately turn in her direction, taking a few steps closer.

"We love our son, officer. We simply do not condone his way

of life. Please…don't hurt him. He will resist you, but please… don't hurt him."

The husband maintained his stance at his wife's side, yet spoke not a word to her or the officer. Rodney nodded his head in her direction, but he would not make a promise he could not keep.

He intentionally did not bring up the true reason for wanting to speak to their son. Even he was reluctant to believe that Zeke was capable of the murder, yet without finding him and relieving his suspicions, he could not close this particular chapter. His window was rolled down and a welcomed zephyr of summer air returned and fondled his cheek, forcing him to look out onto the evening. The cold snap was hopefully over and a return to summer would be most welcomed. He pulled the shifter to D and took the turn-around to the blacktop. He glanced briefly toward the two, who hadn't moved a muscle from what he saw, and in just a few seconds, the house and the couple on the front porch had shrunk as the distance grew between them.

As Rodney drove toward Dells, a thousand thoughts ran through his mind about the brief meeting only minutes earlier. His intention was to stay on course with the questions, and he had done that without arousing negative sentiment from the parents. He believed he'd accomplished that and he mentally thanked the chief for the information about the parents that led him to the evening's meeting with them. However, what he or anyone else in the world could never perceive was what was going on in the storage closet at the Little Roady at this very moment. The chief and Marcy were pounding a huge dent into the same sack of flour that Zeke and Missy had used several weeks earlier, as the new sexual escapades, yet not so new affair, raged on in the heat of passion. As the evening wore on, the after-dark life of nocturnal creatures of the animal and human kind began to stir, making their way to the haunts that tugged at their need to be a part of it, whatever it might be. Zeke and Pozy began their supposed jaunt to town.

—

Without planning, Zeke and Pozy left the camp just after dark. Had they left only minutes earlier, because of the location of the camp and its proximity to the main traveled road, Officer Rodney Torrey's headlights would have illuminated them both when passing. The phrase timing is everything suddenly took on an entirely new perspective where luck and just plain stupid luck intersected.

Being this close to both their family homes and without discussing their personal thoughts, Pozy ruminated on Lost Corner and Zeke on Casket Mountain, as each considered their boyhoods there and the things that country boys do throughout a normal year with the changing of seasons. The very thought of that childhood put Pozy in a jovial mood, anticipating a hopefully fun-filled night somewhere along the coast. *Who knows...maybe we'll hook up with a couple o' out-o'-state chicks and get lucky for a change. Lucky, lucky, lucky,* he thought.

Zeke's thoughts, on the other hand, were violent. Although he was not a coward, his intentions, because of the gun, were dastardly. Sure, there weren't long periods of time on any day that Zeke's thoughts were not of a sexual fantasy; however, tonight his vision of a sexual encounter involved bullying with the revolver—*just the thing a lady wants to make her evening a success*, he thought with a grin.

Both were clad in all-black—Zeke wore his leather, Pozy was without his. The darkness appeared to consume them as they ambled along the back country road toward a town called Sandown. Street lights were nearly non-existent, allowing them to traipse along almost invisible in the night. Most of the conversation was directed by Pozy, uncommon where the two were concerned and due to his being high, he completely dismissed the fact that Zeke had become such a recluse and, in his own words to their friends after he'd pulled his disappearing acts, "Zeke...is a weirdo."

They were approaching a small, dumpy neighborhood known as Spring Valley, where some chick, running up from behind, startled them. It wasn't her intention, but in her running suit with pants that fit her contours tightly, Zeke checked her out, liked what he saw and couldn't help himself to a comment.

"Where'd ya get the buns, Loraine?"

He hollered with a laugh and so did Pozy, but both went straight-faced and silent when she turned only her head and said, "Fuck off, asshole," and kept on running at a speed that made it impossible for either to catch her had it been their intention.

"Lesbian," Zeke hollered back, but she was already out of earshot.

"Well...You seem to be well known hea'," Pozy said with a snort.

"Fuck off, asshole," is all Zeke offered.

After the runner went by them, the two became illuminated by street lights and well-lit homes as the town of Sandown loomed in the distance. The main road through town was packed with mom-and-pop type convenience stores, tiny take-out joints hanging on with a financial thread. Most of the local teens converged on the area, a kind of meeting place to be themselves. Pozy's spirits were uplifted by the sight of them. This was their place, having grown up no more than five miles to the north. Zeke continuously slid his right hand over the inner breast pocket where the .38 rested, for him, uneasily.

The chance of bumping into someone they both knew was good, but less favorable now that they were older and the evening crowd was so much younger. They were reminded of themselves years before. The girls showed more skin now, but they didn't seem as good-looking. The boys looked dumb, but dweebish at the same time; a new generation of night-dwellers.

"Computer freaks," Zeke said, when seeing a small group out front of an ice cream stand. Both kept an observant eye out for attractive women, whether in cars or on foot, yet they all looked like jail-bait to the more mature trouble-makers from Casket Mountain and Lost Corner. Besides, Zeke was looking for someone specific. Not someone he knew, but from away, preferably out-of-state. The hunt excited him. He had the taste of blood now; he felt like a super-power with a .38 Special.

He knew the kids from here didn't have a dollar between them, or maybe that was all they had. Again, they'd be the last ones he'd mess with. But… them from away, they had it and flaunted it. That's what he was looking for. He needed money and hopefully some trinkets he could sell later to extend his summer vacation at camp. He still held onto the watch and ring. Pawning that would have to wait until the heat was off, he calculated. Suddenly, his thoughts raced to Missy and the times they were together. This was the first time she'd come into his consciousness since the last night they'd spent together.

Traffic was heavier this close to town. Out-of-state plates were not, however, making the scene, causing a visible unrest in Zeke's demeanor, with short, snappy responses to anything Pozy said.

Pozy was almost sorry he'd ventured out to camp to be with Zeke, having questioned himself and their friendship on those long, quiet nights alone at the garage, when Zeke pulled his disappearing acts. A couple of times during the walk he'd actually considered turning around and just for the night, going back to the camp for some long sought-after peace, by himself.

The exhaust fans from a back-street grill filled the night air with the aroma of grilling steaks and the rumble from both their stomachs from eating beans and fish for days could almost be heard by each, yet neither offered comment on their need for that type of protein, although they longed to sink their teeth into a bloody, dripping piece of it. Without a word, midway along the main drag through town, Zeke stepped from the curb and put his thumb out to oncoming cars.

"What's up?" Pozy asked.

"This one-horse town's givin' me a royal pain in the fuckin' ass. Let's get down to the coast. This place sucks."

It was still early, but he agreed with Zeke on one thing: this town was a pain in the ass and at least down at the coast there'd be some real chicks to look at, not this farm-stock that looked pale and sickly to Pozy.

"We got anymore o' that smoke?" he asked.

And with a huge smile, as if to indicate Pozy's return to Zeke's reality, Zeke came back to the curb, looked around once, pulled the filled pipe from his pocket and flicked the Bic.

They'd just finished the pipe, and Pozy was about to take a leak between two parked cars, when Zeke noticed a Sandown Police car appear at the end of a side street. The officer saw them immediately and turned his cruiser in their direction. It was 9:30 p.m.

"Flip that baby sausage back in yaw' pants…big boy. The lawman wants ta handcuff it," Zeke said, while displaying a weird look toward the rapidly approaching cruiser.

"Cops?" was all Pozy asked, and the minute he stepped back onto the curb, the cruiser pulled up to them, facing in the wrong direction to the flow of traffic. The cop never got out; he simply looked at the both of them and asked, "What's goin' on here, men?"

"Nothin' sir, I dropped a coin down hea' and picked it up is all." Pozy held up a quarter so that the cop could see it.

"Where are you boys from?" the cop asked.

"Casket Mountain and Lost Corner," Zeke said.

There was a cold silence between the three, but the fact that neither had done anything wrong did not raise much concern. Had Pozy been caught urinating in public, it could have created an issue for them that might have led to trouble.

"Where ya goin' tonight?" the officer asked.

"We're goin' down the coast to stay with friends in Dells for the night. We don't plan on comin' this way no more tonight, or even tomorrow," Zeke said.

The cop looked them up and down, and thought he remembered something about a leather-clad punk, but he just couldn't remember exactly what. It just didn't register right now. "Do you have any ID?" the officer asked.

"Nope," Zeke answered. And without saying a word or getting out of his car, the officer turned toward his dash computer and entered a description of Zeke alone. After all, it was Zeke who kept answering the questions. When he did, they took off running.

There was no traffic, and without saying another word, the cop pulled out onto the roadway after a quick glance over his shoulder. As he crossed the center line he looked back toward the two who had already moved from the spot and out of sight from his vision. His face contorted with a disapproving frown, he pulled a u-turn and circled the block once, but for the life of him, he couldn't see them. This would be another close call for Zeke to go unnoticed, as fate would have it.

—

"Wow…I remember this old path back here now. We used to take it when we played hooky. That truant-fuzz never could find us, could he?" Pozy asked.

"He was a numbskull. He couldn't find his crack if he bent over and looked," Zeke replied; then he got real quiet again.

The evening was dark, so walking the path was difficult because they hadn't been over it for a long time, but staying out of sight for as long as possible was their best consideration, as the local cop would keep an eye out for them now that they'd pulled this vanishing act on him.

As soon as they'd reached what they thought to be the town line, and returned to the blacktop, Zeke immediately stuck his thumb out to passing cars. It didn't take long. The fifth vehicle to pass stopped and picked them up. The first thing Zeke looked for as it came to a stop just ahead of them was the license plate. It read MASSACHUSETTS. They ran up to the passenger side, and saw, looking in, that the driver had a Mohawk haircut with a purple tint, and the passenger was bald. Zeke's heart pounded in his chest as though it might crack a couple of ribs. His breathing became somewhat labored at the sight of them, rendering him speechless. Pozy on the other hand, thinking the night was for fun, greeted them with an exuberant "Howdy."

"Howdy…fuck. Get in the car," the driver said, sarcastically. It was 10:30 p.m.

Zeke nearly burst with the need to take the gun out and shove it up his nose, just for the hell of it. But that wasn't the game he wanted to play tonight. The sheer luck of having been picked up by these guys from Massachusetts was a blessing for him. It was going to save him hours of searching for one or a couple of punks—and here they were: volunteers to meet their fate. Besides, he wanted to feel them and the situation out. Suddenly, remembering Biddeford, he thought, *them twerps had a gun, and it's mine now. What are the odds these two have more than one?*

"Hey...You boys want ta smoke a little weed?" Zeke asked.

"Weed...? Whataya got, some farmer shit? Sure...light it up, farmer boy," the driver with the purple Mohawk said, igniting a flame into Zeke that left even him unsure of why he didn't pull the .38 out right then.

"Well," Zeke responded quickly. "I ain't exactly a fuckin' farmer, but if ya want a little buzz while we drive..." Pozy was surprised that was all Zeke offered in response.

An icy silence fell over the interior of the car as Zeke set a flame to the packed pipe. He really didn't want to share what little he had left, especially with Mass-holes, but he had plans for these two that only he could know. They drove on for several miles sharing the burning herb, when finally the passenger spoke up.

"Hey...man...ya never did tell us where in hell ya wanted to go."

"We're just headin' down ta Route 1," Pozy said. Zeke hadn't even considered a destination until now. His mind raced ahead on the road they traveled and in seconds, he had a plan. He caught sight of the driver's eyes through the rear-view mirror, but wasn't quite sure if he'd noticed. He looked toward the passenger side; Pozy was drawing deep from what remained in the pipe and briefly wondered what he might think when all hell broke loose in minutes. He knew that Pozy would act as dumb as need be to appease him and go along with whatever plan he devised, but he could never know what he planned to involve him in right now. The road ahead was traffic-free. A dark section of country road came along, and Zeke turned slowly to look behind, not wanting to alert the driver to anything out of the norm, and as far as he could see, the road there was the same. Less than two miles from here, a deserted dirt road would go off to the right, and it was Zeke's plan to take the joy-ride on an extended tour of the countryside, whether the driver and his buddy wanted to go or not. All four were feeling the effects of the THC now. It was quiet once again. Zeke took a deep breath and let it out slow.

"Pozy, I think we have us a couple o' armpit dwellers. You from the armpit are ya?" Zeke asked.

"What-tha-fuck are you talkin' about…you dense dunce?" the driver asked coldly. That was all Zeke could take. He slid the .38 from his breast pocket effortlessly and the metallic sound of the hammer clicking back was the only sound heard, until a slight sickening moan came from the driver as Zeke drove the barrel against the base of his skull.

"Welcome ta Maine…Motha-fucka,'" Zeke said with a chuckle, and for no apparent reason he could think of, Pozy's reaction was to place the passenger into a full-nelson hold at lightning speed, and he waited to see what would happen next. What came out of Zeke now sounded like the hiss of an evil snake. "Slow…this… hunk o' shit down. Get ready ta turn in when I tell ya. You make one bad twitch of yaw' ea' and I'll blow yaw' fuckin' head off and I'll drive this hunk-o'-shit from back hea'. Got it, Mass-hole?" The driver nodded his head gingerly, yet not a wisecrack came out.

Flashbacks of the night in Biddeford blazed like lightning through Pozy's mind, and there before him was the very gun they'd stolen from the two from Massachusetts. He looked toward his friend and was stunned at the expression his face displayed. It was the look of a madman. His eyes appeared ready to pop from their sockets; and he didn't even look like himself.

"Slow down more," Zeke said again, and this time it came out sounding gruff. It was a long time since he'd taken the road he was looking for. It ran along the edge of a heath and just north of the railroad tracks, the same track line they escaped on from Biddeford to Dells that night. Remote was the only word to describe the location they were about to enter.

"Pull in here," Zeke commanded. Pozy maintained his hold on the passenger, and several times for effect, but not hard enough to cause real damage, he pounded the guy's head into the dashboard, rousing a fit of laughter from Zeke. Although Pozy entertained his friend with this brutality, he did so in a manner to protect himself from Zeke going wild and completely out of control. He would not challenge him now for fear of his own safety. When it came down to it, these two didn't matter shit to him. If he only knew what was coming...

The darkness appeared to swallow them alive through the thick vegetation on both sides of the rough gravel road that bounced them from side to side, while the dashboard lights offered a warm glow on the foreheads of the two up front, giving the purple tint of Mohawk a fluorescent sheen. It seemed a long way in now, farther than Zeke remembered. He thought the road ended not far from where they were, in a type of turn-around circle, and then there it was just ahead. At this point, the road opened with the clearing of the expanse of heath on the right and a thick growth of low standing fir trees on the left. The area had obviously been cut over several years ago, giving the new growth a stunted appearance. Zeke ordered the driver to circle wide and have the car face in the direction they'd come from. The barrel of the gun created a sore spot on the driver's upper neck where it was planted, and Zeke pushed it harder to make his point. The vehicle came to a slow stop.

"Shut the motor off," Zeke ordered. The sudden silence encapsulated them in their steel cocoon; however, being in an older model car, the lights remained on after the motor was off, illuminating the road ahead of them and offering an eerie sense to the vision.

"Well...ain't this nice and quiet back hea'?" Zeke asked. He expected some smart-ass response from either one in front, yet their silence offered him the taste of dominance he yearned for.

"Now boys, we're gonna' get out o' the caar'...nice and slow. Mohawk-boy here, is goin' first when I say go and remember, fuck-face, you twitch an ea'...I blow yaw' fuckin' head off...ok?" Again the driver gave no verbal response; he simply nodded his head in agreement.

"Pozy, you hold on to the little cock with no hair and I'll tell ya when to get him out and check his pockets for anything that might hurt you and me...ok?" Pozy just nodded his head once, but remained silent. "Ok, stick yaw' arms out the window and don't move," Zeke ordered the driver. When his arms stretched out, Zeke kicked the rear door open and jumped out, sticking the gun barrel between the driver's eyes, ordering him out to kneel before him. He did as he was told. Zeke backed away several steps.

"Ok…Pozy…get out and grab that little pig by the eas' and bring 'im hea.'" Again, the scene in Biddeford flashed before Pozy's eyes, as this was almost a complete reenactment of the same events. With both the driver and passenger on their knees, Zeke ordered Pozy to frisk them and to take anything and everything out of their pockets and place it on the hood of the car. He positioned them so that they were illuminated by the headlights, and Pozy as well, but only when he frisked them. The driver had a wallet; it was empty, and each had pocket knives with small blades, cigarettes and lighters, and the passenger had a wad of folded cash. Neither had any jewelry, except for the driver, who had a cheap-looking gold ring in his left ear.

"Well, you Mass-holes travel light," Zeke said, trying to mimic their obvious, Bostonian accent.

Now, for the first time since the barrel was jammed to the base of his skull, the driver spoke. "So…you're a small-time hood; robbin' people with yaw' big gun? You got the money, now what, farmer-boy?" he asked.

Zeke ignored him and simply asked Pozy if he'd gotten everything off them. Pozy said, "Yah."

Zeke turned and slapped the driver hard alongside his head, sending him toppling over, face-down onto the gravel. Without realizing it, Pozy stuffed the folded cash into his pocket.

"Good, now Pozy, get in the caar' and clean it out. I want everything checked…" He suddenly stopped speaking and said, "Shut up everybody," as he turned a trained ear toward the distant road with an attention-to-detail-look on his face. It was as if even the surrounding wildlife obeyed his command. The entire area became void of any sound. It felt as if the woods themselves closed in around them, screening them from the world outside. Zeke stood for several moments looking intently down the road, yet not a sound came from that direction. When he was comfortable that they were alone, he ordered Pozy to continue his assignment.

While Pozy was rummaging through the car, Zeke taunted the two, who now lay on their stomachs, arms stretched out over their heads and legs crossed. Again, flashbacks of that night in Biddeford haunted Pozy and he continued to convince himself that Zeke would beat the shit out of them, rob them, and then they'd make their way to the railroad tracks and their escape, unknown and undetected. That thought and the fact that Zeke was waving a gun around in everyone's face this time, allowed him to continue ransacking the car with little or no guilt. Then Zeke began beating the driver, because he'd been sarcastic. As he lay defenseless, Zeke kicked him squarely in the ribs with his heavy work boot, and from where he stood next to the car, several feet away, Pozy swore he heard a rib crack.

The Mohawk contorted in pain, only to be kicked again, this time in the legs, and ordered back to his outstretched position.

"There ain't nothin in hea'," Pozy hollered from the interior of the car, evoking a ruffled, angry look from Zeke, and he kicked the baldheaded passenger in the legs.

"Take the key and open the trunk…look in thea'", Zeke snarled and after that order, despite their pain, the two men on the ground looked toward each other in utter disgust, their looks going unnoticed by Zeke or Pozy. All that could be heard, as silence ruled supreme over the entire area, was the sound of gravel crunching under the soles of Pozy's shoes as he went from the driver's compartment to the trunk lid.

Suddenly, a chilling breeze blew across the heath, sending visible shivers into the two lying on the ground who were in light clothing; their injuries appeared compounded by the cold air.

"You can't make us lay here all night. I think you broke my ribs. Let me get up to at least piss," the driver complained.

"Piss yaw' pants…Mass-hole. You get up and I'll beat yaw' brains in if ya got any," Zeke growled. Both men on the ground looked toward each other once again, and this time it was frustration that permeated their expressions. From the rear of the car, Pozy hollered.

"Well, well…will ya look hea'. We got us the jackpot, Zeke-boy. Come look and see," he said.

"I ain't leavin' these two fa' one minute. Whatcha' find?"

"Guns and dope, Zeke-boy. Looks ta me like we got us a couple o' big…city…deala's."

Zeke was grinning from ear to ear. *Financed for the rest o' the year, maybe,* he thought.

"Farmer-shit, he called my smoke. You little punks had all that in the trunk and you call my smoke farmer-shit?" He went directly to the driver, who he'd named the Mohawk in his head. The Mohawk was already face-down, but since his legs were not crossed as originally ordered, Zeke kicked him squarely in the groin, causing an instant blackout and unconsciousness. With one out of the way for a minute, Zeke forced the passenger, who he thought of as Baldy, to get up and go to the trunk area of the car with him. He wanted to see for himself what treasure Pozy'd uncovered. Pozy was still gawking into the trunk when Zeke pushed the guy up against the rear fender, both looking in at the same instant. Zeke's eyes nearly exploded with delight at the vision before him.

Indeed… it was a treasure, for anyone who partook of that type of habit. The thought of having to get rid of it never crossed his mind. With all this lying out before him, a thousand things ran through Pozy's mind: the biggest right now was the fact that his fingerprints were all over this car. Zeke had yet to come near it until now, outside of being in the back seat when they were picked up. This was bigger than the both of them, and not knowing what Zeke's plan actually was, and where his mental state was going, he couldn't be sure of anything right now.

"How cool is this…Pozy-boy? What we have here is winter-long payola. We can stay at the camp or the garage forever now." He went on and on like a dreamer without a clue. He leaned against Baldy, asking question after question, and the guy, with his friend still unconscious, spilled his guts willingly. They were from some town off I-495 in Massachusetts, somewhere neither

Zeke nor Pozy had ever heard of, but Zeke smiled and simply said, "Armpit." They came to Maine regularly, taking all the back roads to somewhere mid-coast, he said.

The Mohawk was obviously driving the car for a reason. This kid was the pounded spike everyone heard of. He didn't know nothin', Zeke thought.

"So…some Maina's buyin' all this shit right hea'? I'll be goddamned. Well, looks like someone from Maine's gonna end up with it after all, but fa' free," Zeke said with a laugh. Pozy had remained quiet as long as he could.

"Zeke…what aar' we gonna do, walk out o' hea with this shit on our backs? We ain't gonna walk the road with this shit. And… what about these two, we gonna let 'em drive outta hea' knowin' who took it?" And he was immediately sorry he said it.

The drugs were in two large duffle bags and there were two sawed-off shotguns. Zeke stared at the trunk's contents for several minutes, disturbed from thought now by the moaning from the Mohawk who was obviously coming around and in much pain. He motioned for the two to follow and when they arrived at the Mohawk, he kicked the legs out from under Baldy, knocking him on top of his partner. Now, Zeke turned his head toward Pozy, with a look that resembled insanity and said, "Get the shit out o' that trunk and let me think."

Hesitating slightly, Pozy returned to the trunk area and did as he was told, placing one shotgun on the top of each duffle bag lying flat on the ground. To eliminate any chastisement later, though he would not stand for any physical abuse from Zeke, he looked deep into the trunk area and even into the spare tire compartment, making sure the trunk was completely empty, then leaving the trunk lid open, he rejoined the three at the front of the car, still under the glow of the headlights. When the Mohawk regained consciousness, about the same time of Pozy's arrival, it appeared that his sense of sarcasm was recharged and he began an immediate, verbal assault against Zeke.

"You… punk-ass farm-boy. You give me one minute…I'll kick yaw' scrawny ass into that swamp. Big man with a gun. Let's see what you can do with your farm-boy fists."

Zeke couldn't believe the nuts this kid had. He continued to stare down in his direction for several seconds, and without saying a word in response or taking any type of aim, he shot him in the pelvis area. The shot cracked through the stillness of the night, reverberating across the soundless heath. Pozy's ears rang from the report and he stood, unmoving, in disbelief, beginning to shake now that he saw Zeke had gone over the edge. Once again, the Mohawk fell still as death, physically contorted in a heap on the ground beside his partner, blood flowing freely from the wound along his beltline. Baldy went into shock, motionless and staring into an oblivion that only he could know.

"What-tha'-fuck?" Pozy asked, then went speechless, staring at his old friend, who he no longer knew. He moved cautiously toward the Mohawk, never taking his eyes off Zeke, who seemed paralyzed to the spot, the .38 smoking slightly from the barrel, still pointing at the victim of the single shot. He wanted to tell him to lower the gun, but for his own safety he remained quiet, keeping a steady eye on Zeke and the weapon.

A lucid evil appeared to cloak the entire area in its spell. Pozy could find no answer to make sense of this bizarre scene. Pozy reached out to the Mohawk in an attempt to find a smidgen of life, and a smidgen is exactly what he found. The wise-cracking Mohawk was beaten, bloody and very near death. It was then that Zeke lowered the gun and returned to his brutal stance.

"Is he dead?" he asked.

"No, but he ain't far from it."

"Here then…cut 'em." And he reached out with his knife for Pozy to take it, yet Pozy remained next to the Mohawk, incapable of speaking or moving. Baldy remained in his trance.

This is all just a bad dream, Pozy thought. *I'm gonna' wake up soon and all this was a bad dream.* But, when he looked down at the Mohawk, the blood had stopped flowing from the wound, and he remembered when deer hunting with his father all those years ago that when the blood stopped flowing, the deer was dead. He couldn't take his eyes from the guy's face.

It had gone into a vacant stare, one eye partially open. Suddenly, he was being pushed to one side. "Get outta the fuckin' way! When I tell ya to motha-fuckin' cut 'em, I mean, motha-fuckin' cut 'em," Zeke snarled, and he proceeded to carve something in the Mohawk's forehead. A sudden urge to vomit took Pozy in the guts, but he just dry-heaved and moved farther away from the dead guy. Through all of this, Baldy never moved. His trance-like state appeared to paralyze him, like a deer in the headlights or the lamb awaiting slaughter.

"Help me with this stiff!" Zeke ordered. When Pozy looked down, the word "holes" was carved in his forehead. Very little blood except for a trickle flowed and the slits looked like when his mother cut slits in chicken parts so they'd cook evenly—exposing the uncooked flesh under the skin.

"What?" he asked.

"Help me with this stiff," Zeke ordered once again in a loud voice.

Unwillingly, but fearing for his own life, Pozy did as he was told, and they lifted the Mohawk, carried him to the driver's side, and sat him behind the wheel, his head flopping coldly against the headrest. Under the dome's dim light, his skin seemed to be changing color and he'd obviously needed to piss when he asked Zeke because now, the entire front of his pants were soaked with urine. Pozy wiped his hands on his jeans and remained speechless.

"Find somethin' ta wipe the fingerprints off this caar'. The last thing we need, right?" Zeke said. And like a robot, Pozy obeyed. In disbelief that there was a dead man in the driver's seat and refusing to look at him, he went around to the other side of the car and searched under that seat, finding a greasy, smeared shop rag and began rubbing the car, mentally detached from his surroundings, in all the places he thought he or Zeke had touched. He heard a muffled discussion between Zeke and Baldy, but he couldn't make out what was said, nor did he look up from his task, until Baldy screamed at the top of his lungs and then another, thundering shot rang out and all was silent once again.

When he finally did look up, he shook like he was in an ice

storm without a coat. Zeke was standing, legs apart, over the guy, who was in a prone position. The back of his head appeared to be gone, and when Zeke turned toward Pozy, even he was splattered with blood, yet there was an uncanny look of satisfaction on his face that might suggest the assignment was complete. There was no doubt in Pozy's mind of the condition of that poor bastard's head, and that there were two dead bodies now and Zeke had killed them both. He was frozen to the spot until Zeke's commanding voice ordered him to come over. Seconds passed that seemed like an eternity, yet when he finally arrived at the corpse, Zeke was carving something in his forehead as he'd done to the Mohawk. Exactly what, he could not see nor did he attempt to look.

"Get his legs," Zeke ordered, and they carried him to his original place in the passenger seat, and they sat him into an upright position. His head stuck to the headrest—it did not move.

"Did ya get the prints?" Zeke asked. Pozy, numb now from his inability to comprehend what just happened, looked up and came face to face with his friend. Zeke's face was covered with hundreds of tiny droplets of blood, giving him a fiendish look.

"Yah…I did," Pozy managed.

"Then let's get the fuck out a' hea'. Head fa' the tracks and the garage," Zeke said as he grabbed a bag and a gun and left, going directly into the woods next to the car, never looking back.

Pozy wanted to throw up as he looked the entire area over, still wondering what had happened to their fun night in town. He couldn't believe he was even a part of what had happened here.

Zeke's crazy. He's out of his fuckin' mind. He just killed two people and he sucked me into it, he thought.

"C'mon!" Zeke's voice echoed through the still night air. Pozy, without thinking and for no apparent reason, hesitated slightly, then reached for the key he'd left in the trunk, the only thing he hadn't wiped clean, pitching it wildly into the heath. He ran toward the remaining bag and shotgun and moved quickly to meet Zeke and a future he could not know after a night of extreme darkness. It was just about midnight.

"Black…bird fly, into the light of the dark black night."

(Paul McCartney, credited to Lennon-McCartney)

1968

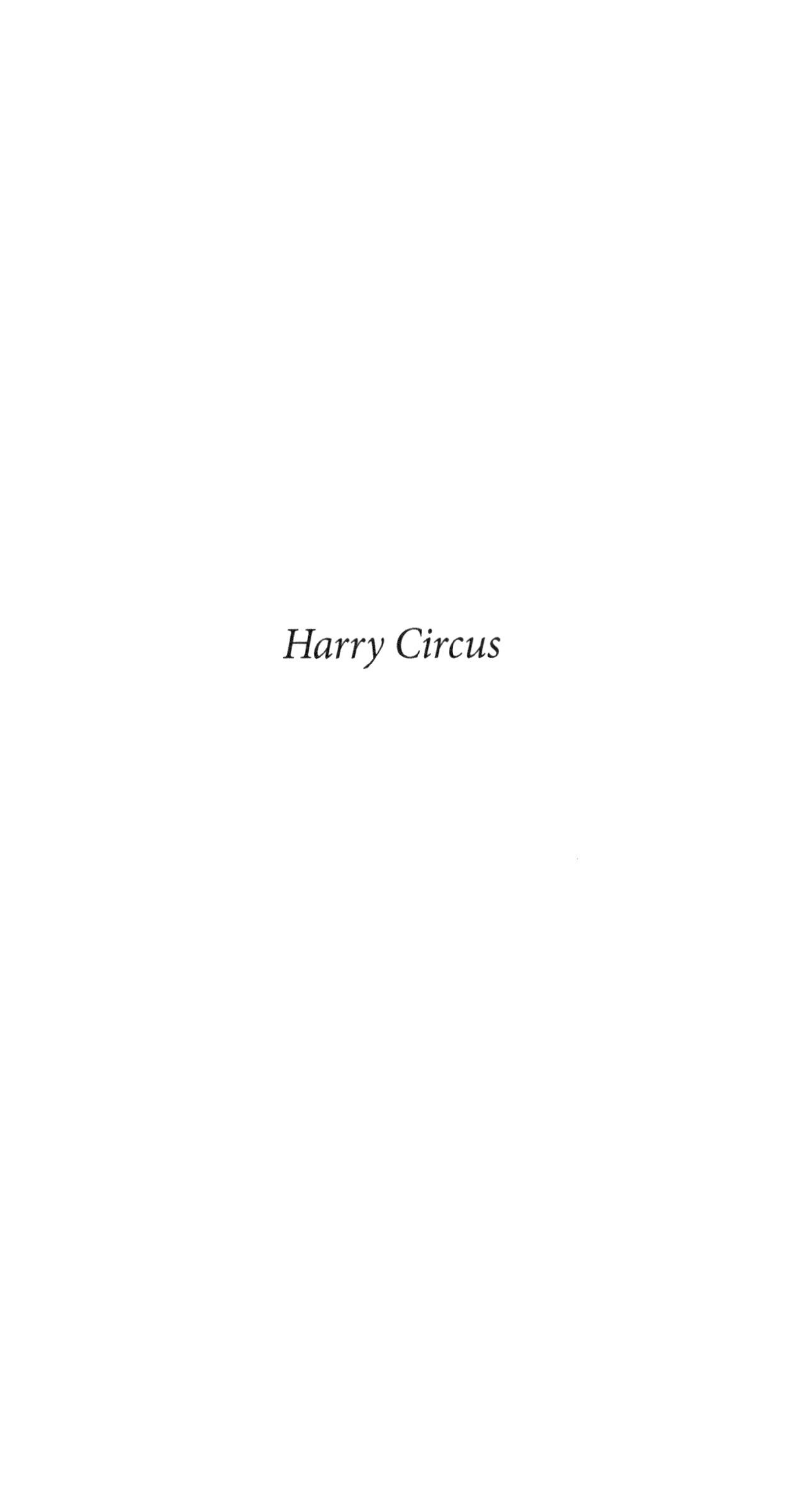

Harry Circus

21

THE EARLY TUESDAY MORNING calm that enveloped the entire heath area was broken suddenly with a shrieking howl from a lone hiker who discovered the bloody remains of the two young men on the dead-end gravel road.

He was unable to immediately dial 911, so it took authorities an hour to respond to the scene. First to arrive was Chief of Police Willard Weaks and Officer Rodney Torrey. Neither man had ever seen anything like this. It was 9:00 a.m.

Following protocol, immediately upon verifying the homicide, Chief Weaks informed the Major Crimes Unit of the Maine State Police of the location and that the individual who discovered the bodies was being detained until they arrived and the scene was secured. The hiker, still unidentified, sat quietly on a fir stump at the far end of the road, about twenty-five yards from the vehicle and the bloody mess that used to be two human beings.

"Be careful, Rodney. From the way that nature-lover looks, there may be some puke around here someplace."

"I'll tell ya, chief...when I first laid eyes on this myself, I had a bit of a gurgle from the midsection," Rodney replied.

"This is a crock o' shit where our department is concerned. Three murders this summer, about a month to the day apart, and we haven't got any more on the first than we did then, and the goddamned leaves haven't even changed colors yet."

Rodney stood silent. *It's unlike the chief to lose his sense of empathy for a situation of this type, but being this close to his retirement and with his impeccable record, it has to be difficult for him,* he thought.

Both men stood in front of the grill looking in at the corpses. Without speaking of it, their focus was on the same thing: the carvings in each man's forehead. The way the bodies were placed, anyone looking in through the windshield at them saw the carvings, which read from left to right or passenger to driver, MASS HOLE

Rodney looked down at the license plate...Massachusetts. He glanced around the plate, then the windshield, and found that all the stickers were legal.

"Do you think this was some kind of...out-of-state hit, chief?" Rodney asked.

"Well...it is awful brutal. Those folks down there are... nuts... as we already know from the way they drive up here on vacation, but this...it's beyond me. I'm not really sure where to start. I don't want to get into something where it causes any trouble for the staties, you know. They'll want to see and touch everything. Why don't we start with a statement from the hiker over there? I'm sure he'd like ta get outta hea."

"Yah, ok, I'll talk to him." And Rodney walked toward the guy, who hadn't moved from the spot since they arrived. As he got closer, it was apparent that he did much of his shopping at either L. L. Bean or the Kittery Trading Post. He was outfitted in what appeared to be top-shelf outdoor clothing. As he neared, the man stood up, but remained where he was.

He looks like a hiker, Rodney thought. His fashionable brown hiking boots matched his British Khaki Cargo pants with a matching dark-brown belt. The Alpine green canvas shirt was a nice way to offset the browns. The closer Rodney got, the more he saw how pale the hiker's complexion was, and it was no wonder that he looked sick. After finding what he'd found, it was a marvel there wasn't puke all over the place as the chief suggested.

"Good morning." Rodney immediately wondered if that was

the wrong thing to say. "I'm Officer Rodney Torrey from the Dells Police Department. How are you holding up?" There was a momentary pause and when the hiker began speaking, it was obvious to Rodney that he'd been very much affected by what he'd found. He spoke slowly, with carefully chosen words, but not about the murder scene. He explained that he was an amateur naturalist, privately studying heaths and peat bogs throughout the state. He had just crossed this heath, taking samples of low shrubs, when he noticed the car at the end of the road. Rodney wrote everything down.

"I'm very familiar with this area, and I found it a bit uncommon to see someone out here as many times as I've come out. As I got close to the car, I slowed down when I noticed the two just sitting there, but after a couple of minutes… and I was in a position that they should have seen me, I though it weird and so…I decided to take a closer look…" he began to retch, and Rodney, believing he might hurl, took several steps back, but as it was, nothing happened and the guy simply apologized.

"Are ya gonna make it"? Rodney asked, but it didn't come out sounding like a wise-guy remark, and the question got no response.

"I'd like to ask you a couple of questions if you're up to it, and then you can probably get on your way. I'm sure you'd like to right now." He never bothered to tell him that the State Police would soon arrive and they'd have their own questions for him. Again, the hiker didn't reply, he simply looked at the officer with a faraway look, demonstrative of someone preparing to be questioned.

"Sorry…I should have shared more with you from the very start. My name is Randolph Quirk. I'm from Bangor and I'm retired. I do this for relaxation." At that point, Rodney queried him on some specifics about Bangor, not that he didn't believe him as much as he needed to take a trip back in time to his college days at the University of Maine, Orono. Bangor was the playground for the young, energetic colligates celebrating victorious mid-term scores.

Rodney looked away briefly from the guy who went on about

things in Bangor and looked toward the chief. He was walking around the perimeter of the police line, eight to ten feet out from the car, jotting notes into a pad he held out in front of him. And out of nowhere, the thought of Zeke flashed into Rodney's consciousness. *A shot in the dark…black leather… the sight of his parents standing on their porch…* He looked back at the naturalist; he was staring at Rodney, probably wondering who might be more affected by this scene.

"I'm sorry," Rodney said. "I've got a hundred things on my mind right now and I'm sure you'd like to get out of here."

"Ya, but if I can help, in any way, I don't mind staying a while longer..." Rodney interrupted him, knowing very well that the sound of approaching vehicles down the gravel was the State Police Major Crime Unit. They would have their own questions for him.

"Look…," Rodney said. "You might want to hang in here for a while. The State Police are coming in now and I'm sure they'll have questions for you." In a murder investigation, the on-scene authority lies with the State Police and it would do Rodney no good to further the questioning of this man.

"No problem," he responded and sat down on the stump and waited. Rodney returned to the car as the trooper vehicles, in what resembled a caravan, blocked the entire area except for a narrow passage along the woods line for any in-and-out traffic like the Medical Examiner and the local undertaker.

Rodney held back and let the chief move toward the first of the investigators to approach the scene. From the chief's arm and hand motions, he tended to give his feelings for the findings up far too easily than Rodney would in most cases, but it was apparent that the chief was not happy and he'd be willing to tell anyone at this point. The two men walked toward the car and the victims inside, followed closely now by a team of State Policemen in blue coveralls carrying items that would hopefully uncover evidence that would lead them to a murderer or murderers still at large. Dells, Maine had become a killing zone, and for no apparent reason other than petty thievery. And who were these two from

Massachusetts? Why did they come here to die on this lonely, dead-end gravel road?

Suddenly, the face of the first victim from Connecticut flashed into Rodney's thoughts. His mind's eye saw Lillian Crandlemyer's facial expressions in the hospital. He remembered telling her that he would call her in a month or so, hoping she'd visit Maine and see him. Now, with a second and third homicide in town, who in their right mind would want to visit after hearing this? He looked back at the man on the stump. He cradled his head in his palms and he hadn't moved an inch that Rodney could tell since he'd left him. He looked back to the car and was being summoned by the chief to come over. The State Police were busy at their task. "Rodney, look at this. These two in the car have sneakers on. Now, look here. These are work-boot prints. We find the foot wearing these and we may find our little bastard with a gun. I'm going to head out of here shortly. Do mind hanging out for a little while longer?"

"Sure, no problem," Rodney said.

Very shortly after the chief left, as if they'd coordinated their arrival, the State Medical Examiner's vehicle pulled to a stop alongside the victim' cars, and the local funeral director pulled in with two large SUV-type vehicles behind him to transport the bodies.

Rodney watched intently as the pros from the MCU went about their assignment, most of the time never speaking to each other. One examined the interior of the car, another dusted for prints, while still another took photographs of everything imaginable. Rodney watched as one approached the man who had brought them all together at this horrific scene and wondered if his questions would be of the same content as the ones he'd never had time to ask himself. At this distance, all he saw were slightly moving lips.

Rodney suddenly became fidgety. Several hours had passed since his arrival with the chief and his place here was simply symbolic, now that the State Police were on scene. There was no longer anything for him to do, realistically. His thoughts ran wild on aspects of the still-unsolved murder of the young man from Connecticut. He flipped back through his notes. Lillian Crandlemyer flashed into his memory. He wanted to see her again. The attraction was still warm and he wondered why he hadn't been more aggressive with his approach, when suddenly, he thought...*Monday... I spoke to Zeke's parents just last night. This is weird. Tuesday...we come out here and find this. We can't be more than six or seven miles from their place right here.*

He looked toward the trooper and Randolph Quirk. It appeared that they were finishing up, as the guy was pointing across the expanse of the heath, obviously in the direction he'd come when finding this. It seemed as though the trooper might be offering something, yet he refused and began walking over the spongy, soft surface of heath, away from the crime scene. He never looked back after leaving. As perceptive as Rodney was, he could never imagine where this guy's head was right now.

After several hours of crime scene investigation the troopers met in a huddle, probably considering whether they'd arrived at a mutual finding of facts; several minutes had passed when one motioned to the funeral director. The Medical Examiner had long since gone, perhaps back to Augusta and most likely an already-waiting corpse and a scheduled autopsy, and the two bodies here would arrive in Augusta in a couple of hours. From the huddle, Rodney was summoned by the investigator in charge and was told that their work was complete, someone would contact his department with whatever findings they needed to share, and Rodney could call a local towing service who would deliver the car to the crime lab in Augusta.

Within minutes, the first of the black SUV's pulled forward after loading the first of the two victims. Rodney looked to the dial pad of his phone, speed-dialed the tow service and when he looked up, the second SUV had started moving, and together they pulled away from the scene in a solemn procession. One by one, the official vehicles pulled away, allowing a strange quiet to wrap itself around the entire area, leaving Rodney standing alone in an emotional body bag of his own. The police tape that he and the chief had strung out upon their arrival swayed slightly in a breeze blowing in from the coast. He began to remove the tape, anticipating the tow truck that he hoped would come soon. His mind sped his thoughts in one direction, then another.

The first murder victim's facial expression. Lillian Crandlemyer. The carvings in the foreheads. Lillian Crandlemyer. The Brailey's on their porch, just last night. Zeke. Lillian Crandlemyer.

He shook his head as if to clear his thoughts when the sound of the approaching diesel laboring its way toward him reassured his own departure soon. This part of the mess was done, but his work was just beginning, though he could never imagine where the next couple of weeks would take him.

22

A State Police spokesperson, flanked by Police Chief Willard Weaks and Officer Rodney Torrey, offered a question-and-answer period for the TV viewing public at the rear entrance to the Dells Police Department. Standing alone in the background was a slender-looking gentleman who remained observantly quiet throughout the proceedings. He would soon be introduced to Rodney Torrey, but neither man could know that now.

Occasionally, simply for not recognizing him, Rodney focused his attention on the stranger standing at the rear of the congregated lawmen. From where he stood, Rodney figured him to be of his own height, six-foot one inch, more slender and probably much older, from the slightly graying temples and the scruffy facial hair, most likely several days' growth. His camo' pullover looked well worn, yet his appearance was not of a dumpy, woodsman type. His black jeans fit his contours; they looked clean and even pressed.

A look of intensity however, overshadowed his appearance and for whatever reason, it was as if he never noticed that Rodney was staring at him. What Officer Torrey would soon find out was that he was being watched by a pro, never offering an inkling of being watched by the officer.

The rapidly pitched questions from the sensationalism-driven media hungry for a scoop were giving some authority figures an obvious headache from the look on their faces, yet they persevered toward a rapidly approaching conclusion of the gathering.

Much to his surprise, when Rodney looked back toward the stranger, he was gone. Without giving any thought to his own appearance, he swiveled his head like a schoolboy who had lost track of something that caught his eye, and when he returned his stare forward to the gathered press, the stranger, with a smiling, "gotcha" look on his face, had mingled with those gathered, staring up at Rodney.

Who in hell is this clown? Rodney wondered.

Suddenly, the State Police official who began the conference brought it to an abrupt end, stating that no further information was available and as the investigation progressed, the authorities would bring the public and the media up to date. A few hectically pitched questions were asked of the group.

"What about the victims, do you have their names?" one reporter hollered out.

"Can you tell us more about the location?" another asked, but no one ventured another response, as the group of policemen moved quickly from the makeshift podium prepared for them by the Dells Public Works Department.

As the police officials re-entered through the rear door, Rodney made it a point to observe everyone entering, yet the one person he looked for was nowhere to be found. Looking for the chief, he realized he'd pulled a disappearing act of his own. Rodney positioned himself near the still-gathered State Police officials in the hallway, listening for any tidbit that might stir his memory, but this was not a gathering to share information. It was just what it was supposed to be…a press conference to update the population on the most recent murder investigation of two young men from Massachusetts.

It was obvious that the officials were pleased that none of the press ventured to ask questions about the still-unsolved murder of the young man from Connecticut less than a month ago. Several minutes passed, one by one the State Police left, and peering out of the rear door, Rodney found an empty parking lot with only the town's police cars and one parked next to the chief's that he'd never seen before. It looked to be a circa 1965 Ford Galaxie 500. He didn't give much thought to the strange car; the dispatcher at times drove different family member's vehicles, so he decided to drop in on the chief, hopefully to get his take on the conference.

He made his way through the maze of walkways that would ultimately deposit him at the chief's office and as he approached, he overheard the distinct sound of two different voices. He recognized the chief's immediately, but the other he did not know. The chief insisted on having an informal policy with his officers. "No need to knock," was his motto and so, Rodney entered without announcement and came face to face with the man he'd thought of as a clown only minutes earlier.

"Rodney," the chief said. "I'm glad you decided to stop in. I want you to meet a very special friend of mine, retired State Trooper, Harry Circus."

—

When they finally arrived at the garage several hours after the murders, there wasn't a paragraph of conversation that passed between Zeke and Pozy, outside of perhaps warning each other of passersby or an oncoming vehicle in one direction or the other. Pozy remained quiet for fear of his life at the hands of a madman who used to be his closest buddy. Zeke was silent because he was completely dissatisfied with Pozy for everything he did or didn't do.

"The garage," Zeke said, "will be the perfect place ta stash the duffle bags and guns." He ordered Pozy to lock the garage doors, something they never did, after he took a sample from each bag. They only stayed a couple of hours to rest, and returned to the camp that very night, but in a direction that avoided Sandown and the local cop there. With all his directions and orders to Pozy, Zeke neglected to remember the wad of cash Pozy had taken from Baldy. He still had it, but had never stopped to count what they had. Before they left and much to Pozy's bewilderment, Zeke opened the cage and freed the Black Racer. "There ain't gonna be no one ta feed ya. Now get the fuck outta hea,"' Zeke said. The snake slithered into the darkness.

—

The news of the two murders spread through the media and also the surrounding coastal towns like a lightning storm along the coast in August. Missy, Marcy, Petey and Dwight sat at the counter of the Little Roady discussing the way things had fallen apart this summer in the little town of Dells, Maine.

"Ya know…it seems funny that through all this shit… that low-down ass-bucket Zeke has been nowhere to be found," Marcy said.

"What's that supposed to mean?" Missy asked.

Petey and Dwight placed their coffee cups down on the counter top and waited for the family duel to start, knowing very well how Missy felt about Zeke, but the very opposite became true.

"Neva', mind," Missy said. "He is an ass-bucket."

It had been some time since Dwight had made an appearance with his older friends, never realizing how Zeke had disappeared from the group, and now it seemed that Pozy had joined him in his disappearing act, but no one was sure of what was going on with the two of them. Petey returned to the garage several times only to find it deserted, without a trace of anyone having been there for quite some time. Missy, on the other hand, being burned as often as she had, was reluctant to share her true feelings with her mother and especially with Petey, whom she knew had always had feelings for her. His body language gave him away. And Dwight, he was just a kid in her eyes, though she kept a warm place for him in her heart.

—

Rodney moved slowly toward the retired trooper, because he didn't know him, and extended his hand for a shake. In his mind, all he saw was the little clown who'd pulled the disappearing act on him less than thirty minutes ago and here he sat now, across from the chief in his office.

"Rodney Torrey, nice to meet you," he said.

"Harry Circus, likewise, I'm sure."

"Rodney…Harry was a trooper Down East before retiring to the southern coast, here…at Kittery Point." He looked toward the trooper. Harry simply smiled back at the chief, nodding his head once, but saying nothing.

"What brought you to our little press conference?" Rodney asked, and it came out sounding a bit smug, yet the chief and Harry let it go unnoticed. The chief spoke first.

"Actually, Rod, I asked him to come when we set the conference time."

"Huh," is all Rodney offered with a heavy exhalation of breath.

Without saying a word, the ex-trooper felt a slight agitation in the officer's tone, thinking back to his theatrics earlier—that it may have gotten him off on the wrong foot with the younger officer.

"Rodney…ok if I call you by your first name?" Harry asked.

"Sure… no problem."

"Rodney, I'd like to apologize for my odd display earlier."

The chief had no way of knowing what in hell he was talking about, and Harry continued.

"I've been on my own ever since I retired several years ago and sometimes I just get a little lightheaded when in the company of troopers and lawmen in general while they do their thing. Sorry if I pissed you off. I was just goofin'," he said.

Again, Rodney said, "Sure…no problem."

The chief still appeared confused at the exchange between the two but he remained quiet, hoping for some type of explanation from either. When none came, he continued, motioning for Rodney to take a seat in the remaining chair opposite Harry Circus. Both were facing the chief's desk at a slight angle to each other.

The chief started with, "Ya know, Rodney, Harry was involved in a couple of high-profile murder investigations in Washington County several years ago." At the mention of them, Harry's gut tightened and he went straight-faced. "And, if I may?" He turned toward Harry now, "he did a bang-up job at solving the first of those cases, oh what was that…a love triangle with the banker, right, Harry? With his right-hand man, Constable Ralph Bailey. No one was ever able to find out who killed that little drug dealer, though…" Harry's face became pale white.

Rodney maintained his focus on the Chief's facial expression, catching a brief glimpse of an award plaque through his peripheral vision on the wall behind the Chief, yet he didn't offer a comment as the chief continued speaking. Looking directly at Harry now, he said, "I never got to meet Ralph. What's he up to these days?"

"Not much at all, chief. As you probably already know, he worked alongside my father for many years and so…getting on with birthdays, he decided to spend some time in the out-of-doors. We get together once in a while, but I don't get down that way much."

When Harry told them that the constable worked alongside his father, he assumed that both men knew that his father was the resident trooper before his son Harry was.

This was like old-home week as far as Rodney was concerned, but he couldn't put his finger on why. His gut, however, would not stop telling him to prepare himself for things to come, that hadn't been spoken of as of yet. He was interested in what the chief said about the "high profile investigations," he just wanted to know what this retired trooper was called about. After all, in his own words, the chief had asked him to come, and sooner rather than later he figured he'd find out why. As that thought crossed his mind, he listened to the chief and Harry converse about those investigations that ultimately came to fruition under Harry's command.

That's all well and good, Rodney thought, *but this investigation is under the Dells Police Department's jurisdiction and the Maine State Police. These two today and Lillian's boyfriend…* He looked toward the chief; and it was as if his lips moved without sound. It was the same for Harry when he looked at him. Rodney's mind was on that path that led to the ocean and that dead-end gravel road.

Suddenly he was jarred back to the reality of the moment by the infernal ringing of his cell phone. He pulled it out and flipped it open. "Hello…Rodney Torrey here." His eyes nearly popped from their sockets at the sound of the caller's voice.

"Hi…It's Lil Crandlemyer."

23

SEPTEMBER 1ST. All seemed lost to those who relied on tourist dollars to survive. Those that had made enough were already making their snow-bird plans for winter. The Dells Police Department could not leave for winter. It remained locked into an investigation that at times seemed hopeless, except for the soon-to-be-revealed investigative gift of a motivated and inspirational thinker: Harry Circus.

He was extremely reluctant to get involved in a murder investigation, and he made that point very clear during the meeting, but as the meeting progressed, it became clear to Harry that the Chief had invited him to be there for a very specific reason. But he hoped it would just all go away. Willard Weaks, however, had an extremely persuasive manner about him that made it difficult to say no to an almost impossible task while sitting in front of him in his office. Rodney on the other hand wanted nothing to do with it. He did not make his opinion known, and the last thing he needed was the chief badgering him now, knowing very well the chief's disposition regarding the cases. What Rodney had on his mind was Lil Crandlemyer. He excused himself, going out in the hallway to take the call. Had someone taken his blood pressure then, it would have been through the roof.

"Wow…you may not believe this, but I was just thinking about you." Rodney neglected to tell her that it was because he was thinking about her late boyfriend and the two most recent victims on that lonely gravel road.

"I'm sure you were," she said, and Rodney thought it sounded like she was snickering.

"Well, I was. And the reason being I never called you when I said I would. I'm sorry about that," he said.

"You don't have to worry about that. I've been very busy with counseling. I..." She stopped suddenly. Rodney was thrilled that she had gone to see a counselor. There are some things that no one should try to handle alone, and the murder of someone close is one of them.

"I'm glad you did," Rodney said. "How are you doing?"

"I'm doing well, thank you. It's going to take some time. I'm sure you know how it all works, being the police and all. I'm sure you see this all of the time."

If she only knew what he was thinking right now. This job didn't get any easier with time. He handled it better now than when he started, but as time went on, he wondered if he shouldn't seek some kind of counseling himself.

"Well, on a lighter side," she said, "I really thought you might have forgotten about our last conversation." Rodney's stomach began to flutter with the rise of butterflies. "I wonder if that invitation to come up for a short visit was still open..." she said, and the receiver went silent.

"Hello," Rodney said.

"I'm sorry; you must think I'm pretty forward inviting myself up like this. I..."

He interrupted her. "Not at all," he said. "I actually wondered the same thing...you know...if you'd forgotten about me and Maine. I..." he went silent as she interrupted him.

"No, I couldn't forget you. You were so kind at that time when I needed kindness the most. No, I didn't forget."

Rodney's heart fluttered at the sound of her voice this close to his ear. He was lifted out of a near-depression caused by the conversation in the chief's office minutes ago, with the nightmare of the unsolved murders and the gore that emotionally affected all of them. They talked and talked of things that neither knew from where they stemmed, and Rodney actually lost track of time as he weaved his way through the maze of hallways in the bowels of the Department, walking and talking, finally finding himself at the farthest end of the building from the chief's office, at the rear door. Rodney felt like a schoolboy, smitten by the emotions of love. Although he knew very well that he was much older than Lil, the thought had crossed his mind only once, at the hospital that night in Biddeford.

He was suddenly lighthearted. He stood with his back against the wall; a nervous left foot tapped a rhythm onto the tile floor. His face radiated a glow like a boy seeing his presents under the tree on Christmas morning. His body language spoke volumes, had he been observed by the right person. As his heart soared to new heights, he saw the chief and Harry Circus approach from a corner of the maze. He turned when hearing the distant footsteps, and saw them, deep in conversation, yet their words were still inaudible to Rodney, and they hadn't noticed him leaning against the frame of the rear door. It hit him headlong that the strange car parked next to the chief's belonged to…

"Is everything ok?" Lil asked.

"Oh…yeah, I just saw someone and it distracted me, sorry."

It wasn't as if they'd intended to leave Rodney out of whatever it was they spoke of, they simply nodded at him and made their way out the door as he moved to let them pass.

A chilling air blew in as they left, giving Rodney a sense of urgency for the investigation, though the last thing he wanted to do now was to hang up with Lil. Rodney listened intently as she went on about possible dates she might visit, and while he remained attentive to her, specifically the formation of her words, he focused his visual attention on the two men in the parking lot, deep in conversation, probably on the same subject begun in the chief's office while he was still there.

"So…how does that sound to you, Officer Torrey? One week from this Friday."

"Good, real good," he said. *One week would give me plenty of time on the case,* he thought. And he was pleased with himself for having maintained the attention to her that he had. Now, with a few well-placed compliments and an eagerness to see her in person, Rodney reluctantly ended the conversation on cloud nine. He couldn't wait for her to arrive, but in the same breath, he wanted to be in on the talk between the chief and the retired trooper that appeared to be, from where Rodney stood in the doorway, coming to an end. The cars were parked less than five yards from the door and Rodney, though he did not want to appear anxious, exited quickly and made his approach known to the two men who turned and looked in his direction.

"I'm sorry, but I had to take that call. If I remember correctly, Harry…you were saying something to the effect that you didn't want to get involved in a murder investigation…" He was stopped dead in his tracks by the chief.

"Rodney, what if I told you that Harry would be willing to be a consultant on the case? You know…look at this, maybe look at that, but only if we need him, though. How's that sound to you?" The chief said it knowing very well how his officer hated interference. "I'm sure that every tidbit of info uncovered can only help," the chief offered as an afterthought.

Rodney felt a twinge of bile rise from the pit of his stomach. The last thing he wanted was a retired trooper prying around in what he'd already uncovered on his own, as little as it might be on either case. Both men now looked to Rodney for a response to the chief's comment, yet he appeared to be off on that cloud again, this time on his own. With the chief's comment, there could be no doubt in Rodney's mind where the inner-office conversation had led after his departure and telephone conversation with Lillian. The trooper would get a piece of this investigation as long as the Willard Weaks had anything to do with it, and until he retired, officially, this was his department. He could consult anyone he chose, and he obviously chose retired State Trooper, Harry Circus.

24

THE WEATHER REMAINED DRY and no rain was forecast by the Portland meteorological wise-men. Because of the dry spell, the murder scene remained untouched by Mother Nature, and the fact that Rodney had strung out a police-line tape and barricade at the beginning of the gravel road before leaving yesterday kept the area virgin-like, awaiting his return today. As he arrived, however, it was obvious to him that someone had moved the barricade and entered.

Just past where the tape was, he passed the old Ford he knew now to be Harry's car, and moving farther in, he immediately recognized the camouflaged shirt and black jeans. Harry Circus had arrived before him. At the sight of him, Rodney slowed his cruiser to a crawl, his stare focused on the retired trooper, who as of yet, made no notice of the approaching car. Now, as Rodney came to within several feet of him, Harry, without apparent concern, nodded toward the officer with a look that might suggest, *what took you so long?*

Rodney's jaw muscles bulged under the pressure of his clenched teeth. *All respect where respect is due, but this guy is going to cause me some heartburn,* he thought.

He pulled the cruiser wide along the woods-line so as not to disturb any prints or other evidence that might remain in the gravel, since he wanted to scope that area out today, and from the looks of the manner in which the trooper trod, it was obvious that his intentions were similar. Rodney exited the car but did not slam the door. Instead, he allowed it to come to rest against the jam, simply to silence the door-peep. Both men remained silent—Rodney, for fear of losing his cool in the face of the former trooper for having jumped the gun on this. But the chief's words echoed in his subconscious thought... "*Actually Rod, I asked him to come.*" Those words burned a huge hole in the process he'd planned for the investigation. *And what was he thinking...calling in some retired trooper? I don't care who he is or what he's done...* Right then, in mid-thought, Harry called out to him.

"Rodney...will you have a look at this?" He was pointing toward the ground in the area that the victims' car was parked when they were found. Without a doubt, Rodney was curious, but the last thing he'd do now was to show interest by stepping up his pace on his way to where Harry stood. Harry's stare to the earth was intense. He never blinked that Rodney saw and he appeared to study the dirt as if it was the most interesting thing in the world. Upon his arrival, Rodney looked to the earth and believed he saw what the trooper saw, but exactly what he did not know until Harry spoke up.

"See this print... See how it appears to twist, as if someone pitched a ball or something. Watch my feet over here." And he stepped to one side so as not to disturb the print. He stood as a pitcher on the mound might when getting ready to let the games' fast-ball whip toward the batter. He was right-handed. As he pretended to let it rip, his right foot, placed to the rear of his stride, twisted as he imitated the pitching motion.

"Will ya look at that?" Rodney said. "Your right foot made almost the same mark as that print. What's that all about?" They moved toward the original print, more cautiously this time, careful not to disturb the dirt.

—

At times, Pozy continued to dry-heave when the vision of the two young men in the front seat of that car, bloodied and dead, flashed before him. They couldn't have been much older than he and Zeke, and his mind would not allow him to venture as far as subconsciously picturing himself dead at his age. And then the thought of them faded. Whenever he looked toward Zeke, it seemed he was smoking the stuff they took from the trunk, oblivious to all that had happened. He suddenly wanted to be home, on the farm—the place he hated the most when growing up. Now, it had become his mental refuge from the hysteria that was his life.

Suddenly, September ushered in a chilling breeze from across the pond, slapping him directly in the face: a reminder of the changes to come and a Maine winter which would settle in as cold as death. He knew that Zeke would never allow him to leave, especially to go home.

—

Rodney was impressed at the trooper's acumen for uncovering the footprint and the potential outcome from the subject's posturing. Without sharing the thought, their actions seemed rehearsed as they both looked in the direction of the possible throw, the heath. Rodney's cell phone rang, disturbing their train of thought. "Rodney Torrey here," he answered.

"Rod… It's Willard. We just got a fax from Augusta. Are you ready for this? It's the same gun that was used on the kid from Connecticut."

Rodney was speechless. His mind raced with the thought of Lillian Crandlemyer. *Was her boyfriend part of some out-of-state drug ring or something? Am I getting involved in something I should stay out of?* he wondered.

"Hello…hello… you still there?" The chief hollered into the phone, thinking the cell connection was broken.

"Yeah—I'm here, chief. It just felt like I passed a stone or something after that one. So, my thought on a possible out-o'-state hit wasn't that farfetched. By the way, I'm out here at the scene with Harry right now. I'm sure he'll want to hear this..." He was about to continue and was immediately interrupted by the chief. "Rodney, look...I've got to go. I'll be in touch later or I'll see ya when you get back to the station." Without another word and with the click of the receiver, the chief was gone. After overhearing Rodney's end of the conversation, Harry looked eager to hear whatever it was he'd told the chief Harry would want to hear. Rodney glanced toward Harry as he slid the phone back into its holster.

"I'm not sure what you've been told of the earlier homicide near the beach this summer." Harry appeared to draw a blank. Rodney continued. "Ballistics on the weapon just confirmed that this is the same gun used then. It looks like we have a nut on our hands."

Because he was from Kittery Point, one of the southernmost locations in Maine, the trooper would be hard-pressed not to have heard of the murder at Punquit Beach. He did not, however, know any specifics where the investigation was concerned. Rodney continued. "Ballistics from the first murder confirmed that the gun was used in a holdup and murder in Massachusetts. This gun is getting around," he said. Rodney told the trooper of his finding the hand-grip screw at the scene of the first Dells murder investigation, hoping that the trooper would at least raise an eyebrow, but getting absolutely no response, he concluded with the fact that the lab was only able to confirm that it came from a weapon of the same caliber: a Smith and Wesson .38. At the same instant, they looked down at the footprints in the gravel and again visually traced the possible direction something might be thrown from the spot. Without speaking, they moved to the edge of the soft, mossy bog.

"You know, there's no telling what, if anything was actually thrown from that spot and how far it went. Are you game for a little experiment?" Harry asked.

"Sure—I've got nothing but time," Rodney answered, and he followed the trooper toward his parked car, considerably farther than Rodney remembered. As they walked, each quietly reflecting their own assessment of the phone call from the chief and the fact that for sure now, they knew the same person or persons were involved in both homicides, yet this particular one left no indication of a reason other than hellish brutality. Again, Rodney's mind traveled at the speed of light to every crevasse of these investigations that his memory allowed him to navigate. Harry, on the other hand, felt a tremor from deep within his consciousness as he remembered the vision of Lester Sawyer tied to the drying rack, disemboweled and partially skinned. And Kenny Collins, the small–time drug dealer and wife-abuser from Chesterfield—the case that remained unsolved to this day—flashed before his mind's eye, the last one being the reason he retired.

For the life of him, Rodney could not imagine why Harry had to return to his car, but as they arrived and he opened the trunk lid, it became clear to the officer that Harry Circus came prepared. The trunk was filled with neatly wound coils of rope, heavy black bungee cords with thick, sturdy hooks and tools of every assortment. There were work gloves and a toolbox pushed close to the rear seat that was as large as the trunk was wide, and there was a sawed-off shotgun affixed to the trunk lid. He didn't give that much thought—a retired trooper usually had a concealed firearms permit.

Harry removed one of the coils of rope, hanging it around his shoulder. "This is a hundred-foot coil," he told Rodney. "I figure… if one of us holds fast at the footprint, the other can string it out and follow in the approximate direction something thrown might go, maybe..." Rodney shook his head in the affirmative, but remained silent. The thought was as good as any, and as he'd said earlier, he had nothing but time.

Harry slammed the trunk lid; it echoed through the silence of the woods and heath and as they turned to make their way back toward the prints, Rodney's cell phone rang again.

—

For the second time in as many days, Petey stopped in at the Little Roady, and it appeared that it was for the purpose of just hanging around to talk with Missy. There was a closeness that seemed to bind them now, if only in a strictly platonic way. Petey, however, continued to feel the tug of a physical attraction. Although he could never get up the balls to tell Missy, he'd been having sexually charged dreams of them for quite some time. If what's been said is true, "The eyes are the windows to the soul," his were wide open for love.

Missy never wanted him to pay for his coffee, as they hugged the counter for long periods of time, she drinking as much as him, but he always left a five-dollar bill on the counter when leaving and that more than covered the cost. The reason she liked it when he stopped in was that he always listened to what she had to say. He never interrupted her no matter how long she ranted on or about what. Slowly however, as time passed, she was getting off of her regular subject…Zeke; and Petey couldn't be happier.

"Have you seen Zeke or Pozy around?" she asked.

"No…I haven't. The last time I saw either one was that night we had a few beers at the garage; then Queer-Eye showed up and Zeke vanished." *I told her that a while back, but she probably forgot,* he thought. He knew how it was to be down on something or someone. He'd been there before. Much to his surprise, she went on to something else, never mentioning Zeke again, but there was something in the way she dropped the subject that left a big, empty spot in his wide-open soul.

Just then, a small group entered the Roady, taking up two booths. When he turned to see who they were, he felt a twinge of loneliness when he saw they'd taken the boys' familiar booth by the window. And from the look on Missy's face, the feeling was apparently mutual.

—

"Rodney Torrey here."

"Rod…It's Willard again. Hold on to your hat, big-boy."

Rodney was momentarily taken aback by the chief's comment but he said nothing. "I just got off the phone with the Sandown Chief of Police. He said that one of his officers stopped two individuals on the night of the murders. He considered them vagrant, and when he tried running a description on his computer, they high-tailed it out o' there and gave 'im the slip when he turned the cruiser around." Then he said, "Hold on a second." The earpiece went silent and when Rodney looked up, Harry was already in the area of the footprints. It felt like an eternity before the chief finally came back on. "Rodney…are you still there?"

"I'm here, chief."

"The Medical Examiner just faxed in the approximate time of deaths." He stressed the word, deaths. "Early Monday morning, like just around midnight. It appears they died only minutes apart." And he went silent again. Rodney waited a moment. "And what about the Sandown Chief's call?"

"Oh fa' Christ's sake. Yeah…get this. One o' them was dressed all in black with a leather jacket. That ringing any bells for ya?"

"Just one…thanks, chief. Oh, by the way…did he happen to mention what time that was?"

"Yep…about 9:00 p.m."

Without saying another word, Rodney punched the red button and slid the phone back into its holster. Right now, his full concentration was on what, if anything, had been thrown out onto that heath, and Harry was already stringing out his line. As he walked, a dozen images flashed through his mind's eye. The most prominent was a black leather jacket.

Harry uncoiled the line, while his memory ushered him back to Berryville and the Lester Sawyer murder and then, in the blink of an eye to Chesterfield and Kenny Collins. All of the pieces of the first investigation fell into place. All of the players were right in his face, one might say. He knew most of them personally. He didn't know anyone here except the chief. Suddenly, the need to recoil the rope, get in his car, leave, and never look back was overwhelming. *This is someone else's problem,* he thought, and then he saw the look on Rodney's face as he approached and the thought of leaving passed.

As they came together, both men remained quiet, but it was as if they'd rehearsed their movements. As Harry moved to one end of the rope, the end closest to the footprints, Rodney took up the slack and walked, sliding the line through his hand toward the heath. As the officer moved forward, Harry guided him onward with, "a little to the left," or "No, a little to the right," hopefully following the trajectory path of the supposed object thrown. Several times Harry stopped him in his tracks, replaying his stance and throw, then picking the rope up and re-guiding the officer. They did this until the entire one hundred-feet were out. At that point, Harry told him to lay the rope down, then, Harry walked out and joined him about fifty feet out onto the heath. Each man stepped gingerly, always looking down so as not to disturb or conceal anything that might be waiting to be found. Rodney watched as the trooper made his way toward him and he was taken by the expression of total commitment on Harry's face, giving him, because of his civilian clothes, the undeniable look of a P.I. at work. Thinking back to the meeting in the chief's office, Rodney was less intimidated by Harry's presence, but he was unable to fully let go of his resentment at the chief's invitation for him to assist. He had to admit, however, if only to himself, this footprint-in-the-dirt thing was pretty damned good, and he couldn't help wonder if he'd been able to see it as Harry had.

—

Zeke had hardly eaten anything since their return to camp. Forgetting that Pozy still carried the wad of cash, he never suggested they get a fresh supply of grub from the local store down the road. Pozy finished the beans that remained and now that Zeke had passed into a drug-induced sleep, he counted the cash: two hundred and fifty bucks, all in reasonably small bills of tens, fives and a few ones. He left, knowing very well that if and when Zeke came to before he returned, his only salvation would be a huge grocery bag full of food and a bunch of beer. And that's what he intended to do. Besides, he couldn't slide another bean down his throat for any amount of money or threats, and boiling pond water to drink was old. Fear alone of what Zeke was capable of kept him at the camp, and never once did the thought of turning Zeke in enter Pozy's mind

—

As Harry neared the end of the rope, Rodney filled him in on the chief's call and the Sandown cop's run-in with a couple of vagrants. At that point he told him of his inability to locate Zeke Brailey and that he seemed to be wearing his black leather jacket every time someone got killed. Not knowing who Zeke Brailey was or anything of his past, Harry appeared confused at the officer's report, and at this point, it meant absolutely nothing to him, except that Rodney was extremely concerned in what he said.

"So…you think there's a connection with this guy and the Sandown officer's report and these murders?" Harry asked.

"I'm not sure of that exactly, but he just seems to be at the wrong place at the wrong time, all the time. I'll give you a copy of my notes when we get back to the station, if you'd like to have a look at them," Rodney offered.

"Oh…yah…I would." Harry responded without hesitation. *Yah—I would. Sure, get involved right up to your eyeballs, Harry,* he thought. But he was already involved and he'd known it the minute he spoke with the chief.

—

About an hour after leaving, Pozy returned with a huge paper shopping bag full from the variety store down the road. His heart leapt into his mouth upon entering the camp, as the first thing he saw was the .38 pointing at his head. The look of insanity on Zeke's face was as he'd expected, yet being threatened by the murder weapon, which should have come across as the major concern, had never entered his mind until now.

"Eeeasy, buddy," he stammered. "I just went down ta get us some grub and beer." He reached in and pulled out a frosty cold beer, his hand shaking with nerves.

"Have one," he said.

25

A DEATHLY CHILL RAN DOWN POZY'S SPINE, his shaking arm stretched out offering the cold brew to his friend. Without saying a word, Zeke slid the .38 into the belt line of his jeans like an outlaw might. Besides, who needed a holster for a gun when you had a large breast pocket in your leather jacket? Zeke's stare was intense as he popped the top on the can, and because of Pozy's shaking, the beer foamed, spraying suds into the air around them.

It wouldn't take a huge brain to figure out where Pozy had gone during Zeke's stuporous venture, yet he just had to say something.

"Did anyone…fuckin' see ya?"

"Just the old geezer and his wife…at the variety store."

"They ask ya any questions?"

"No…I've—we've been there a thousand times for just this kinda shit. Why would they ask questions?"

It wasn't good enough for Zeke.

"Did anyone follow ya?"

"No!" Pozy responded, and now he became agitated with being questioned and distrusted with such vigor. *But how else should a criminal who helped to kill two men feel?* he thought.

—

The two lawmen had spent several hours combing through the

low-lying vegetation on the heath, finding nothing that might signify a lead to what was thrown, if anything, outside of a couple of discarded beer cans that, judging from their condition, had been there for some time.

It was Thursday, three days after the murders. Harry sat peacefully on the blue slate patio behind his home at Kittery Point, reading and re-reading Rodney's notes. The property was not extremely close to the ocean, yet when the tide and the direction of the wind was right, the crashing surf on the rocky coastline became a distinct and welcomed avalanche of sound. The house had been built at the base of a slight knoll with southern exposure at the rear where the patio was installed. It was this seclusion that Harry and his wife, Annie sought often from the onslaught of what they both described as the out-of-control fanaticism of an over-medicated southern seacoast society—a lifestyle they'd never known in Washington County. She joined him now with two steaming cups of coffee.

"I thought you could use a break. You've been at this for a while now," she said, handing him the hot brew.

"Ah—thanks, Annie. I sure can use this right now. You know… all week I've been plagued with flashbacks from Chesterfield. It's been a while, but I think this case is bringing all of my shortcomings back into view," he said.

"You really need to rethink this whole…consultant thing if this is the way you're going to deal with this…" He interrupted her, but not in a bold way.

"You're right, Annie. I should be able to put all of that behind me... you know…the Kenny Collins thing and the fact that it's still unsolved."

"And you really have to stop putting yourself down," she said pointedly. "You were an awesome trooper, dedicated to the cause of justice, and besides, I loved you in that blue uniform." Harry rolled his eyes, taking a sip from the steaming cup, and then looked out onto the surrounding privacy of their little sanctuary by the sea.

After a few minutes of quiet he said, "You're right. There's no sense to get my blood pressure up over this. I only agreed to consult, not to lose sleep or anything. You're right," he said again. "I think I'll head back out to that heath after coffee. There's something out there and I should at least put in some time to try and find it." She looked at him from the side of the face but knew better than to add something, like her thoughts. It was her turn to roll her eyes now from him back to their solitude, and she sipped her coffee.

—

Rodney appeared overwhelmed with the tasks laid out before him on his desk. He shifted his vision from his handwritten notes to reading the fax print-outs from the M.E. and other State Police findings from their investigation of the two murders. Occasionally, the name Melvin Nisbet appeared, sending him on a guilt trip, thinking of Lil. He knew, and so did the chief and Harry Circus, that the State Police MCU was in charge of the investigation and they were comfortable knowing they would go the distance in making every effort to find the killers or killer and eventually solve the case, but in their own jurisdiction of Dells, this small town police department could and would conduct their own detective work in any criminal investigation to help matters along. And it was Rodney's intention to do just that.

Today he would be back at the heath for another go at finding whatever might be out there in relation to Harry's suspected throw from those prints in the dirt. As deeply as he immersed himself in the reading, a very vivid impression formed itself in his subconscious of the fact that Lil would be here next Friday, and if everything worked out, for the entire weekend. He made mental plans of places he wanted to take her. A nice restaurant or a lobster pound—there were lots of those around—and maybe just a quiet walk on a deserted beach, which were rare on the southern coast, but some, known to the locals, remained. His desk phone rang.

"Rodney Torrey here."

"Rodney, it's Harry. I was thinking about heading out for the heath. The thought of something waiting to be found is eating away at me," he said. Rodney felt slightly intimidated at the first sound of Harry's voice, but the feeling faded quickly and he was suddenly invigorated by the trooper's determination to be a discerning participant in searching for potential evidence.

"Sure, in fact, I was heading out that way myself, probably within the hour."

"I'd like to meet you there…if you don't mind," Harry said.

"No…not at all. In fact, I was thinking about calling you just before you called." It was not his intention, but considering the possibilities…it sounded good.

"Great," Harry said. "I'll meet you there in about an hour 'n' a half. If that works for you?"

"See you then," Rodney said. They hung up simultaneously. He sat quietly for a moment and couldn't get over the retired trooper's politeness and respect whenever dealing with him or the chief. It was obvious he did not want to overstep his bounds, at least as to where the authority rested.

—

This time it was Pozy who suffered from a confounding restlessness, yet he did well to mask it whenever Zeke was coherent enough to converse in a communicative manner. For the second time since they'd arrived at camp, Zeke complained of hunger pangs but it wouldn't be Pozy this time that would make him something to eat.

"What-a'-ya got ta eat…fuck-face?" Zeke asked in a manner that might suggest he was ready to be the jokester again, but Pozy found no humor in his sudden need for laughter.

"I never thought about it, but I never knew that smokin' that much made a fella go blind. Whateva' we got fa' grub is right up thea' on them shelves," Pozy said as he pointed up toward the food. "Oh...yah," he said. "There's still some beer in the cooler." Since he was so wasted and had slept so much, Zeke never knew that Pozy had gone back to the store for more supplies. Several minutes of silence passed between them, as Zeke ate with a ravenous appetite, and Pozy watched the food and beer being slurped with smacking lips; he now thought the time right to suggest a small excursion away from here.

"Ya know...the last thing we need is to have people start askin' where in hell we might be. We've been layin' low fa' three days now and no one knows how long you've been out hea'. We could make an appearance somewhere," he said to the deaf ears of his friend who continued to devour huge amounts of groceries. "Zeke, are ya hearin' me? I'm startin' ta go stir-crazy hea'. I'll be climbing the friggin' walls if I don't get out-a' hea' soon."

With his mouth full and his words bordering on unintelligible, Zeke sprayed several morsels of food onto the table and said, "Why don't ya jump in the fuckin' pond?"

Pozy knew then there would be no sense in trying to communicate on an understandable level. Zeke was set in his ways and Pozy would not change him, not now anyway. The door to the camp was always open now, so that any sound would carry over the silence and through the open door. They had become masters of distinguishing natural sounds from those distant, man-made ones. Pozy knew that it could only be a matter of time before he would not be able to control his need to leave, no matter what the cost to him or anyone else. As long as Zeke swung that gun around like Billy the Kid, nobody was safe around him.

—

As luck would have it, Harry, arriving from a northerly direction and Rodney in his cruiser approaching from the opposite direction, reached their destination simultaneously. This was the first time that Rodney was glad to see him. What Rodney couldn't make out at this distance was the type of trailer behind the former trooper's car. Rodney pulled in first and, looking through his right side rear-view mirror he saw, tagging along behind Harry, what looked to be some sort of high-intensity lights. They proceeded slowly over the gravel, and having marked the area of the footprints with fluorescent orange paint before leaving from their first visit, they stayed well to each side away from the center where the car and the prints were. Harry, with the trailer, stayed close to the edge of the heath, jackknifing the trailer and stopping within inches of the soft, low-lying vegetation. He got out and went directly to the trailer. It was a mobile light tower with four high-intensity lights, capable of lighting up seven acres. Each light could rotate 360° and the tower was attached to a 6,000-watt generator for powering the lights. Harry looked like a kid with a new toy. He immediately opened the control panel door, looking intently at the directions for use, and never noticed Rodney, who was now standing alongside of him, peering in at the controls. Harry jumped slightly at the sound of his voice. "What are you going to do with this?" Rodney asked. Harry did not answer directly, which caused Rodney to frown, but he remained quiet.

"This…I hope, will give us the brightest opportunity for a reflection off anything that was thrown into this God-forsaken swamp. Besides, I know the manager of the rental place and he owed me one. This is how I'm taking payment."

Harry flipped a couple of switches, illuminating several lights on the control panel and with a push on the start button, the generator sputtered to life with a spasmodic spewing of thick, black smoke from the exhaust. The machine rattled for a moment until it reached its agreeable operating temperature and then the engine smoothed out and began to purr.

"Ya ready?" Harry asked, and without a response, he flipped the switch and daylight took on an entirely new intensity of brilliance.

Wow… Rodney thought, remembering back to his ordeal in searching for and eventually finding the tiny screw from the hand-grip. *That screw would have lit up on that path to the ocean had I known these lights even existed.*

Harry carefully twisted each light for the optimum use of their beams; each light was aimed toward the vegetation. They assessed the lighting as it engulfed the entire area.

"I feel as though I need sunglasses and an SPF 30 before

walking out there," Rodney said jokingly, but either it was ignored or simply went right over the trooper's head as Harry wasn't normally a jokester. Even back in Washington County, as many times as Constable Ralph Bailey offered humor as an anecdote to a serious situation, Harry had remained straight-faced, thrusting himself and anyone involved headlong into his work and the investigation. Nothing had changed. Harry was Harry and always would be. Rodney just didn't know the full extent of it yet.

Without another word spoken from either man, and at the same instant, their heads turned and they looked out on to the expanse of heath before them. Their approach to the search was different this time. As they stepped out, they were almost shoulder to shoulder. This way, their vision was equal going forward and each focused on the area to their own side. As they went out, Harry went left and Rodney went right. They marked the possible trajectory from the footprints to the heath with the fluorescent orange paint, and then set out from the farthest edge of the light beam at the right of the trailer. Harry's idea was to walk a back-and-forth grid to the farthest end of the beam from the gravel and to encompass the distance of a decent arm's-throw from an adult male. It was all they had to go on regarding the theory that something was thrown from the area of the prints.

The back-and-forth went on for an hour. Stiffness in the shoulders and neck began to plague each man, yet neither would admit to it by complaining. For whatever reason, conversation was held to the bare minimum—concentration was…quintessential. At a point about three-quarters through their planned grid, Rodney exhaled a sigh that might indicate frustration, and the second that Harry considered a comment in response, he was silenced by Rodney's explosive and abrupt command. "Stop!"

Both men stopped as if chained to each other, and Rodney pointed toward the vegetation with a look of total determined surprise. Harry remained in his place watching, as Rodney went down on one knee, took a latex glove from his pants pocket and reached slowly, poking his finger through the low bush plants as if trying not to upset anything that might live there. All that could be heard now, had it not been for the wail of the generator, was the wind, blowing softly through the treetops surrounding them.

"Well... Will ya look at this," Rodney said as he pulled a little gold key from the heath and held it up to Harry's smiling face.

26

It was shortly after 1:00 p.m. when Harry pushed the stop button on the generator, bringing the machine to a rattling silence. The afternoon shadows were already engulfing the areas sundrenched only an hour ago. For a second time since the retrieval of the key, Rodney heard the chief's phone access his voice-mailbox. The chief wasn't answering. They conferred for a short period of time; both men appeared fulfilled at uncovering the key, and Rodney felt the investigation was reinvigorated. The two lawmen made plans on how they would proceed from this point. Priority One: the key had to go to the State Police Crime Lab ASAP.

Harry wanted to go now, but he would not allow himself to ask the big question. Rodney's perception was keen, but he didn't want to share in the glory at first, but as the conversation between them continued, as they stood near the heath, Rodney couldn't help feeling like a chump suddenly, for wanting to hog all the glory. After all, they might never have found the damned key had it not been for Harry's light trick.

"I was thinking—ah…Harry, what if we take your car and the trailer back to the station, you know, for safekeeping? I'm sure the chief will want to hear the news…then, if you want, you could hop in with me and we'll deliver the key to the Crime Lab in Aug—" He never got the chance to finish the word Augusta.

"I'm ready right now if you want to leave from here," Harry

said, obviously eager to go. They decided, however, that Rodney would feel better with the car and trailer being left at the Dells Police Department lot and at this point, Harry would make no waves, so they left immediately. It was a short drive to town from the heath, and both men had made the trip several times now, but neither was more happy to be on their way to Augusta, so to make better time, Rodney turned the lights and siren on, giving Harry a charge of adrenaline as he tried to keep up.

As they pulled in, finding the space reserved for the chief's car empty, a feeling of disappointment came over Rodney; the key could be a crucial link they all hoped for, but a simple call to the chief would do the trick. Without being directed, Harry pulled his vehicles to the farthest end of the lot so as not to obstruct any flow-through traffic to the station, and met Rodney at the dispatch desk within minutes of their arrival.

Upon speaking with the dispatcher, Rodney was informed that the chief would call in periodically during the course of the day. It was common knowledge that the chief's wife was in failing health and everyone respected their need for privacy. Rodney was completely capable of running the show in the chief's absence and Willard, knowing that both Rodney and Harry were on this case, was enjoying much peace of mind. The fact that the summer cops were still on duty gave both senior men the opportunity to pursue other interests. For Rodney, it was this investigation. For the chief…no one knew that the chief was shacked up at a far-away camp with his long-time lover, Marcy Griffin.

—

"Do you think folks are talking about us, Marcy?" Willard asked. They were naked on top of the sheets, warmed by the two-foot flames in the fireplace several feet from the side of their bed.

"Outside from maybe the hurt on your wife if she knows, I could give a rat's ass who knows or what they think about us." She leaned over him and kissed his chest. He remained silent as he looked up toward the rafters. The cabin had been handed down long ago to his father before it became his. Having had no children, he couldn't help wonder who might end up with this little hideaway in the woods. "You still hea'?" she asked.

"Yah'...I'm hea'. There's no place I'd rather be than right hea', right now and with you."

—

Rodney made contact with a lab tech, informing him he believed that a solid piece of evidence had been uncovered in the Dells murder case, and that he would be on his way to deliver it shortly. He wondered when listening to directions from that person how the time might pass during the trip to and from Augusta with Harry Circus in the cruiser. Rodney was generally a solo act. He and the chief worked well together, with the chief giving him all the room a cop needed to progress and not be afraid to make mistakes while learning the ropes of police investigating. Harry, on the other hand, was also a solo act, seasoned to a consummate professional. What Rodney could not know was that, as they stood at the dispatch desk preparing to leave for Augusta, Harry's thoughts were exactly the same.

It was 2:00 p.m. straight up when Harry looked up to the big clock across from the dispatch desk. One hour had passed since he'd silenced the generator for the light tower. Both men were ready to leave, with or without speaking to the chief. Harry made one call to Annie from a phone in a small office to one side of dispatch. He still did not carry a cell phone. Rodney gave several phone numbers to the dispatcher, and without saying another word, both men went directly to the door and walked out. Only time would tell how each man would handle being cooped up in the tight quarters of a cruiser for the better part of four hours for the round trip and however long they needed to stay at the Crime Lab. For all practical purposes, it would be a late night for everyone concerned.

—

Zeke had a way of dismissing people, either by simply ignoring them or coming on with his frightening outbursts of anger. But he wasn't a stupid person. It sometimes took much processing over what someone said before he was able to act or react on the subject matter. He knew, but made no effort to allow Pozy to believe that he even made a mental connection with him about his need to get away from the camp for a while, but he did process what his friend suggested: that they get out of the camp and make an appearance somewhere. The last thing he would do, however, was to let Pozy in on his own need to leave. After all, he'd been here far longer alone than the amount of time Pozy was here with him. Besides…they both could use a good bath and some fresh clothes. Neither one would jump in that pond at this time of the year.

The big decision now was where in hell would they go? Several hours had passed since Zeke had told Pozy to jump in the pond. Zeke was still seated at the table, and from the expanse of his stomach he probably would not eat for the remainder of the day. Through the open door he looked out on Pozy who was sitting on the stump at the edge of the pond, which was generally used as the repository for the .38 revolver whenever Zeke fished—something he hadn't done much of since Pozy arrived to assume the position of chief cook and bottle washer.

Zeke, not being of sound mind when seeing his friend near the water, jolted his memory to improvident periods of their young lives, when neither one cared for anything or anyone but each other. For as long as he could remember they'd covered each others' backs and now, without a reason except for seeing his friend sitting alone, Zeke had an attack of conscience; not for his crimes, but for his abandoned friendship with the only person on the planet who always stood by him, no matter what the situation. He hollered out through the doorway.

"Hey…fuck-face, what-a-ya doin'…takin' a shit?"

Pozy immediately looked toward the cabin but remained silent. He just didn't know what to expect from Zeke any longer. He'd proven time and again he could blow a gasket without warning, and as long as he walked around with that gun in his pants, Pozy felt as though he needed to walk on eggshells around him. He watched as Zeke stepped out from the cabin and strutted like John Wayne heading for a gun-fight with the pistol grip swaying with his hips as he walked toward Pozy.

—

Willard and Marcy remained in a passionate embrace, kissing, touching and making love for hours. Not once did Willard look toward his phone, nor did he make any of his promised calls to dispatch or Rodney. He and Marcy had talked many times about how they felt destined for this moment, though neither wanted to rush things along; at least, Marcy would never force him by any type of persuasiveness. She knew the situation with his home life.

It's not inconceivable for a man to love two women. When he's ready, he'll come to me and I'll be there for him. She couldn't remember how often she'd told herself that every time she watched him walk away from her at the Little Roady and wondered if he would ever come back. Maybe he'd come to his senses upon arriving home and seeing his wife ill. But a man needs to be comforted and loved. A man needs physical contact with a woman, and he can only go so long without it. They lay beside each other, physically spent from an entire afternoon of great sex and togetherness. "Are you hungry?" she asked.

"I think I'm too weak to tell," he answered, and they burst into laughter. It was a happy laughter—something he hadn't felt for a long time. With his personal troubles at home and a triple-murder investigation this close to his retirement, he had finally been brought down to a point where he just couldn't say no to her, and now it was difficult for him to even care. Marcy offered him what no one else could: Escape. Not from his life, but from the brutality that seemed to suck him in. They shared something special, and this time, nothing would come between them. And then, she felt something against her thigh—she reached down and took it into her hand. It was huge and hot, and she smiled at him, got up and slid herself down onto her heaven.

—

Rodney gassed it onto the turnpike from the Dells northbound on-ramp. He felt comfortable driving well over the posted speed limit; no patrolling trooper would mess with a local cruiser that appeared to have a purposeful destination. The two men made small talk, seemingly trying to size each other up, considering they'd be spending the better part of the rest of the day in the close quarters of a police cruiser. Before leaving, they'd both filled large coffee mugs, and in about a half-hour of driving, which put them north of Portland on I-295 northbound, the click of connection snagged them and they began sharing things from their pasts, which allowed an understanding to flow between the two, enlightening them to the realization that they were very much alike, not only in law enforcement but in their personal beliefs. The chatting allowed the time to fly and suddenly, Rodney took the exit ramp off I-95 onto Western Ave.—one of the only two, multi-numbered routes through the capital city.

Harry thought back to his own solo trips to the State Police Crime Lab, coming in from the opposite direction and Washington County. Within minutes the traffic flowed well to the Memorial Bridge, then to the familiar Circle onto Stone Street and finally, Hospital Street and the Crime Lab, directly next door to the State Police Headquarters and Traffic Division. It was old-home experience for Harry—the area came back to him with such familiarity.

Rodney looked at his wristwatch and smiled slightly. He was proud of the good time he'd made in getting here—something that Harry loved to pat his back over. Thoughts began to drift through Harry's memory banks to this very lab and a particular Lab-Tech who'd worked closely with him on the Lester Sawyer investigation, wondering now if he might still be here. He thought back for a moment: *What was it that I called him then?* But he could not remember.

Rodney swung the cruiser into the driveway entrance on the right, and finding a parking space toward the rear entrance, he parked. Harry immediately felt a pang of butterflies in the pit of his stomach. It had been a long time for him with much water over the dam. Each man sat with their heads facing the building, yet neither had anything to say. Rodney was first to open his door; following suit, Harry did the same and they exited together.

—

Missy had never felt so alone since her best friend and her family moved away while they were in first grade. Her teacher, Ms. Agnes, never discussed why a friend had to move and Missy asked, but was put off. A kid who loses their closest friend wants to know why the friend left. The kid who leaves hasn't got a clue. They know they're leaving because their parents told them they were and the next day…they were gone. For Missy, it was every other stray cat she ever brought home. Like Grandma used to tell her, "When it's time fa' them ta go, ya just can't handle the leavin' part…Missy. Missy—honey, you'll have to be careful out thea'… men folk aar' like the strays ya bring home. They're all just pigs. Mind-ya, if ya ask 'em…and they'll tell ya; they all love women. They' ain't a one that can hold 'emselves back when it comes to a cute smile, a wiggle from their little tushes, or some gravy on the mashed potatoes. They're all just pigs, Missy." But, back then it was all about Missy losing her friend.

These days, it didn't matter to her how long Zeke wanted or needed to stay away or why. She just wanted him back, and she'd fight off any little whore he had on his arm or break his arm to get the bitch off, but she wanted him back.

She loved Petey like a brother, and he was on her mind a lot, but a love relationship with him—she couldn't see it happening. It wasn't as if she wouldn't do it with him; she saw him as a very sexy younger guy, but she just wasn't turned on by him in that way. That day-dream began to fade while standing at the corner of the counter, close to the kitchen entrance and the swinging doors. She looked back at them now and could mentally picture Zeke plowing through them on his way to the kitchen, but when she looked back toward the outside, she saw Petey's car pull up to the curb out front.

—

Rodney led the way toward the rear door; it was as if Harry deliberately hung back for whatever reason. It was a short walk from the car to the door and the second Rodney opened it, the sights, sounds and smells of the Crime Lab exploded in Harry's senses. It was like he'd never left. The hallway walls were the same color he remembered, and everything was as neat as a pin. The offices to each side of the hall had the same furniture or were replaced with the same type and color. It was a blast from the past. After several more steps farther into the building, Harry lost his feeling of inadequacy, and yet there was no reason he should feel that way. Perhaps he felt like the second cog in someone else's machine, but up 'til now neither the chief nor Rodney had ever downplayed his being on board with them.

Annie was right. I really have to stop putting myself down, he thought.

Suddenly, some guy with a white three-quarter length lab coat came barreling out of an office from the right of the hall, nearly colliding with Rodney.

"Oh…I'm so sorry," he said.

"Well, well…if it isn't the nutty professor," Harry said. His previous inability at recalling the name he'd called him disappeared, and the name rolled off his tongue at the sight of him.

"Oh, my God—Harry."

"Remember," Harry said. "You don't have to call me that in public," and then he laughed out loud.

Rodney seemed a bit confused, but from the sound of their banter, it was obvious they knew each other. They slapped each other on the back and appeared glad to see each other.

Rodney had been here several times during his tenure on the Police Department, but he'd never had the pleasure of meeting this particular tech. He stood to one side, not wanting to interfere with the reunion, and this was the first time he'd noticed Harry display any type of sentimentality.

"I'm sorry…I don't remember your name," Harry asked.

"It's Robert, but I got used to Professor during all of your trips from Down East. Come to think of it, I never did make it down there for a visit," the lab tech said.

For the life of him, Harry had no clue what he was talking about and he wasn't about to ask. "By the way, this is Officer Rodney Torrey of the Dells Police Department." The two men shook hands and said hello, forgoing any formalities. The tech looked at Rodney. "How long have you known Harry?"

"Just over the last few days. The chief called him in as a consultant in our investigations." He intentionally left out any specifics. "One of the reasons, thanks to him, is why we're here in the first place." Rodney held up the baggie with the key.

"Oh…you think you've found something connected to the case? Great, only I haven't been working on your cases." When he said cases, it became apparent that he knew of them. "I've been tied up with that little-kid disappearance up north," he told them. They both knew of the missing kid, though neither offered a comment; it was a sad situation they didn't want to get into with the tech. "So, I've heard that you retired, Harry. How's that going for you?" And without saying another word about the key, the tech went on and on about nothing, just like the old days.

The great time Rodney had made on their way to the lab was not, apparently, good enough. The department assigned to the Dells cases were in the field today, and so the key would be catalogued and placed into an evidence folder, awaiting that team's return. Rodney filled out the appropriate form indicating who, what, where and why in regard to the key from the heath in Dells. Not being able to achieve the results they'd hoped for, their work was done here, though they both enjoyed the off-beat humor offered by the Professor.

The trip back lay before them. Both men pushed hard for a quick departure from the lab, but the tech was obviously starved for companionship and made it difficult for them to simply end the little reunion, until the door they came in from opened and a well-dressed woman with a determined walk entered and made her way toward the three men, who remained congregated in the middle of the hallway. From the very second of entry, her visual focus was an eye-to-eye contact with Harry Circus. The instant recognition was mutual.

Suddenly, at the sight of her, the bitterness of bile began to flow upward and freely through his esophagus, bringing a visible sign of discomfort to his face.

"Harry Circus…this is a real surprise. You'd be the last person I'd expect to find here, at this time of the day," she said. Her tone was almost dictatorial. This was Wanda Lane of the Channel 2 News team from Bangor—the last person on earth Harry expected to see at the Crime Lab today. Needless to say…Harry was freaked out. She was the puissant correspondent he'd given the slip to during a press conference by the then District Attorney in Machias over the Lester Sawyer case, which seemed like a million years ago until a few by-gone seconds when he laid eyes on her again. He raised his eyebrows and smiled, but remained speechless. Both Rodney and the tech appeared confused. Wanda looked toward Rodney. "Harry, aren't you going to introduce me to the handsome officer?" Rodney disliked her immediately.

"I'm sorry…this is Officer Rodney Torrey of the Dells Police Department."

"I gathered that with the cruiser out back. I just didn't…"

Harry interrupted her. "What brings you…down hea' this time of day?"

She seemed less than concerned at the interruption. "Oh, you know me…if there's some diggin' ta do, I always carry a big shovel," she said, then choked out a silly little giggle.

Harry was visibly uncomfortable in her presence. The lab tech spoke up. "Wanda is here in regards to that missing child I told you about."

It was Rodney's turn this time. "Any leads on that? I've been getting some stuff from the evening news, but that's about it," he said.

"Not really," the tech responded. "Many think the father had something to do with it but right now, we're still digging."

Wanda chimed in. "So…Harry, are you on the Dells cases? Because, if you are, I'd love to interview you," she snickered, "but not like the last time…you know, back-door Harry…remember?" He remembered all too well and wanted her to disappear. Just the sight of her forced him to mentally travel back in time, excavating the players who'd been buried, deep in the bowels of his conscience, which ultimately led to his retirement and now, having to deal with it all over again. He would not let this tack onto her score-board.

"Ya know…Wanda. People change and so do circumstances. I'm not the same person I was then, and I'm sure you've made changes also, surely for the better. Why don't we leave what's buried right where it is?" Rodney liked his style. He couldn't have done better himself. He glanced around at the faces that encircled the hall and it was Wanda who looked most like throwing up, but she just had to get the last word in.

"Sure…Harry. Let's leave the dead right where they are." She smiled then.

Once again, without sharing their thoughts, Rodney, Harry and it appeared—at least from his facial expression—the Professor were happy that the key was placed in the envelope out of sight from Wanda Lane. Several times she did her best to incite conversation over the Dells cases, and each time both Harry and Rodney evaded the question by asking her another question. They were good at it, and they seemed to be enjoying the back and forth of prevarication. After several minutes of the hugger-mugger shuffle from the two lawmen, Wanda gave it up as a lost cause.

"Well…boys, it looks as though I'm gonna get nothin' outta you two. Nice ta see ya, Harry. Maybe we'll run into each other on another—case," she said, stressing the word. "Nice ta meet you… Officer Torrey," she said, and walked away from them toward the far end of the hall.

Finally, seeing her turn at the far end of the hallway and move out of earshot, Harry spoke up.

"Whew!" he said, followed by, "Judas Priest… that woman makes me nervous."

It was comical to see the reaction of both Rodney and the Professor when hearing Harry say, "Judas Priest." Their eyes met with intense confusion. Both men had a different perception of the name, yet neither chose to ask any questions. They made small talk and ultimately the return trip to Dells was imminent. When saying their good-byes, Harry and the Professor man-hugged, and the feelings were again mutual as to the sincerity of the reunion. Harry was revitalized from the visit to the Crime Lab. It offered him a release in many respects from the cross he felt he needed to bear for his mistakes of the past or the skeletons in the closet or whatever a person needs to make them a martyr for what they did or didn't do.

Rodney drove with less intention than on the trip to Augusta. His speed was prudent from the lab to the Circle, then on through to Western Ave. and ultimately I-95 South. There was, however, an important stop on Western Ave. Just behind and out of sight of the Capitol Building, which was directly across the river from the crime lab, was a wonderful Dunkin Donuts where a couple of large coffees and some plain doughnuts would allow conversation to flow during the trip south. And flow it did. Harry was wealthy with information and thought-provoking ideas. He produced from his briefcase copies of Rodney's notes and reports he'd given him after their first day at the heath.

What he focused on was the Sandown Police Officer's report on the two suspected vagrants he stopped, the same night of the murders. His question to Rodney was, "Is there a connection with those two and the two victims?" He quizzed Rodney on the area surrounding the heath since he wasn't familiar with it. They simply brainstormed on the possibilities of how it all might have come about. Finding the deserted gravel road should have been something more obvious to a local than two young transients from Massachusetts—but then, maybe not. Whoever directed them down that God-forsaken road had a plan—but then…maybe not.

"It'll be just around dinnertime when we get back," Harry said.

"What do you say we go out that way tomorrow, starting at the heath and trace our steps in reverse, if we can, back up to where the cop stopped the vagrants? If we get the time, we could even talk to the cop, ya know. He might be able to light something up for us."

"Yeah, why not," Rodney said, and was overwhelmed with Harry's energy and insight on avenues to follow. They were well on their way south when Harry finally started to run out of steam, and much to Rodney's pleasure. He could settle back now and let the cruise control whisk them on their way. Just as Rodney sat back and took a welcome breath, his cell phone rang. It was the chief.

"Rodney Torrey here."

"Rod—Willard."

Rodney's thoughts were a hundred miles from here. He wondered what damned good reason the chief had not to have called before now. He hoped his wife was ok.

"Chief…I've been expecting your call. Is everything all right on the home front?"

"Fine, Rodney. Thank you for asking. How'd it go for ya in Augusta?" he asked.

Wow! Rodney thought. *This is so unlike Willard not to have said more than, "Fine, Rodney, thank you for asking."* But he let it go.

"The group that's on the case was in the field today. It would have been nice had they told us, but we got the key in and from the looks of it, Harry got a real nice blast from the past." He looked toward Harry, who smiled. The chief was obviously very tired as his conversation was nothing less than short-sentenced, almost off the subject all together.

"Well…chief, it sounds as though you've been drained of all bodily fluids," Rodney said with a touch of laughter in his tone. He meant it as a joke, but it was taken much differently by Willard Weaks.

"What the fuck does that mean?" he barked.

"Nothing…chief, I didn't mean anything by it. I…" but he never finished. With a click, the chief hung up.

27

FRIDAY MORNING BEGAN WITH THE MOST beautiful sunrise off Kittery Point. It also found Harry Circus on his patio with a huge mug of coffee and Rodney's handwritten notes spread over the wooden table top, next to the fire-pit. His face-off with Wanda Lane allowed him to see a new horizon in his ability to dig into a case. It's what he was all about.

The morning chill offered a prelude of things to come. Even the southern coast at times served up bouts of cabin fever for those inclined to domesticity during the long winter months of isolation. Harry would be the last to admit it, but Annie had researched the reason for his lack of ambition as winter approached. The symptoms pointed to a condition known as Seasonal Affective Disorder (SAD). Being born and raised in Washington County, the long winters and the lack of natural light had an effect on many, but in the absence of professional diagnosis and understanding, most times it went unchecked.

The cordless phone rang and before the ring-tone completed its chime, Harry snatched it up from the table.

"Hello?"

"Harry... Rodney Torrey here. How ya doin' this mornin'?"

"Actually…meeting up with old Wanda yesterday really got a huge snarl out o' my hair, you might say."

"Well…I'd think you were ready. Unless you have something

else on the calendar, I thought we might take a spin out toward the heath and… from your suggestion, trace a route back to Sandown and maybe have that chat with the local cop. I've already checked… he's on duty today."

Harry was excited by Rodney's ambition and drive toward the pursuit of justice. His father's words rang clearly in his mind: *The law must sustain a monumental patience to apprehend the offender.* It was true, especially after the Kenny Collins unsolved case, which eventually led to Harry's early retirement and his outward signs of religious devotion toward all life, at times alienating those close to him by giving some the impression of fanaticism. Over time he became aware of choosing, as time passed, to soften the public practice of his beliefs.

"Are you still there?" Rodney asked.

"Sorry, something was tugging at my inner skull for a moment."

"Yeah, no problem, Harry. What do you think about meeting an hour and a half from now at the station?"

"I'll be there," Harry said. "Do you need me to bring anything?"

"Just you," Rodney answered.

Both men hung up simultaneously and without realizing it, reached for their mugs of coffee and sat back in their respective chairs giving the day and what they might find much contemplation.

It was the fourth day since the murders. Along with the key, very little was turned up in regard to the investigation. As of yet, no motive was established other than perhaps robbery. No wallets were found on either victim. The car's interior and trunk were completely empty and from the most recent fax from the crime lab, there were no fingerprints anywhere on the vehicle, including the steering wheel, which should have been loaded with the driver's prints, had the victims, when found, been in their original seats. It was obvious that the entire vehicle had been wiped clean before the assassins left. All they had were boot prints in the dirt, and those could have been made by any work boot sold in Maine—or New England for that matter. For the two justice-seeking lawmen, today would prove to be very trying.

—

"So...Where's all the fuckin' cash, Pozy-boy?" Zeke asked.

"I...spent...it...on grub and beea'. You eat like a hause' when you get the need. Ya want more eats, go fishin'. I ain't got no more than what's left," Pozy said and reached into his pocket, pulled out a wad of bills left from the stolen money and threw it on the table. Zeke took a giant step, grabbed the cash and counted it.

"One-hundred and twenty bucks", he said. "Shit...this ain't as bad as I thought. How much did we get from them...Mass-holes?"

"There was two-hundred and fifty. It went fa' beea' and grub since we've been hea'."

"When-the-hell did you go down ta the store?"

"Every time yaw' ass was unconscious," Pozy replied.

Zeke remained quiet and walked to the open door, looking out onto the pond. The silence inside the cabin matched the calm from their outside surroundings. Pozy believed it best not to add anything to what he'd already said about the money, the groceries and the beer. And he figured it wouldn't take long for Zeke to put in his own two cents' worth. He was right.

"Ya know, Pozy-boy, ya might be right." At that, Pozy's eyebrows rose up to meet his forehead.

"I think we oughta get the hell outta hea' fa' a couple o' hours. Not right off, mind ya, but wait 'til dark. We'll take a stroll toward the coast. Maybe find us a couple o' lollipops and have us a little time tonight." And the second the word lollipop came out, all that his mind's eye allowed him to see was Missy.

"Huh, ya know," he went on, "I haven't seen Missy in quite a spell. She must hate my guts by now. How long have I been gone?"

"I don't keep tabs on ya. A couple o' weeks, I guess."

"Um...I could use some o' that. She's such a sweet, little thing. I think she loves me, ya know? At least she puts out like she does."

Pozy wanted to block his ears from the words of this moron who used to be his friend. He couldn't believe a word Zeke said any longer. In fact, anything he said now should be considered a lie.

He's a fuckin' murderer and I helped him, Pozy thought. *We're going to hell for this one and there ain't a goddamned thing anyone can do about it unless I want ta join them two Massies down in their holes.*

Zeke yawned and stretched. "I'm gonna take a little nap." And he turned from Pozy, who remained at the table, as Zeke went toward a bunk and that was the last Pozy would see of him for the next couple of hours. After several minutes of quiet, Pozy decided to take a hike around the pond. It had been a while since he'd gone all the way around. It might do him some good to look at a different scene, even if it was just to the other side of their private pool.

—

Exactly an hour and a half after they spoke, Harry pulled into the Police Department lot and this time, he pulled his de-commissioned '65 Ford Missouri Sheriff's car into the spot next to Rodney's cruiser and went in. He greeted the dispatcher and without a word, he pointed toward the office where Rodney was, obviously anticipating Harry's arrival. Ever since they'd met, Harry never saw a smile as huge on the officer's face as what appeared at this moment. He walked in as quietly as possible so as not to disturb his telephone conversation and sat himself at a desk opposite Rodney. The desk was obviously used as some sort of location- or destination-finder for the area, as maps of the seacoast and surrounding topography were laid out for easy access. The maps centered on the desk were of the area encompassing the heath. Harry began studying them and realized that Sandown was the closest and largest town to the murder scene, which enlivened his senses to the fact that he was in the neighborhood when suggesting they retrace the possible footsteps of the two vagrants stopped that very night by the local cop. Rodney's low tones on the phone were nearly inaudible now, as Harry's focus remained on the maps.

For the first time since Harry entered, though he saw him come in, Rodney acknowledged him with the lifting of his index finger and a raised eyebrow. Harry left the desk then and went directly to the coffee pot, pouring two mugs. Both men took it black, making the pour quick and easy. He was about to deliver one to Rodney when he said his goodbyes, pushed the end button on his phone and came to get his coffee.

"Yah…I can use that right now," Rodney said. Although it was his nature, Harry refrained from asking who the caller was; after all, it wasn't any of his business unless it was about the case he consulted and Rodney offered no comment.

"I noticed…" Rodney said after taking a large gulp, "you seemed to be tracing a direction on that map. Did you find anything interesting?"

Harry smiled. "Very much so," he said. "I couldn't help but notice that the heath and several secondary roads are on a close-to-perfect direct path from Sandown, paralleling the main road, with access to the heath. And I'm not sure how this might fit in, but I'm sure you must have noticed how close the location is to the Boston and Maine RR tracks, which lead right back here to Dells."

"I have considered it and I haven't discounted the possibility of taking a hike along those tracks, simply out of curiosity," Rodney said.

Both men looked to the map now and if thought had sound, the office would clang with it. They consumed another large mug of coffee each and began to follow up on the original plan, tracing out a potential route that the murderer most likely took had he or they traveled the path outlined on the map. Right now…it was a crap-shoot.

The autumn sun was as high in the sky as it would get. The air was cool and the day-star struggled to heat a defiant, turning world. The longer the clock ticked, the colder the trail would get in the pursuit of justice. One or a couple of murderers were walking around with a weapon that they were very willing to use. They'd used it three times that the investigation had revealed to this point. Hopefully, Harry Circus, Officer Rodney Torrey, or for that matter, the MCU of the Maine State Police would soon pick up the scent of a killer. Rodney folded the topographical map and took several others from the desk and the two lawmen, all coffee'd up, headed toward the waiting police cruiser for what would turn out to be a day-long jaunt into the potential life of a murderer.

—

Willard Weaks was spending as many waking hours as possible with Marcy at the Little Roady or at her home, or if time allowed, the rustic old woods-camp, far from the beaten path or any watchful eyes. There wasn't much he could offer his dying wife, who was being cared for by hospice workers, and who for the most part never knew if her husband was home or away. His frustration stemmed from his inability to just be with her, as he knew she would do for him had the tables been turned. Although they were very much in love, he shared little with Marcy of the trials his home-life dished out for him, and though she knew, she never pried into his affairs, but it felt ludicrous when she considered her involvement with him; in retrospect, she was his affair. She cared very much about him and his welfare.

Missy was now well aware of her mother's involvement with the chief. It was impossible for her not to see that slight touch on an arm as he prepared to leave or a look that might say, let's get together soon. She was happy for her mother. At least she had someone; even though he belonged to someone else—and Missy was well aware of Willard's home-life. She felt as though she'd had a life once, or at least thought she did. She saw herself in that picture with the tender touch of a hand or the look that might suggest everything. But with so many unanswered questions about Zeke, she could not continue the charade where her life mattered. She could only stare at times when seeing the two of them together and feel good for her mother's happiness, but what was it all about? If the family history played its familiar card, her mother was destined to be hurt.

—

They discussed their strategy on the drive to the heath and the systematic following of their designated route to Sandown. When

Harry said, "Rod… according to this map…" it was the first time he'd called him by anything other than Rodney. He continued, "The RR tracks come before the heath. Do you know the way to get us into that area first?"

"No sweat on that, Harry. I've hunted that section many times." Harry's eyebrows rose in a happy curl, being an avid hunter and fisherman. "There are a few trails, if you feel like walking a bit, and a couple of discontinued roads that lead to the tracks—and if memory serves me, one goes directly to the heath…in a roundabout way."

"Yeah…I think I'd like to start at the beginning. I have a strange feeling about those tracks."

—

While Zeke took his usual mid-morning nap, Pozy, having stayed completely away from the stash, took a sampling from the little box they kept it in and went for his walk around the pond. His sentimentality was stirred as he stepped onto a patch of swamp-grass, flushing a good-sized garter snake from the warmth of its sunning place. Suddenly, he wanted his boring little life back. He had been free then, to lie on the stinky couch, look out of the garage doors, (his garage doors, he remembered), and listen to the Black Racer rustle through the leaves and sawdust in the cage, then watch stupid Dwight and his torn, baggy jeans bring mice for Rowdy. He missed Petey's car in the bay next to the couch and just the plain, old hanging-around without a care in the world.

—

It took less than fifteen minutes to reach the dirt road that would lead them to the RR tracks west of town and just off the road to Sandown. This particular road hadn't been maintained for years and was used predominantly by nature hikers and hunters. It paralleled the tracks, although they were well-hidden by the overgrown vegetation. They went as far as Rodney dared with the cruiser after several bottoming-out hits to the frame. Harry preferred the walking, as it allowed him a better opportunity to scrounge around for whatever reason he thought he needed to. Along the way, several areas opened up, revealing a slight glimpse of the heath in the distance, but through those clearings, it was obvious to both that the going would not be easy.

Harry was convinced that through them an escape to the tracks would have been a quick departure from the murder scene, giving the culprit an easy exit to the north or south from here. Harry was like Sherlock Holmes except he didn't have a magnifying glass. His stare was intense on whatever area of their surroundings he chose to examine. And he never rushed. As they went in farther, the heath was no longer visible through the thick forest that grew along the tracks, but there were sporadic game-trails that would allow travel without much difficulty from the heath to the tracks.

"You say you've hunted out here, Rodney? Do you suppose these trails lead out to the heath? I'm sure the deer would find much feed along the way and probably on the heath as well. There is cedar out there," Harry said.

"Oh…there's no doubt, Harry. I've actually shot several deer over the past three years right off these trails. And they do lead out to the heath." But with all of Harry's intensity, they were unable to find anything that might lift a smidgen of evidence. The better part of an hour elapsed like the blink of an eye.

Harry shook his head finally. "There is nothing here that will help us. Maybe we should head toward the heath," he said. Rodney agreed and so they walked back toward the cruiser, never realizing they had gone as far as they had. When passing one of the open areas where the heath became visible, Harry stopped as if an unseen force caused him to contemplate going in that direction. "Rodney," he asked. "If I went down through here and you drove to the heath, we would…eventually hook up somewhere near where the car and the bodies were found, ya think?"

"Yeah, I do."

"Let's do it then," Harry said, and before Rodney could add another word, Harry was well on his way through the opening, going toward the heath.

It took several minutes for Rodney to reach the cruiser. Knowing the terrain as he did and considering the way Harry looked at everything, it would take him much longer to walk than the ten minutes or so to drive, so he needn't rush. *This is the perfect time. I'll call Lil, h*e thought. The vision of her in the hospital bed flashed before his mind's eye. *She has the most beautiful face I've ever seen.* He hit the number 7 on speed dial. Lucky number 7, he hoped. The first ring never finished.

"Hello." Her voice sounded somewhat subdued. His stomach flipped. *Bad time to call,* he thought.

"Hello, I hope I haven't caught you at a bad time," he said, and his stomach flip-flopped again. He couldn't figure out why he felt this way.

"No…no," she said. "I was—and I hope you don't mind—thinking of you just then."

His heart pounded in his chest. "I'm glad. It seems as though we're on the same page, anyway."

From the tone of her voice, he could picture her smiling through the receiver…he wanted her here, now. "Are we still on…for the weekend?"

There was a tiny pause. "Yes—absolutely. It's all good with you…right?" she asked.

"Oh, it couldn't be better. I'm looking forward to it. Any special time you might be thinking about?"

"Later in the afternoon, maybe…four-thirty?" she said.

"Great. Call me after you cross the high-rise, you know, the big I-95 bridge between New Hampshire and Maine."

"Ok…I'll call you then."

"I'm looking forward to it," he said. It was quiet for a moment and then she was gone. He sat motionless for several minutes, mentally chastising himself for letting her go that quickly, when reality hit him suddenly with the thought of Harry trudging his way toward the heath. He started the engine, ending the silence that surrounded him. From where he'd parked, the tracks were visible, but not physically close, and the sound of a southbound

Amtrak train on its way to Boston shook the earth beneath it. It brought Rodney back to a happier time—summertime as a boy swimming with friends in the river beneath the old train trestle. It was a calming moment for him. It felt good suddenly to feel a nostalgic tug at his memory. The short train rolled by quickly, leaving the sound of the last car clacking along the line, fading into the distance. Then Rodney pulled away from his daydream to the present and drove slowly over the rough road to the second stop on their planned trip.

—

It was as if nothing had come between them when Zeke appeared at the door—his heavy-eyed look was immediately recognized and his jolly-jester demeanor was sickening to Pozy, who'd returned from his little jaunt around the pond and was again seated on the stump.

"Well—mista' man. I'd be thinkin', for as long as yaw' ass been sittin' on that stump, yaw' hemorrhoids should be hangin' quite low by now."

"What?" Pozy asked. Without saying another word, Zeke opened two cold beers and brought one to his friend by the pond. He cracked a few dry attempts at his own style of humor, but getting no response, he became concernedly quiet. Their silence and that of their surroundings suddenly became ominous.

"I was thinkin'," Zeke said. "Why not, after dark…ya know, you and me, if we were to take a little walk into Dells…" Pozy remained speechless as he knew more would come and for this he would put up no argument.

"Missy must be wonderin' where in hell I went. Ya know—me and her…we're an item in case ya didn't know." Pozy wanted to lance into him for that stupid remark. The only person Zeke was an item with was—Zeke.

"Yeah…I'd like that," Pozy said. "We could hit that China-joint you worked at. Um, pork fried rice and some hot mustard." But Zeke remained in his thoughts a million light-years from the moment and never responded. As time passed, this day would be like all the rest. The afternoon shadows would darken the landscape around the little pond in the woods. Pozy's silent thought of wanting his life back superseded all others. They sat there with few words passing between them, almost as if they truly enjoyed the peaceful ambiance of Mother Nature's solitude, yet it was strange nevertheless to Pozy that everywhere Zeke went, the gun was tucked into the waist area of his jeans. Pozy had one thing on his mind: getting out of here. As far as Zeke was concerned, no one could know where his head was from one minute to the next.

—

There was no sign of Harry when Rodney pulled the cruiser onto the gravel turn-around at the murder scene. Out of habit, he steered clear of the area once taped off, pulling close to the heath, offering him a clear view of the woods-line he believed Harry would exit from.

What a lonely place to die, he thought. At that very moment, his cell phone rang. As he lifted the phone, seeing the chief's name on the caller ID forced him to think back to the last call he and the chief had shared and the cold-tempered hang-up on Willard's part.

"Rodney Torrey here."

"Rod…Willard. How's it goin'?"

"Ok," he said, thinking of how blunt the chief was being. He'd never known him to be this way. "Harry and I are tracing some steps back toward Sandown. Why, do you need me for something?"

"No…no Rod, it's all good here. I just wanted to fill you in on a fax I pulled a few minutes ago from Augusta. Toxicology on the two vics indicated they both had high levels of THC in their bloodstreams and both did some drinking before they died. Oh, by the way, they got one good print off the key, but nothing's turned up on it yet."

Both men remained quiet for a moment, then the chief went on. "Ya know…Rod—the last time we spoke…I—ah, was a bit short with you, but I didn't mean anything by it. I was just tired..."

"You don't have to explain anything to me, chief," Rodney said, and then he saw Harry exiting the brushy foliage with a trip and near fall. Rodney coughed a slight laugh.

"What's that?" the chief asked.

"Nothing, chief, I simply held back a sneeze is all," he said.

The two men made small talk, mostly about how little they'd been able to find on the cases. As far as the chief was concerned, the kid from Connecticut was rapidly becoming a cold case as they had nothing on it to date except for the hand-grip screw and a vague description from Lillian Crandlemyer. The closer Harry came, the sooner Rodney wanted to end the call with Willard. He thought, *The less I say, hopefully the less he will want to*. It paid off.

As Harry came within twenty yards of the cruiser, Willard Weaks ended the conversation with, "Keep me posted, Rod," and he was gone. As Harry approached, the smirk on his face might indicate a successful walk over the trail, but to what extent Rodney could not know. He also wanted to share the tox results and the fingerprint findings on the key.

"What-cha-find?" Rodney asked.

"A twenty twisted in some broken branches about midway of that game-trail. It's hard for me to imagine some hunter digging into his wallet in the middle of a hunt," he said. Rodney took a moment to wonder why someone with such intuition for investigation could retire from the one job to allow that person such freedom to dig into a case with very little restrictions. And he kept that thought to himself. Both men pondered over the twenty on the trail and how it might have been lost there. If Harry's original theory was right, the murderer, alone or with an accomplice (which the footprints indicated), left the scene through those woods and most likely via the RR tracks. After several minutes of silence, Rodney produced a plastic evidence bag, and deposited the twenty for a later delivery to the C L Right now, it was time for them to move north toward their ultimate goal of speaking with the Sandown Police Officer. They climbed into the cruiser and bolted out to the black top.

28

AUTUMN WAS IN THE AIR, despite the lingering summer heat of some days. It seemed that even the progression of nature's death through the process of photosynthesis this year was slowed and the leaves stubbornly refused to change colors, outside of a few deciduous species in low-lying areas like swamps and heaths where a scattering of flaming intensity began to appear at the very tops. The inevitable would come soon however, as life continues until death.

The lawmen decided to go directly to Sandown and meet with the officer who'd stopped the two vagrants the very night of the double murder at the heath. Wisely, Rodney called ahead; making sure the officer was informed of their arrival and free to spend some time with them. Harry perked up with enthusiasm as they passed the sign that read, Welcome to Sandown. Being an avid fisherman, he'd dipped a line many times in the surrounding lakes, ponds and countless streams in this area, but for whatever reason, he always traveled the back roads and never made it up or down this main road to the city. Upon entering Main Street, the Police Department was a short drive. It was also one of the county's largest Police Departments, experiencing the lowest crime rate of all York County's larger towns.

The clock was closing in on late morning when they arrived at the station. Rodney had been here many times before for whatever police business brought him. Harry, though he kept many of his thoughts to himself, after looking the place over with a keen eye, realized that during his years as a trooper Down East and having visited many of the state's police departments, he'd never had the opportunity to stop here in Sandown. As they approached the dispatch desk, which was behind a security glass, the officer they had come to see walked in behind them.

"Well…" the officer said.

"That's a deep subject for a shallow mind," Rodney answered quickly, displaying a broad smile. The two men met in the central area, Rodney taking two large steps toward the officer, and they shook hands like two long-lost friends. After a brief exchange, Rodney turned toward Harry and made the introduction.

The younger officer appeared to know who Harry was, yet for the life of him he couldn't figure out why. Then, Harry got right to it.

"Rodney and I are working on that double murder at the heath down the road. We're wondering if you might share anything you have with us on the two…vagrants you stopped on the side of the road that night."

"Absolutely," the officer answered. "I have my notes right here," and he reached into a side pocket in the leg of his uniform pants. Harry, without saying a word, examined the location of the extra pocket, and quickly considered it to be a useful tool in the growing needs of an officer in the field. While the policeman produced the notes and flipped to the pages in question, Rodney's thoughts wandered to when Lil would cross the bridge into Maine and finally, in just a few hours—they would meet.

"Here it is. I stopped them at 9:12 p.m."

"Why?" Harry asked.

"Well… I'd just pulled out of Tilton Ave. It goes through a small neighborhood on the south side of town. That's when I saw them next to a parked car on Main Street. Actually, it looked like one was getting ready to take a leak beside the rear of that car, so, I decided to say hello. When I stopped and asked what was going on, I realized I was dealing with a couple of wise-guys."

"Why do you say that?" Harry asked.

"Well..." The officer had a habit of starting a sentence that way. "The guy with the leather jacket didn't say a word, but the other one next to the trunk said right off, 'Nothin' sir, I dropped a coin and picked it up.' At that point he held up what appeared to be a quarter. That's when I asked where they were from. I didn't recognize them as being from here and the one in the leather said, 'Casket Mountain and Lost Corner.'"

The second he heard Casket Mountain, Rodney's gut began to churn with anxiety. Although he felt strange about the fact that Zeke's family home was near Casket Mountain, he listened attentively and never faltered from entering into his notes what the officer continued saying.

"Well...we had a small exchange then and I realized they probably weren't doing anything wrong, so I decided to pull away. It was the quickness with which they disappeared that gave me some concern."

"Whaddaya mean?" Harry asked immediately.

"The area we were in—ya know," the officer hesitated momentarily, "is a low-income part of town. We've had trouble there before. They're close to wooded land and they consider themselves out of the community, so-to-speak. They try to make their own rules. But anyway, I think the boys bounded into the woods along the road, and I didn't think it was necessary to follow after them at that point."

Harry and Rodney looked toward each other, and both knew that unless the officer had something else to add, the wooded area near Tilton Ave. would be their next stop.

"Can you think of anything else that might have taken place that night that might connect the two in some other way to things that went on in town that night?" Rodney asked.

"Not really," the officer answered.

—

A noticeable agitation began to envelop both young men at the camp. Being secluded there for this long caused cabin fever to set in. It was midday now, and the thought of having to wait until after dark to leave caused Pozy to spiral downward into a depth of depression, making it difficult to breathe at times. From an early-morning inventory, the cabinets were low on supplies once again. *It won't be me that will make the trek to the store this time,* he thought. As it was, he'd turned over the remaining cash when Zeke questioned him on what was left and he had no intentions of asking for any back to go shopping. He was jarred from that notion suddenly by the popping sound of a beer top being opened at his side.

"Here…get it in ya," Zeke said, and handed him one of the last remaining beers. He stood over his friend like a towering menace, the gun tucked into his waistline, eye level to Pozy as he sat on the stump. He hated the sight of that weapon now. *I wish I'd never found that fuckin' thing in those punks' car in Biddeford that night. Had I left it there, where it was, maybe, just maybe, none of this would have happened. We might be sitting in the garage with nothin' to do,* he thought and brought the cold brew to his lips and drew deeply from the can. He remained seated, and Zeke stood beside him; neither spoke. Though they did not share their thoughts, it was as if they both took in the tranquility of their surroundings like the calm before the storm. It was Friday. Not a cloud masked the endless blue of the sky.

"Ya know…the old man used to say, when ya don't see any clouds, wait a while. There's a storm a-brewin' somewhere," Zeke said. Pozy didn't answer, but it was a familiar saying in his home also, except it was his grandfather who said it.

"Ya still thinkin' o' goin' ta town?" Pozy asked, but the only response he heard was from the wind whistling through the pine needles in the treetops.

—

Rodney and Harry drove directly to the Tilton Ave. location. From the look of some of the houses it was obvious to Harry, who'd seen many homes in Washington County in various stages of disrepair, that the officer was being kind when he described the location as low-income. Rodney parked the cruiser just beyond the intersection of Main Street and Tilton Ave. He turned the engine off and took the key from the ignition, locking the doors as they got out.

When Harry looked toward him with what could be considered a questioning stare, Rodney simply shrugged his shoulders and met him on the sidewalk.

"I see what the officer meant by saying they were close to wooded land. From the way he described the area and how quickly the two vanished from sight, I'd say they headed down that path right there," and he pointed toward a down-hill, well-worn walking path through the thick, low-lying fir trees. At that point they walked back to the cruiser and pulled out several maps, spreading them over the hood of the car. The topographical map Harry had found on the desk earlier was the one he was most interested in seeing. It was a 1:24,000-scale map and should offer a detail of the area they most wanted to see. Rodney looked at his watch, simply out of habit, and Harry noticed immediately.

"Is there a problem with time, Rod?" he asked.

"Absolutely not. It's just a nervous habit is all," but his thought-habit was on one thing right now...Lillian Crandlemyer. It was closing in on 1:00 p.m. The afternoon was moving too quickly for him. Soon she would be here, and he didn't want to meet her while still in uniform, but how could he hurry Harry Circus, who was now totally consumed with the investigation? They studied the map for several minutes, finding an indication of the path, but with no apparent direction leading away from their location. At this point in time, several young people, seeing the police car at the intersection, came to within speaking distance. Harry was the first to notice and immediately focused his attention toward them. Not wanting to scare them off, he waved first and then asked them if they would come closer. They looked inquisitively at one another, and said nothing, but came slowly to within several feet of the cruiser, then stopped.

"How ya doin', ya live around hea'?" Harry asked, putting on his best Down-East accent. Being in his camo' shirt and black jeans seemed to take the heat of a police questioning out of the equation, but they did not verbalize an answer, they just nodded their heads…yes. Harry, alone, took several steps toward them and when they appeared uncomfortable, seemingly familiar with the drill, he stopped.

"I'm not hea' ta get anybody in trouble, I just wanta ask ya about this path, over there."

"Ok," the taller of the two said. Harry gave them no more than fifteen years old.

"If I got on this path here..." and he pointed toward it again, "Where would it take me and how far from here?" he asked. Again, the taller of the two spoke up.

"Not faa'. Maybe…half-mile or so through the woods, then… back to the road," he said.

"It looks to me like a lot o' folks use it. Is it a short-cut to somewhere?"

At that point the look on both of their faces told Harry what he had from them was all he would get. He thought, *this is probably a hole in the wall for young-uns' to drink beer and smoke whatever it was they needed to smoke.*

"Yah…well, ok—you've been a big help," Harry said and held out a couple of five-dollar bills, but for no takers. The two boys looked somewhat puzzled, turned and walked away back down toward the Tilton Ave. neighborhood.

"Wow, that's a first. They were probably worried they'd be seen taking something from cops," Rodney said.

"Yeah, just as well, I guess," Harry responded.

"Ya know…if they did ditch down this path and it leads back to the road, they may have run into those two from Massachusetts after reaching the blacktop," Harry said, and that's when Rodney mentioned Casket Mountain.

"Listen, Harry. Remember that kid I told you about, ya know… the black leather jacket and my gut feeling? He and his family are from Casket Mountain. I talked to his parents the very night of the murders."

With beaucoup anticipation, Lillian Crandlemyer loaded the trunk of her older, mid-sized car with one suitcase and a couple of shoulder bags. She always loved being in Maine, but the thought of spending Mel's last day together suddenly popped up in her mind and almost caused her to remove the contents of the trunk and call the whole thing off. She knew that Rodney Torrey was a reasonable man and he'd understand if she decided to stay home. But in her heart, it was the last thing she wanted to do.

She'd been very close to Mel, but their relationship had never developed in to real love. The sex was fantastic, but she'd truly needed to move on. Besides, Rodney Torrey had become an everyday thought for her; whether his feelings were the same, she couldn't get him out of her mind. His mild mannerism was very attractive to her and she looked forward to being with him, even for just an out-to-dinner date. She slammed the trunk lid, looked around to see if she had everything, took a deep breath, got in the car and drove onto the road and never looked in the rearview mirror. She was on her way to Maine.

—

In the back of his mind, Rodney knew his last statement to Harry would cause the retired trooper to develop numerous questions about the residents of Casket Mountain. The investigation was paramount, but Rodney needed and wanted the distraction he knew Lil and only Lil could offer, even for the short time he expected, not wanting to push her in a direction she might not want or be ready to go in. The last thing he wanted now was to venture back to the Brailey farm today, knowing very well that Lil, at this very moment, was probably getting ready to leave for Maine. Never giving it a thought, he looked to his watch, and again was noticed by Harry. Now…Harry became somewhat sarcastic—in a sing-song voice, he sang, "I'm a clock watcher… I'm a clock watcher, hear the ticks fly by, my, my, my."

Rod took a deep breath, exhaled and offered a reason why he

was so distracted by time.

"Harry..." The ex-trooper stared, but remained quiet. "I'm sorry I've been...I guess you might say, mentally somewhere else today. There's this young woman..."

"Oh, for God's sake, there it is, Rodney. That's all you needed to say. I understand. When are ya supposed to meet her?" After that, the two lawmen spoke little as they buttoned up a couple of loose ends at the site of the walking path on Tilton Ave. They agreed, only because Harry wanted to and hopefully, Rodney would be involved with other important matters this weekend, that Harry would return to the path on Saturday morning, alone. He could not stand for any loose ends left undone. Rodney made it perfectly clear, however, that he would be available at any time if Harry felt the need to call him. They agreed once again and made their way toward Dells with a happy, but nervous Rodney Torrey at the wheel. As he drove, he could not escape the distraction of another walking path and a young male victim resting, but not in peace.

29

FROM THE MOMENT THEY ARRIVED at the Police Station and Harry got into his own vehicle, the afternoon took on a time-warp sensation for Rodney. He looked at his watch once again: it was 2:00 p.m. The next time he checked, an hour had passed.

He'd shaven, showered and now sat on the side of his bed with a flutter in the pit of his stomach each instant a vision of Lil entered his thoughts of where she might be, right then. He went over his plan of what he might say at the first instant they met, but it sounded all wrong, now.

During their telephone conversation she'd mentioned that she planned on arriving around 4:30-ish. He would tell her, when she called, to meet him at the RR station at the Dells exit off the Maine Pike. That would give him plenty of time to drive from his place, about a ten-minute trip, and be waiting for her when she got there. He paced in his room now and when he ran out of cubic feet, he went downstairs and paced there.

It was a small house, left to him by his last surviving parent, his mother. The place was on seven country acres, located several miles from the center of Dells on the Village Road. It was far enough from the hustle and bustle that when Rodney needed to run away, you might say he simply went home. Suddenly, the thought of where she might stay, which had never entered their conversations previously, now gave the young officer a trembling sensation throughout his entire body. The solitude inside the house, however, always gave him a sense of security, and only after his mother passed away did he love being in his own world.

I decide who gets to come in…although, that thought does not include loneliness, he always said. He realized suddenly that he'd forgotten to put his watch on and was heading directly toward the stairs when his cell phone rang and the caller ID indicated… Lillian Crandlemyer.

—

Without mentioning that he would, Harry immediately returned to the sight of the walking path at Tilton Ave. It was just the way Harry worked. Although there were no outward markings on Harry's vehicle, it looked as if at some point in time it had been a police vehicle, and the moment it appeared on the scene, so did the two boys.

This time, taking Rodney's lead from their earlier visit less than an hour ago and considering the contents of his car's trunk, Harry locked the doors upon exiting. He immediately recognized the two boys, wondering why they had nothing better to do, when the taller of them came close after what might have been perceived an impish wave from Harry. If for no other reason when describing himself, which he never did, Harry believed he had a keen intuition for facial expressions. Right now, as the boy approached, alone…Harry detected a slight change in his outward appearance, and his curiosity forced him to remain where he stood, delaying his entry to the path. It was Harry who looked at his watch now, and then realized it may have made him look more official than he wanted. But when Harry investigated, there was no time as far as he was concerned. It's just the way Harry was.

—

In comparison to Rodney's assimilatory reaction to time-passing, Pozy's afternoon also flew by. With every tick of the clock, the day faded closer to the darkness that would free them from their prison. Again, little to no conversation passed between them, yet both displayed an eagerness to escape the confines of their once-cherished hideaway in the woods. Although there was a noticeable chill in the air and neither had a clean change of clothing, Pozy stripped naked, took the remaining sliver of Ivory soap and plunged himself into the cold pond water in preparation for their evening's jaunt into town. The icy water shocked him into awakening, surpassing any amount of caffeine he could consume at any one time. He scrubbed himself and lathered his long hair, then dove deep into the chilling water and came up refreshed and ready to begin anew, until he came face to face with the begrudging stare of his once-closest friend.

Again, neither had anything to say to the other, and it was apparent to Pozy that Zeke had entered into one of his oppressive moods and wouldn't be ready to share anything, especially small talk about the temperature of the pond water. It wasn't as if Pozy was shy about getting out of the water naked in front of Zeke—there was simply something about his stare that made the water comfortably palatable. As he began to move away from the shoreline, treading water backwards, it was then that Zeke decided to speak. "What-a'-ya, nuts? That friggin' water must be ready ta ice-over and yaw' swimmin' in it?"

Pozy didn't respond, feeling it would do no good to debate water temperature with him and at that point, Zeke turned and walked back to the cabin, allowing Pozy to exit the water. Surprisingly, his body had adjusted, and the air felt colder now. At the very second Zeke disappeared into the darkness of the camp, Pozy dried the water from his rapidly chilling body and re-dressed himself in his less-than-clean clothing. What he had on his mind was leaving this stink-hole in the woods, and he would not share his deepest thoughts with Zeke any longer.

When they did finally leave, it was Pozy's intention never to return here, with or without Zeke. Now that he was physically clean and having swam as long as he had, the exercise gave him a need for food so he returned to the cabin to forage through the cupboards for whatever might quell the hunger pangs, and wait for the darkness of night to set him free.

—

The boy approached at what seemed to be a cautious pace, maintaining eye contact with Harry. If he knew nothing else, Harry knew the eye contact was a sure bet the young-un', as he'd referred to them earlier, had something on his mind, and Harry hoped that he'd be willing to pass it along.

"Is that a police car?" the kid asked.

Harry was taken aback somewhat, but not completely surprised with the question. His belief in eye contact appeared to be paying off.

"It's a decommissioned Missouri Sheriff's car, actually. Why, does it look that much like a cop-car?" Harry asked.

The kid did not respond verbally, he simply shrugged his shoulders and moved a couple of steps closer to where Harry stood. Then, he displayed a type of twitch that might indicate nervousness, but when he spoke, his voice was robust.

"Are you a detective or something?"

"No…I'm retired," Harry said. "I help out sometimes when I'm needed for things."

Harry had no desire to give the kid too much or to lead him away from where he wanted him to be by having him think Harry was a police officer, but he truly believed the kid was worth the time and he went for it.

"The last time I was here…about an hour ago..." he looked past the kid to the other, shorter kid who now stood with several others who had come with this one before. "…you seemed to want to say something, but did the cop I was with make ya nervous and make ya leave, then?"

"You could say that," the kid answered. Harry looked now toward the path, hopefully instilling in the youth the reason he'd been here before and was here again now. From where the boy stood, his view was straight down the path, and now he looked in that direction. Several moments passed, and no one spoke, yet there was a murmur from the group who remained gathered a short distance away; then, the boy spoke up.

"Why ya so interested in that path? It don't go nowhere."

"Well..." Harry responded, "I'm a curious kind of guy. I look for things that most people don't think about and where they don't think about looking. The first time we met, I thought right off...now there's a young man...who sees things differently than most folks. Am I right?"

Again, the kid did not respond verbally, he simply shrugged, but this time he added a quick nod.

Rod gazed open-mouthed at the caller ID, but collected himself before the end of the chime of the second ring. "Hi...How's it going on the big road?" he asked, in regard to I-95.

"Fine. The traffic's a bit heavy, but when isn't it on a Friday?"

"Where are you?" he asked and his words came out sounding a bit short, to him anyway.

"I'm just now on the Maine side of the big bridge like you asked," she said, and there wasn't an inkling of agitation in her voice.

"Great," he said and proceeded to give her directions to the Dells exit, which he thought to be the best place for them to meet. She agreed, and as they said their goodbyes, if the sound of their voices was any indication of things to come, both, without sharing their thoughts, began to look forward to a very smooth weekend together. It was 4:30 p.m.

—

As Harry continued speaking, the kid made his way closer to him. Now, he was within a couple of feet and he appeared more attentive than ever. Suddenly, he spoke up. "Whaddaya want to know about that path? Why don't ya just go down there and see for yourself?" the kid asked.

"Well..." And as soon as Harry said it, the cop from Sandown flashed into his thoughts, and how often he said that when starting a sentence. He cleared his throat. "I plan on doing just that, but I thought, you…" Harry stopped speaking then. He didn't want to push the kid too fast. "I guess I'm wondering why you keep coming back here every time you see me." The kid remained still, then looked back over his shoulder to the group a short distance away. Then he came right out and asked, "You still offerin' that cash…like before?"

"Yah…I can be," Harry said.

30

As usual, the onslaught of tourist traffic clogged the northbound interstate route to Maine all day Friday. The tourist season never really ended. One simply followed the other through the months of the year. The summer folks went home when school started, came back to Christmas-shop, then went home, got their skis, snowmobiles and winter clothes and came back for their extended stay in Vacationland. Most folks from here considered it the familiar out-of-stater insurgence that never goes away.

One person from here, however, did not consider any type of stink when thinking about a particular part of the tourist traffic. Rodney Torrey, in civilian clothes, stood nervously beside his personal car out front of the Amtrak Station in Dells. The last thing he wanted was to look obvious, but he glanced at his watch all too frequently not to be. She was late.

It was 4:45 p.m. His hand just had touched his phone's holster when he noticed a vehicle pull in from the roadway at the entrance. It was a mid-sized car and the moment it came to within a hundred-feet, he immediately recognized her. His heart thumped like a bass drum in a parade and he could barely keep his emotions in check at the sight of her. The closer she came, and smiled as she recognized him, the weaker his knees felt.

Take a hold o' yaw'self, Rod… you idiot. Make a fool o' yaw'self now and you can kiss this one goodbye, he said to himself, as she pulled the car up right next to him.

It seemed to take her forever to get out, but when she did, Rodney felt that she was more beautiful now than the first and last time he saw her in Biddeford. She appeared more slender than he remembered, but he never did see her out from under the hospital covers on the bed. Her jeans hugged the contours of her long legs and the thin, white pullover top extended down past her waistline, covering her butt. She moved toward him and immediately put her arms out, and they met in a cordial hug. The very scent of her was intoxicating, and he could have held her for hours.

"Hi," is all she said.

"Hi. I'm glad you made it safely," he murmured.

They looked deep into each other's eyes, hypnotized momentarily with infatuation, neither wanting to be first to sever the bond.

"It's so nice to finally see you in person. It feels like so long ago now, but then…" She stopped mid-sentence. He examined the smoothness of her skin and the facial expressions that made her so appealing to him.

"I'm glad you're here. This is so much better than a phone call. You look fantastic," he said, and once again they froze to the spot. Several moments passed when suddenly, as if cued, they both, because of where they stood, became a bit self-conscious of their surroundings and finally let their hands slide apart, yet they remained in their trance, focused on each other, standing close for several more minutes, not wanting their first contact to end. They made small talk about her trip up and he shared a smidgen of his plans for tonight. She told him of her reservations at a small Inn near Punquit Beach and his emotional high suddenly deflated with the thought that possibly she'd stayed there with Mel.

But that was then. She's here with me now and we'll make the best of the weekend, together, he thought.

—

For no apparent reason, the thought of seeing Zeke after one of his long disappearing acts caused Pozy to suddenly remember him showing up at the garage with all-new clothes; the very night Queer-Eye showed up and Zeke dissolved into the woods. The blue jeans and white sneakers were an odd sight, and he wondered what had happened to that outfit. Since he'd arrived, all Zeke had worn was his black stuff with the gun tucked into the waist. He knew better than to ask stupid questions, but he wanted to know.

Approaching the cabin, his need for something to eat was overwhelming, but the thought of Zeke's clothes remained indelible in his mind's eye. Many memories flowed through his thoughts. He missed the way their life used to be. Thinking about food…he could almost smell the burgers and fries Missy served up for them. But what he saw upon reaching the open door was a total mess: anything and everything edible was laid open or smashed on the cabin floor. Zeke had finally gone over the mental edge. With this type of behavior, Pozy knew it was only a matter of time before he would have to defend himself and until then, he would remain vigilant and never turn his back on Zeke.

—

The late afternoon shadows were tall enough to inject a chill into the air, especially where the sunlight did not penetrate. After several minutes of chatting, and Harry's promise to turn over the bills he'd shown earlier, he persuaded the young man, who had introduced himself now as Roger, to guide him down the path. During their discussion about money, Roger turned toward the small gathering he'd arrived with and motioned for them to leave. Without a word spoken between them, they turned and vanished quickly into the village of tiny houses. With the speed at which they obeyed, Harry found a new respect for Roger and no longer did he consider him a "young-un."

Harry made his way down, following at a distance behind Roger and taking in as much as he could of the area. The path immediately sloped downward after only a few steps, then gradually leveled off in an area that allowed for open and long-distant views. They were low enough from the upper grade that no sound from the traffic on the road to Sandown could be heard.

What a perfect escape this would be if the two stopped by the cop came this way to evade further questions, Harry thought to himself, while a hundred notions ran through his mind. Yet he didn't have much to go on at this point, and nothing grabbed him enough to consider any single particular thing. The going wasn't all that bad, but Harry watched every step he took where tripping might be possible. Roger was quite agile and moved steadily forward. At a point several hundred feet into their walk, Harry called out, stopping his young leader, allowing Harry to catch up.

"Wow…this is nice down here. A guy could come down here and hang out all day and never be seen," Harry said.

Without saying a word, Roger looked Harry straight in the eyes, and nodded his head slightly, with an almost contemptuous twisting of his lips.

This guy is obviously well-groomed with a disposition toward law enforcement. Probably a family background of law-breakers, Harry thought; when all of a sudden, a vision of Kenny Collins' body lightly covered with a dusting of fresh, powered snow on that early morning in February flashed into his memory. His inability to solve that murder caused his heart to speed up, and his focus drifted off to the distant view that lay before him. Oddly enough, while Harry was regaining his composure, Roger stood in the middle of the path taking a leak, and apparently never gave it or Harry a second thought. Not that it was any big deal—Harry could hold his bladder longer than most—it was simply not his style to be that impertinent in the company of a stranger and probably not even with a close friend. They stood for several minutes without speaking; Harry remained in awe of his surroundings until his young guide spoke up.

"Ya never did say any more about the…cash."

"Ya—Ya, let me ask you a couple o' questions first, then…" Harry was about to continue when he was interrupted.

"Look…I ain't no squeak," he said.

"I never thought you were," Harry fired back without a breath. "I just want to know more about this path, that's all."

The boy looked attentively at Harry, but remained quiet.

"Now...don't get me wrong, but it seems a bit strange that whenever you and your friends back there see or think you see a cop-car, you all come out and have a look. Would I be wrong in thinking that?" Harry asked.

"No, I guess not."

"Right," Harry said, but he was searching and apparently in the right place now.

"I've got one question, then I'll hand over the cash. About a week ago, the local cop stopped a couple o' guys back at the intersection where my car is now." Roger bobbed his head in the manner that might suggest the affirmative. "Did you and your friends come out that night?" he asked. This time the head-bobbing was a definite "Yes." With that wordless response, it was as if Harry'd been injected with a huge dose of caffeine. He was wide awake to any possibility, knowing all along that the young man would allow him to move forward, but he needed to keep him on his side of town.

"Ok...ok," Harry said and could almost feel his face develop a smile, but he had to slow it down. He didn't want to lose the only potential witness he might have.

"Can you tell me who and maybe...what you saw that night? And I promise...I won't think you're a squeak and I'll give ya the cash."

—

Rodney was nervous, but he remained the perfect gentleman. He knew exactly where the Inn she'd reserved a room in was and he led the way there in his car. He helped her with her luggage, waited until she registered and allowed the Innkeeper to take her bags up to her room. They stood in the lobby, away from the desk in front of the fireplace, which was cold from the lack of being stoked.

"Why don't you freshen up from your trip...call me when you'd like. I'll be home, and I'm not far from here. I'll pick you up and we'll have a nice dinner and relax. How's that sound?" he asked.

"It sounds great. I won't need all that much time, but thank you for your patience, Rod," she said. When she called him Rod, his stomach tingled.

"It's my pleasure. I'll see you when you call." He could hardly contain his emotions at being this close to her after so long, because she had only been a voice on a long-distance phone call. But, she was right here at Punquit Beach, and he'd be less than three miles up the road. *It's going to be a perfect night...* he thought, when suddenly, the last thing he wanted to think about flashed into his mind: the investigation. Harry's presence and discernment eased the pressure that was once an overbearing frustration for the young policeman. He wanted to know what Harry was doing at the moment—that was Rodney being himself—but he truly hoped that Harry would not call.

—

"Did ya really think you were gonna get ta eat...this shit?" Zeke said as he pointed the barrel of the .38 at the rubble of discarded remains of what was left on the open concept shelves before Pozy had gone swimming. The shelves were empty and bare as he stood motionless in the doorway in disbelief of what lay before him on the floor.

"What-tha'..." Pozy began and was immediately interrupted.

"Sit...down," Zeke ordered and pointed the barrel toward the single chair at what might be considered the head of the table. Everything was moved around in the camp. The three remaining chairs were up against the wall opposite the stove. It looked like moving day; had they discussed moving? Pozy wondered.

"What...is going on here?" Pozy asked. "I take a bath and come back to a friggin' mess."

Zeke remained silent, but his stare could have spoken a thousand words without him moving his lips. "You think I'm nuts, just like everybody else, don't ya?" And his voice rose with the last word. "Well, you'd be right. I'm as nuts as a friggin' coyote with ticks. You thought you were gonna' keep this money..."

“I don’t want the friggin’ money,” Pozy hollered out suddenly, not believing that he was still on the subject of the cash, then he realized who he was dealing with. “I didn’t mean that like it sounded,” Pozy added.

“Sit there…shut-up and listen ta me. I’—got some shit ta say before we leave.”

Zeke began talking a blue streak, about things that made no sense to Pozy. Things like, two farm girls in a pickup truck and how bad she drove; his need to see Missy in the next sentence; then, how he didn’t give a shit about her with his next breath. He told Pozy he was thinking about burning the camp when they left tonight. He said he didn’t want any finger-prints to show up. He went on and on until the natural light from outside faded to almost darkness. At that point he began to frighten Pozy when he rubbed the barrel of the gun, speaking to it as if it understood him. It wasn’t until he abruptly mentioned shooting the little-shit while his girlfriend watched when it finally sunk in that Zeke was talking about the kid from Connectaclit, killed on the walking path at Punquit Beach during the height of summer.

Pozy stared at him, fearful now for his life. It all fit into place. The blue jeans and white sneakers, the money and the beer he had the night Queer-Eye busted up their little campfire party at the garage and Zeke so magically disappeared into the woods. The clothes were his way of not being identified by the girl, who he read was still alive.

Zeke was staring at him from across the table where he’d stood since telling Pozy to sit down and shut up.

“So…ya proud o’ me, or what?” Zeke asked, and you could have heard a hatpin had one bounced on the floor, as the silence strangled out any sound in the cabin.

“Proud?” Pozy asked.

“Yah’…Proud! I got rid o’ three out-o’-staters this summer, all by myself. You should be proud, ya little moron.” The smile he displayed now bordered on the macabre—a look they’d seen in old monster movies—and here one was, staring at Pozy from within a demon murderer that used to be his closest friend since boyhood. As darkness encapsulated them, the need for food became insurmountable. Then, as if an electrical switch had flipped, Zeke became a self-appointed caregiver—concerning himself now with Pozy's need for sustenance.

"C-mon, buddy. Let's get ta town, get some grub in us and have fun tonight. What-a-ya say…Pal?"

"Sure," Pozy responded in a voice tremulous with fear.

—

Harry was all ears as his escort along the path relayed to him what he and his friend had seen that night when the Sandown cop had stopped to chat with the two vagrants. His accounting of the events were almost verbatim to the officer's report, reaffirming in Harry that the young man had far more potential than what his neighborhood possibly allowed him to believe of himself. Harry remained quiet throughout his recollection of what he saw, but when he got to the part where they came down to the path, silence was no longer Harry's virtue.

"Where were you when they came down this way?"

"Right next to the entrance to the path, but…funny as it was, they never saw us standing in the thick jack-fir. They went right by us, fast!"

"Then what happened?" Harry asked.

"They kept right on goin' and like I told ya before…the path winds around for about a mile, then hooks back up to the main road, down that way." He pointed to the far reaches of the path, going deeper from where they stood.

"So…you got a pretty, good look at 'em as they passed you and your buddy?"

"Yah, you could say that, but the two of 'em had all black on—the big guy out front had a real nice leather jacket. It felt a little warm, but I would o' wore it, too."

It was Harry's turn to nod his head in the affirmative, yet he spoke not a word to his hiker companion. His first thought was to give Rod a call, but after their earlier exchange, there wasn't a chance in hell he'd be disturbing him tonight. He considered calling Willard, but he also seemed preoccupied lately, so…

"Tell ya what." Harry reached into his pants pocket, pulled his wallet out, and along with a ten-dollar bill he grabbed one of Rodney's business cards. On the back, he printed his home phone number, purposely neglecting to tell the young man where that particular call would ring, and handed them over to him.

"If you remember anything about those two in black, call me." And he pointed to the number on the back of the card. They turned toward the Tilton Ave. intersection, and Harry thanked him for his help, telling him if there was anything he could ever do to help, not to hesitate to call. By the time they reached the car, darkness was upon them. Harry had had a full day and was just about done in, and though he hadn't found anything substantial, he had more than when he came.

He got in the car and turned the key, and the big engine came to life, settling at a fast idle. He jotted notes and checked previous entries, killing time to let the motor reach operating temperature. When he was satisfied that all he had done today was all that he could do, he tapped the shifter lightly into the D position and began his ride to Kittery Point. What he would never know—and it was probably just as well that he didn't—was at the very minute his car began to move forward, Zeke and Pozy, no more than five miles from the Tilton Ave. intersection, placed their feet onto the blacktop for the first time since arriving at the camp after the murders. They were on a get-to-town mission that should have been a happy time, but it was like a death-march for Pozy, who felt like a prisoner to an old friend and a .38 special.

The murderer and his accomplice walked into the darkening evening.

—

It was seconds away from 6:00 p.m. Rodney was in a mental state bordering on collapse, not having heard from Lillian since escorting her to the Inn. Obviously, unless something had gone very wrong, freshening-up took on an altogether different meaning between the sexes. He began to pace again, his nervous stomach gurgled with acid-reflux, and heartburn was simply several swallows away when his cell phone rang.

"Hello."

"I'm starving," she said as if the elapsed time since they spoke last had been only minutes. Rodney wanted to scream from his frustration, yet he held it in check and thanked his lucky stars that she was here and calling him. He took a slight breath so as not to reveal his bafflement at the time she needed to get ready.

"Yeah…I'm starving, too," he said. Again, he remained calm with his next question, not wanting to appear anxious. "I can pick you up if you're ready."

"I'm ready!" she said with an obviously new-found energy.

"I'll be right there," he responded, in a voice eager with anticipation. He was only minutes away.

They met in a hug, and he found her scent entrancing. Suddenly, food was the last thing on his mind. They exchanged small talk briefly and Rodney suggested they leave. "I have a table reserved at a small place I think you might like. Shall we?" he said.

"Yes," was all she said, and the word came out as a whisper from heaven itself to his ears.

It was an uncomfortable situation for Rodney—a bit surreal being a police officer, having had hundreds of impersonal interactions with strangers, which had never made him feel less than in control of his emotions. It's not that he hadn't dated, but the young woman at his side was definitely making him nervous.

They traveled an area of the coast she'd never seen before; the road wound its way very close to the ocean in places. It was something he thought she'd like. She found it very romantic. Suddenly, they arrived at a small restaurant at land's end. The building was perched high, overlooking a broad expanse of an open and bold Maine coast. The parking lot was relatively large and open, so he parked at a distance, allowing for a short walk, before and after. The view was splendid from all locations. Upon entering, she immediately fell in love with the quaint, dim privacy emitting from throughout the interior. The topper came when they were escorted to their private table for two overlooking the water, across from a crackling, slow-burning fire.

—

It was difficult for Pozy to maintain the speed at which Zeke walked. Having no idea of where he intended to go, Pozy followed, trying to keep pace, offering little in the way of conversation. They stayed clear of all the familiar routes to the coast, even though they had no reason to believe they were suspects in the double murder or the murder at Punquit Beach that Zeke had confessed to, if in fact he was telling the truth and not grand-standing to make himself out as the big, bad guy. Pozy had seen Zeke murder with his own eyes, and right now, Pozy was his accomplice. In fact…it was Pozy's guilt forcing his belief that they were suspects, but only he believed it. Zeke acted as if he couldn't care less.

The miles seemed endless as they wound their way from one back-country road to another, occasionally crossing a cornfield, ending up on another road, going in an altogether different direction. Without food, Pozy was tiring rapidly, yet Zeke appeared unfazed from not eating. For a short period of time, Pozy lost his sense of direction and had no idea where Zeke led him nor did he pay much attention to where they were at any given time. The dim lights from distant and partially secluded farmhouses seemed to hypnotize him, allowing his thoughts to drift back in time and dwell on his need to be free. Finally, in a clearing, he recognized the location they were in, forcing a chuckle from him, which he didn't hear himself. But Zeke did.

"What ya laughin' at?" Zeke asked.

They were less than a mile from the Chinese Restaurant they'd spoken of earlier and now, just the thought of being here forced Pozy's stomach into spasms of hunger pangs. Being this close to the coast, it was as if they'd rehearsed their maneuvers at ditching out of sight from any oncoming vehicles, making their progress even slower. After all…it was Friday night on the southern coast of Maine. Every fool and his brother was out tonight and without knowing it, any fool who got in Zeke's way was likely not to live to tell about it. That was Pozy's biggest concern until he was able to free himself from Zeke's control, and he would wait as long as needed, making sure the time was right then…he would make his move. He had or knew of as many places to hide as Zeke did, and by the time he found him, just maybe it would be too late for anyone to worry about anything of what had taken place.

From a slight knoll overlooking the ocean, the twinkling lights of the seacoast appeared in front of them. Pozy began to feel the strength of his need for freedom tug at his getaway plan.

Out of thin air, the thought of something his mother had told him many years ago flashed into his memory. Something about his grandmother dying and what her children did when finding the body. *It was sad when we found mother's lifeless body, but knowing very well that it hadn't been all that long since her passing, we opened the window next to her bed so her spirit could fly free. We were happy then, knowing her spirit was all around us.* When first hearing that, all those years ago, he gave it up to his mother's spiritual need to be connected or whatever in hell he thought then. But now, the idea of a spirit flying free was the connection he needed to maintain some level of sanity within himself. He would keep that memory from the past with him until he set himself free from the clutches that held him captive.

Perhaps it was his imagination, but Pozy began to smell the aroma of cooking food, steaks especially, even though he had a hankering for Chinese. In the time it took to exhale the breath, Zeke spoke up for only the second time since they'd left camp.

"Ya smell that…rum-dumb? That's the smell o' that Chink-place I worked at. Ya want some o' that China-mush, do ya?" he asked.

Pozy said nothing, yet he truly wished he could come back with something sarcastic, just to spite Zeke, but to what end? He was too hungry to put up a fight. After all, Zeke had all the money and he'd play that card as long as he held it in his hand.

31

The warming air blowing in from the south mixing with a radiational cooling from the waters of the Gulf of Maine created sea smoke that rolled ashore eerily as the early evening flowed into night—a phenomenon that at times was solely responsible for slowing the pace of traffic on the roads of the seacoast. People drove fast along the coast, the theory being that whether or not you would have to stand in line wherever it was you intended to go, you still had to get there first.

From the single window beside the table where Rodney and Lil sat, only the reflection from the fireplace could be seen. The outside world had vanished, leaving only the distinct sound of a distant fog horn.

"So." Rodney asked, "What do you do in Connecticut? We never got around to talking about…us."

She smiled and paused, as if she might consider holding something back, and then she said, "I'm a medical transcriptionist." Rodney released a sigh of relief that went unnoticed.

"That's a good job. I have a friend whose wife does that." And for a moment, he felt a bit uncomfortable. She breezed right into the next question.

"How long have you been a co— um, police officer?"

"Ten years," he said, and was about to continue when the waitress came to the table.

Their conversations continued to flow over many subjects, lighthearted and about them, not intellectually driven. They were everyday people, driven by the wheels of life. Rodney did not drink alcohol, ever, but Lil sipped on a French Chardonnay, with ice on the side before, during and after their Surf n' Turf dinner, which included a thick and creamy clam chowder to start, PEI oysters on the half shell, followed with a one-and-a-quarter-pound Maine Lobster and a thick, juicy New York Strip Sirloin. They both opted for the duck-fat, deep-fried French Fries on the side.

For the first time in what felt like forever, Rodney's mind was on the evening, Lil, and their togetherness, and not the grisly endeavors of the murder investigations that had ruled his entire existence for nearly two months. He sat back now, sipping his black coffee, admiring the young woman sitting across from him at the quaintly set table. He knew that his selection for dining out was well received. As it is with time, however, the minutes ticked away unnoticed, and before long, the reality of a wonderfully shared experience must be accepted as...all good things must end.

The polite waitress placed the bill on the table in front of him, telling them not to rush, but she was unable to hide the anticipation of what might await her cordiality on the tip line of the merchant's copy. Although he was enjoying himself and wanted the evening to be special for them, he could not dismiss his desire for Lil sexually. They were compatible in every way, resurrecting his belief in mutual attractions. It had been so long since he'd been involved with someone, he thought it best not to rush things and move the evening onto the next level of her visit to quickly. It was difficult for him to reach out for the bill, as the peaceful environment was appealing to both their needs for calm, but the time had come to move on. They remained comfortably seated for a reasonable amount of time after the waitress collected his signed receipt. Without much to say, neither appeared uncomfortable with the silence.

"Shall we?" he asked, and without a verbal response, she nodded her head and they moved slowly from the table by the window and made their way toward the exit. Feeling the dampness from outside, without sharing their thoughts, each wished they were only just arriving to begin the experience. Remaining silent, she looped her arm through his, feeling that comfortable in her place beside him. The air was thick with fog, much different than when they'd arrived. Being a woman, though she said nothing as they strolled toward the car, she worried how her hair would frizz from the dampness of the night air, yet her thoughts were now on the fact that she was arm-in-arm with the police officer who'd investigated the murder of her former lover, and she forced that thought from her consciousness almost as fast as it appeared. Neither had given any thought to time since he'd picked her up at the Inn, somewhere around 6:15 p.m. It was closing in on 9:00 p.m. Although each had wound down from a long day, complaining of being tired was not an option. The evening was young and so were they.

"There might be a nice fire in the lobby this time of the evening," she said and tugged at his arm, forcing him to a complete stop facing her.

—

It was history repeating itself as Zeke, with his one-man accompaniment, entered the huge, temple-like front doors of the Chinese Restaurant. They were greeted by the woman co-owner, and Zeke simply nodded his head but remained silent, walking past her and going toward the lounge. Pozy, knowing the woman, though not as well as Zeke, stopped to chat briefly, but finding her somewhat indifferent, shrugged his shoulders and followed Zeke. He was already seated at the bar when Pozy entered.

The out-of-staters filled the atmosphere with an almost oppressive level of sound, far different from what they'd accustomed themselves to at camp. Pozy knew that pitch would eventually get to Zeke; how he might handle it after a couple of beers remained to be seen. The bartender on duty tonight was not the usual one. It was one of the Chinese waiters, obviously filling in. Zeke would not make small talk tonight. They both seemed out of place next to the still summer-clad tourists all around them, yet it barely fazed either one.

Upon placing an order for drinks, Pozy was carded by the young Chinaman, forcing a scowl to form on Zeke's face, yet he remained thankfully quiet as Pozy willingly produced his State of Maine ID. The beer was so cold it went down like a little taste of heaven. Suddenly, the need for food superseded the need for alcohol.

Ever the joker, Zeke poked his friend, exposing what remained of the pot in a plastic bag from his jacket pocket. Always the big-shot, he never feared reprisal. He downed the first beer, clanked the empty bottle hard onto the bar-top, motioning for the bartender to replenish the brew. Now, the scowl being displayed belonged to the Chinaman. Waiting for his second beer, Pozy's need for food became overwhelming.

"You gonna' order somethin'?" he asked, but in a tone of passive disposition so as not to rile Zeke more than he already was. Not having eaten much while at camp, after Zeke's food-cleaning act, it wouldn't take much to fill Pozy, but when Zeke started eating…there was no telling how much he'd want. Their beers were delivered under what might be considered a questioning eye from the bar-keep, yet he remained politely quiet.

"We're gonna' order some food," Zeke said in a gruff voice, his manner ignored by the man as he immediately took out an order pad and waited to hear what they desired.

—

Harry and Annie sat by a crackling fire, the only light from a darkness that encapsulated the patio behind their home. They both quietly absorbed the solitude. It was this quiet time they always looked forward to, as it brought them back mentally to a different way of life they knew and cherished. Although Harry's previous job had stressed him out to unsafe levels of depression, the memories were good overall. Harry's mind, however, was not fixed in the solitude of the moment or their past. His concentration was on the young man he'd spent the earlier hours of the day with and how skillfully he'd described the two men walking down the path, especially the one wearing the leather jacket. Oh, how he wanted to call Rod. His description was exactly the same, word for word, and his need to find this guy…who Rod called Zeke Brailey was now número uno on Harry's list. It was a gut feeling. For all anybody knew, the murderer or murderers were long gone from Maine, but what stuck in the lawmen's craw was a reasonable motive. Harry's mind raced over the possibilities, forgetting he wasn't alone.

"Which planet is it this time, Harry?" Annie asked, but said nothing else, she simply continued staring, her eyes absorbing him from the corner of his left eye, the one closest to her if he continued to look forward, to the tip of his chin, and she still loved what she saw.

He looked toward her, but said nothing for a moment.

"This thing keeps me going back in time, Annie. I should be over all that by now, but it still bugs me."

"Remember," she said. "No one twisted your arm into consulting. You said it was because you were friends with Willard and you knew how he felt at not being able to…wrap it up this close to his retirement." He knew she was right with that last comment, but down deep he was still a cop and probably always would be, one way or another. The fact that he and Rodney had been unable to reach Willard recently was beginning to cause Harry some concern. He knew his wife was ill, but that's all anyone knew about it. Although he did not know Willard's wife personally, he had no reason to doubt his good friend, but there was something about all of this that just didn't set well with him. Again…

He couldn't overlook the fact that it was Willard who had given him carte-blanche where the investigation was concerned. When faxes or other communiqués arrived at the Dells Police Department, a fax with the same information was sent to Harry's home fax machine as soon as it arrived at Dispatch. He was looking at one this minute. The crime lab in Augusta had found no prints on the twenty-dollar bill he picked up on the path near the heath. He had to get himself back on course and leave the past right where it was.

—

Rodney and Lil remained facing each other for what seemed an endless moment. Their physical closeness was warming, not only bodily but emotionally. He looked deep into her eyes, the color somewhat faded from the darkness, and his heart began to race. Her face was serious, yet her eyes, beaming with anticipation and unblinking, focused on his with an intensity that said it all. Rodney was pleased with himself for having chosen a parking spot at the farthest end of the lot. Since they'd arrived, there weren't many spaces left to choose from closer to the restaurant.

He finally tore himself away from looking at her, and changed direction slowly, walking directly to the car, and they got in. With the dampness of the fog, the dry, quiet interior of the car was welcomed by both. They were relaxed after a meal of gourmet quality. Being in the car evoked a sense of privacy, allowing them to speak openly—not that they hadn't conversed freely while enjoying their little table by the window, but a sense of intimacy began to chart a new direction for conversation to flow. They were even closer in the mid-sized car, giving a physical closeness without either invading the other's personal space.

The light scent of Lil's perfume entranced Rodney once again. He moved closer to her and her eyes widened, suggesting a willingness to be approached, and without hesitation, they met with a kiss—a soft and tender touching of the lips at first, and as the moments passed, with their breath on each other's cheeks, they felt the passions of their libidos rise simultaneously—and for Lil, the willingness to give herself to him became apparent as her breathing intensified with her desire for sexual gratification. They were both very needy and their lips were pressed ever tighter. They wanted each other.

—

The fact that Zeke still had a-hundred and twenty-five dollars, thanks to Pozy's frugality, ordering whatever they wanted would not be a problem. They never asked for nor were they offered a menu by the Chinese bartender, but the two young men knew what they wanted. Zeke ordered first.

"When we get done with these beers, you bring more," he demanded in a less-than polite tone, and the expression on the man's face spoke volumes about what he thought of this young man's "politeness," a trait most Chinese honored. Zeke continued.

"Spareribs and fried rice," he ordered abruptly and sipped from his beer, looking away toward the TV screen across from their bar-stools.

Pozy, feeling somewhat embarrassed—though he was no saint when it came to being rude—ordered Egg Rolls, fried rice and chicken wings. He offered a "please" after ordering, but it went unnoticed by the man. Neither one was particularly interested in sports, although the clientele, obviously from away, were very much interested if the sound of their hoots and hollers was any indication, leaving no doubt as to what their viewing pleasure was, and it irritated the hell out of Zeke.

Like many busy restaurants, many of the menu items were prepared in advance, making the serving of the food, especially on weekends, an enjoyable experience for patrons and moving them in and out for a good turn-over. An observant waiter and bartender, he brought their food quickly, and with each order came a fresh bottle of beer. For whatever reason, however, it wasn't the right thing to do as far as Zeke was concerned.

"What…did…I tell ya?" Zeke said in a condescending voice, forcing a questioning look on the waiter's face, drawing the attention from several patrons on the other side of the bar.

"I said…when we get done with the beers, bring more. We ain't done yet," he said.

Pozy could see and feel the tension building in Zeke, but there was no logical reason for it.

Here we are, comfortable in a nice Chinese Restaurant, a place Zeke worked for a while. We've got cold beer, good, hot food and we're finally out o' the freakin' camp, he thought.

With a nod from Pozy, the waiter placed the orders, including the beers, in front of them and left quickly. Occasionally, Pozy caught a glimpse of Zeke reaching into his jacket pocket, simply to feel the gun—a routine he'd become accustomed to now, but he'd never learned to live with the fact that he always carried it and it was always loaded. They both consumed the food before them as if a vacuum formed from just breathing in. With Zeke, it was a mouthful and then a guzzle from the beer. Pozy, on the other hand, though he ate fast, appeared to cherish the flavors. As their stomachs became filled, Zeke seemed to calm down somewhat and as far as Pozy could tell, he paid little or no attention to what went on around him, easing Pozy's fears of an outburst. But he was a realist where Zeke's demeanor was concerned, and he knew it could only be a matter of time before something touched him off.

I just hope I can finish my hot meal before any explosions lift us off these bar-stools, he thought.

"How's yaw' grub…buddy?" Zeke asked, with a gluttonous smacking of his lips.

"Good, real good, and it sure beats pond-fish, don't ya think?" Pozy answered, but got no reply. They were on their third beer each, and a good buzz had crept into their heads when that dreadful look of anger began to disfigure Zeke's face.

"Come ova' hea'!" Zeke ordered the bartender, causing a look of complete displeasure, if not anger of his own to form on the bartender's face. He came, directly, yet maintained a safe distance from the edge of the bar where Zeke sat and said nothing upon his arrival. For a moment, Zeke remained quiet, his stare appeared focused on nothing in particular as if he were in a dazed state of mind and a blank look formed on his expression. Not knowing what to expect, the waiter's eyes shifted from Zeke to Pozy as if he might be able to explain the behavior, but Pozy, never having seen this particular type of behavior, was at a loss. At this point, neither dared to speak and release him from what might have been considered a self-induced state of hypnosis. He was that far out there. Pozy couldn't take another second of this.

"Zeke?" he asked in a low, concerned voice. Zeke blinked

his eyes, shook his head slightly as if shaking off the cobwebs, and looked around the room in an obvious attempt to regain his composure. And he did, quickly, but not in a passive way.

"What the fuck do you want? Get away from me...you, friggin' Jap. If you ain't in my face, you're up my friggin' ass."

Both Pozy and the waiter wanted to melt into the floor and get away from him as soon as possible, but unfortunately, Zeke was the only one in dreamland, mentally leaving whenever he wanted. Still appearing somewhat unsteady, though he remained seated, Zeke turned to his friend after the waiter left again and asked, "What did he want?"

"You...called him over, then ya just sat there. You didn't say anything to 'im. You ok, or what?" Pozy asked.

Again, Zeke continued looking toward a reflection of himself on the mirrored wall behind the shelved bottles of booze in front of him and remained in a trance-like state, only seconds after speaking to Pozy. Suddenly, he reached into his pants pocket and pulled out the wad of bills, handing it to Pozy.

"Pay that fucker," he said, then he got up and walked out the back door, the same door he'd exited the night of the first murder. Pozy sat quietly, confused and by himself, motioning for the waiter to bring the bill. What he could not know at this moment was that as he watched Zeke walk out, the back of his head and the leather jacket would be the last of Zeke he would ever see. Pozy looked toward the Heineken Beer Brand clock on the wall over the bar. It was 9:00 p.m. Without realizing it, Pozy had been freed.

—

The kiss seemed to last an eternity, yet in reality, it was several minutes. As their lips parted, neither one could break eye contact, allowing the heat that began with the embrace to continue while simply holding hands.

"Wow," she said with a smile. *His lips are so soft,* she thought.

"Right back at ya," he said, and felt a slight flutter throughout his entire body. He kissed her again, and this time she pushed her lips firmly against his.

Oh…God, his lips are so soft and warm. I want this night to last forever, she thought as a weakness overpowered every sense of her being. *His arms are strong, yet he can be so gentle with me. I want him now,* she thought, but then he moved from her and their gaze on each other melted them to the spot, as a light rain began to tap on the windshield and the encircling fog encapsulated them in their metal cocoon.

"Take me back to the Inn," she said, softly, with no indication that everything but wonderful was the order of the evening. Without a word in response, he started the motor, but before pulling away, he looked toward her.

"Was everything ok with the restaurant and all?" Rodney's self-imposed inadequacy in a sexual or personal relationship plagued him once again.

"It couldn't have been better," she said and moved toward him, their lips meeting, this time with the moistness of a deep, passionate kiss, and neither of them noticed the minutes passing. Their closeness was arousing. She placed her hand gently on his thigh; suddenly awakening a need in Rodney that had been sleeping for a long time. Thinking the moment right, gently he cupped one of her petite breasts in his left hand, and she gave a slight moan of satisfaction. Her firmness and warmth excited him to the core.

—

The transaction between Pozy and the waiter took less than a minute. Paying in cash, having no idea of what to leave for a tip, he threw three twenty-dollar bills down and hurried out to meet Zeke, who he felt would be in a world of panic and anger by now and probably ready to kill something or someone again. Upon exiting through the same side door, he looked around, but Zeke was nowhere to be seen. Pozy dashed to the rear corner of the building, seeing nothing and no one, he bolted toward the large temple-like doors they had come in from, yet all that he saw were tourists, parking their cars and entering the restaurant. Now… it was Pozy who panicked. As much as he'd contemplated being on his own, he'd become through his fear somewhat subservient in his reliance to be told what to do by Zeke, who had suddenly vanished. Pozy felt psychologically and physically stranded, and had no idea what to do next. At this point, he never gave it a thought that Zeke might have taken off, leaving him behind.

I'm a witness to the murders. And with that thought, he shivered with the fear of what would happen when they got caught. His fear was so intense now, it made him feel ill each time it came to mind. He wanted his freedom, but he knew better. It wasn't if… it was when they got caught. Pozy ditched into the woods behind the restaurant. He knew the back way to the garage from here.

—

The traffic was typically heavy for a Friday night. The fog slowed it down a bit, and it appeared that no one attempted to make a fool of themselves on the road by taking unnecessary chances. Rodney drove slowly, nervously hoping the ride would build some level of self-confidence in him before arriving at the Inn. Lil made it easy for him, however. Her soft voice and even temperament was enjoyable for Rodney, who had become used to the high level of stress and sometimes anxiety that went along with his job. Rodney turned left at the first crossroad, affording them the road less taken. She slid toward him now. The road was dark and few cars appeared. The scent of her hair mixed with the essence of her perfume made it difficult for him to concentrate on his driving, yet his self-confidence, if only from his desire for her, began to build in strength. They were within several miles of the Inn. It was obvious from their faces that both were anxious to arrive, and without speaking of it, though it was not possible to disguise, their need for each other dripped with the desire to be sexually satisfied. She pushed herself tighter against him, placing her hand on his thigh, feeling his manhood and causing him to exhale a deep breath.

"Are we very far from the Inn?" she asked.

"Oh…not at all," he answered quickly. "No more than a mile, now."

She smiled at him, exhaling a breath of satisfaction. The street lights loomed hazy in the distance through the fog and she nuzzled against his neck. Suddenly, the darkened shadow of a figure appeared in the underbrush, moving quickly from view, forcing a scream from Lil, causing Rodney to swerve wildly as he slammed the brakes on, first swerving to the left, then to the right, then fishtailing slightly before getting the car under control on the damp road surface and stopping at the edge of the steep shoulder.

"Oh…my God! It was him," she cried. "The guy who shot Melvin just ran into those bushes," and she pointed in the direction she saw him run.

"What…?" he asked, confused. Rodney had seen nothing, leaving him bewildered for having allowed his guard down for that short period of time.

"Are you sure you saw the same person? The one…"

She interrupted him. "I've never been so sure about anything in my life. I'll never forget what that bastard looked like. It was him and he was wearing the same goddamned clothes."

The heavy, gray fog made it difficult to see things only feet on front of him. The going was rough, even for Zeke, but having heard the screeching tires and what he made out to be a faint scream caused him to move even faster than when trying to avoid being seen by the oncoming car. But he was obviously too stoned and drunk to move his own weight. In the distance now, he heard the sound of a slamming car door, but he never slowed to hear that anyone followed. Even if they did attempt it, he had a much greater head start, and through the foggy, wooded darkness, it would be almost impossible to follow without a decent spot-light or a good bloodhound. What bothered him as he ran was *who and why would someone have stopped so quick after seeing me?*

The darkness was a real problem. Zeke stumbled several times, not a hundred yards from the road. The last topple forced him down on his knees, and he thought he might have sprained his ankle. After several minutes to rest, and keeping his espial senses tuned to his surroundings, realizing he wasn't being followed, he stayed put for a few minutes, occasionally testing the ankle, giving him time to rest from his run through the thicket. His mouth and throat had gone completely dry, making swallowing difficult, and he wished to himself out loud, "If I only had one more beer." He was hot and wanted to take the jacket off, but then he'd have to carry it. If he tucked the gun into the waist-line of his jeans, he knew if he fell again the gun could cause him a world of hurt. He began speaking to himself as if Pozy sat beside him. His young mind was shattered.

"Ya know…if we sit here too long, them fuckers up thea' aar' gonna' get us." He laughed out loud then. "Let 'em come. I'll plug the hell out of 'em with my tiny….38 hea'," and he pulled the gun from his inside breast pocket and pointed it at nothing in particular, then swung it toward shadows of trees in the direction of the road. Suddenly, Missy's face appeared in his mind's eye, and he needed to see her. He strained getting himself to his feet—the pain in his ankle was harsh. He listened intently to the world around him, then moved slowly in a direction that would parallel the road. He was far enough in to remain hidden. He was on his way to see Missy.

—

After seeing who Lil thought was the murderer, the one who came to life occasionally in her nightmares, unfortunately…there would probably be no further immersion into a possible romantic interlude that evening. Rodney was pumped with adrenaline upon his return to the car, unable to see or hear anything in the woods. He immediately began an attempt at reassuring Lil, but she appeared to be in a state of shock, and reassurance would not be easy. They remained parked along the shoulder for some time and he slowly put his arm around her shoulder and with the other hand, took his phone out and hit the preset-set speed-dial number for the Dells Police Dispatch.

"Rodney Torrey, here. I'm on the South Side Road, just off Route 1. I believe..." he hesitated for a moment, not sure of how to report the sighting, as he'd seen nothing. Thinking another second..."We think we've spotted the subject in the Melvin Nisbet case. Send a patrol car down, ASAP. I'll be here when they arrive," he said.

He could feel Lil tremble in his arms. He wanted to kiss her and tell her he would make it all go away, but he knew the time was all wrong, and it wasn't the reality of what he did as a cop. She just needed to be held and let the passage of time get her through this. *She's a strong-willed young woman, she's proven that,* he thought. Without saying a word to her, he immediately called Harry. While the ring-tone filled his ear, he looked at his watch. It was 9:30 p.m. Suddenly, he remembered that Harry was an early-to-bed person, but the phone was picked up.

"Hello...this is Harry."

"Harry, this is Rod. Sorry to bother you at this hour, but..."He was interrupted.

"No bother. What's up, Rod?"

"I believe we just saw the murderer jump from the road and into the woods, about a quarter-mile off Route 1 in Dells. I'm waiting for a cruiser to respond now," he said.

"What murderer?" Harry asked, sounding somewhat confused.

"Melvin Nisbet's murderer," Rodney answered.

At the sound of the name Melvin, Lil became suddenly saddened, knowing how much he hated to be called Melvin. *He said it made him feel old. It's what his parents and elder family members called him, but he insisted on being called Mel by his close friends,* she remembered.

"I'm coming to meet you," Harry said and before Rodney could speak, he heard the click of the broken connection on Harry's end. Without realizing it, and at the same moment, Rodney and Harry wanted to call the chief, but the fact that he'd been so out-of-touch or simply unreachable made it a second thought to follow their chain of command. But this was a police investigation and

Willard Weaks, no matter how distracted or removed from the case he became, was still the Town of Dells, Maine Chief of Police. Protocol took precedence.

—

By the time a cruiser arrived on scene at the South Side Road location to meet Rodney, Zeke had long since re-crossed Route 1 and continued, with a slight limp, toward his destination, Missy's place. He and Pozy knew the wooded areas outside of Dells as well as the back of their own hands. From where he'd been seen just off the South Side Road to Missy's was less than one mile cross-country. Normally for Zeke, it wouldn't take very long to travel that distance through the woods, but having to accommodate his ankle, it would take a considerable effort and a goodly amount of time.

As he progressed, his thoughts ranged from leaving the restaurant and Pozy behind with the cash and how stupid that was and the stash of drugs and guns at the garage and how he'd get them out. At times, for no reason at all, knowing well that he was far enough from dwellings or the road, he would burst out with loud, angry fits of yelling and once, he pulled the gun out and fired one round into a tree stump he'd tripped on. Realizing suddenly what he'd done, he sat on the ground after the shot, listening to his surroundings. Surely the firing of a gun after dark, especially in Dells, would be cause for alarm and undoubtedly a call would be made to the cops. He was rested. It was time to move and move fast. He changed directions, moving closer to Route 1, but not close enough to be seen, yet close enough to see whatever came from the reporting of the shot, if anything. If the cops did respond, they would most likely arrive at the home of the caller, and getting there, Route 1 would be the most likely route and that would not be where Zeke was when they did. He walked quicker now, his ankle limbered and the pain subsided.

I'll bet she missed me. She'll be pissed at first, but after a little kissy-feely, she'll come around ta my point of view, he thought as a police car went past him, about a hundred feet away, going toward the South Side Road.

Well...whoever it was that saw me out thea' must a' called 'em, he thought, but it was a second police car responding to the call about the shot from the woods. But he had no way of knowing that.

—

Pozy wandered along aimlessly, clueless as to what had made Zeke cut out the way he did. At any moment, he expected him to pop out of nowhere, ending the cherished freedom he now enjoyed with some skepticism. He continued on a path that paralleled the road, whichever one he chose to travel. His destination goal was his garage, even though he knew it would be Zeke's plan also. In his mind, he knew they would eventually meet up. After all, the drugs and guns were there and Zeke would want to make good use of their potential value and support his need to be free.

As he got closer to the garage, the fog thinned somewhat through this section of wooded land. He was close to the road that would lead him there when a Maine State Police car raced past in the same direction he was walking. He stopped, his ears immediately tuned to his surroundings, and his old, paranoid fears that the law looked for him came alive once again through his guilt. He agonized over whether or not to go to the garage now. There was no telling what kind of mess Zeke had got himself into after leaving the Chinese restaurant. As he stood, silently listening to the world around him, his mental process inspired him to turn around and head toward the old family homestead, where he knew no one would think to look for him. Not even Zeke would venture there. Although his belly was full, he could almost smell the homemade soup simmering on the stove in his mother's kitchen, and he longed for that simple security that came with a life he'd become so far removed from.

—

Zeke stood angrily in the shadows of the thickly grown section of trees and bushes, left deliberately untrimmed for privacy along the border of the property. From here he had an unobstructed view of Missy's home and the driveway to the side. Marcy's car was not there, and the source of his anger was the big Mopar parked in its place. The lights throughout the house were dim and he saw no visible signs of movement from within. He remained where he stood for quite some time, his anger stewed to a boiling point.

What-tha' hell is that little—fuck-a-diddle doin' hea' at this time o' night? The minute I take a day or two at camp...the cockroaches come outta the woodwork. And what is she doin' seein' him this time o' night, the little whore? he thought to himself, but some unseen force held him where he stood. His hand went directly to the .38, and the second his hand was upon it, he took his first step toward the house, still hiding in the thicket. The fog remained dense, allowing him to move undetected while his eyes stayed focused on the windows so that he might see anyone inside who might choose to pass in front of them. No one did. He knew the house and the entrances, front and rear, and the rear was the best choice for him to be unseen by any passersby. He moved like a Black Racer whose vision was riveted to the location of its prey. With no sound about him, Zeke paid little attention to his surroundings as he neared the building. It was 10:00 p.m., late for a working-class neighborhood. The partiers were at the beach and the solitude encapsulated him and the chaos of his intentions.

There was a three-step staircase to the rear kitchen door and he looked around intently before placing a foot on the lowest step, and then he went up. He hesitated only a second, placed his hand on the knob and entered. Even after warnings from the police and the media, folks around here still never locked their doors.

Immediately, the familiar scent of the house filled his senses, and he moved slowly, his ears perked to any unsuspected or unfamiliar sound and he stopped abruptly when a floor-board creaked underfoot. The house remained as quiet as a morgue, and seeing nothing on that level of the house, he continued toward the staircase leading to the second landing and the bedroom area. Upon reaching the ornate banister at the staircase of the old house, he cased his surroundings like a burglar in the night. It was so quiet he believed that perhaps no one was even in the house. It grew darker the farther up he went, but as he reached the second level, the familiar voice of his so-called friend tugged at his ears, while the aromatic essence of Missy's perfume filled his nostrils, causing his jugular to pulse with an anger, the depth of which had slept within him until now.

The sounds came from Missy's room at the far end of the hall. He moved silently like a big cat preparing to pounce on an unsuspecting sparrow. The sound of their voices became clearer, each one distinctly familiar. A dim light glowed through the partially open door, and he crept to within inches of it and peered inside the room. His emotions at seeing them took control. He planted his heavy boot hard against the door and kicked it open with a force that slammed it against the wall, the doorknob bashing a huge hole into the plaster with an explosion that forced the couple, naked on top of the sheets, to jerk their bodies in fear in the direction of the destructive sound. The sight of Missy's naked body completely exposed to him instantly turned him on, yet the gun in his hand, pointed in their direction, was more compelling to him.

"Well…well, well. Missy and Petey, ain't this a sight for sore eyes? From the look on yaw' faces, it looks as though you two aar' gettin' ready ta use the same bedpan. Is this…true love?" Zeke stressed the word "love."

"Oh...you have such a nice body, Missy baby. I've been missin' ya, but it don't look much ta me that you've been feelin' the same," he said.

Petey began to speak when Zeke hollered out, "Shut up!"

Missy and Petey were stunned into silence. The gun was pointed at Petey's head.

"My close friend and my girl. Did ya'll think I wasn't comin' back?" he asked, but this time there was no attempted response from either Missy or Petey. Missy covered herself in embarrassment with a blanket, yet Zeke, much to their surprise, had nothing to say. He simply stared at them, one after the other, and his silence was enough to make his point. The barrel of the gun only reinforced the idea that perhaps their time had come. After a sickening silence, Zeke burped and began laughing, sending shivers of fear through Missy. And then he spoke up.

"Ya know…Missy, yaw' actin' like some scabby Jane from the Portland waterfront. How long has this been goin' on? You two been squeezin' like this for awhile now?" and then his voice took on an eerie depth in tone. It was as if someone else spoke.

"I think I'm gonna' whack the both o' ya and wait 'til ya bleed out like the rest o' them fucks who thought I was some retard or some stupid farm-boy, with cow shit all ova' me." They would have no way of knowing what he meant by that last comment, and neither would ask any questions now. Zeke paced back and forth at the foot of the bed then stopped, centering his stare on them.

Without warning, Zeke began to shake. His hand, the one holding the gun, shook uncontrollably and his body seemed to respond in spastic twitches. His face contorted into an unfamiliar person's. It lasted for a minute, not much more, but a minute that seemed to last forever. As fast as he came, and without another word, he was gone, leaving the two wondering why, but speechless. All of it lasted less than ten minutes if it was possible for either to tell time.

32

THE FOG WAS AS THICK as pea soup when Harry reached the South Side Road. A Dells cruiser had already arrived and was parked in front of Rodney's car, its blue strobe lights illuminating the fog several feet above and to the side of both cars. Approaching at a prudent speed, it was difficult to see the surroundings well because of those lights, but it would certainly slow any oncoming vehicles to the scene. Harry couldn't wait to be filled in, for during his travels through the beach area, he'd been passed in both directions by State Police cars. It pumped him with his former sense of self-reliance seeing and being a part of all this.

He parked, staying well behind the police car, leaving plenty of room in the event the officer had to leave in a hurry. He was blinded by the blue lights, yet for the life of him he couldn't remember it happening to him when it was his own blue lights stopping someone for whatever reason. Rodney spotted him as soon as he arrived, and reassuring Lil first, he got out to meet him.

"Good evening. It looks as though you're having quite a date," Harry said, but remained straight-faced, knowing very well how Rodney had looked forward to this evening.

"It went well until about a half an hour ago when she..." Rodney paused momentarily, looking back toward his car and the silhouette of Lillian sitting in the front seat, alone. "She said she saw the guy who killed her boyfriend back at the beach early this summer."

"Did you see him?" Harry asked.

"I saw a shadow and took off after it, but…I couldn't keep up in all of this," he said, sweeping his arm about him to indicate the fog. They both looked back toward the car. Lil, who Harry had never met, was looking out toward the wooded land where the shadow vanished.

"Is she going to be ok? This has to be a jolt to her system," Harry said.

"She's a toughie. She'll get through this, she's strong, but tonight's a bust for us now. I'll stay with her as long as she needs me, then we'll play it by ear, ya know?" Rodney said.

Harry stayed right with it. "Did she get a good-enough look at him, you know, description of any kind?" Harry asked.

"Yah," and Rodney lifted the notepad he was holding. He always kept one in his civilian car. Rodney relayed the description from Lil's sighting and wasn't quite finished when Harry interrupted.

"Sorry, Rod, but check this out." He now opened his own notepad and read the young man's description on the path only this afternoon at the Tilton Ave. location. As far as he was concerned, he was either describing the same person or this was a very unlikely case of mistaken identity.

"Well…I'll be…" Rodney's voice trailed off as he looked toward his car again. Suddenly, he looked back at Harry, whose eyebrows were lifted to the highest point of his forehead.

"Are you thinking what I'm thinking?" Harry asked.

"I'm thinking I am," Rodney answered.

Just then, the officer who'd responded to Rodney's call came out of his cruiser and approached the two men.

"I just got off the radio with dispatch. Nothing turned up from that call about a shot fired."

"What shot?" Harry asked.

"Sorry, Harry," Rodney interjected. "Someone called the station shortly after we saw the shadow…" He paused momentarily. "Someone uptown heard a shot in the woods outside of their home and called it in. The troopers are in on it also," Rodney said.

That explains all the activity with the troopers, Harry thought. He feared that another rampage was being set in motion, and it was probably the same renegade who was now an even more out-of-control murderer. He did not share that thought with either man standing next to him. He glanced now toward Lillian Crandlemyer and hoped Rodney was right when he said she was strong-willed. Being here tonight was throwing the nightmare right back in her face.

From where they stood, the officer on duty heard his radio and excused himself, going back to his cruiser.

"So…Harry, when did you go back and talk to that kid on Tilton Ave.?"

"Right after I left you off at the station. I wanted to call you, but I knew how important this evening was for you…" and he looked toward Rodney's car and the young woman.

"By the way," Rodney said. "I called the chief. There's something going on with him and it's more than his wife's illness."

"You got something eatin' at your gut, Rod?" Harry asked, but Rodney remained quiet as if to indicate his uncertainty on the subject. Right now, both men had attained an enormous respect for each other's acumen in their approach to the investigation, and Harry remained quiet.

Several minutes passed as both Harry and Rodney struggled for something constructive to say.

Seemingly in a trance, Rodney looked out toward the wooded land where the shadow of a potential murderer had escaped only a short time ago, when Harry began to ask a question.

"How sure is she?" he began, when the officer came back from his cruiser and interrupted him.

"Rodney…Do you know a kid by the name Petey Harriman?"

"Ah…yah', I do. What's up?" he asked.

"Well, he just called in to dispatch and said—Zeke stole his car and to tell you. What in hell do you think that means?"

From the looks on their faces, the two lawmen knew exactly what was meant by the statement.

—

Petey had a bad habit of leaving his ignition key over the sun-visor. *Out-of-sight, out-of-mind,* was his theory, but when you tell the wrong people, even if they're your friends, it can come back to bite you on the ass. The second the big motor rumbled to a start, Zeke was on his way to the garage. He knew that Pozy would eventually get the message that he was gone, and he had every intention of picking him up later. Right now, however, Petey's Mopar would act as a pick-up-and-delivery vehicle for the stash they'd left at the garage. He was totally psyched up to be behind the wheel of a car again. He'd lost his license five years before, and never attempted to get it back. As long as good-old Petey was willing to cart their asses around, it was fine with him.

—

"Slap 'er in ta second and give 'er the turkey!" Zeke hollered at the top of his lungs—the old back-country saying he'd heard from an old farmer years ago while plowing a corn field on a tractor felt appropriate.

Unexpectedly, a vision of Missy and Petey, naked in the same bed he'd spent so much time in with her himself, flashed through his subconscious mind, and he pushed hard on the gas pedal. Flinging his left arm out the driver's-side window, he fired a shot across the hood at a road sign on the shoulder, never knowing if he'd even hit it, he was going that fast. The doors to hell were wide open for him now, and he was one crash away from getting there. Had he been thinking at all, he should have known, with all his exposure and as many times as he'd fired the gun tonight that the countryside would be crawling with cops answering complaints of someone shooting up the world and stealing cars. Zeke, however, was too far gone for that. It was all about him, as it had always been, but now, his desires took on a deadly energy.

Missy remained in a state of shock, in bed, her knees tucked firmly against her chest, held by her encircling arms. The blanket she'd pulled over her while Zeke pointed the gun at them covered her nudity. In her mind, the stupid thing about all of this was not being caught in bed with Petey, but the fact that she still loved Zeke and couldn't believe that he would point a gun toward her and threaten her the way that he did.

Sure…it's my fault again. Zeke can do no wrong and it's always the other guy who screws up. But that gun. Where did he get that and what has he done with it already? she wondered, when the sudden sound of Petey's voice startled her back to the present.

"Are you all right, Missy?"

"No, I'm not," she said, and paused momentarily, then went on. "I'm not sorry that you and I got together like this. I'm sorry for the way it all went down. I can't believe he's carrying a gun." Petey pressed his lips together. He'd omitted that information when he'd called the police about his stolen car. "And with his temper, there's no way to tell what he's gotten himself into…not to mention he was aiming it at us," she said.

Petey, thinking almost the same thing, but seeing the gun through his mind's eye with the cold, round end of its barrel pointing at him…and then finding his beloved car gone, thought, *I want to take her by the shoulders and shake some sense into her and tell her that Zeke has always been bad. I'd like to tell her how he'd give the boys the details of their relationship and the things he made her do sexually.* That wasn't Petey, however. He felt sorry for her, not in a way that would hold him captive to a sexual relationship, because for Petey…it was much more than that.

—

"Well, Marcy…It looks as though the shit is finally hitting the fan. I think Harry is stirring the pot with a big spoon," Willard said.

Although it was wishful thinking on his part, the fact that Harry had helped to uncover evidence that either was overlooked or just unable to be found by Rodney was a good thing; together, they were a remarkable team. Lately, because of his involvement with Marcy and the failing condition of his wife's health, Willard Weaks, if only for reasons of self-preservation, could only think of himself and his retirement. The fact that he'd become difficult to find was intentional. Call it pride or simply a denial of reality, he was keeping himself out of the public eye, and there was no happier person than Marcy. She had detached herself, in a way, from her own responsibilities also, and it was just the way she wanted it. Right now, however, all Willard and Marcy knew was that the possible killer of the kid from Connecticut had been seen by a young woman riding with Rodney. There was no putting two plus two together for him. What they would not know until much later was the event that took place at Marcy's home with her daughter and Petey Harriman, which would probably be a turning point in the direction Chief Willard Weaks chose to go.

—

Both Rodney and Harry conferred for several minutes at the location of Zeke's sighting, and agreed that the responding officer would take Lillian back to the Inn. Before they left, Rodney reassured her that he would return there after meeting with the young man who'd reported his car stolen, never mentioning the connection between Petey and Zeke. After all, she didn't know either one except for the brutal connection with Zeke. It was agreed that the officer would remain outside of the Inn until Rodney returned.

Rodney went to the car to console Lillian, while Harry got the name and address the caller gave from the young officer, making an entry into his notes on the same page where Rodney had described Zeke to him earlier. As of yet, Harry had never met any of these people, but it was obvious to him that Zeke was a renegade killer, and all the little pieces of this puzzle began falling in and around Dells, Maine. The radio chatter over the airwaves to police cars throughout the area and beyond gave the description of the stolen car, and more importantly, a description of the driver. It was 10:30 p.m. An hour had passed since Harry had been called.

Unaware of anything that had happened since they'd parted company at the Chinese Restaurant, Pozy came to within a mile of the garage. He was totally exhausted. Because of the enormous police presence each time he attempted to cross a road or open area, he would pause for long periods of time, waiting and listening, and it took him over an hour to travel the relatively short distance. A strange feeling ruled over him: one of being completely alone, like those periods at the garage during the heat of summer when Zeke had pulled his disappearing acts and Petey and Dwight were off to their jobs. That one time when he visited the family homestead, as far as he could tell, was a turning point in his life that had never reversed itself. Now, he longed for the quiet security that his little garage would offer him, but his paranoia about the murders would not allow him to rest easy. At any moment, he truly believed he would be encircled by police cars and arrested.

Finally, without knowing what time it was or how long it took him, the garage, still as dark as when they left it to return to the camp, came into sight. From where he stood, it was obvious from the forsaken appearance that no one was or had been there. Surprisingly enough, he thought… *With all the cop cars around, why isn't Queer-Eye, being the cop of cops, not here waiting for someone to show up?*

After observing for several minutes from his lookout, he decided to move toward the garage. With every step taken, he listened intently to his surroundings for any unfamiliar sound, especially any vehicles slowing suddenly at the entrance to the gravel leading to the garage. There was nothing. *Soon, I'll be fast asleep and I'll worry about tomorrow when it comes,* he thought. He was at the double doors now. He'd taken the key from its hiding place and paused once again, this time looking over his shoulder toward the road, simultaneously yanking on the door. He was home.

The first thing to catch his eye was the empty space where they'd left the duffle bags filled with drugs and the sawed-off shotguns, just inside of the doors. His first thought at seeing the empty space was, *how did Zeke carry it all away without my help?*

He couldn't imagine, as tired as he was right now, that Zeke would have the energy to carry it all back to camp without waiting for him to get back here. But knowing how fierce Zeke was when in one of his moods, he wouldn't put anything past him. He looked around the garage, and seeing nothing out of place except the bags and guns, he threw himself headlong onto an old chair he'd brought from his parents and within minutes, was fast asleep.

—

"Petey," Missy asked in a subdued, questioning tone, "With your call to the police about the car being stolen, you know they'll send someone over to ask questions. Do you think the chief will put it all together…you know… you and me?"

They sat on the side of the bed staring into each others eyes, yet remained speechless at the thought. "You know damned well it will only be a matter of time before the chief and my mother get the news and it'll be you and me being asked more questions. I don't care, for me, but how are you going to handle it?" she asked.

Petey suddenly arrived at the end of his romantic rope. He was not going to play second fiddle for anyone any longer, especially Zeke Brailey.

"Missy, you need to know that I've always kept a special corner of my soul just for you, but down deep I know you'll never stop loving him no matter what I say or do for a relationship with you. But don't ever talk down to me where my emotions or the strength of my ability to deal with the freaks of the world is concerned. That…would be your biggest mistake," he said.

She looked at him, stunned. She'd never seen this side of him before. He always displayed a kind of passive approach to life, a follower as opposed to the leader.

It's probably the stolen car bringing all this out, but I like it on him, she thought.

"Ok…ok, I didn't mean it like it came out, sorry," she said.

He remained looking toward her, and his face softened as a hard knock came to the front door.

—

With Lil being escorted back to the Inn by the officer, Rodney, though he found it difficult to leave her, was comfortable being with Harry on the front step of the location given of the stolen car. What he knew, however, was that Petey did not live here.

Harry knocked on the door, giving even Rodney a start in the midst of the quiet of the night. From inside, footsteps were heard by both lawmen approaching with a brisk intention to answer the knock on the door. When the door finally opened, it was Missy who stood before them. Knowing that Petey had called the police, she expected to see a uniformed officer, but finding both Rodney Torrey in casual, civilian clothes and another man she did not recognize in camo' attire, took her aback for a moment until Rodney spoke up.

"Missy…I was surprised to see your address come up from a call on a stolen car."

He knew exactly whose car was stolen and who the caller had been, it was simply his way of coming to the point without having it sound like an official stance. All three stood for a moment, seemingly uncomfortable, until Missy spoke.

"I'm sorry, please come in," she said, and she stepped to one side allowing them to enter, closing the door after looking outside. Her fear was that Zeke was still in the area, watching.

The downstairs of the house was as neat as a pin; it appeared that everything had its place. Missy pointed to a large sofa in the center of the room facing the fireplace, long since cooled during the heat of summer. At the invitation, each man chose a spot closer to the center cushion rather than toward each armrest. Conversations could flow between the parties without much head-turning, keeping eye contact easy. Much to Rodney's surprise, Petey came down the staircase, seemingly comfortable with his surroundings. The last time Rodney had seen him was during his traffic stop when he pulled Petey over looking for Zeke. What Rodney thought of first was, *Funny how some things never change.* The second thing he thought of, however, was the doughnut caper at the beginning of summer.

"Petey…long time no see. Had any good donuts lately?" Rodney asked, much to the questioning eyes of both Harry and Missy. Neither knew of the incident.

"No, I don't eat 'em…Officer Torrey. Besides…" He was interrupted by Rodney.

"I'm just kidding. We're here because of your call about the car. You told the dispatcher that Zeke stole your car. I'd be curious to know whatever you could tell us," Rodney said. He turned toward Harry for a moment, then back to Missy and Petey.

"Please forgive me. This is Retired State Trooper, Harry Circus. He occasionally consults with the Dells Police Department."

Harry nodded his head in their direction, but remained silent, letting Rodney lead the way with two people he was obviously familiar with. Harry looked at Missy now, and for whatever reason, she looked vaguely familiar to him, but he gave it up to his many years of interrogating characters in the past. Rodney took the perceptive cue from Harry and began.

"Tell me the specifics of what led up to Zeke taking your car. Why do you think he stole it? I thought you all were friends." Petey remained silent. The question was an in-your-face type, causing a visible discomfort from the two who, until now, hadn't found a place to sit. Simultaneously, each took their place in respective chairs at each side of the fireplace facing the two officers. Both Rodney and Harry remained quiet after that last question, especially after seeing their reaction. It couldn't have been quieter, and the only sound came from the ticking of an antique mantel clock over the fireplace.

Harry, never having met the two young people in front of him, looked around the room simply because he liked the layout. Seconds continued to tick away; Rodney cleared his throat and appeared ready to ask the same or another question when Petey spoke up. "We got into a bit of a spitting match when Zeke…" he hesitated, then continued. "He'd been gone for quite some time and didn't know that Missy and I…well, ya know, we've been seeing each other. When he came in and saw us together, I guess he—kind of lost it."

"Lost it how? Did he get physical with the two of you?" Rodney asked, and from their facial expressions it was obvious they were holding something back.

Both officers had learned long ago that sometimes silence on the part of the questioner is a better tool to get the subject of an interrogation to open up than an aggressive approach. Harry, seeing their faces, was ushered back in time to a drab, color-faded questioning room in Machias, where two stepsisters had held his questions at bay until he backed off a little to finally win their trust and get them to open up to him. It was obvious, if only to themselves, that the two lawmen were on the same page. After the last question, seeing their expressions, Rodney maintained his silent stare, this time toward Petey and after several seconds—much less time than Harry expected—Petey opened up.

"Ya know…Rodney, Zeke's a bit of a wild-man when he gets wound up." He was hedging on the direction he should have been going with this and Rodney saw right through it. Petey looked to Missy, and the look on her face would not allow him to betray her by covering up for the things Zeke did any longer.

"No…that's a bunch o' crap and I think you know it," Petey said. "He pulled a freakin' gun on us. He's out of his mind. From what he said, he came here to see Missy. When he found us… ya know, upstairs," he pointed to the staircase as if to strengthen what he said, "he lost it and made some scary threats." His body language spoke volumes in the minds of the two men sitting across from him. It was Harry's turn to ask a question.

"Besides the gun—and I'm not trying to make light of that fact—what kind of threats, exactly?"

"Well…what scared the hell out o' me, and I have no way of knowing what he actually meant by it, but he said… 'I'm gonna whack ya both and watch ya bleed out like the rest o' them fucks who thought I was some retard with cow shit on my boots.' He's out of his mind, I'm tellin' ya," Petey said.

At that point, Petey wasn't quite sure if he'd relayed to the officers word for word what Zeke had said, but in his mind, it was damned close enough to get his point across to them that Zeke had gone over the edge.

"And he stole my car, goddammit!" Petey added.

The two men glanced toward each other, yet remained quiet after that last comment. After several uncomfortable minutes as Missy and Petey watched Harry look around the room as if he'd never seen furniture before and Rodney scribbling things in his notepad, both now thought the two to be somewhat eccentric in the manner in which they conducted a question-and-answer period that seemed to have gone nowhere. But the fact that both Missy and Petey felt the need to add more to what was already asked of them was a good indication the officer's silence-in-questioning technique had worked in their favor. Petey was burning with the need to get his car back and couldn't figure out why they hadn't asked more about it or about the type of gun Zeke had pulled on them.

"Don't you want some info on my car…or the gun I said he pulled on us?" Petey asked, frustrated.

"Sure, sure…" Harry said. "What kind of car is it?"

Finally, Petey was fulfilled in his need to tell all that he could.

"It's a 1964 Dodge 880, white, four-door."

"Nice…" Harry responded, adding… "Are we talking .361 cubic inch big-block here?"

"Yeah," Petey said gleefully.

"I'm thinking… push-button on the dash, automatic tranny?" Harry asked.

"Wow, you're definitely up on the old cars. Not many folks would know about the push-button on the dash shifter." They had each other's interest now.

"Well, hell yah, I'm up on the old stuff. It's the only good stuff if you ask me," Harry said, and he began telling the young man about his de-commissioned 1965 Missouri State Police car, which was just outside in the driveway.

33

The questioning of Missy and Petey went on for about half an hour, and although the young couple did not feel as if they offered enough to help the men in pursuing Zeke, they could not know the full extent of the officer's interest. During the questioning, and without them recalling when they offered it, both Petey and Missy at different times mentioned the garage—a location that Rodney was most familiar with, yet on his approach to finding Zeke, had always found it to be a dead end. Now, however, he felt a strong sense of certainty about the little hideaway, and he would fill Harry in on it as much as he could where needed. Petey felt as though the retired trooper could relate to the loss of his antique automobile, and he was right.

As their questioning came to a close, Harry looked toward Petey as if another size-up of the young man was in order. His acumen of Petey's personality was that of a caring, giving, yet somewhat industrious person. Even without knowing him personally, his estimation was right on. Harry looked to Rodney now and saw a look of revitalization on his face.

"We're close to wrapping this up, right?" Harry asked.

"Yes, we are," Rodney answered.

Harry looked at Petey. "Look…Peter..." Harry called him by his given name, causing him to look to the trooper intently. "Would you like to take a close look at my '65 Missouri Trooper car?" he asked.

"I…yah, I would," Petey said.

Rodney smiled from the corner of his mouth, looking toward Harry, and nodded his head in approval, knowing very well that without entrapment as a plan he'd won the young man's support if simply through their love of antique cars.

As they left for the driveway, Petey looked back toward Missy. She looked anguished, yet she might have just as easily been longing for his return. Rodney just happened to catch their expressions and waited until Petey and Harry went out before offering a comment.

"You know…Missy, I've been watching your facial expressions change each time Zeke's name was mentioned. You never tried to keep your feeling for him a secret. Is Petey just a…" and was about to say, a rebound from a lost love, but then he paused, and well that he did, as it would have come out sounding all wrong hearing what Missy had to say now.

"Look, Rodney. I've always loved Zeke. He saved me, emotionally, a long time ago, but he's fallen by the wayside, you might say. I've seen it coming for a while now and so has Petey and Dwight, although Dwight has gone his own way, I guess. It's when he pulled that gun on us and the look on his face, then that shit about letting us bleed out and all…." And then it was as if the dam broke and she began crying like a little girl. The tears ran freely down her face, covering the back of her hands as she tried to support her head.

Suddenly, Rodney was wrapped up in the emotions, and his steel facade turned to mush for different reasons, but caused by the same man, Zeke Brailey. He reached into the back pocket of his pants and removed a neatly folded and pressed white handkerchief and offered it to Missy. His frustration, however, stemmed from his failure that he'd never been able to even catch a glimpse of Zeke each time he went out to find him. Several minutes passed, and Missy regained her composure, looking toward the officer as though she should be guilty for allowing herself to break down in that way in front of him, but Rodney's perception was again keen and the last thing he would do now was to say something stupid. Silence was his best tool, but the last thing he expected was what Missy asked next.

"Do you think he's involved in any of those …murders this summer?" she asked.

Rodney hesitated a long moment, not wanting to take the conversation anywhere that might compromise what the authorities already believed to be true.

"Well…we have some information, but right now, we couldn't say." He stopped then, hearing Harry and Petey returning from outside. From the look on Harry's face, Rodney couldn't wait to hear what Petey might have told him. As they entered the living room, Petey went directly to Missy, keeping the reunion to a slight touching of their hands. Petey seemed more relaxed now that he'd spent some time with Harry and his car, but he and Missy could not hide all of their emotions. There was an obvious nervousness about them, but anyone who's had a gun pointed at them are usually never the same, and these two were obviously psychologically affected by the experience. Now, it appeared that the officers, who'd apparently been recharged by the direction the questioning had gone with the two people who were, without a doubt, former friends of Zeke Brailey, were ready to leave. Rodney, being the local cop, spoke first.

"Is there anything else you might think of that could lead us in the direction that Zeke might go besides the garage?" He paused momentarily, looking first at Missy then at Petey. The overpowering silence again seemed to encapsulate the entire downstairs of the house with a funeral-home atmosphere. At that point, all four seemed to fidget in their seats, and it became obvious that the interview was finally over when Missy looked at Petey, then Rodney, and apparently remembered something.

"You know, they had a camp somewhere out in the woods," she said. Her face seemed to contemplate an intense memory of sorts.

"I think his grandfather built it, but…for the life of me—I can't remember where it is."

"You mean, Zeke?" Rodney asked, surprised, looking toward Petey

"What about you, Petey? Zeke must have said something to you about it."

"No, I have no idea where it is," he said.

Upon finishing the questioning of Missy and Petey, Rodney offered a card with the name and number of a counselor that could help them deal with the gun-threat against them.

"It's a real problem you'll have to face eventually," he told them.

The two officers left at that point, standing outside in the driveway for a while as Rodney filled Harry in on the comments they'd made about the garage, telling him of the times he'd tried to find Zeke there and how conveniently he would vanish. It was Harry who suggested they make a quick stop there, for as Rodney said, it was on their way—back home for Harry and hopefully to the Inn for Rod.

—

It was dark. So dark that nothing in front of the car, to the sides or rear could be seen through an encapsulating, all-consuming darkness. The roar of the engine and the deafening sound of the big tires whining over the blacktop echoed through this eternal Erebus. The two lifeless bodies bounced peculiarly on the back seat, as the vehicle, seemingly out of control, moved at high speed over the curvy and at times uneven road. Faster it went as it approached the high-rise bridge at a rate of speed that it might never had gone before. The wide-open eyes of the dead appeared to be the only ones to see what was about to happen.

The upright posts of the guardrails flashed by as if animated. This time Zeke was at the wheel, laughing his fool head off. Without warning, the car began to fishtail wildly out of control, sideswiping the guardrail, and because of the centrifugal force caused by the speed the vehicle maintained, it hugged the rail, sending fiery sparks from the clash of metals into the darkness below, until the front wheel lodged against a rise in the curb, thrusting the car over the rail into the awaiting abyss.

"I'm sorry…I'm sorry. I didn't want to kill them. It's not my fault."

What should have been a silent fall into oblivion ended suddenly with a distant, continuous pounding. A pounding that would not stop. Pozy was being ushered out of his nightmare.

"What—what?" Pozy was wrenched from his restless sleep. He was drenched in sweat as he stumbled toward the voices that called out to him to open up. He tripped twice before reaching the garage doors. When he finally opened it, he couldn't have been more stunned at the sight of Queer-Eye and some other guy he'd never seen standing before him in the darkness.

Seeing Pozy and the condition he was in after hearing him holler as they knocked on the door, both men were happy now that they'd decided to follow through with the plan. All three faced each other; the expressions on their faces identical questioning stares, yet at this point, only Rodney chose to ask a question.

"Is everything all right, in there?"

"Yeah...why wouldn't it be?" Pozy answered, in a tone bordering on sarcasm, yet in a way that might indicate a willingness to cooperate with the two men standing before him. Rodney, knowing the young man, found it quite strange and spoke up.

"We couldn't help hearing you holler in there." Rodney pointed toward the interior, still dark without lights. Pozy remained silent, looking briefly over his shoulder into the sombrous cavity that lay behind him. For whatever reason, Pozy looked to the floor as he was standing in the exact spot that the duffle bags and shotguns had sat, probably only hours earlier, yet he had no way to know what time it was at the moment. From simple instinct, both lawmen followed his gaze to the floor and saw the same: nothing.

Harry couldn't resist. "Did you lose something down there? By the way, my name is Harry Circus. I work with the Dells Police Department from time to time. I hope you don't mind if we ask you a couple of questions." And he motioned toward Rodney to let the young man in front of him know they were together.

"Wha'...what kind of questions? I'm kind of tired, and ya woke me up from a sound sleep." Pozy was about to add something when Rodney interrupted him.

"Well, a sound sleep in this case leaves a lot to be desired. After all, we heard you hollering in there," he said, and he pointed to the inside of the garage. "Can we come in…for a minute?" he asked.

Pozy hesitated for a second, then muttered, "Yeah, I guess so. Hold on a minute." He went to light a candle. As they entered under the gloom of one lit candle on the work bench, both men's natural curiosity forced them, through past experience, to scan, as best that they could, each corner of the garage so their eyes allowed them to see the contents of the building, which was much larger than its outside appearance. After lighting the candle, Pozy remained where he was, but Rodney moved to within several feet of him. Harry remained closer to the doors, keeping an observant eye on their surroundings, inside and out.

"So, once again…Is everything all right? You seemed a bit…" Rodney was about to continue when he was abruptly interrupted by Pozy.

"I said…yeah, before—nothing's changed since then," he said. Rodney's patience was thinning at that point, but he had no reason right now to cause Pozy any grief. He and Harry were here to find Zeke. Knowing how close the two were as friends he couldn't help wonder why Pozy would be here alone. His police mind considered the separation of these two mock-Siamese twins to be a tactic they might have planned to divert the police. They stared into each other's eyes in silence. Rodney was ready and willing to go the distance with this one.

"Ok…I didn't mean ta get ya riled up. I wonder… do you have any idea where Zeke Brailey is?" Rodney asked and returned Pozy's silent stare.

Suddenly, Pozy's guilt from the murders came back to haunt him; he swallowed deep with no satisfaction from his dry mouth and throat. He became noticeably uncomfortable in the eyes of both lawmen and it appeared that a chord had been struck with that question.

"Well, no…why should I? I ain't his keeper. He comes and goes," he said, and it was Rodney's turn to interrupt.

"Ok, no problem. Maybe he's out to the camp? I heard you two go out there a lot." Rodney was searching with that one, but he did get a rise out of him and that's exactly what he wanted. It was as if he'd swallowed a stone, yet he remained quiet, though his eyes formed a squint, looking first at Harry, who remained by the doors, and then at Rodney. The scowl that formed on his face now actually appeared to collapse his eyebrows onto the bridge of his nose.

Rodney was rapidly tiring of the game these young people had played with him most of the summer now, but this was not a game. Three people were dead. Zeke had a gun, and for all anybody knew was the one who'd killed them. This gig was up as far as he was concerned. He could feel his anger rise through his jugular and he took one step toward Pozy. His enlarged eyes demanded attention.

"I'm going to say this one time. You put your listening ears on and keep your trap shut while I'm talking," Rodney said.

The remark took Harry by surprise, as he'd never seen the officer lose his temper, but in a way, he was glad to see this human emotion.

"Your buddy, Zeke, has a gun. He made some scary threats with it toward your other buddies, Missy and Petey, then he stole Petey's car. There are lots of police looking for him right now and if you know where he is or where he might go, it would be real smart for you to share your thoughts," Rodney said.

Without saying a word, Pozy realized now how Zeke was able to move the duffle bags and guns without help. He had Petey's car.

From where he stood, seeing the young man's reaction to Rodney's statement, the retired trooper was extremely happy that they'd decided to make this their first stop after leaving Missy and Petey. Harry looked at his watch. It was 11:45 p.m. The strain on the two officers who'd been at it since early that morning began to weigh heavily upon them. Lawmen and women have been known to put in extremely long hours, supported by gallons of caffeine and devotion to seeing that justice was done. Sometimes, however, fatigue can cause mistakes to be made or crucial evidence to be overlooked. This thought crossed Harry's mind as he looked at the confused, concerned look on the face of a young man standing before Rodney. The silence in the garage was intimidating.

Finally, overcome with the need to know and plagued with his own guilt, Pozy spoke up with a question. "Are Missy and Petey all right?" It was a question that took both Harry and Rodney by surprise. At least Rodney, though he did not share his feelings for obvious reasons, expected sarcasm from Pozy.

"Yeah, they're ok...a little shook up, but who wouldn't be after a gun was pointed at them?" Rodney said, coldly. All Pozy could feel now was the fear he'd experienced at having that same gun pointed at him as often as it had been.

Silence ruled over them all once more, until Pozy's feelings for his friends and the need for his own freedom dominated his psyche, through fear, to protect his long-time friend, and he was about to speak when Rodney's phone rang, causing all three to be startled by the sudden loud sound. It was Lillian.

"Hi…hang on a second," Rodney said in a low voice, and he excused himself. Walking past Harry he went outside. Now, Harry moved closer to Pozy. Not having met him before this, recognizing the farm-boy look in his stance, he sized him up, not in a threatening manner, but in a way that might suggest…"I'm on your side." The concern he'd heard in his question to Rodney about Missy and Petey's welfare rang familiar in his ears and he would not overlook the long-ago promise to himself to never again dismiss the potential of any prospective witness, despite their demeanor or his first impression of them.

"I couldn't help but notice you might have been ready to say something when Officer Torrey's phone rang. You can feel free to share that thought with me…if you'd like," Harry said softly, keeping his eye-to-eye contact as passive-looking as he could.

Rodney had remained silent until he reached an area he felt was out of earshot of the garage. "How are you holding up?" he asked, with much concern in his voice.

"I'm ok now. I hope you don't mind, but I've been sampling the Chardonnay I brought with me." She giggled slightly. "I guess

I'm finally mellow."

He chuckled, feeling good that she was at least relaxed after all that had happened, realizing as he looked at his watch that it had been less than two hours ago.

"Things are moving…a bit fast right now. I'm not…" And was about to say he wasn't sure he'd make it back at a reasonable time, when she interrupted him.

"Rod, you don't have to explain to me what you need to do. All I hope is that you catch that…son-of-a-B and put him where he belongs. Right now, I'm pretty tired, and for all we know that jerk has no idea that I'm even alive, never mind here in Dells. Why don't you tell that officer out front to go home to his family? I'll be fine 'til I see you in the morning," she said.

With those words, *'til I see you in the morning,* Rodney felt a pang of happiness jitter through his midsection, while the thought of her concern for the officer out front of the Inn eased his weary mind somewhat. They chatted for several more minutes, as his mind ushered him to her room at the Inn, when a sudden sound from inside of the garage distracted him from the conversation. The sound of her voice revealed her fatigue from the long day of travel and the wonderful evening together, though it was cut dreadfully short, had finally gotten the better of her. The essence of her perfume lingered in his thoughts, and he wanted to be there with her, but the business of murder would have to keep him where he was for now.

"I'm sorry we had to split up the way that we did. I'll make it up to you tomorrow," he said.

""I'm not worried," she said, and there was a pause that led Rodney to believe that she might have nodded off, then her voice returned to the receiver with a slight giggle. "I'm sorry this time…I think I've had too much to drink. Seeing him…well, you know—it was tougher than I thought, after I had time to play it over in my mind. I hope you understand." she said.

"Listen," he began when he heard some louder-than-normal talk coming from inside of the garage. "Lil, I've got to go. Something's come up. I'll call you midday tomorrow. Get some rest," and with that, he hit the cell button to hang up.

He was no more than fifteen feet from the door, and he couldn't imagine what had taken place since he'd left. He rushed to the door and within seconds he entered the garage, coming face to face with Pozy, still leaning against the work bench, seemingly out of breath and quiet. Harry, standing over him in a manner that suggested a non-confrontational stance, took notes while listening attentively. Rodney moved closer, picking up on the conversation, leaving him speechless at what he heard before Pozy went quiet. Harry, not wanting to take his eyes from Pozy, looked briefly toward Rodney, nodded his head while displaying a smirk of approval, writing as fast as his fingers could move the pen.

"Then what happened?" Harry asked.

There was a long, breathless pause from Pozy. At that point, it appeared that all three held their breath. Pozy dummied-up the second he saw Rodney, and Harry wondered why. Rodney had never shared anything that might suggest hostility between the young people from town and the Dells Police Department. Right now, however, this guy just shut down, and it was crimping Harry's style.

As Rodney entered, Pozy had been sharing his thoughts about his relationship with Zeke and how long they'd been together, that they were more like brothers than friends. He was about to share an incident that took place early on as boys when he went quiet. Harry looked to Rodney, then back to Pozy. Again Harry asked, "Then what happened?"

Pozy remained silent. Harry reassured him that it was ok to go on, then it was Pozy's turn to swing his stare between the two men standing before him. Rodney stayed by the door.

"Go ahead," Harry said. "It's ok.

Another moment passed, then Pozy cleared his throat and began to talk again. His voice wavered with an obvious nervousness.

"Well…even when we were in school…he'd make threats to the teachers then…when the principal was called in…ya know, and because of his size, the principal would back off. He finally got kicked out o' school and I quit about a year later," he said, and stopped talking again, looking all around the garage as if he'd misplaced something, then he looked back toward Harry.

"I guess I started thinking he was off his rocker this summer. We were headin' for the beach—check out some lollipops..." Harry looked toward Rodney with a confused gaze, and Pozy caught it immediately.

"Sorry...lollipops are girls. Well, this guy and his woman pull up alongside us in a traffic jam. He seemed nice enough...ya know, a fuckin' preppie type in a Volvo." Harry squinted at that one, but said nothing. "Well, Zeke looks over at him, the guy rolls down his window, smiles at Zeke and says, 'Hi!'—kind of warm...and Zeke, without taking a breath, interrupts and says, 'What-the-fuck do you want?' real angry-like, ya know? He freaked the guy right out. What the guy couldn't see, though, because he pulled away from us as soon as he could, was that Zeke was tappin' tha blade of his huntin' knife against his palm. I could see it from the back seat, and he kept starin' at them two in the Volvo. And then he got real quiet for awhile."

Harry remained expressionless, writing as much as he could in his notes. Rodney, on the other hand, never wrote a word, and for him, that was most unusual. He simply looked stunned at hearing what Pozy had just said. Pozy went on for several minutes, saying things that seemed, in a way, juvenile—pranks pulled by kids as opposed to young adults. It wasn't until he began relaying the night In Biddeford that Rodney's curiosity spiked, and he decided he'd stood by the door long enough. He strode toward the empty snake cage, looking occasionally back toward the doors, if only for his own peace of mind. It was Rodney's turn to speak.

"So...when I stopped by here," Rodney looked away from the cage and directly at Pozy, but not in a way that might cause him to clam up, "You know—when I asked the two of you if you'd been to Biddeford lately—that was the night you two were there, right?"

Pozy simply nodded his head in the affirmative, though he

remained quiet. Rodney knew of the ruckus at the old mill site in Biddeford, only because of the beer banter with a friend and fellow officer, but what Pozy offered now set the two lawmen on their heels.

"Yeah—well, after he beat the hell outta them two Mass-holes, that's when he got the gun," Pozy said. The term "Mass-holes" did not seem to faze either officer, because they were both from Maine, though they refrained from using it.

And then, it was as if Pozy had seen a ghost walk in through the double doors. His face drained of all color and he stood upright from his crouch against the bench, which he'd held since lighting the candle. An eerie hush fell over the interior of the garage; as if an unseen spirit had entered, taking control of Pozy's vocal cords, silencing him from continuing his escape to freedom. Both lawmen knew that they could not pressure him if they expected him to tell them what they needed to know about Zeke's mental state or where he might be.

Rodney moved away from the cage, walking softly so as not to disturb Pozy from his daydream or whatever it was he'd slumped into. Harry, on the other hand, stood in his place directly in front of Pozy. The silence became intimidating for all. Without coaxing, Pozy spoke up after several minutes of silence.

"He pointed that gun at me, a lot. That's how he got me to… do shit for 'im. I can't imagine how little Missy and Petey felt with it pointed at them." He laughed then, taking the two men completely by surprise. The fact that he'd been as serious as a heart attack only moments earlier and to laugh now, when thinking about his friends having the gun pointed at them, was beyond their comprehension.

"Are those two playin' with each other?" Pozy asked, but got no response from either man. Then, he began where he'd left off without blinking an eye. "Yeah…so, like I said…He likes pointing that gun at people. I was scared of 'im, but not as much as when he mentioned shootin' that kid while his girlfriend watched. I knew then that he was talkin' about that Connectaclit on the path to the water."

Rodney's mind raced to Lillian. It was Zeke she'd seen, and he had killed Melvin Nisbet.

Though Harry's attention remained focused on what Pozy said, his thought was, *What in hell is a Connectaclit?* And he came right out and asked, and got sarcasm.

"Yeah…we had nicknames for out-a'-state morons," Pozy said, and picked up where he'd left off, without hesitation. "D-ya know what he asked me?" He paused slightly. "If I was proud of 'im. And then he said…'C'mon, buddy, let's get ta town and get some grub in us.' He's whacked, I tell ya."

Harry needed more. There had to be more than what Pozy offered.

"What else did he say? I mean…from asking if you were proud of him, he must have said something else before inviting you to town to eat."

Suddenly, it seemed to Harry that the unseen ghost was prowling around and Pozy was the only one to feel the spirit's presence. His face drained of color once again and if Harry was right, vomiting was imminent, and the moment he thought it, though he did not vomit, Pozy began a series of dry heaves, formed either from a thought from the past or something he ate that was obviously turning his stomach. Both men looked in his direction with puzzled looks on their faces.

With the questioning and Pozy's revelation of the Biddeford incident about when and how Zeke had acquired the gun, sleep was the last thing to cross anyone's mind. No amount of coffee could have sparked such an awakening in all three. As late as it was, however, they knew they could not push Pozy and risk having him lull himself into an inability to continue. Harry's stare was relentless. Finally, Pozy cleared his throat and began, but what he offered now came as a huge surprise.

"He made me help him carry that poor bastard back to the passenger seat. He shot them two fuckers!" His voice rose with the end of the statement. "He carved that shit in their foreheads after they were dead, or at least they sure looked dead."

"What about the driver? Did you help to carry him, too?"

Harry asked.

"Yeah," he said, flatly.

Zeke's face immediately appeared in Pozy's mind, and he raced toward the door. Rodney was thinking he might try and run, and was right on his heels, but Pozy stopped abruptly when reaching the outdoors and let loose with a disgorgement of violent proportions.

Rodney stood with one foot in the garage and one out, looking toward Harry, who remained as if planted to the same spot he'd been in.

"How in hell did you get him to open up like that?" Rodney asked.

"While you went out to talk on your phone…I told him you were quitting the force and I was thinking about taking your place. He seemed to like that idea, so I went with it," Harry said while smiling broadly at his counterpart. Rodney scowled at Harry's approach to get Pozy to talk, yet he remained silent, amazed at Harry's ability to dig in.

Pozy remained outside for several more minutes, giving the two officers a chance to quietly discuss what they'd heard between the sounds of dry heaves. Finally, Pozy reentered the garage, Rodney stepping to one side as he did. This time he looked like the ghost that Harry perceived had entered and haunted the young man earlier. Until now, neither man noticed, probably from the lack of lighting, the small refrigerator in the corner, from which Pozy removed a plastic bottle of water, drinking deeply from it. Harry was noticeably anxious to get back on course with the questioning. After several more gulps, Harry began again.

"You gonna' make it?" he asked, but got no response from Pozy, except for a vacant stare.

"Ok, you said that Zeke got the gun from a couple of guys after he roughed them up in Biddeford. Then, you said that you knew he killed that…'Connectaclit' as you called him while his girlfriend watched," Harry said as he looked toward Rodney, who stood stone-faced across from him.

"I knew," Pozy said.

"Were you there for that murder?" Harry asked.

"No," he said coldly.

"What about the two, as you called them…'Mass-holes'? Did Zeke kill them while you watched?" Harry asked, sternly.

"Yup," was all Pozy said to the question.

Rodney had moved to a central point between the two garage doors after Pozy returned from blowing Chinese food all over the side of the garage. He stood now, without knowing, in the very spot where the bags of dope and sawed-off shotguns had been before Pozy's return several hours before. Pozy's stare was now focused on the area around Rodney's feet, so much so, that at one point during Pozy's silence, feeling somewhat uncomfortable from his stare, Rodney looked down thinking he might be standing in vomit residue that he'd missed. That's when Pozy offered a most important piece of information.

"Them two Mass-holes were drug dealers. We grabbed what they had in the trunk…after they were…" he couldn't finish the sentence. "…And we brought it all back here." He nodded his head and pointed to the spot where Rodney stood. "There were two duffle bags full o' pot, and by the way…Zeke-boy has three guns now. We took two sawed-off shotguns from the trunk and left 'em right where you're standing." Then he went silent, displaying that vacant stare once again.

With the information about the drugs and guns that Zeke had in his possession, Rodney called dispatch immediately, requesting an officer and cruiser to be sent to the garage, giving the location and reason. At that point, Rodney placed Pozy under arrest as an accomplice in a double murder. Because both Rodney and Harry drove their civilian cars, they could not transport Pozy for booking at the County Jail. He told the dispatcher to notify the appropriate State Police assigned to the case and that he, Rodney would notify Chief Weaks.

After ending the call, Rodney could hear the low-volume conversation between Pozy and Harry. Harry was doing his best to keep him calm, obviously hoping to get as much from him as possible that might help them to find Zeke quickly and end this murderous rampage. Rodney looked at his watch. It was 1:15 a.m. Physically, he was toast now, and wondered how Chief Weaks would respond at hearing the news of what they'd just uncovered. He hit the speed-dial for the chief, but the call went immediately to voicemail, and a wave of disappointment flooded over him, yet he refused to think poorly of the chief, hoping the chief's wife hadn't taken a turn for the worse. He did not leave a message, and turned his attention to the two men in the garage.

During their wait for the cruiser, Pozy relayed to them, willingly, things they couldn't imagine that Zeke would do, though surprise was not the emotion they felt. Harry had seen too much of the wrong side of humanity to be surprised. Shortly after 1:30 a.m., the sound of the cruiser was heard as it left the pavement and entered the gravel drive that would lead it to the garage. At the sound, Pozy's eyes enlarged so much it looked like they might burst, and he realized that his part in a hellish rampage of murder was over. This however, was not the freedom he'd envisioned in his daydreams. He was given his rights under the law, handcuffed, and walked out to the waiting police car. Harry walked alongside, speaking in low tones, hopefully instilling a sense of confidence that would keep the young man on their side and help to alleviate the fear of what was about to rule his life.

Within minutes he was whisked away, leaving the two men in a cloud of dust from the gravel in front of the open garage door, tired, yet overflowing with the success of their accomplishments today. They shared small talk as they secured the area. The State Police would arrive, probably at daybreak, to fine-comb the entire area. This would be considered a crime scene, if only because of what Pozy had offered about the items taken from the murder victims' car at the heath. Tomorrow was another day. Right now, Officer Rodney Torrey and retired trooper Harry Circus were going home for a well-deserved rest.

34

POZY WAS PROCESSED AT the York County Jail early Saturday morning. Going through the normal booking procedures, he was fingerprinted, and because of his involvement and his association to the crimes he confessed to, his prints were immediately sent to Augusta. The fact that he'd never been arrested before this meant that no matching prints were on file. The process only took an hour. They had a match. The prints taken from the key in the heath had Nigel (Pozy) Linscott's name all over them.

With no sleep, though he'd calmed down considerably from his time with Harry Circus and Rodney Torrey only hours earlier, Pozy was astonished, as morning arrived, to see many men that he knew pass by the detention area, all wearing the orange suits inmates are issued. His many brushes with the law while associated with Zeke had never culminated with an arrest or imprisonment. This in itself was by far the most intimidating experience he'd ever faced outside of being on the wrong end of Zeke's .38-caliber revolver.

From somewhere in the facility came an institutional stench of food being cooked, and Pozy's nostrils filled with the nauseating aroma to the point of feeling the need to vomit once again, yet his stomach remained empty from last night's episode with sickness, and he buried his head in his arms to avoid the smell, but nothing he did could alleviate its permeation throughout the jail. His mind wandered to any thought that might free him from this new physical imprisonment. Psychologically, he'd been a prisoner of sorts for as long as he'd known Zeke, but all that his mind would allow him to conceive was the fact that all of his plans to be free and on his own were dashed as he fully realized he was now in the York County Jail, a prisoner once again.

—

With very little sleep, Harry was up at the crack of dawn reading from his notes and gulping coffee like he used to as a younger trooper. For a long time now, he had eased himself off the caffeine in large doses, but with the lack of sleep and a newfound enthusiasm for the investigation, it all just seemed to fit well together. The early morning was cool, while a sea breeze added to the slow rise of the thermometer. The hot coffee simply warmed the moment.

Harry's ability to judge facial expressions was impeccable. Reading his notes from only several hours earlier in the garage with Rodney, Pozy's expressions to questions posed offered Harry an intuition that Pozy had been strong-armed into aiding his long-time buddy to be an accomplice to murder.

Even when he read back on statements made by Missy and Petey, they tolled the mark when Zeke spoke. Harry sat now, his thoughts transported back in time to another young man who had ruled his world and all those in it with fear. He wasn't able to reach that one, but he would, to the best of his ability, try and reach this one. His plan, since it was Saturday morning, knowing Pozy's arraignment on the charges would probably take place first thing Monday morning, was to call Rodney after a reasonable time, as their evening had ended early this morning, and visit Pozy at the jail for the only reason they would have: Finding Zeke Brailey.

He began jotting notes for his plans and how he felt they should proceed. He'd compare his thoughts with Rod when they spoke, and then his thoughts whisked to a new rendezvous with unfinished business: Chief Willard Weaks. The chief had disappeared from contact. Although Harry had not made as many attempts at contact as Rodney had, he thought it was extremely unlike Willard to neglect Harry as the relationship had spanned many years in and out of police business. For him to vanish from his duties, considering his nearing retirement during a most troublesome time for his department was quite unexplainable as far as Harry Circus was concerned. At this point in time, however, Harry was unsure of the proper approach to contact him. *Probably my first step should be the chain of command,* he thought. *I'll bring it up with Rod, when the time seems right.*

—

Rodney, at this very moment, was sipping coffee with Lillian Crandlemyer at the Inn. Sleepless nights seemed to be fashionable these days, at least with a small group in and around Dells, Maine.

They sat on an antique divan situated in a hallway between the dining room and library. No guest had ventured down as of yet, giving them a quiet moment alone.

"Did you sleep much?" Rodney asked.

"Yeah…once I finally got there, I stayed there until a bit of light filtered in through the blinds. That's when I…selfishly called you," she said.

"There was nothing selfish about it. I'm glad you did call," he said.

Several minutes passed, and neither drank from their cups, because they couldn't stop staring at each other. Lil was wearing a snug-fitting pair of blue jeans, with a light gray sweatshirt. The blue flip-flops on her feet seemed somewhat out of place for the chilly morning, but the Inn, as they both agreed, was much too hot for them.

They each took their turn talking rapidly, thinking the same, though not sharing their thoughts, that their time together would probably be cut short once again. Without realizing it, they were approached suddenly by the Innkeeper carrying a tray with a steaming pot of fresh coffee with creamers, sugar and packets of calorie-free sweeteners. They passed on the additives, since black was their favorite brew, but thanked him for the re-heat and resumed the conversation.

After several minutes, Rodney interrupted Lil. "Sorry, but if I'm right and I think I am, Harry will most likely want to make a run to the jail. There are a few things we couldn't cover last night, ya know…we ran outta steam, you might say. But, I…was thinking…maybe, if you'd like…no pressure by the way, but I have plenty of room at my place if you'd like to move your stuff there. Just in case I get called away for a time, you could have the run of the place, you know, make yourself comfortable," he said.

"Well, well…mister policeman, are you trying to get me…" she stopped then, her smile was as broad as her lips could stretch.

—

For the first time in weeks, Chief Willard Weaks was unable or unwilling to be reached by phone because his wife had actually taken a turn for the worse. During the early morning hours of Saturday, he sat at the bedside of a woman rapidly failing, barely clinging to life. Although he truly loved her for all that she was to him, he had another lover who meant as much. Not many can understand how love is shared, nor can it be explained by those who find that kind of love.

While his hand caressed his wife's hand, hopefully offering her the compassion he had no longer been able to give her physically for some time now, his thoughts were of Marcy, and he longed for them to be together openly.

—

Marcy knew better than to call Willard at this time of his wife's need for him, having been with him until the early hours of

Saturday. Upon her return home, however, she was shocked at the news given her by Missy at the horror she and Petey had faced with the threats made by Zeke with the gun and the goings-on in her home while she was away. It wasn't until Saturday morning when Marcy arrived downstairs getting ready to leave to open the restaurant that she came face to face with Petey and Missy at the kitchenette counter sipping coffee that she realized he'd stayed the night. It wasn't until it was time to leave that Missy told her mother she would be late to help open the Little Roady. Considering the distance from here to Petey's grandparents' home, she would not let him hitchhike. Without wheels, Petey was a fish out of water.

Aware of Marcy's return and at the suggestion from Missy, he'd spent the night in the downstairs guest room, away from any path that Marcy might take from any part of the house to her own bedroom upstairs. As they all prepared to leave, chatting about the events of last evening, the more Marcy heard, the angrier she became. She couldn't count the times she'd told Missy that Zeke was a no-account loser, but it all had gone right over her head. Love is blind, so they say, and who was she to talk? But right now, she and a lot of other people wanted Zeke to be found.

—

Zeke was running wild and completely out of control. He was dangerous but not stupid. During the early morning hours of Saturday, while his closest friend was being booked and fingerprinted as an accomplice for his crime of murder, he began what would prove later to be a massive cover-up of everything and anything that was Zeke Brailey and Pozy Linscott.

First, through his personal flow of illicit contacts, he got rid of both sawed-off shotguns, and except for a sizable, useable amount for himself, the rest of both duffle bags of the pot. On such short notice, he was unable to cash in on what everything was truly worth and he expected as much, but with what he did get for such a large quantity of the drug and the condition of the guns, he had more than enough to survive for several months as frugally as he'd accustomed himself to until now. No one, however, could have calculated the extent he would go to become invisible, or at least in his warped mind, remove himself from the face of the earth. He even offered Petey's car for sale, but found no takers. As it turned out, the vehicle came in very handy for at least a few more hours.

With as many miles as there were between the extreme rural area where Zeke and Pozy called home and the bustling seacoast, it was only a matter of hours before word of Zeke's threats and Petey's stolen car reached the ears of Zeke's parents. It wouldn't take long for the authorities to stop by. Zeke's father was beside himself with anger, swearing that he would help the law in any way that he could to end his son's rampage against life. His mother, as most mothers would, prayed that no harm would come to her son and that he would not harm anyone—not knowing at this time the extent of her son's madness—and be given the opportunity to come to his senses. Sometimes, however, bad things come to bad people, no matter how many good people pray for them.

35

HARRY WAS EXTREMELY SURPRISED to hear the phone ring this early, and he truly hoped it was Rod. From where he sat and with the amount of caffeine he'd already ingested, he bounded toward the phone like an athlete over hurdles. At the very moment of his competitor's exhibition through the living room, Annie, still under the spell of somnolence, saw with disbelieving eyes her husband's leap of unbridled energy.

"Harry Circus, here," he answered the phone, as one leg pulsed out a nervous rhythm as he stood in place.

"Good morning, Harry. It's your favorite police officer, Rodney Torrey." A smile formed on Harry's face at the sound of his voice.

"Wow…I never expected a call from you this early. Is everything ok?"

"It couldn't be better. I just wanted to beat you to the punch, that's all. I've got a few questions for Mr. Linscott before his arraignment. I've jotted down a few things we might ask."

While Rodney spoke, Harry's thoughts brought him to a new high where Rodney was concerned. The young officer was eyebrow-deep in it, and Harry couldn't have been more enthused.

"You still there, Harry?" he asked.

"Yah, yah, I'm listening," he said.

"Ok, I'm thinking…mid-morning. Say, ten o'clock? We could meet at the station and head up there in my cruiser. I'm sure you have some Q's all ready to go for our young man."

Suddenly, the term "young man," when hearing someone else say it, flashed in Harry's mind and brought up the time when he and Ralph Bailey had used that same term to identify with another out-of-control young person from another time and place. That young man had been murdered on his watch. This one was alive but involved in the murder of two, possibly three young men. Harry hurried to shut the door on that particular thought. The past was a huge part of him, but it alone would not direct him and Rodney to a resolve they needed to solve this case and bring a young out-of-control man to justice. He remembered his father's words once again:

"The law must sustain a monumental patience to apprehend the offender."

Although a newfound energy pulsed through his bloodstream, he would be patient and allow the process to take its course. Through his mind's eye, he saw Lester Sawyer's silver casket and remembered his own promise. *I will leave no stone unturned. I will never shy away from questioning anyone I feel needs to be questioned.*

"Harry," Rodney called out. "Are you still with me or what?"

"Yeah…yeah, I'm still here. I was just jotting something down in my notes, is all," he said.

"So…10:00 a.m. ok with you? I'll meet you at the station then," Rodney said.

"Gotcha," Harry replied. Both men hung up simultaneously.

Annie was just arriving at the dining room table with a steaming cup of coffee when Harry placed the receiver into its cradle.

"If you drink any more of that stuff, you'll be able to fly over to Dells and wait for Rodney to arrive by car," she said. They remained silent for several minutes before Harry began to speak, disregarding her comment about flying.

"Did you remember that Rodney had a young woman friend visiting for the weekend? I know we've never found the time for you to meet Rod, but I thought…if we have time, we could have them over for dinner tonight, or even Sunday midday for a light lunch. All things considered, and if it works for you, Annie?" he asked.

"It's fine with me, what about the young woman? She might have something to say about it. They may want to find the time to be alone," she said. "Just let me know with enough time and I'll put it together."

"Great," was all Harry added before getting ready to meet Rodney.

—

At 10:00 a.m. straight up, both men pulled into the rear parking lot of the Dells Police Department simultaneously. Rod parked and went directly to dispatch, Harry parked and walked to the cruiser, waiting for his counterpart to return. Harry was leaning against the cruiser when Rodney exited the building. A deep sense of envy filled Harry at the sight of the young officer in uniform. He had always taken much pride whenever he wore the blue uniform of a Maine State Police Trooper. It was his career. He lived to be a Trooper, following in his father's footsteps. His father had passed on two years after the murder of Kenny Collins. He'd never offered an opinion when Harry decided to retire. When his son made a decision, it was his to live with. Both father and son wanted it that way. Now, however, he wished his father could see him, at least as a consultant to the police; most of all, their good friend, Willard Weaks, thinking of whom, Harry decided to speak with Rodney about his sudden disappearing acts on their way to the County Jail.

As Rodney arrived, both men nodded without a word passing between them. They got in and left for the jail. The route they took was very familiar to both, and as they came upon and passed the gravel road where the two victims had been found at the heath, together, as if rehearsed—both men looked down the road, but remained quiet. About a mile past the road, Rodney spoke first.

"Harry…I've been in contact with the D.A., and he'll have a search warrant for Pozy's garage when we get back to the station.

Are you…"

He was immediately interrupted by Harry. "You'd better believe it. It's funny how I was thinking about that and made notes to ask you during coffee, just before your call this morning." He flipped through his pad and the first name that popped up was Willard Weaks.

Rodney was a determined driver, as Harry once had been: foot to the floor, whether he was going somewhere or with no particular place to go. Within a short period of time, they were several miles from the heath, and Harry had stalled long enough before bringing up the Chief. He took a deep breath and began.

"Rod, I'm concerned about Willard, since we haven't been able to reach him with all of this…stuff that's been unfolding with the case. Is he having some problems we should know about?" He paused a moment; then, getting no response, he continued. "He's been a good friend for a long time and if I can help in any way, I would hope he would feel comfortable enough to ask."

"I feel the same, Harry, but I'm thinking—and this is simply a gut feeling on my part—that along with his wife's failing health, and I'm sure that alone has him on the edge of the cliff of life, but I can't seem to shake the thought that there's something else eating away at him."

With that said, both men appeared to ponder that thought silently for several minutes. Now, it was Harry's turn.

"Look, if we can't raise him by phone today, you know…when we get our business done and only as a friend, I'm considering going to his place. I need to know if he's ok. You, probably better than I right now know this is not the Willard Weaks of only a few months ago. If it were either one of us, I can't imagine him not… sticking his nose in." Rodney nodded his head yes.

With the speed at which Rodney drove, they arrived at the County Jail sooner than Harry expected, going directly to a secured police officer entrance. The facility was a considerable distance from the main road, on a down-sloping drive. After several curves on their approach, the County complex came into view. It was a reasonably new facility. Harry had only been to the old County Jail, several miles from this location years earlier, on an official visit as a trooper. Seeing the new jail appear before him, and for no other reason than feeling behind the times, it forced a gurgle of pensive sadness through his mood, but only for an instant. There was work to be done inside the building with a young man that needed to be questioned.

Rodney swung the cruiser to a spot reserved for police vehicles, no more than fifty feet from the police entrance to the side of the building. Both men exited the cruiser together, slamming their doors at different intervals. Harry carried a briefcase. Upon entering, they came face to face with a secure thick glass entry. One of the guards recognized Rodney and buzzed them in through the thick security door. Rodney informed the guard of the reason for their visit and they were escorted to a private questioning room to await Pozy's arrival.

They made themselves as comfortable as one might in a room such as this one. It instantly ushered Harry back, mentally, to a similar room at another County Jail at what seemed a lifetime ago now. Both men shuffled through their notes, and without the sound of approaching footsteps to forewarn them, the door swung open, and standing before them was a handcuffed, tired and almost sick-looking Pozy Linscott.

"Will you need me to hang on here?" the slightly overweight and bored-looking guard asked.

"I'm thinking we'll be fine…just the three of us," Rodney answered, and the guard walked the prisoner to a seat opposite the two lawmen, turned and went straight to the door.

"I'll be just outside. If you need me, just call out," the guard offered and left. Rodney simply nodded his head but said nothing, while Harry's stare, though non-threatening, was focused on Pozy, who remained silent, but his questioning eyes and pinched face spoke volumes to the retired trooper. As the door closed, Harry reached into the briefcase and pulled out three still-cold bottles of Poland Springs water and placed one before each man. Pozy was the only one to say thank you. Harry moved his head in an upward swing, yet remained quiet. He had a few more goodies in the case, but time would dictate if and when he offered them. The officers remained quiet as Pozy pulled on the water bottle.

The silence was suddenly sickening, and Harry was again mentally guided to his long-ago promise. *I will leave no stone unturned.*

"How ya holdin' up, Pozy?" he asked.

Pozy took a deep pull from the water, then answered. "I could think of a hundred places I'd rather be right now, but the grub ain't bad."

Rodney couldn't believe his answer, but knowing the young man as he did, he expected some form of sarcasm. He remained quiet and hopeful, watching Harry work his magic.

"We have a few questions that came up since we saw you at the garage," Harry said. Pozy remained silent and simply shrugged his shoulders. Before leaving the garage, Pozy had told the officers where the key for the doors was tucked and Harry thanked him for that now, something Rodney never considered. Harry informed him of the warrant and their plans to return to the garage later. Again, Pozy shrugged his shoulders and remained silent.

Harry continued. "You'll be held here until Monday morning, assuming you won't make bail." Again he shrugged. "You'll be arraigned then on an accomplice to a double murder charge." It was obvious that now, Harry had his undivided attention. "If what you told us is true, however, and if you get a half-decent lawyer, you may be given the opportunity to plea-bargain."

Pozy looked toward Rodney, his eyebrows rising in a questioning curve. Harry found the attention he was looking for, but he waited a moment longer. "Do you understand what I just said?"

Ever the wise guy, Pozy shrugged his shoulders, making both men think they might be losing him.

Harry reached into the briefcase once again, and this time he produced a Baby Ruth candy bar and slid it over the tabletop toward Pozy, while displaying an impish grin.

Pozy wasted no time opening the wrapper and devouring the candy bar in a couple of bites. Harry looked to Rodney then, getting go-ahead approval with a single nod of his head.

"Where do you think Zeke would go…now that he has Petey's car?" Harry asked. "The camp? Maybe someplace on his parents' farm or maybe your…parents' place?" Harry knew of Zeke's family farm from conversations with Rodney; he just threw the one about Pozy's parents in for good measure.

Pozy hesitated for a long minute, and when Harry was about to offer a different approach, Pozy offered an answer, but not what they expected.

"It ain't easy rattin' on a friend," he said, and Harry shot right back.

"Oh…I'm thinking doing time for one is much better," he said while looking Pozy straight in the eyes without a single blink. The young man looked toward the tabletop and swallowed deeply, looking first to Rodney then to Harry.

"He…he would go to the camp is my guess. Everything we own is there." Using the term "we own" sparked a new sense of understanding between the lawmen of how close the two had been, at least in Pozy's eyes.

"Well." Harry nodded briefly. "Just for the hell of it…if he decided not to go to the camp, where else would you guess he might go?"

Pozy answered quickly this time. "The only other place is the garage. He'd have to be some constipated to go home to his mama," and then he began to laugh, giving the lawmen some concern as to his mental stability, finding humor in the situation at this time. "No, he'd go to the garage or the camp. I would have said Missy's, but right now…you and me know better 'n that," he said with a slight snicker in his tone. Rodney wrote everything down. Harry noticed that Pozy's water bottle was empty and he reached for another one and gave it to him, much to Rodney's surprise. *How many of those does he have in there?* he wondered as he pulled from his own bottle. Then Rodney stood, excused himself and walked out into the hallway, closing the door behind him. He looked to the guard, then immediately called dispatch.

"Rodney Torrey here. Has the search warrant arrived for the Nigel Linscott garage yet?"

"Yes, it has," the dispatcher answered.

"Fine. Do you have an officer free to send to that location, and wait for me to get there? I need that place secured in the event that Zeke Brailey happens by. Remember...the officer needs to know that he is armed and extremely dangerous. I'll be in touch with whomever you send shortly. By the way...have you heard from the chief yet?"

"No," was the dispatcher's only response.

"Please notify the State Police of the location of the garage. I'll be in touch, hopefully with another location, shortly," he said, and ended the conversation. He went back into the questioning room to find a sickening silence throughout. Harry, however, did not appear to be perplexed. Pozy, on the other hand, looked bored as hell.

"Great," Harry said as he entered. "I'm glad you came in. Pozy was just about to tell us how to get to the camp," and he looked toward Pozy again.

I always seem to miss the part where he gets them to talk, Rodney thought.

"You've been a big help. If what you told me just now is the truth, you have nothing to be ashamed of. You deserve your freedom as much as anyone else," Harry said.

Rodney seemed a bit confused, because in his absence, Pozy had told Harry that he had made several attempts to set himself free from Zeke, and even now that he was locked up in the County Jail, he felt free. After several minutes of silence, Pozy went into detail with the direction the officers should take to get to the camp. Rodney was familiar with the area he spoke of, but to his surprise, he'd never known that a road or a camp existed in the deep woods surrounding the variety store. What surprised him more was when Pozy said it was built by Zeke's grandfather many years before and forgotten by most family members.

The back-and-forth went on for another fifteen minutes before the all too familiar smell from the kitchen began to fill every corner of the jail. Lunch was about to be served, and unlike earlier, Pozy's tastes were now becoming used to institutionalized food. All meals were served at the same time each day. A man's stomach becomes accustomed to that schedule and when that time arrives...

From the look on his face, Pozy wanted them to leave, and they felt the same. For them, it would be another long day. For Pozy, it would probably feel even longer. They left immediately, exiting through the same secure section they had entered, wasting no time on their way to the camp. Rodney's thoughts brought him back to the evening he'd questioned Zeke's parents when he specifically asked if they knew of anywhere Zeke might go; then in the next thought, Missy's comment to them as they prepared to leave after the questioning about Petey's stolen car, *They had a camp somewhere out in the woods.*

"The more I think of it, Harry, the more I feel we need to be ready to find old Zeke at this camp," he said. He shared his thoughts with Harry, who nodded his head in agreement, that time and the need to make good use of it was essential now. Rodney hit the strobes, with an occasional blast from the siren, clearing the way through the late-summer traffic. The camp, from Pozy's directions, was not very far from the York County Jail, but their anticipation at arriving there seemed to literally bind the hands of time itself for these two officers of the law. Leaving the main traveled road and finding themselves on a back-country thoroughfare, Rodney cut all warning signals, yet continued at a high-speed drive toward Zeke's camp, which was now less than a couple of miles ahead, and he told Harry to get ready. Neither man could know what awaited them. Rodney slowed the vehicle.

"The area Pozy told us about, you know...the path, is just past the little mom-and-pop store up on the left," he told Harry. Once again Harry's acumen was keen.

"It smells like someone is burning a shit-load of brush somewhere close. Can you smell that?" Harry asked.

The moment the words left his mouth, as Rodney negotiated a slight curve in the roadway, both held their breath at the sight of a huge fire truck on the shoulder in front of them. Out in front of it was a Maine State Police car. There were several civilian cars.

Rodney suspected they belonged to the small-town volunteer firemen. Rodney remained silent as he pulled the cruiser onto the shoulder and well behind the truck, looking intently as to where the path might be, realizing now that Pozy was right when he said it was well-concealed.

As they exited, the rancid smell of smoldering wood filled their nostrils. It wasn't difficult to follow the path, since it had been widened by the firemen and their equipment. The path couldn't have been better identified on a map. Every twist, dip and turn was exactly as Pozy had described the terrain. Had it not been for the firemen, and without direction, the path would be completely hidden from any unwanted foot traffic. As a clearing began to appear through the thick vegetation, the pond and what remained of the burned-out camp came into view. The firemen continued to hose pond water onto the smoldering embers; the sound of their pumps was deafening to the newcomers' ears. Simultaneously, Rodney and Harry saw what they assumed to be the white hat of a Fire Chief emerge from a dense section of underbrush, replacing the straps of his suspender-hung trousers. The stupid-looking grin he now displayed toward Rodney, whom he'd known for ages, made it obvious what he'd gone into the bushes to do. He maintained the grin as he approached the two.

"Well…it doesn't matter where ya are when Nature calls," he said with a chuckle.

"How are ya, Chief?" Rodney asked and immediately introduced the two men, wasting no time with his next question. "When did all this happen?"

"Very early this morning is when the first call came in, to my place, ya know." It seemed the chief wanted them to understand that he got the first call.

"I hope everyone got out ok?" Rodney asked.

"We'll have to wait 'til the Fire Marshall gets here, but… so far…we ain't seen nothin' that might suggest, ya know…any remains inside the rest of it."

"Ya know," Rodney said. "I've been coming out this way for years and never knew this place was even here."

"Yeah…this is one o' them long-forgotten little places. Old man Brailey built it. Ya know…the grandfather, not the one that runs the farm now," the chief said. Rodney simply nodded his head. He wanted to dig for more information without giving too much up to the chief, but the chief had to be a wealth of information on the goings-on in a small town like Lovell.

"I though the family was from up around the Casket Mountain area," Rodney said.

"Oh yeah, they are, but the old man used to like to get off by himself, and so he built this place. I think they still own it and all the land around it to the road."

"Did anyone get in touch with them? Because if not…we might consider going up that way," Rodney said.

"Aar' ya lookin' for that little scum-bag, Zeke?" the chief asked, shocking both Rodney and Harry. "He was livin' out hea' for a time with that other dirt-bag Pozy Linscott. They figured no one knew, but every time they went into the store down there them folks would call me to make sure they didn't burn the place down. Looks as though they forgot to call me last night."

Rodney and Harry looked toward each other; their eyebrows rose simultaneously. Their naturally suspicious minds escorted them to the mind of an arsonist, and murderer, Zeke Brailey. It was just too coincidental that they'd gotten the directions to the camp less than an hour ago and now found it burned to the ground, along with anything that might have helped to close the gap between them and Zeke. Zeke was apparently working and thinking much faster than they were. As far as a cop's intuition goes, it didn't make their day. The only solid lead besides the garage was now a smoldering heap of embers.

Harry went directly to the trooper on scene and informed him that the site should be preserved as evidence in the Dells murder investigation of the two young men on the heath, and asked if the trooper could notify the CID of the site's importance. With that done, they left immediately for the Brailey farm at Casket Mountain. They hardly spoke a word on their return to the cruiser and even less as they made their way toward the Brailey farm.

Harry was plagued once again with thoughts of his failed Kenny Collins' murder investigation, and he felt the rising of bitter bile from his nervous stomach into his esophagus. Then, Annie's face flashed into his consciousness and he remembered her words to him regarding this consulting endeavor.

Remember Harry, no one twisted your arm into this. And again…he knew she was right. The past was the past and this was the present, and there was a murderer on the loose. He reached into his shirt pocket and pulled out a cell phone. His action did not go unnoticed by Rodney.

"Ah...yeah, I thought you didn't carry a cell?"

"Ah…yeah," Harry responded with a humorous tone. "Annie gave me hers. She wanted me to carry it today."

Rodney had no comment. He simply nodded his head and now, he thought of Lil. He was glad she'd decided to relocate to his place. As long as she planned to stay on in Dells for a few days, it could prove to be most convenient for them both. He focused on his driving and whatever questions he might have for Zeke's parents, while his peripheral vision caught the movement of Harry's hand as he clumsily fingered over the keypad in his attempt at calling his wife.

The midday traffic was relatively thin, and the drive to the farm was an easy one. It seemed like yesterday to Rodney when he had traversed this same road through an ensuing darkness and conversed with an obviously assiduous couple on their porch. He wondered if a weekend for a working farmer was like that of a police officer, if they would find them in the field. It was now that Rodney turned onto the gravel drive to the farm, and Harry said his goodbyes to Annie and focused on the country terrain that lay before him.

"Wow, this is a well-maintained place," Harry said.

"Yes it is," Rodney responded. "I was here around sunset once before and I can see now just how well they keep it."

They remained silent as the home came into view. Harry, though he said nothing, felt a pang of envy for the solitude that must be offered this far in from the traveled road. There was a tractor parked in front of the porch and Rodney hoped it was lunchtime for the farmer. Suddenly, it was history repeating itself for Rodney as they neared the house. He recognized Mr. Brailey immediately from their first meeting, and following right behind was his wife as they came out of the house and onto the porch, standing almost exactly where they'd stood the first time. They remained like porcelain dolls, unmoving and erect, focusing their stare on the approaching police car. Rodney pulled the car to a spot directly behind the huge John Deere tractor, the usual bright green paint dulled from years of outdoor use. Just before exiting, Harry asked if these were the parents.

Rodney said, "Yes."

This time, Rodney was met by the father with no attitude and no slang for the officer's name.

"Officer Torrey. We've been expecting you. Seems to me there's a lot more activity from down your way than what we get out hea,'" he said, looking toward Harry with a questioning stare.

"It seems that way," Rodney answered, remembering the curt manner in which their last conversation had gone. "Good afternoon, Mrs. Brailey. Sorry to have to disturb you like this. Please, let me introduce retired State Trooper, Harry Circus. He's been working on some things with us at the Dells Police Department." He was about to continue when Mr. Brailey interrupted him politely.

"Excuse me, but we've been told of Zeke's stupidity… ya know…stealin' young Petey Harriman's car like that." Rodney was amazed at how fast news and gossip traveled through small towns. "We won't stand for our son goin' around makin' threats against his friends or anyone else for that matter," he said.

"We appreciate that," Rodney said, thinking the parents might be ready to give the kid up, with as few words as possible. "At this point, we think he may be carrying a gun, but we're not sure what he's willing to do with it," he said, staying as far away from the truth about Zeke's actions as he could, if only for the sake of the woman standing before them. It was Harry now who stepped forward.

"You obviously have not heard about your father's camp back down in Lovell."

"What about it?" the gentleman on the porch asked.

"It burned to the ground just this morning. We were made to believe that Zeke had been staying there, but as of yet, he's nowhere to be found..." and was about to continue when Mrs. Brailey burst out in a tearful voice.

"Oh...my...God! Was he in it when it burned?"

"There is no sign that anyone was inside, but the Fire Chief is waiting for the State Fire Marshall to arrive. They'll know more then," Harry said.

The couple looked to each other as grieving parents might when having received bad news about a loved one. With each word that passed between them, Rodney and Harry felt that sadness, especially from the mother, evoking a heightened energy which began to pound through their bloodstreams. As Rodney had before him, Harry now became entranced by the woman's calm elegance. It seemed, to Harry anyway, somewhat out of place on the farm, but who was he to judge? And then she offered her thoughts, taking both men off guard.

"For the life of me, officers, I find it hard to believe that you would come all the way out here from Dells to tell us that our camp burned and that our son stole his friend's car while making some threats." There was an uncomfortable pause and then she said. "Please...won't you both come in for coffee? I have more that I need to ask," she said.

Both men went onto the porch willingly. Their need for caffeine was strong now, as none had been made available at the jail. Instinct told them that the couple before them was willing to offer any help they could to find their son, and they might just have the key to a door that had been slammed shut for the police for some time now. They followed at a polite distance, avoiding any behavior that might suggest oppression, both keeping in mind the need to direct the questioning and in some cases even the conversation toward the ultimate goal of finding Zeke.

As they entered the archaic farmhouse, which looked like it

had been built in the 1800s, they noticed that it was completely preserved in its original condition, right down to the conveniently placed kerosene lanterns, though it was obvious the house had its modern conveniences of electricity. The woman led all three, her husband following close behind, to a comfortable little breakfast nook that looked out onto the fields to the side of the home, forcing Harry into a daydream of sorts when coming upon the vision.

"Please, gentlemen, have a seat," she said, and pointed to the chairs surrounding a small table by the window.

The inside of the house emitted a familiar country smell to the officers, both having the roots of a country upbringing, and it would be hard to describe to anyone whose rearing focused on city life; however, the most predominant aroma was freshly perked coffee. It appeared now that the couple was preparing to have the brew when the officers arrived. It gave both Harry and Rodney a sense of comfort to be in the home, regardless of their reason for being here.

Mr. Brailey sat in his chair at what appeared to be his regular spot by the window. A notepad, pen and several ledgers were there, and it was as if he intentionally avoided eye contact with both officers until his wife arrived and snuffed out the tension from the room. She carried a tray, and placed a cup, saucer and spoon gently before each officer, then her husband, and finally one at her place. In the center of the small table she positioned a sugar bowl, a small pitcher of cream and a thickly sliced loaf of homemade bread, still warm from the kitchen, and beside it a bowl of whipped butter with a short-handled butter knife stuck into the creamy spread. Each man looked to the bread with hungry eyes, yet no one made an attempt as Mrs. Brailey returned to the kitchen for the steaming brew that would complement the little lunch. When she returned, she was smiling. It was the first time any emotion from her other than a solemn expression was seen. She proceeded to fill each cup and took her seat, her back facing the view to the fields.

"Please gentlemen, help yourselves," she said. Harry was the only one to respond quickly.

"Please…Mrs. Brailey, after you."

She smiled at that and took a dollop of butter for her plate and a slice of bread. Her husband followed suit, and Rodney began to salivate, waiting his turn. She never buttered her bread or drank from her steaming cup. The moment Rodney reached for the bread, she spoke up, looking toward him as she did.

"Officer, during your last visit here, I told you of our disappointment over our son's behavior. Now, that emotion has turned to fear for those who may be or have been assaulted or harmed by him. We do not have all of the details and you're probably not willing or able to share more than you have with us. We may not be able to cope with the truth of our son's rampage on the seacoast. One thing is certain. We will help the police in any way that we can to bring our son to justice," she said.

"Justice." The word magnified itself in Harry's mind as a subliminal message from his past, and his own words, *Justice awaits him, like every evil that wanders the Good Lord's earth.*

"It's what we all want, justice for all. Our son is out of control, and I pray for those he may have hurt," she said.

With the arrest of Pozy Linscott, Rodney knew the media would offer ambiguous reports to the public, within professional guidelines, confusing them even more over what the truth actually was, but until the truth was known and the police were convinced of what that was, Rodney would not lay open the already bleeding wounds of this couple who seemed so far removed from the world. He would not reveal their son's morbid actions, but to find Zeke and end his reign of evil that besieged the little town of Dells, Maine, he would have to win their support.

"Did you ever consider the possibility that Zeke might have been staying at the old camp in Lovell?" Rodney asked. It was the husband's turn to speak up.

"Ta' tell ya the truth…I thought that old cabin fell in on itself a long time ago. The road was all grown up and I never really had the time to check it," he said.

"Well, according to Zeke's friend Pozy—do you know him?"

Rodney asked, and getting a simple nod of yes from both parents, he continued. “Pozy said that he and Zeke lived there for some time after a thinning of the trail and a bit of sprucing up. I’m sorry, but with what we know now we think it may have been Zeke who burned it down last night. I know I’ve asked this of you once before, but do you know of any other”...and he used the term this time...“hide-out where Zeke might go to remain out of sight?”

“Well,” Mr. Brailey responded, “We do have an old fishing shack on Moose Pond, but that’s over near the New Hampshire border.” He gave Harry the directions while Rodney finally got to fill his face with the still-warm bread and coffee. He gave the trooper meticulous turn-by-turn directions, saying that it had been years since they’d ventured out that way. Mrs. Brailey seemed pleased at Rodney’s obvious love for her homemade bread, and she wrapped what remained on the table for the officers to take with them. After several minutes of questions it became obvious that they could offer nothing else that might help to locate Zeke. Rodney stood and offered his sincerest gratitude for the information they did give and the wonderful little lunch and wrapped bread. As they walked toward the door, Mrs. Brailey spoke up as she had the last time Rodney prepared to leave.

“Officers...if it is at all possible, when you find him, please don’t hurt him.”

Neither man would lie. No one knew what would happen when they did find Zeke. They simply nodded their heads in her direction, but remained quiet and went out.

Arriving at the cruiser, knowing the distance between the farm and Moose Pond near the NH border and the fact that an officer with a warrant was waiting for them at the garage, Rodney called Dispatch requesting that a State Trooper assigned to that area of the state be sent to the Moose Pond location, giving the details of the case.

He pulled the vehicle around to the front of the farmhouse and again, like his first visit and departure, the couple stood motionless on the porch watching until the police car vanished around the final curve in the driveway. They had just returned to the blacktop when the dispatcher's subdued voice crackled on the speaker. Chief Willard Weaks had phoned in shortly after Rodney's call was answered. His wife had just passed away.

36

THEY HAD STAYED LESS THAN AN HOUR with the couple and were several miles from the farm before Rodney uttered the first words between them since receiving the news of Willard's wife.

"This sheds some light on where the chief has been spending most of his time," he said.

Harry simply nodded his head in agreement, but his facial expression, had Rodney taken his eyes from the road to see it, might have indicated a lesser harmony with the officer's statement. Neither man, however, wanted to disturb the chief with the trivial matters of this investigation, now that their focus was on a small garage in the woods and a search warrant in the hands of a waiting police officer.

The men became quiet once again, Harry jotting notes as Rodney hit the strobes, minus the siren, and whisked them toward their destination. Both men were consumed with their private thoughts. The investigation had found them with many hours and miles behind them, and although the time-frames of the murders had taken place through the not-yet finished summer, it was taking a toll, physically and emotionally, on everyone who was involved with them.

The minutes ticked away unnoticed. Without realizing where he was, when Harry looked up from his notes, he saw that Rodney was pulling the cruiser onto the gravel driveway to the garage.

The second town cruiser came into view, parked just to the side of the double doors, and the officer who sat in the driver's seat got out at the sight of the approaching car. Rodney made a wide, swinging u-turn and backed the car's trunk area up to the doors, stopping a few feet away. Both men got out quickly.

"Good afternoon, Rodney," the younger officer greeted them, with a simple nod of his head toward Harry. They had never been introduced. Without hesitation, Harry walked directly to the young officer, put out his hand and introduced himself as Harry.

"It's nice to finally meet you, trooper. I've heard a lot about you," he said.

"Really? Probably all bad," he said, then laughed. The officer echoed his laugh, but said nothing further.

"Has anyone come down the driveway since you've been here?" Rodney asked.

"I haven't seen a soul," he said, then added, "but when I got here, that police tape was already strung around the perimeter."

"We..." and he motioned toward Rodney, "strung that out before leaving. We thought the CID would have swarmed this place the minute we called in the arrest."

Without a word Rodney went under the tape and into the garage, leaving both doors open, remembering how dark it was inside. Harry and the officer followed and upon entering, the overwhelming redolence of burned green wood filled the atmosphere, so reminiscent in Harry's memory of life Down East. Nothing had obviously changed since Pozy's arrest only yesterday and he wondered how thorough the State Police would be in their search of the building. This time, the garage was under the scrutiny of Rodney Torrey and Harry Circus. Every corner, every crack in the concrete floor would be examined.

Rodney turned and looked toward the officer. "If you don't mind," Rodney said, "it would help tons if you stayed outside. I don't want someone unexpected or otherwise popping in on us as a surprise."

"I understand," the officer said, and stood just outside the doors.

They wasted no time, starting at opposite ends of the garage, working their way to a central point where they might meet. They went over everything as if with a fine-tooth comb. Rodney went to the small fridge in the corner, Harry, to the wood stove. Both men wore latex gloves. Upon opening the door, the first sight was of a pile of unburned hardwood coals. Nothing out of the ordinary for a stove, and he was about to close the door when his eyes fell upon an iron poker.

No harm in pokin' around, he thought, and began stirring the unburned embers slowly. On his second stir, an object other than wood became visible. His eyes widened and he placed the iron down, reaching in with his bare hand, being careful to lift it by the edges. No one would ever know everything Zeke threw in the stove that night after the first murder, and until now, all they had was a vague description of the assailant from Lillian Crandlemyer.

"Rod," Harry called out. "Come have a look at this."

"What did you find?" Rodney asked, with much concern in his voice.

"This looks like an unburned portion of what looks to be a Connecticut driver's license. See here...There's a part of a photo."

Rodney's heart thumped in his chest as the thought of Lillian entered his consciousness. This was not something he wanted to share with her after last night. As of yet, neither man knew what Melvin Nesbit looked like, but there was a real good chance that Harry had found another spike for the lid of Zeke's coffin. As Rodney was about to call out to the officer to bring an evidence bag, his cell phone rang.

"Rodney Torrey here."

"Officer." It was the Dells Police Dispatcher. "I've just received a call from the State Trooper you asked to go out to Moose Pond. The camp is smoldering. It burned to the ground."

37

Rodney called out to the officer, who immediately poked his head into the garage.

"Officer, please get me an evidence bag from my car, would you?" The officer went directly to the vehicle. While he was gone, the two men spoke candidly. Harry was first.

"It looks like Zeke is cleaning up anything and everything that may have been a stop-over for him and Pozy or just him alone. Pozy never mentioned the Moose Pond place," he said.

Surprisingly, Rodney appeared to be a million miles from where they stood, and he was alone with his thoughts. *I can't believe that the chief called dispatch instead of me with the news about his wife. I can understand him being...Oh ta hell with it. He'll always be the chief to me and no matter where his head is at now, I understand. Huh, I guess that makes me the acting chief in his absence.*

Then Harry cleared his throat and brought him back to the present at the very moment the officer walked in with the evidence bag. Harry carefully placed in it the remainder of what was once the driver's license belonging to a living young man, hoping that perhaps a smidgen of a fingerprint might be left, but the fact that it was found in this particular stove meant that a fingerprint probably wouldn't matter much.

"How does that sound to you, Rod?" Rodney looked toward

Harry, with a confused look on his face.

"What?" he asked.

"I said, while you left the planet before, it looks as though Zeke might be cleaning up places that might connect him and Pozy for whatever reason he thinks he should."

"Yeah," Rodney said. "Do you think he's thinking about this place?"

"This was their home, you might say. I can't understand why he would be starting as far away from it as he's been, if those are his thoughts," Harry said.

"It's hard to figure how a mind like his might work, but it might not be a bad idea to have another chat with Pozy before Monday morning. He may have been holding something back, but from the sound of his details, I kind of doubt it," Rodney added, then looked toward the officer with a sternness of face and said, "Officer…would you get this to the station and notify the CID, whom we expected here by now, that we have some additional evidence in this case?" He looked more closely at the officer's face. "Huh, you must be ready for some home-time by now. We'll wait here until you send a replacement for yourself, and thank you for your patience," Rodney said.

"It's all part of the job," the officer replied, and went directly to his cruiser and sped up the gravel toward the blacktop. It was 4:00 p.m.

An eerie silence encapsulated the entire area after the officer left. Harry thought, *It's so different here as opposed to the seacoast and the constant clamor of everyday life there. Being this far removed could offer much time to just think.* Although Harry had uncovered an important piece of evidence only minutes earlier, and because they had nowhere to go until the replacement came to stand guard, both men continued their search through the inside and outside of the garage, looking at and touching everything they could put their hands and eyes upon.

Harry stumbled through a thicket close to where a stone fire pit was constructed, finding a heap of empty beer cans in the bushes. *An easy toss without having to leave your seat next to the fire,* he thought, and then he returned to meet Rodney, who had gone to the cruiser. All either man had eaten since they'd hit the road this morning was what Mrs. Brailey had offered at the farm. They met at the entrance to the garage, and Rodney held out the unwrapped bread. Their stomachs growled at the sight of it.

They had just begun eating when a car came onto the gravel from the roadway and as it did, Rodney's phone began to ring. Both men looked to each other inquisitively, then back to the approaching car. It was their replacement officer in a Dells Police cruiser. At the sight of it, and only after the third ring, Rodney answered his phone. It was Lil. He looked to Harry with an uplifted index finger, as if to indicate for him to wait a minute, so Harry proceeded to greet the newcomer to the scene, while devouring his piece of bread.

"Hi…Is everything all right?" Rodney asked, with concern.

"Oh…I'm fine. I just woke up from a badly needed nap and wondered if you were all right."

"A little tired, but I'm fine. We've had a busy day, but it looks as though we'll be able to wrap this part of things up…very shortly now," he said.

"Well, I've been looking through your cupboards and it doesn't look as though you do that much in the kitchen." She giggled then.

"Huh…I guess I don't, come to think of it."

"If you don't mind, I'd love to cook you some dinner tonight—that is, if you think you'll get the chance to eat it."

"I think I will. What did you have in mind?" he asked.

"You leave that to me. I'll be gone for about an hour. Whenever you get back will be fine."

"Great," he said. "Do you need me to pick anything up on my way?"

"Nope. Just bring yourself home and we'll have a great evening at your place."

Rodney's midsection tingled at the sound of her voice and invitation. He couldn't wait for the day to end now, although his mind would never allow him to rest from the investigation completely. They said goodbye, and Rodney went to meet the two men standing beside the cruiser. As he approached, he noticed the drawn, tired look on Harry's face, and he was convinced they both needed a good night's rest. He would suggest it as soon as they filled in the officer now on duty.

Harry and the young officer had met previously, and they made small talk about fishing, something Rodney, although he was born in Maine, had never found appealing. Sitting on the bank of a slow-moving stream or river usually made him fall asleep, and generally awake to find the hook had been cleaned of its bait and it was time to go home with only a few mosquito bites for his trouble. As he approached, both men focused their attention on him, thinking the call might be pertinent to the case, but as he began, it was obvious that it was not.

"Did the officer fill you in on why you're here?" Rodney asked.

"Yes. It's all about that little punk, Zeke Brailey, right?" he asked.

"Yeah," Rodney said. "He is armed and extremely dangerous right now. You might position your car and yourself facing the entrance," and he pointed toward the blacktop. "We have reason to believe that he may drive down here with a car he's stolen. If he does show, call dispatch that second. They'll get in touch with me. I'm thinking when he lays eyes on your car; he will beat feet out of here. Follow him, but remember…he has a gun and maybe more than one." Rodney's face was determined and concerned, giving even Harry a pang of worry for the young officer, alone at this secluded post. It was 5:00 p.m. when Rodney looked at his watch, and now he looked toward Harry, whose stare toward the woods appeared to have placed him under hypnosis.

"Are you going to make it?" Rodney asked.

"Oh…yah, I'm a little tired…a little low on caffeine is all. We have put in some time on this one, haven't we? I'd like to have a crystal ball to see just where Zeke is right now. I hope he doesn't hurt anyone else."

Rodney remained quiet and wondered how Harry could empathize with such a violent character as Zeke Brailey, and then, Mrs. Brailey's request entered his thoughts. *He will resist, but please, if it is at all possible, don't hurt him.* Rodney nodded his head. But the action went unnoticed by either man.

"I'm for callin it a day," Rodney said. "I could use a little pick-me-up myself, and Lil said she's cooking me dinner at home." He stood now looking directly at Harry, but it was his turn to stay quiet.

Harry asked, "Any chance for me to take that map we have in the cruiser home with me…you know, look it over again?"

"Yeah, I think I put it in the trunk. Take it if you want. Remember…you can call me anytime, Harry."

"Thanks."

Without saying another word, Rodney went to the officer, and Harry to the trunk of the cruiser and then the passenger seat. They left immediately upon Rodney's return from his chat with the other cop for a long-awaited rest.

38

The house was empty and quiet when Rodney walked in, encapsulating him with a sense of foreboding, but he gave it up to his involvement with the murder investigations and the sudden knowledge of the chief's wife added to the list of the deceased.

Knowing very well Lil's intentions to go shopping, he went directly toward the upstairs and a long-awaited and relaxing hot shower. His uneasiness from his day-long encounters with so many and the fact that Zeke remained at large forced him to scan every corner of the small house on his ascent. Now, he had only one thought on his mind. Lillian Crandlemyer and their long-anticipated evening together.

Within minutes of arriving home, Rodney stood under a steaming hot shower, loosening the knot of tension that had become painful in the neck and shoulders area. He relaxed, thinking of nothing in particular, and after several minutes of bliss, suddenly he thought he heard the sound of a creaking floorboard. His ears perked to any potential movement from outside the bathroom, giving no thought to the beautiful woman he'd given his key to. He wiped a slow hand over the steamy glass shower enclosure, quickly eying his service pistol, which he'd placed on the bath towel in the center of the vanity.

"Rod," the soft voice called out from the still-closed bathroom door. He let out a breath of anxiety, relieved now that it was her.

"Glad you made it back," he said.

All but the shower at this point could be heard, while a shadow moving in front of the clouded glass door was all Rodney saw, until the door slid open and Lillian's beautiful, naked body stood before him. He was speechless in awe as his eyes ran over her beauty.

"Can I come in?" she asked, as the smile caused her entire face to beam under the radiance from the overhead lighting.

"Oooh, ho-ho, yes," was all he could get out.

—

Because of the distance between Dells and Kittery Point, at about the same time that Lil stepped into the hot shower, Harry Circus stood in the doorway of his home, embracing his beloved wife, Annie, as if he would never let her go. Although it had been only a short period of time since Chief Weaks had asked Harry to help with the investigation, much water had cascaded over the proverbial dam. Both felt the stress of being apart for the long intervals of Harry's absence. Since his retirement, most of their time had been spent together, doing whatever they felt like doing.

The evening was cool and the warmth of the house and the enticing aromas from within signaled to Harry that an almost ready pot-roast would be enjoyed for dinner. The smell of freshly perked coffee told him it was time to settle down.

"You look tired," Annie said, as she tried to smooth out the fatigue lines on the side of his face with her fingertips.

"I am," he said, then took her in his arms once again, breathing deep with the essence of her fine hair. She took him by the hand and led him away from the open door into a hopefully quiet evening together.

—

In Marcy's living room, dimly lit from a slow-burning fire, Willard Weaks sat uncomfortably as his lover consoled him during his time of mourning. Marcy knew his wife, though only as an acquaintance. She didn't have the stomach for more than that. After all, Willard was her lover and that was that. *All's fair in love and war,* she thought.

They were seated on the couch half-facing the flames, half-facing each other; their knees touched slightly and their feet were flat on the floor. They looked like they were already in the funeral home.

"I loved her, you know. I just fell in love with you a long time ago," he said.

Marcy remained silent, looking toward him and knowing the battle raging within him now was guilt; a natural human reaction to his infidelity, and having to face the tragic end to his marriage. There was much she could add, but she knew it would probably come out sounding all wrong and so she opted for silence. *The only way he can get this out of his system is with the passing of time, and I'm not going to make a fool out of myself by saying the wrong thing,* she thought. "Have you talked to Rodney and the boys at the station? Rodney's been a good friend to you through thick and thin. I'm sure he's been thinking about you since you called dispatch with the news."

"No...I'll wait until tomorrow for that. He's a good guy. He'll already know why I haven't called him or Harry." With that said, they looked toward the flames, held each other's hands, and waited for the moment to pass.

—

After fifteen minutes in the hot shower together, Rodney was sapped of whatever physical ability remained of his constitution. They were wrapped tightly as the water trickled over their naked bodies. Smiling seemed to be all that either of them had the energy to do.

"Are you hungry?" she asked.

"I'm famished."

"Good. You take your time up here. I'll get dinner started and you can relax with the evening news and a tall Pepsi before we eat," she said and was out of the shower and gone in what seemed like seconds.

Rodney moved in slow motion. The long day and the round of shower-love had just about finished him off. He knew one thing: he was so glad that Lil was here, and the last thing he wanted to think about was when she would have to leave. He put the electric shaver to his face, combed his wet hair down, and slipped on a pair of sweats and a T-shirt and went out to meet his new love.

The stairs seemed difficult to go down; his legs were weak and so he took his time. Lil heard him from the kitchen and told him to get comfortable and she'd bring him a frosty, cold drink.

This is so good, he thought as he sat in his favorite chair, grabbed the remote and pushed the power-on button, and almost changed the channel when finding himself at the tail-end of an all-too-common, hateful car commercial. Suddenly, the image of news reporter Wanda Lane, who he'd been introduced to by Harry Circus on their trip to the State Police Crime Lab, was now broadcasting a live report from the heath.

"This is the location of the grisly and still unsolved double murder of two young men from Massachusetts. This reporter has tried, unsuccessfully, to make contact with the Chief of Police here in the town of Dells for any updates on what the police have found to date. I was unable to reach him or any of his officers. When I contacted the State Police, they declined comment, informing me that it was still an active crime investigation. To the families of these two young men, we offer our sincerest sympathy and let them know that we...the dedicated, investigatory staff of the Channel 2 News Team, will continue our own investigation. Live, from a lonely heath in Dells, Maine...Wanda Lane, Channel 2 News."

"What in hell is she doing down there?" Rodney said in an obviously agitated voice as Lil carried his iced Pepsi in.

"What's wrong?" she asked, seeing the deep furrows in his forehead and on his face.

"That was a news reporter from...as far as I know, Bangor. I just can't understand why she's reporting on a..." He hesitated, not wanting to say the word murder. "...crime in our area. As Harry might put it, having dealt with her in the past, she is trouble with a capital T."

She placed a soft hand on his shoulder, as Rodney reached for the phone and immediately dialed Harry's number, though it was the last thing he would have wanted to do after the day they'd had.

Annie and Harry were just sitting down to a pot-roast dinner with browned potatoes, carrots and onions in a bouillon. The aroma lingered throughout the entire house, along with the freshly perked coffee and homemade bread. Annie had refused to let Harry do anything except talk with her since he'd arrived. When the phone rang, he nearly upset the entire table in his attempt to answer it. Annie was unable to hide her disappointment.

"Harry Circus here."

"Harry...I am so sorry for this call, but I've just been knocked for a loop with what I just saw on TV. Your...old friend Wanda Lane was doing a live-shot from the heath. She said she'd tried to reach the chief for a comment, but failed to reach him and the Staties had no comment. What in hell do you suppose she's doing down here, besides getting ready to start trouble?"

Harry was dumbfounded, and in a rare display of character, he remained silent, contemplating what he'd just heard. Then he asked, "Have you heard from Willard yet?"

"No, but I think now...might be a good time to call." Had Lil been able to see the look on Annie's face, they would have been able to start some sort of wife's and girlfriend's cult to keep their men at home. Annie's was an identical stare to the one Lil was wearing.

Both men exchanged their thoughts as to why a news reporter from the Bangor area would have come to the southern coast to report on a series of murder investigations; and right now, neither man could sum it up with a viable reason.

"Well...there isn't much we can do about it now. A good dinner," Harry looked to his wife, but found no response, and he continued, "a good night's rest and we'll probably better understand in the morning," he said.

"Yeah, I'll let you go and…ah…call me in the morning. Have a good night," Rodney said.

Both men hung up simultaneously, to the quiet relief of both women.

Dinner for Harry became a bite-and-gulp meal; much to his wife's displeasure. She knew that nothing she could say could matter now. Harry was on the scent.

—

Rodney sat, somewhat despondent about his surroundings. Lil, thinking only of him, turned the TV off then, and only then did he reveal any notion at having any life left in him.

"I'm sorry for that," he said. "I…just lost it when I saw that woman on the screen."

I need to change the subject and in one hell of a hurry, he thought.

"Oh, what is that wonderful smell filling my entire house?" he asked, getting up and taking her in his arms, where they stood for the longest time. Seeing her, touching her silky hair, soon made him forget his troubles and even his thought of calling the chief. Dinner was forgotten for these two young people. She took him by the hand and led him to the upstairs bedroom where they made love as if time stood still, until Rodney finally collapsed from exhaustion, falling fast asleep, though it would prove to be a restless night.

—

There were two people who made themselves scarce during the activity in and around Dells. Missy and Petey had not been seen, nor had they made contact with anyone except Marcy since Petey's car had been stolen and Zeke's threats were made toward them. Though she said nothing to anyone, Marcy was concerned for her daughter.

39

WITH A SLIGHT BOUT OF INDIGESTION from his rapidly ingested dinner, Harry sat quietly on the couch under a dim lamp, studying the map he'd taken from the trunk of Rodney's cruiser. He slowly traced, in pencil that he might erase later, a line that could suggest a definitive route Zeke might have planned at his obvious attempt at eliminating any evidence that might connect him to the murders. With the evidence already in hand, however, and Pozy's revelatory statement, there remained little doubt in the minds of the authorities that their only suspect, who remained at large, was still Zeke Brailey. The question on everyone's mind, however, was where he was now.

Annie looked in on Harry occasionally from the kitchen and the clean-up of their hastily finished meal, putting leftovers in the fridge; knowing well that Harry would probably want them for breakfast in the morning. Her thoughts ushered her back in time to their home in Berryville through those long nights when Harry had sat on the couch looking over his notes, or preparing some duties for Ralph Bailey to carry out while Harry was preoccupied with other matters.

I guess history does repeat itself, she thought. *Once again…I want him back, all of him.*

She looked toward the clock on the kitchen wall. It was 9:00 p.m. She wondered where he found all the energy. As it was, he'd begun his day very early this morning looking over his notes and when Rodney called, she thought he'd break his neck getting to the phone. And then he left and was still at it now.

"Would you like some coffee, Harry?"

"Um, I would," he said without looking up.

All she could do was smile and shake her head slightly, going back into the kitchen.

Suddenly, Harry's vision blurred and his sight became lost in the topographical drawings on the map, while recalling the news of Willard's wife, which he'd forgotten to share with Annie. An unexpected vision now appeared clearly in his memory of a funeral scene that felt like a thousand years ago, of Lester's Sawyer's silver casket through a dulled daylight and his promise. The thought of a similar promise he'd been unable to keep, ultimately failing to solve the Kenny Collins murder, tormented him as it did then and he wished quietly that he'd never agreed to help Willard. He saw so much of himself as a young trooper in Rodney's character, and he became again mentally motivated with the thought of the young officer. His gaze remained clearly centered on the map before him when Annie arrived with his coffee, startling him from his transcendental journey to the past.

"Annie…my God, I forgot to tell you. Willard's wife passed away this afternoon. Rodney was called from dispatch with the news on our way back to Dells."

"Does that sound a bit…strange that he would call the dispatcher and not Rodney directly? Have you talked with him yet?"

"No one has been able to reach him." Harry looked at his watch. "It's too late now. I'll call him in the morning. I'm sure he'll need this time alone." He took a careful sip from his coffee, looking up at Annie, who remained standing in front of him.

"You can't imagine how many times Rodney tried to get in touch with him over the past few days. It's as if he didn't want to be found, but knowing him like I do, it just doesn't make any sense. I know his wife has been ill for some time, but I can't shake the thought that there's something more to it and I haven't been able to get my head around it," he said.

"I'll get a sympathy card ready and get down to the florist first thing in the morning," she said. "I'm going upstairs to watch TV. Are you staying down here for a while?"

"Yeah…I'm looking this map over. I'll be a while yet," he said.

She kissed him softly on the lips, then smiled down at him and thought how she never wanted him to change. *Harry will always be Harry and that's who I fell in love with.*

The house became deathly quiet after several minutes. Harry's drifting thoughts from the past subsided and he again focused on the map in front of him. He scanned his notes periodically about conversations with Rodney, Pozy and the young man on the path in Sandown, and they became a constant mental refresher.

The caffeine began to circulate through his bloodstream, triggering an evening awakening. He wasn't as tired as he'd been on arriving home several hours earlier. He retraced the pencil lines once again, validating his theory of Zeke's movements. There could be no mistaking his earlier conclusion. He looked toward the front window—the curtains remained open to the darkness outside, unusual for this time of night. Annie generally closed them right after dinner. A faint display of stars in the northern sky became visible, and it sparked a thought of Willard's wife, and a long-ago verse from an unknown poet leapt into his memory.

With the loss of a friend
The emotion rests,
Sometimes on the soul

One soul wings its way to eternity,
One soul remains to embrace the thought forever.

A new energy beat heavily through Harry's rising determination. He would not fail the victims of these horrific crimes. He would bring Zeke Brailey to justice, and he would resurrect himself from the humiliation and consternation that had plagued his soul all these years.

40

Harry looked at his watch. It was midnight, October 4th, and it seemed like only yesterday that the earth had been drenched in the sweltering humidity of summer. Soon, all of the leaves would begin to change colors. Tomorrow morning, Monday, Pozy Linscott would be arraigned before a judge in York County as an accomplice in a double murder. Depending on his court-appointed lawyer and the information he willingly shared with the police, he would undoubtedly be given the opportunity to plea-bargain. Doing so could significantly reduce his sentence if he was found guilty by a jury. That could be months from now. Zeke Brailey remained a free man and retired trooper Harry Circus intended to change all of that, very soon.

From habit, he looked toward the kitchen, thinking...*coffee*, but if he followed through with his plan, the coffee he'd already downed would be more than enough. After all, what he would not need within a very short time from now was the necessity to relieve himself periodically.

He went to the stairs and climbed slowly, worrying about the events to come and whether his theory was correct. As he approached their bedroom, in the semi-darkened hall, the sound of Annie's breathing filled his senses. At first, he didn't want to wake her, but he also did not want her to awaken to find him gone. That would be the very worst for her. Besides, he wasn't sure where she'd left her cell phone. He would be taking it with him.

He stood over her silently, watching her chest rise and fall from her shallow breathing, and he wanted to climb in with her for a desperately needed rest. He was about to call her name when she stirred restlessly and noticed that he was standing there.

"What is it, Harry? What's wrong?"

He coughed out a slight laugh. "It's all good, Annie. I need to take your cell phone for a while. Is it charged up?" he asked.

She immediately threw the covers off and attempted to get out of bed, when Harry motioned for her to stop with a raised hand and said, "I didn't intend for you to get up…I only need to know where the phone is."

"Where are you going at this hour?" she asked, glancing at the digital clock on the night stand.

"You know me, Annie. I can't leave well enough alone. I have a theory and I'm going to have to chase it down until I prove it right or wrong," he said, while looking deep into her worried eyes through the meager light in the room.

She got out of bed then. Annie was not the type to lay back down and helplessly await a phone call while her man potentially placed himself in danger. "Let me make you some coffee," she said and was taken aback with his response.

"Ah…no thanks, I've had enough for tonight. I'm pinging off the walls right now. Look…I don't want you to worry," he said, and the second he said it and saw the look on her face, he realized they were simply wasted words. "I'll be gone until…daybreak. As soon as I realize it's all ok, I'll call you that instant. I love you, Annie."

Annie said what she had always said when she wanted to cling to him to keep him from going. "I love you, Harry. Be careful out there."

She went downstairs with him, took the phone from the charger and handed it to him.

"Can I pack you a lunch or something?" she asked.

"No, that pot-roast will stay with me for a while. I'll be fine, don't worry," he said and began collecting what he would need to arrive at daybreak.

In Dells, Rodney stirred himself into awakening. Only a few short hours ago he had succumbed to physical exhaustion. Now, the intensity of the investigation and the knowledge of the chief's wife forced his mind to deprive him of sleep. He still felt weak, and preferred to stay with his head on the soft pillow, but his thoughts raced through his mental notes of the days and weeks that had passed rapidly with no apparent resolution in finding Zeke Brailey and putting an end to his reign of terror. He began to find fault with his approach in the early stages of his detective work before Harry had arrived. Guilt began to overshadow his dedication as an operative in law enforcement.

A restless energy forced him to get out of bed, moving slowly so as not to disturb the beautiful young woman at his side. The house was warm and he walked barefooted toward the hallway, closing the door gently behind him. Without a second of time passing upon entering the hall, the gruesome vision of finding Melvin Nesbit on the path during the heat of summer flashed before him, causing him to blink rapidly as if attempting to see through the lack of light in the hall and finding the origin of the vision.

Upon reaching the downstairs, Rodney immediately looked toward the kitchen clock. It was shortly after midnight. What he could not know was that at this very second, Harry prepared to leave his comfortable home to follow a theory. Had either man realized that the other was awake and thinking the same things, without a doubt one would have called the other and shared their thoughts. Rodney, however, just couldn't get his head around the fact, even this far along in the investigation, that it had taken help from Harry Circus to get them to where they were and so, for the young officer, it would become a night of unsettling perplexity.

—

The night air was chilling as Harry slid into the driver's seat of the old trooper car. He made mental notes of what he wanted with and on him before starting the motor. It hardly cranked before firing to a low rumble. He sat, contemplating the possibilities in the next couple of hours, as the engine purred to a low idle. For the first time ever that he could remember, he found himself stalling for time, adjusting the rearview mirror, looking back toward the house for whatever reason other than to see if maybe Annie was looking out the window. She was. That little gesture on her part made it all the more difficult to leave and caused him to feel a sudden nostalgic need for an earlier time in their life. Although she'd never shared her sentiments about his job then or now, if she had, from that earlier time, they would have been identical to his at this very moment.

He looked back at her, put his left hand with open palm against the window and mouthed the words, I love you. He turned, placed the shift lever into drive and pulled out of the driveway. This time, however, it was not the same: he was no longer the foot-to-the-floor Harry who had once patrolled the highways and byways of Down East Maine.

—

Harry arrived as the CID was just finishing up at the location. They were loading their equipment into a van they worked out of on crime scenes when Harry recognized one of the investigators he'd worked with years ago, and approached.

"I don't believe this," the investigator said. "Harry Circus. What are you doing on the southern coast at a crime scene…in the middle of the night?"

"You know me. I always seem to get my nose into something I shouldn't," he said, and they shook hands, smiling intensely. After several minutes of catching up, he relayed to the investigator how he'd been asked to help with these as of yet unsolved murders and where they all stood in regard to gathering evidence. He did not, however, share his theory or the reason he was here at the garage at this time of night.

"Well…Harry, have a look at this," said the CID officer, pulling a small plastic bag from his briefcase. "We dug this from the dirt," he said, then pointed to a spot just out front of the garage door and held up a ring. "It may have been walked on or driven over and we almost missed it had one of us not shined a flashlight over it."

Harry immediately scanned his memory banks, remembering Rodney's list of victims' items, and vaguely remembered a ring, but without his own notes, he couldn't picture it.

"Other than this, and we were lucky to find it, we didn't get much more than a few fingerprints. We'll take it all back to the lab and run everything."

The two men made small talk until it was time for the CID to leave. Both men shook hands vigorously, and then they were gone. Whatever light remained was from the headlights from Harry's car, which the Dells Police officer who'd been here since Harry and Rodney left about six hours ago was looking over with much interest. The entire area fell under an almost hypnotic silence, broken now with the officer's voice.

"Is this a '65 decommissioned police car?" he asked.

"Missouri Trooper," Harry responded with a broad smile, but wasted little time over small talk.

He went on, "Officer, you must be pretty tired and hungry by now. I've come to relieve you. Go home and get some needed rest," and he thought, *It might be a good thing for me also.* "There is something I'd like you to help me with before you do, though. Help me pull all of this police tape down and take it with you, if you would? Then I'll have you follow me up the road where I'll leave my car. You bring me back before you leave. Ok?"

It only took a few minutes to gather the tape. Harry removed his sawed-off shotgun from the trunk of his car and placed it in the Dells cruiser, much to the officer's surprise. With the tape stuffed into the cruiser's trunk, both cars pulled out immediately toward a location where Harry would leave his car.

Harry had placed the shotgun on the back seat, and with every opportunity to look back, the young officer nearly broke his neck to get a glimpse of what the gun looked like. It was just too dark to see. They hadn't gone far. There was a slight turn-out on the gravel shoulder and Harry pulled in quickly, turned the lights and engine off, got out, locked the car and immediately jumped into the rear seat of the cruiser.

Harry was dressed in military fashion: his trousers were tucked into his camouflaged paratrooper boots. The vest, as it appeared to the young officer, was police issue with armor plate, and Harry looked prepared for a riot. And, considering his hypothesis, he might as well have been.

Upon their return, the entire area out front of the garage emitted a solitude that exemplified foreboding, as they entered into a darkness that seemed to encapsulate them. The vehicle came to a stop just outside of the garage door, and a pang of uncertainty crawled around in the pit of Harry's stomach. The officer got out immediately; being in the back seat, Harry had no means for egress. There are no door handles in the back of some police cars. His perception of the officer's desire to have a closer look at the shotgun was precise—as he began to slide out, Harry handed it to the young officer, whose eyes gave him up.

"Whoa!" he said. "Where did you get your hands on something like this?"

It was a Mossberg, Model 500 Tactical Light Forend, a pump-action 12-gauge shotgun with an 18.5-inch barrel and side-touch pad to a fixed-on or strobe-beam white-dot sight.

"I've had it for quite some time," Harry said, but he was not in the mood for chit-chat about the gun he would soon carry to an engagement with infamy. "You're the only one who knows I'm here. For what I'm about to do, it has to remain that way…for at least the rest of the night. I'll call Officer Torrey and the chief at daybreak, ok?"

"No problem, trooper." He used the term "trooper" with the utmost respect for the man and the reputation standing before him.

"Thank you for all that you've done, officer. Now, it's best that you leave right this minute."

Without another word, the officer got into his cruiser and did as he was told. The distant headlights and the brilliant red glow from the taillights faded into the night, and Harry was finally alone with only Annie's cell phone, his thoughts and his gun. He looked around the property, and the beauty he saw in the silhouettes of trees surrounding him offered little in the way of perhaps soothing the troubled waters of his mind, yet for the most part he had chosen this particular cup of his own volition. He took a deep breath. "It's now or never, Harry," he said to himself at just above a whisper. He looked about him once more, saw nothing, and went directly into the garage.

As he closed the door behind him, the dank smell of mold filled his nostrils, though he had not noticed the fetid air when he was here last. He stood motionless, allowing his eyes to adjust to the darkened interior, and pondered the best location that might offer a more advantageous view of the devil, should he choose to make his entrance.

The minutes ticked into an hour; each second became the pounding of a heartbeat. Harry sat in the darkness, twitching in a nervous spasm as the sound of a falling pine cone hit the roof above him, or a vision of a past event flashed before his mind's eye, as if an unseen volume dial had been turned up full. In one such vision, he found himself standing in front of his blue trooper car in horror at the sight of Darcy Richards' body impaled on the jagged splinters of the utility pole. He flinched suddenly, then rapidly looking through the empty darkness again, he found nothing except the interior of the garage.

"Stay awake, Harry," he said out loud.

And then the ticking of his watch echoed through the still night, but once again the flashbacks came. He had been sitting in the snappy early morning air for nearly two hours. It was 2:30 a.m. The cold tended to slow his metabolism, causing his dreary head to nod with fatigue. Out of nowhere, a vision of Kenny Collins' lifeless body and his bloody, pockmarked face and upper torso from the shotgun blast that had taken his life flashed before Harry in living color.

"Dear God!" he hollered out. "Let this cup pass from me." It was as if he'd returned to the river bank to preach to the ears of the forest. As it was then, no man could hear him now. His religious upbringing began to surface from the depths of his soul and he wished he could share his thought with his father or even Ralph Bailey, anyone who might listen, and then he wished he'd called Rodney.

They'd become so close over the last couple of weeks, and he admired the young officer's stick-to-it detective work. *His notes are what brought me here tonight,* Harry thought.

It was now that Harry began to doubt himself and his theory. Being alone and this tired could only create a dysfunction in an alert and calculating mind. For Harry, it was now ticking away on eighteen and some-odd hours since he'd begun his day. The caffeine he'd had with dinner had long since been absorbed and expelled. Sleep was the only thing now that could return any normal person in his condition to the fullest extent of their potential. He reached into his pocket and latched onto Annie's cell phone, cupping it in his palm. Suddenly, that little piece of her was enough to stir a new awakening in him, but how long it would last, remained to be seen.

Tick…tick…tick. The infernal ticking of his watch began to irritate him, yet in a tiny way, it also began to hypnotize him into a lull in consciousness and he was there, in the arms of Morpheus.

The rowboat glided over the mirror-like surface of the remote pond. The distant, yet eerie call of the loon was calming. The red and white fishing bobber danced lazily in the distance, the sun was warm on his face. This is what life is all about. No worries. Few things troubled a man in this solitude. Relaxation… It's all good. Out of nowhere, the deafening sound of a low-flying helicopter burst through the serenity, but as hard as Harry looked…

Harry was thrust from the tranquility of the dream into the sudden reality of the throaty pounding of Petey's hot-rod exhaust. Zeke was flying down the driveway toward the garage in the stolen car. The headlight beams showed sparsely through the spaces in the doorframe. The excitement of the chase suddenly resurrected itself in Harry's thirst for justice.

He backed himself firmly against the wall, and placed the shotgun in a defensive position, aiming it toward the garage door, the only means for entering or exiting. He could only assume that since he hadn't heard the sound of a slamming car door, Zeke remained like a rattlesnake before striking: observant to its surroundings. The devil had arrived.

Harry made one last visual check of the garage, helped now by the infiltrating headlight beams. Mentally, he had no way to know how it would all go down, but the last thing he wanted was to be killed or to kill this obviously mentally tortured and distraught young mind.

The car door finally opened and then slammed. Zeke's heavy, booted footsteps approached the garage slowly. Harry took a final gulp of saliva and waited for the door to open.

The seconds felt like an eternity before a smidgen of a crack became visible between the doorframe and the door. Zeke was extremely cautious, moving almost in slow motion. He had left the headlights on with the motor off, knowing very well and obviously from memory that the garage would be near to blind darkness. Harry had considered his position well, and he was tucked in the corner behind the snake cage. This location would shield him from the obvious insurgents of light, soon to fill the cold interior, and hopefully long enough to take Zeke completely by surprise. Harry, however, was no fool. He knew that the best-made plans are sometimes doomed to failure due to one forgotten iota in the mix.

And then…there he was: Zeke Brailey, standing in the doorway as big as life. Because he'd never seen the young man in person, Harry had only descriptions of his physical attributes, and had never realized how big a man he was. The inside of the building was suddenly flooded with light. Harry held his breath. His eyes were focused on the big guy's hands while they hung, seemingly lifeless, at his sides.

Good. Harry thought. *No gun in his hand, but I doubt very much he left it in the car.*

Zeke walked determinedly now, toward the stove or more likely toward the candle on the top. Within seconds, the interior was awash from the new and added light, and when he turned to have a better look at the garage, he saw Harry's outline in the corner and immediately went for the gun, tucked into the waist of his black jeans.

"If you pull that out, even just to show me what it looks like, there's gonna' be a lot of blood all over your…nice jeans, there," Harry said with an affirmative tone in his voice.

Zeke let his arm drop to his side. When he did, though the light was sparse, Harry immediately noticed the tape around the pistol grip, confirming Rodney's finding of the screw on the path at what seemed a lifetime ago, now.

"And…who the fuck are you?" Zeke asked.

"Oh, I'm sorry. My name is Harry Circus. I work with the Dells Police Department, occasionally."

"Harry Circus, ya say," Zeke responded sarcastically. "Well, I see a clown, but where's all the fuckin' elephants?"

"Hey now, that's pretty good. I've never had anyone reference my name in that way," Harry said, laughing slightly.

"What?" Zeke asked as if what Harry said went right over his head.

Zeke swayed then as if preparing to move from the spot. It was then that the light from the candle reflected off the large silver watch on his left arm—another item from the list they had looked for.

"I meant what I said earlier about the blood on your jeans. Don't even blink without asking me permission first," Harry said.

And, in an almost cat-like hissing voice, Zeke replied, "I don't ask permission from no one. Not even a clown."

As he looked to the floor, perhaps contemplating his next move away from the sudden imprisonment, it was then that he noticed the white dot on his knee. "What tha' fuck is this?"

"That my friend is an L3/Insight light fixed on your knee-cap, signaling the direction of the 00 buck-shot from my little 12-gauge, here."

Ever confident and sarcastic, Zeke asked, "Hey…where can I get one like that? Let me have a look at it, will ya?"

And without hesitation Harry came back with, "Maybe later, but for right now, you and I have some unfinished business to talk about. You don't mind, do you?" Harry was being flippant in the face of Zeke's obvious smart-mouth question.

Zeke pointed toward the tall stool beside the work bench. "Ya mind if I sit while ya fire a few my way?" he said, again, with the smart mouth.

"Yeah…I do mind, but what I'd like for you to do now, is reach…slow with your finger and your thumb and pull that pistol from your pants. Real…slow now," Harry said, with purpose.

A look of hatred formed on Zeke's face, yet seeing the shotgun pointing at him, he did as he was told. When the gun was free from his clothing, Harry barked another order.

"Now…put it on the floor, and kick it to me. Remember…00 buck shot is going to make a real mess of everything you consider to be yours….personally and physically. Do you understand?"

Zeke never spoke a word, never breaking his stare of eye-to-eye contact with Harry. The kick was intentional and the gun slid to within Harry's reach, but he did not move a muscle to seize it nor did he look down at it. His eyes remained riveted on Zeke's. Zeke's stare however, was on the .38 caliber revolver that had become an extension of his arm. He wanted it back.

Harry went on. "Your friend, Pozy, is living at the York County Jail." Zeke appeared unfazed by the news and remained silent, but it was obvious to Harry that his total concentration was on how he would get the gun back. Unhesitant, Harry continued.

"He told me that you…well, he thought you'd gone off the deep end this summer. Ya know, pointing that gun at everyone the way that you did. Oh, by the way…Missy—"

At that point, Zeke hollered out, "You leave that little bitch out o' this. She ain't nothin' ta me…no more," he said as a bit of spittle flew from his mouth. At the quickness of his anger, Harry considered another approach: his mother.

Harry's mind was lifted to a higher authority. *Dear Lord. Do not let me fail this time if thy will allows it. This young man can be saved. Give me the strength to save this one. I pray in the Holy Name of God, Amen.*

"Ok…ok, Zeke. We don't need to speak of Missy. I did however, with Officer Torrey, meet your mother and father the other day. They sure have a nice farm up there." But his efforts seemed useless.

"Hey…dry up, mister policeman. You ain't hea' ta make small talk about the old man and the farm. Ya got somethin' on yaw' mind, spit it out."

Harry remained frozen to the spot. If he moved now, it might, after sitting this long, put him just enough off balance to allow Zeke to get the upper hand. That was not going to happen if Harry could help it.

"No, really…Zeke, your mother is very concerned for you. Your father, well…that's another story, but your mom, you know how mothers care. She wishes you might stop by once in a while. Maybe have a hot meal and some of her homemade bread. I had some. It's awesome with her butter."

Zeke was silent now. If a hard-assed punk could be softened with the thought of his mother's home-cooking, it appeared that Harry had found that soft spot. Several moments passed, which seemed like an eternity, but Harry waited and Zeke spoke up.

"Yeah…she always was a good cook. The old man, though, he wanted another mule on the farm after grampy died. I worked my fuckin' ass off for him, but he wanted more. Yah, Ma used to stand up for me…like moms do, but he'd have none of it. Rah, rah, rah. 'The boy's gotta work fa' his keep.' I hope he shits himself. I had enough o' that place. Me and Pozy came ta town and we weren't goin' back." He stopped for a moment. "What about Pozy? What's he got to do with all this?"

That's as good of an opening as any, Harry thought. "We, Officer Torrey and I, found him here the night you scared the hell out of Petey and you know, the other person, the night you stole his car. After we talked a while, right here in this garage, he opened up about his need to be free. He said he'd told you about it several times, but you couldn't be bothered. Did you know how bad he wanted to be free? Well, as it went, he gave us a bunch of info about the two murders out on the heath. He made it pretty clear what went on out there, about how they died and how you both carried them back to their car, but not before kickin' some serious ass, right, Zeke?" And without hesitation Zeke responded.

"They were a couple o' Mass-holes. I saved the poor slobs o' Maine from the shit they were peddlin'. You people oughta be happy I got rid of a couple o' drug dealers from away. I should get a medal for it."

"So…You're not denying you killed them?" Harry asked, and now, he moved his right leg out and hooked the heel of his boot onto the gun as Zeke appeared to have entered a fog bank, gazing toward the ceiling. One quick jerk and the gun slid to within his grasp. He had it. With the sound of the cold steel being dragged across the concrete floor, Zeke looked quickly back toward Harry, yet displayed no facial expression that he even noticed that the gun was gone.

The interior of the garage became deathly silent once again. The dancing flame on the candle reflected a dull sheen over the arm of Zeke's leather jacket. From where he remained, Harry as of yet had not gotten a good look at Zeke's face. No light had hit him frontally and so far all Harry had was a silhouette. Harry was not ready to let it all go just yet.

"You look tired, Zeke. Have you been sleeping in the car?"

Without responding to the question, Zeke asked one of his own. "Did my mother say much when you talked to her?"

Not wanting to share all of what she'd shared, particularly, her request of, "Officers, if it's at all possible please don't hurt him," Harry chose his words carefully.

"Well, like I said… she wishes you would stop by for a nice hot meal. She said she missed you and she hasn't seen you in a while. That's pretty much it—ya know she's worried about you," Harry said while looking intently at the young man's face. It was a blank.

Knowing very well the level of violence this person was capable of unleashing on others with such callous abandon, Harry had to assume that it was all a façade for the purpose of distraction, and he would not fall prey to it. He retightened his grip on the shotgun and brought it back to its original defensive position. Zeke apparently never noticed.

"Ya know," Harry said. "Petey really wants his car back. Did you take good care of it?" he asked, hoping that Zeke might be coming around to his side, after they'd spoken about his mother. He couldn't have been farther from the truth.

"That old shit box couldn't get out of its own way. He and that little tramp can have it back…" And, without warning, Zeke lunged at Harry in a last-ditch attempt at regaining the control he thought he had upon entering the garage.

As if gravity had no pull on him, Zeke literally flew through the air toward Harry. As it was, the wood stove was no more than ten feet distance between the two, but what Harry had missed, due to fatigue, was that each time Zeke played possum at Harry's comments by looking toward the ceiling, he actually inched himself closer, narrowing the gap. Although the distance remained considerable, taking his height into account, the space closed rapidly. Harry never got the chance to blink. Zeke had him by the neck with one hand and the back of his head with the other. Because of the momentum gained from his leap, they hit the wall hard with Harry's back as he only had the time to reach out with one hand in an attempt to slow the hit down, to no avail.

With a violent twist of his head, Harry was toppled to the floor, with all of Zeke's weight upon him. The shotgun went flying across the concrete, while the metallic sound of it forced Harry to want to vomit, having been overtaken by the young man he'd held that gun on only moments earlier. Another grab by Zeke was deflected, and a punch thrown was blocked and Harry was now the man on top. All of the training at the Criminal Justice Academy that Harry remembered years ago came back as if it were yesterday.

The last thing Harry wanted was another death, this one by his hand. There were no more flashbacks for Harry. He and Zeke were happening right now. Harry sucker-punched him to the temple; knocking Zeke against the wall. Before he could regain his equilibrium, Harry pummeled him with a series of rights and lefts all about his face, neck and finally one hard right to the nose. Blood exploded from both nostrils. The finishing blow was a left hook to the area just above the Adam's Apple, rendering Zeke into a lifeless prone position directly under the snake's cage. The battle lasted less than five minutes.

There was quite an age difference between the two men. Zeke lay in a heap, still unmoving after the beating, but he was alive. Harry struggled to catch his breath, and he was very much alive. Still out of breath, Harry reached into the black leather double-cuff case on his belt and pulled out a unique pair of handcuffs. One end fit snugly around Zeke's wrist, the other, somewhat larger and connected with a heavy chain, fit securely around his calf. He wasn't going anywhere. Zeke Brailey's reign of terror on the southern Maine coast had come to an end.

After securing the prisoner, Harry reached for Annie's cell phone and made the call he'd hoped could have been made sooner. The call never finished the first ring.

"Rodney Torrey here."

"Don't you ever sleep?" Harry asked.

"Oh…about as much as you do. Is there a problem, Harry?"

"I've got a surprise for you. Are you dressed?"

"Not yet, but it won't take long. Where am I going and what's the surprise?"

"Just get down to Pozy's garage. It won't take you long to find out."

With that, Harry was gone. He took a deep breath, picked up both guns, thankful that neither one was discharged, and he walked out into the early light of the new day. This was the first time he'd seen Petey's car, and from first glance, Zeke had not done it any harm. He would ask Rodney, if he, Harry, could be the one to call Petey and give him the good news.

He placed the guns at his feet, stretching now, feeling a pull in the area of his shoulder-blade from the tussle with Zeke, but the fresh air of the outdoors re-kindled his awareness. Several minutes of quiet passed.

Just then, he turned toward the sound of Rodney's rapidly approaching police car. It was at that very moment as his eyes fell on Petey's car that a broad smile appeared on Rodney's face and he began shaking his head in a playful way at Harry. Both men burst into laughter at the sight of one another. It was done. The nightmare in Dells Maine was over.

Epilogue
Two years later

TWO DAYS AFTER ZEKE was arrested for the three murders, Harry and Annie, Rodney and Lillian stood solemnly at the graveside of Willard's wife. He stood alone beside the silver casket. Harry's thoughts were ushered back to another funeral with a silver casket, but this time there was no head-trip for him. No promises to be made or kept.

Shortly after the funeral, Willard made his retirement official, and left the Department with a clean and honorable record. He also made it known then that Marcy would now be his main squeeze, but not in so many words. The revealing of the affair shed much light on his whereabouts during the investigation, but it was all good now.

Missy and Petey had moved out to his grandparents' farm shortly after the incident with Zeke. She never went back to the Little Roady; Marcy finally sold it. Petey still had the Mopar. Outside of the filth, Zeke had never hurt it mechanically. There is one thing they added, though: a child restraint seat in the back. Missy had gotten pregnant around the time Zeke pointed that gun at them. They got married the same day Zeke was sentenced, and stayed right on the farm. Petey took over the day-to-day needs of the old spread, and Missy and grandma got along beautifully in the kitchen. Theirs was a happy ending.

Dwight Betters seemed to fade out of sight as things happened.

No one really knew what happened to him or where he went. It was just about a year after it all went down that he showed up at the farm. He had gone and got his GED, and enrolled in dental school, following in his old man's footsteps.

As for Pozy, he turned State's evidence and plea-bargained for time. After all was said and done, he did a year and a half at the County Jail as an accessory to the murders. As it was, Zeke had told him of the first murder, and the law knew how he was involved with the other two.

He finally found that freedom he longed for. When the old lady finally died, with no family, she willed the entire property to him. With a little help from family, they refurbished the old house and turned the place into a real nice piece of real estate. The garage, however, due to an improperly installed stove pipe, burned the first winter he was there. He figured it was a small loss in comparison to what he ended up with.

Nothing ever came of the affair between Rodney and Lil. Sure, they spent some quality time together after Zeke was put away, but Rodney could not spread himself between two loves. His first love, police work, won over, but they ended it with a kiss and they remained good friends and still communicate. After the chief retired, the town was more than ready to offer Rod the chief's position, and he took it. He never again considered applying to the State Police. Chief of Police Rodney Torrey has a long future with the Dells Police Department.

Free at last! Harry and Annie made an extended trip Down East the day after Zeke was sentenced. Not once did a flashback from his past make itself visible, nor did Harry speak of anything that did not involve him and Annie—at least fishing, hunting and Annie. They visited old friends and he went fishing with Ralph Bailey. There was no more police work for him. All in all, life was good once more. When they finally returned home, Harry had accustomed himself to screening all calls from Chief Torrey. Although the two men were at times inseparable, there would no longer be consultant work for Harry.

It's funny how things go. Not long after that night in the garage with Zeke, Harry went out and bought himself a cell phone. He continues to give thanks for having been able to subdue Zeke without another killing and salvage his lost ability to end the Kenny Collins story peacefully. He also made as many connections as he could, and found out that Wanda Lane had simply filled in as a volunteer at the local TV Station in Portland. It just so happened that her assignment that day was the murders on the heath in Dells. In actuality, neither man had anything to worry about, but as far as Harry was concerned, if it involved Wanda…

Zeke Brailey was sentenced to twenty-five years to life at the Maine State Prison at Warren, with no chance for parole. His attitude for dominance remained the same. He was the prisoner who spat at the guard just because he wanted to. He got inmates to do things for him, including getting beer and drugs from family members who smuggled them in under the watchful eye of the guards who got a little for their trouble. And so goes the politics of prison life.

His mother could never bring herself to see her only son behind bars, and probably never will. His father, however, went only once, just to tell him that he hoped he rotted there for the disgrace he'd brought on the proud family. Zeke attempted to spit in his face. Luckily, the glass divider was between them.

After a year or so in jail, Zeke got into a jail-yard gang fight. He loved those. Unknown to him, the fight had been set up by the friends of the two Massachusetts boys he'd killed on the heath. One had a jail-made shank in his shoe and stabbed old Zeke right in the heart. He fell dead on the spot. The old saying goes… "Live by the gun, die by the gun," but it was a homemade knife that got Zeke Brailey. What goes around…comes around.

The chair sits empty
The notebook is blank
The music is silent
The writer pens no more

E.D. Ward

Feb. 14, 1950 - Dec. 3, 2016

www.ingramcontent.com/pod-product-compliance
Lightning Source LLC
Chambersburg PA
CBHW070833020826
48982CB00019B/1046/J

* 9 7 8 1 9 4 4 3 9 3 8 6 1 *